W9-AAS-037

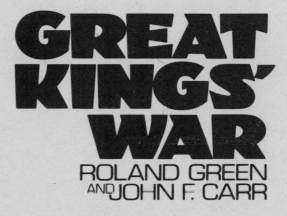

GREAT KINGS' WAR

ROLAND GREEN
AND JOHN F. CARR

ACE SCIENCE FICTION BOOKS
NEW YORK

To the memory of H. Beam Piper,
and with special thanks to Jerry Pournelle,
who brought the two of us together on this path.

GREAT KINGS' WAR

An Ace Science Fiction Book / published by arrangement with
the authors

PRINTING HISTORY
Ace Original / March 1985

All rights reserved.
Copyright © 1985 by Roland Green and John F. Carr
Cover art by Alan Gutierrez
This book may not be reproduced in whole or in part,
by mimeograph or any other means, without permission.
For information address: The Berkley Publishing Group,
200 Madison Avenue, New York, New York 10016.

ISBN: 0-441-30200-9

Ace Science Fiction Books are published by
The Berkley Publishing Group,
200 Madison Avenue, New York, New York 10016.
PRINTED IN THE UNITED STATES OF AMERICA

There was a cry from ten thousand throats—

"KILL THE DEMON'S SPAWN!"

The billmen began their charge.

The Hostigi reply came—

"DOWN STYPHON!"

The two forces collided with such impact that the first Hostigi ranks disappeared before Xykos's eyes. He was eight ranks deep into what had once been the enemy line before he came to a stop with his thirty-six inch pike head buried halfway into a billman's hip. . . .

"My friend Beam Piper would have liked this book."

— Jerry Pournelle

"GREAT KINGS' WAR is a lot of fun, a fine adventure story in the tradition of the original H. Beam Piper works."

— Poul Anderson

"We both enjoyed the book very much. When is the sequel coming out?"

— Robert Adams and Andre Norton

"The first of all the requisites for a man's success as a leader is that he be perfectly brave. When a general is animated by a truly martial spirit and can communicate it to his soldiers, he may commit faults, but he will gain victories and secure deserved laurels."

— Jomini: *The Art of War*

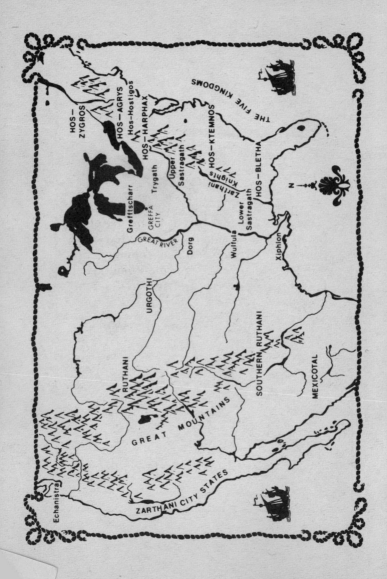

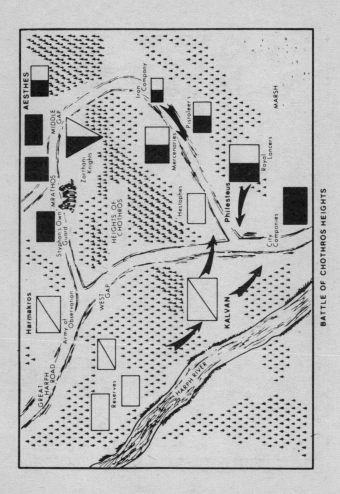

BATTLE OF CHOTHROS HEIGHTS

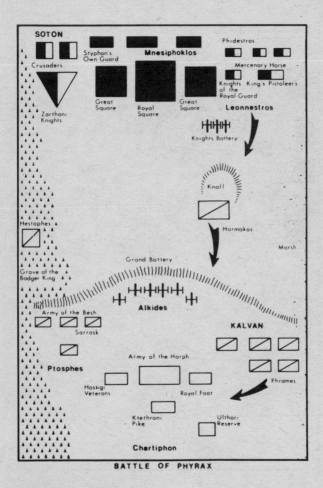

BATTLE OF PHYRAX

ONE

I.

The howl of a wolf floated down from the wooded hills to the right of the trail. A moment later several more howls replied from farther off.

"Your Majesty! That first one's on the scent of prey. He's calling the pack!"

Kalvan reined his horse to a stop and looked back at the bearded trapper riding behind him. He might be Great King of Hos-Hostigos, but when it came to hunting wolves he would yield to Hecitides's forty years' accumulation of knowledge.

"The forest's too thick for us to turn off here," Hecitides added. "We'd best ride on a bit."

"What about his scenting us?" asked Kalvan.

Hecitides pulled off a glove and held a finger up in the icy winter air. "Not enough wind. With the wolves this hungry, they'll eat anything. They got their minds on something."

A shot came from ahead, then the sound of hooves at a canter. One of the buckskin-clad scouts came plunging back down the trail, his horse churning up the fine powder snow into a silvery spray.

"Your Majesty! There's a fire up the hill and to the right. Not too far. A big fire!"

As an intelligence report the scout's words left a lot to be desired, but they told Kalvan enough to make him think about his tactics. Wolves could be ridden down with lances or swords, or shot from the saddle with pistols. A fire could mean bandits, and they could shoot back. Two of this winter's worst problems seemed to be abroad tonight. At least they were also the two easiest to deal with.

"Musketoons to the front," called Kalvan. That was ignoring the chain of command, of course, and one of these days he'd have to start being more careful. Right now he wanted to save time. Besides, nobody would argue with the Great King of Hos-Hostigos, as long as he obviously knew what he was doing.

As the scouts fell back on the main body and troopers rode forward to reinforce the line, Kalvan had a moment to listen to the wolf howls again. He also had time to wonder, not for the first time, if the confidence these people had in him was entirely justified. *Did* he really know what he was doing?

Kalvan had known what he was doing when he shot his way out of that—call it a cross-time flying saucer—that scooped him out of 1964 Pennsylvania and landed him here-and-now. Of course most of that was self-defense, a fairly simple job for the trained reflexes of Corporal Calvin Morrison of the Pennsylvania State Police and former sergeant, United States Army.

It was when he landed that things started to get complicated. Here-and-now was still Pennsylvania, but nothing like the one he knew; it was an alternate Pennsylvania that had never heard of William Penn or even George Washington. From what he'd been able to deduce in the past year, this was an alternate Earth where the Indo-Aryan invasion had gone east across China, then in ships to the northeast along the Aleutians, instead of moving into Greece, India, and the Near East as they had in Kalvan's home world.

Here they had built city-states in all the natural harbors along the Pacific Coast as far down as Baja California. Later arrivals from another migratory wave had settled the Great Plains and the Mississippi River valley. Then, about five hundred years ago, there was a large-scale migration from the Pacific Coast to the Atlantic seaboard, where there was now a gaggle of what Winston Churchill had called "pumpernickel principalities."

It was a late-medieval to early-Renaissance culture, with gunpowder and good hand weapons, using a modified back-acting flintlock. The monopoly of gunpowder gave enormous power to Styphon's House, a here-and-now theocracy whose priests claimed that gunpowder (or "fireseed" as they called it) was a magical secret they alone knew. Any ruler who defied them was cut off from any supply of gunpowder—and that meant disaster.

Prince Ptosphes of Hostigos was under such a ban from Styphon's House when Calvin Morrison landed in his Princedom, helped rout an enemy cavalry raid, and was accidentally shot by Ptosphes's daughter Rylla. He'd spent his convalescence in Tarr-Hostigos as a guest of the Prince. Calvin Morrison might not then have told them what he thought of Styphon's House and taught them how to make their own fireseed, but when the alternative was having Rylla's lovely blond head stuck up on a spike over the gates of Tarr-Hostigos—well, that was as good as no alternative at all.

After that, developments had followed one another more or less inevitably. While the new Lord Kalvan had sometimes felt he was riding a runaway horse, he'd known there was no dismounting in midjourney. More important, he could look back and say that he hadn't made too many avoidable mistakes.

Taking the castle Tarr-Dombra was easy; that was craft and common sense, as well as a few new tactics, all used against an unwary and complacent opponent. The Battle of Listra-Mouth against Prince Gormoth of Nostor was a lot bloodier, but not that much harder. Stupid generalship by Kalvan's opponents helped. So did new field artillery, with trunnions and proper field carriages, able to outshoot anything else in this world.

Then came the Battle of Fyk; Kalvan still sometimes wondered how anybody had come alive out of that blindfolded slaughterhouse on a fog-shrouded field where the eventual outcome was more due to luck than skill. Still, that outcome was a victory for Hostigos over the Princes of Beshta and Sask, and a resounding defeat for Styphon's House.

Now Hostigos was a power, whether it wanted to be or not. There was nothing else, really, but to proclaim it the Great Kingdom of Hos-Hostigos. And who was the only man everyone would accept as Great King?

Corporal Calvin Morrison, Pennsylvania State Police (Forcibly Retired).

That was as far as Kalvan's memories took him when he

realized that his escort and the hunters were waiting for his orders. They were also crowding close to him on either side, making a wall of horseflesh two or three ranks deep. Most of them were troopers of Queen Rylla's Own Dragoons; they'd far rather be eaten by wolves or shot by bandits than return home and report to their colonel-in-chief that they'd let her husband be killed.

"Forwarrrd!" shouted Kalvan. The hunting party moved up the trail at a walk, until the trees to the right started thinning out. As they did, the wolf howls came again. This time it was the whole pack, closer than before—much closer.

Now Kalvan could see the fire for himself—a wavering orange glow from near the crest of a low hill to the northeast. In the light he could also see a zigzag trail leading downhill, ending among a dozen sleek gray shapes. Whatever had made the trail, it was down now, with the pack ready to dine.

"Follow me!" The old infantry command turned everybody's head toward Kalvan as he swung his horse off the trail. In the lee of the hill the snow lay only a few inches deep on hard-frozen ground. Kalvan's horse barely broke stride as it plunged in among the trees. He bent low to keep snow-laden branches from scalping him and cantered out into the open field while drawing a pistol from its saddle holster.

A dozen wolves made a target impossible to miss even from horseback. Kalvan's shot drew a howl from the pack, and one rangy specimen yelped and jumped up into the air as if it had been kicked. About half the wolves drew back with snarls and bared teeth, while the others turned from the blood-spattered mess on the snow to face Kalvan. A quick look over his shoulder told Kalvan that he'd outdistanced his escort by a hundred yards or so. For the moment, he was going to have to face this pack alone.

He cocked and fired his other pistol. The gray wolf he hit dropped as if it had been poleaxed.

The other four charged Kalvan, led by the biggest black wolf he'd ever seen. Even half-starved, it was still the size of a Shetland pony. Kalvan dropped the empty pistols, pulled two more out of his boots, and discharged them both just as the wolves reached his mount.

Kalvan never saw what his shots hit; he was thrown back in his saddle as his horse reared and struck out at the attacking wolves. The next thing he knew, Kalvan was on the ground and the black wolf was worrying at his left boot. Kalvan tried to pull out his sword, but it was caught in the scabbard now pinned under his left leg. He found his knife at the same moment the black wolf realized its prey wasn't dead or stunned.

The wolf lunged and Kalvan threw his knife. The knife sank into the wolf's shoulder, but the oversize beast never even flinched. Then Kalvan could smell its carrion-laden breath, stinking like the hell his father had so often and so eloquently described. He closed his eyes and braced himself for terrible pain.

Instead of pain, he heard a deafening explosion. Then the wolf smashed into him, knocking the wind out of him but not sinking its teeth into his flesh.

He opened his eyes to the blurred movements of someone throwing off the wolf carcass. The next thing he saw was the face of Major Nicomoth, his aide-de-camp.

"Your Majesty! Are you hurt?"

Kalvan looked down and saw bloodstains on his breeches. He quickly felt his legs. No gashes or pain; the blood must be the wolf's. He shook his head and sighed with relief. The prospect of a bite-wound without reliable antiseptics was bad enough, but more than a score of people had died this winter of rabies. That prospect frightened him more than all of Styphon's armies.

"Your Majesty," Nicomoth stammered. "I don't know what to say. . . . I can't understand how you could have ridden so far ahead of the rest of us. What will I tell the Queen?"

"Nothing, Major. She has a breeding woman's fears, and I want nothing to upset her." *Particularly since I'll be on the sharp end of her tongue, not you.* "Understand?"

"Yes, sir."

"How about our men? Anyone hurt?"

"Yes. Petty-Captain Vrantos. He was badly mauled by one of the wolves. He will probably never use his left leg again."

If he survives, thought Kalvan, cursing mentally. One more victim of the harsh winter. One less trooper to fight the war that would follow in spring.

"Mount up," Kalvan ordered. He waited until Vrantos had been strapped into his saddle before giving the order to move out. He examined what the wolves had left behind: the body of a heifer calf, dead and already half-eaten in the few minutes the wolves had been at it. Kalvan could also see the fire more clearly now; it was the thatched roof of a log barn, blazing merrily and quite out of control. In the glare he saw figures in peasants' clothing darting among the other farm buildings, beating out embers with old sacks or dousing them with buckets of snow. Two stood guard over what looked like a cow and a couple of pigs.

No bandits, just an accidental fire and an escaped calf to draw the wolves. They had paid a high price for their half-meal, too. Now what could he do for the people on the farm? Kalvan dug in his spurs and set his horse at the slope.

He didn't find any surprises at the farm: animals with their ribs showing, a father and two grown sons with eyes too large in thin faces, the plaintive cry of a baby from inside the house. The men stared at Kalvan without making the slightest sound or gesture of respect. Was it because they didn't know him, or were they too awed by his presence? Or maybe they just thought their being hungry was his fault.

A long war or a big war in an agricultural society always meant trouble; some parts of Germany never recovered from the Thirty Years' War. Last year's war had been both long and big, with raids all over the place even when the main armies weren't in the field. There'd also been a high percentage of the peasantry sucked into the poorly trained militia, where casualties were always highest. Crops that weren't burned by the enemy or trampled down by either side rotted in the fields because the harvesters were dead, on campaign, or had run away. Hostigos had harvested barely half its normal crops, Nostor still less.

The people of Hostigos were facing a hungry winter even before the snows began and the temperature dropped. It was the worst winter in living memory, so everyone said, and Kalvan wasn't about to argue. He hadn't felt cold like this since Korea.

All winter long snow had clogged the roads, so there was no carrying food from those places that had a surplus to those where rations were short. To fill their larders, people went out and hunted; even a winter-thin groundhog could keep a family from starving. More animals died of hunger, unable to find food under the ice and snow. Wolves that had grown fat on escaped livestock and battlefield dead suddenly found themselves going hungry.

It was inevitable that the wolves would turn on the hunters, then on travelers, then on isolated farms and even small villages. Men who might risk a blizzard and death from exposure wouldn't face being dragged down and eaten alive by starving wolves.

Kalvan realized that for this winter, the main enemy wasn't Styphon's House. It was the wolves, who were going to gnaw his Kingdom out from under him if they weren't stopped. That was what had brought him to swear a public oath two days ago that he would bring an end to the wolves' reign of terror. Hunting parties would go out everywhere the wolves were a problem. That also meant leading one himself, to set an example, which was why he was out here tonight, slowly freezing in his saddle and doing a cavalry lieutenant's work.

"We took seven wolves as the price of your heifer," Kalvan told the farmers. "You may have the skins, and the bounty for them."

Wolf-bounty was five ounces of silver, or five rakmars—a silver coin about the size of a silver dollar, with a two-headed battle-ax on one face and a stamped image of a young King Kaiphranos on the other. Kalvan had added an official gold coinage, a one-ounce gold piece called a Hostigos crown, minted from the loot of Styphon's temples.

Maybe the silver from the bounty would keep the farmers alive until spring, and maybe not. "Also, I will have soldiers come and rebuild your barn. In the spring," he added; there was no hope of finding fresh thatch in the dead of winter.

"Dralm bless you, Your Majesty!" said the father. He bowed his head. "It has not been easy, this winter, and we have prayed to Dralm and Yirtta Allmother . . ." His voice trailed off as the baby started crying again.

"Go on praying," said Kalvan. "When you can spare a prayer for someone else, pray for Great Queen Rylla. She is with child too."

The three men managed a smile at that news, which lasted until the ridgepole of the barn cracked and fell into the fire. Sparks flew up again, and they dashed madly for the buckets and sacks they'd left to greet Kalvan.

Kalvan thought of writing out his promise and leaving it with the farmers, then he remembered they probably couldn't read. Also, parchment was scarce and expensive. Which reminded him he'd better stop off at the paper mill on the way home and give *those* poor bastards some encouragement.

They were working hard with what little knowledge of paper-making he'd been able to dredge up out of his memory. All their results were still various grades of foul-smelling mush.

That too would eventually change; there were already quite a few people learning their way around Kalvan's new world. Rylla, of course. Ptosphes, First Prince of the new Great Kingdom of Hos-Hostigos. Count Harmaknos, Captain-General of the new Royal Army. Trader Verkan the Greffts-charrer. Count Phrames. Chancellor Xentos, also highpriest of Dralm. Brother Mytron, the healer priest who had listened with great interest to the lecture on antiseptic technique Kalvan delivered the day after he learned Rylla was pregnant.

There would doubtless be more. And the child who would be born in July, he or she would grow up with all these changes, learning to ride the runaway horse from the cradle. Now that he had a real stake in here-and-now's future, Kalvan was much more careful about what changes he introduced. After all, he didn't want to start a stampede, just save Hos-Hostigos from Styphon's House and King Kaiphranos. Kalvan's own world's history was full of examples of technology changing the world faster than people's ability to adapt to those changes.

He was going to make mistakes, of course. Probably already had, but only because he'd been running hard ever since he'd arrived here-and-now. Maybe when—if—this Styphon menace was ended, he'd have time to think of ways to help these people adjust to the changing world around them better than the people he'd been snatched away from had done. Anyway, even uncontrolled social upheaval was better than the type of theocratic despotism Styphon's House was using to enslave the peoples of the Great Kingdoms. Much more of that, and they'd be worse off than the Chinese!

Right now he knew more than anyone else here-and-now. So he had to be out in front, leading the battle against Styphon's tyranny, even if he barely knew what to do himself.

There wasn't anybody else who knew it at all.

Kalvan was glad to turn his mind from that thought, to concentrate on getting his horse down the hill without its stumbling, and rejoin his escort.

II.

In the flickering torchlight Archpriest Anaxthenes, First Speaker of the Inner Circle of Styphon's House, searched the faces of his fellow conspirators to see if they shared his growing anxiety. Only Archpriests Cimon and Roxthar looked comfortable in the white robes of village priests, the mark of conspirators fit only for burning or dismemberment.

Archpriest Neamenestros was two candles overdue, and the atmosphere in the cellar of the abandoned winery in Old Balph was damp and oppressive. At any moment Anaxthenes expected to hear the tramping feet of Temple Guardsmen coming to arrest them. Anaxthenes knew that half the Inner Circle would have smiled to see the discomfort on his usually expressionless face.

"How much longer are we going to wait?" asked Archpriest Euriphocles, a trace of hysteria raising his already high-pitched voice.

"Another quarter," replied Anaxthenes, pointing to the notched candle flickering in a niche in the rock wall. "We must know now if we can count on Archpriest Heraclestros's support."

As highpriest of the Great Temple of Hos-Agrys, Heraclestros was a man of some influence in the Inner Circle, especially among the uncommitted moderates—the group the conspirators needed most to court. Archpriest Dracar, who already saw himself in the flame-colored robe of primacy as each day Supreme Priest Sesklos's voice grew weaker, was panting hot on their heels. Dracar! Anaxthenes wanted to spit at the name. Were Dracar to become Styphon's voice, he would quibble and quiver until the Usurper Kalvan had Styphon's House drawn and ready to quarter.

It was the mistaken belief of Dracar and too many others among the Inner Circle that King Kaiphranos the Timid should be the principal agent of Kalvan's destruction. The witless fools! Didn't they realize that Kalvan was a warlord of the stature of King Simocles the Great, who'd led the Zarthani people to victory over the Ruthani Confederation of the Northern Kingdoms? They would have to scourge the Hostigi heresy with fire and sword as Simocles had scourged the Northern Ruthani.

Were it not that Kaiphranos employed so many food-tasters, Anaxthenes could have solved this dilemma long ago. Not that Kaiphranos's sons were any better; the older was too rash, while the younger was a debauched fool. Duke Lysandros, the old king's half-brother, was the only man in the dynasty with any mettle.

Suddenly the candle flared brightly, showing that the quarter had ended. Anaxthenes began to rise from the barrel he'd been using as a seat, when he heard the sound of footsteps on the stairs above. Without willing it, he found himself holding his breath.

There was an audible sigh of relief throughout the chamber when the bent and hooded figure of Archpriest Neamenestros entered. "I am sorry, Brethren. I was followed, so I took the alternate route."

"Are you certain you were not followed here?"

"Yes, First Speaker. I lost him when I entered the ruins of the Old Temple of Dralm." Everyone in the cellar but Anaxthenes and Euriphocles drew an imaginary circle on his breast at the mention of the false god Dralm. "As you foresaw, he thought the Old Temple was my destination, for when I slipped out the back I waited for two quarters and no one followed."

Using the deserted Old Temple of Dralm as a decoy had been another of Anaxthenes's ideas. As always when one of his plans went well, he felt a sudden surge of mental pleasure. For Anaxthenes, the joy of a well-wrought scheme brought to completion overshadowed the lust for gold or even for the willing women that other men so highly prized.

"Is Archpriest Heraclestros with us?" asked Euriphocles, no longer able to contain his curiosity.

"Yes. He knows King Kaiphranos the Timid from Great King Demistophon's court. Not even with all of Styphon's Host and treasure would Kaiphranos be able to smite the Daemon Kalvan. He will support our policies even though he distrusts our fervor."

Anaxthenes shared Heraclestros's reluctance even while he used the True Believers for his own ends. They were useful tools as long as one remembered that they were sharp and double-edged. Before Kalvan had arrived out of what seemed to be nowhere, the followers of Styphon's Way had attended their worship in private, fearing the ridicule and even persecution of their peers. The only openly known True Believers in the Inner Circle had been Cimon, the Peasant Priest, and Roxthar, the self-proclaimed Guardian of the True Faith. Cimon had proved a useful spokesman for the more devout lower orders, while Roxthar had his own small but fanatical following, and ill luck was known to befall those who blocked the Guardian's way. The most feared man in the Temple, he was not only surviving but prospering.

While the Temple was strong, feared, and respected, it could still survive the cynicism of its higher orders. Now Kalvan had appeared, disclosed the fireseed mystery, and turned the wretched little Princedom of Hostigos into a Great Kingdom under his leadership. Yet it was not Kalvan's military victories that had shaken the very foundations of Styphon's House on Earth; it was the callous and self-serving defection of Archpriests Krastokles and Zothnes.

How could Styphon's House expect the laity to put out the Temple's fire when its own priest fought their way out of the doors?

That both Archpriests had accepted baronies and a share of the gold looted from Styphon's temples made matters even worse. Even the most faithful of Ktemnoi peasantry were beginning to question their faith, as well as the rule of Styphon and his earthly representatives.

Neither gold nor armies could return that which Krastokles and Zothnes had stolen from Styphon's House. Only the physician's lancet could bleed the Temple of the corruption that threatened its doom and destruction. As its only servant who saw clearly what must be done, it was up to Anaxthenes to act as that physician, even if it meant dealing with the unpredictable and not always trustworthy believers.

When Styphon's House was once again healthy, Kalvan could be disposed of easily. With Kalvan out of the way, it would be time to consolidate Styphon's dominion once and for all over the Northern Kingdoms and think about extending it to the Middle Kingdoms of the Great Valley as well.

"Heraclestros's support in the Great Council is good news," said Anaxthenes. "It will go a long way in helping us convince the moderates that we need a better weapon than the blunt sword of Kaiphranos to rend the army of the Usurper.

Now, Archpriest Roxthar, have you been able to clear the vision of our blind brother Dimonestes?''

Roxthar was a tall man, well over three rods in height, thin to the point of looking gaunt but known to be almost supernaturally strong. His eyes were his true strength; they burned with an intensity not right for one of this earth. Of all Anaxthenes's tools, Roxthar had the sharpest blade, although there were times when he was not sure whose hand gripped the hilt.

"I have restored his vision," said Roxthar with a grin that made him look even more cadaverous. "He now sees what must be done, although one eye had to be sacrificed to save the other."

Dimonestes was a physical coward, so Anaxthenes wasn't sure just how literally Roxthar's words were to be taken. Nor did he really wish to know. Roxthar had no peer among those who understood the mastery of fear and pain over other men. Had he understood the power of loyalty and love as well, it would have been he who ruled this conspiracy.

"I hope the others have done as well," Anaxthenes said. There were a few confirming nods, but most of the Archpriests averted their eyes.

Anaxthenes turned to Archpriest Theomenes. Theomenes was King Cleitharses's palace priest, their window into the royal chambers of Hos-Ktemnos.

"Where does your Great King stand in the fight against Kalvan?"

"The Infidel's disclosure of the fireseed mystery has sorely tested the Great King's faith. The weakness shown by Styphon's servants has weakened him even further. Where he was certain, he now doubts."

King Cleitharses was one of the major pillars of Styphon's House on Earth. "Did you tell the King that the traitor Krastokles is now dead?"

"Yes, First Speaker, but his thoughts are still troubled and he questions what was once unquestionable."

Roxthar's harsh voice cut through the rising babble in the chamber. "Anaxthenes, why do you not release your viper upon the Daemon Kalvan and thus remove the sting from the impious armies of Hostigos?"

Anaxthenes cursed silently at having to reveal that which was best kept secret. "It is because my snake values its skin too much to commit itself wholly to either one side or the other. Krastokles was old and not in the best of health; his death was easily explained. Furthermore, as a member of the Inner Circle, his knowledge of the secrets of the Temple was more a threat than all of Kalvan's armies."

"Yet Zothnes was spared?"

"Zothnes was long a creature of Sesklos, but not one privy to the Inner Mysteries. He was but an infant to the adult Krastokles. Yet were my snake not so coy I would have had him silenced as well. But enough of this. Theomenes, will King Cleitharses release the Sacred Squares of Hos-Ktemnos upon the Usurper?"

"Cleitharses has little love for mercenaries parading as Great Kings. The Usurper Kalvan vexes him mightily. Yet Hostigos is far away, while the Mexicotal march on Xiphlon stirring up the barbarians is in the Lower Sastragath. I have weighed his words and do not believe he will march upon Hostigos unless so directed by the Great Council."

"Then our path is clear. Brothers, we must impose our will upon the Council, or this time next year it will be our heads upon the walls of Balph."

TWO

I.

      Paratime Commissioner Tortha Karf stepped through the sliding door into the outer office of the Chief of Paratime Police in the Paratime Building. The door hissed shut behind him, cutting off the drumming of the rain on the landing stage. He unhooked his cloak and presented it to one of the green-uniformed Paratime Policemen on guard duty. It dripped water as the man headed for a closet, and the janitorial robot in one corner let out an electronic whimper as it detected the damage to the carpet.

For at least the hundredth time, Tortha Karf wondered why First Level civilization couldn't manage weather control. A handful of Second Level civilizations and one or two Third Level ones managed it; it was talked about and sometimes experimented with on a few of the more advanced Fourth Level ones. On First Level, however, they'd conquered space, controlled gravity, converted mass directly into energy, learned the ultimate secret of Paratemporal Transposition, and still endured rain dripping on rugs.

Also for the hundredth time, Tortha Karf came up with the answer almost at once. Any agreement on what the weather should be over a whole planet could only be a fragile, artificial one, sure to break down sooner or later. The human animal wasn't made to come to enduring agreements. The best Tortha

14

Karf had ever seen it do, in more than three centuries of watching its behavior on thousands of different time-lines, was to limit the extent of its *dis*agreements. (He'd also seen the ruins, usually radioactive, of a good many civilizations that hadn't even gone that far.)

First Level humanity had at least outgrown a higher percentage of the silliest delusions about itself than any other level. Not that this made it well behaved, let alone completely trustworthy—otherwise both Tortha Karf and the man he'd come to see could have spent their lives as something other than policemen. Yet a race that knew avoiding artificial agreements was worth a few wet rugs wasn't completely hopeless.

That, Tortha Karf reflected, was probably about as high as the human animal could reach, at least until the next evolutionary step was achieved. Waiting for that day to arrive would keep the Paratime Police busy for the next four or five hundred millennia.

Ex-Chief Tortha straightened his neckcloth as he approached the familiar secretary's desk beside the door to his former office. He wore a civilian tunic and breeches, although as a former Chief of the Paratime Police he had the right to wear the uniform for the rest of his life if he wanted to. However, it was only ninety-two days since people had stopped calling him "Chief" and started calling him "Commissioner." The less he wore his uniform, the faster they would think of him by his new title and remember the man now called "Chief."

The secretary was already on the screen, informing Chief Verkan Vall about his visitor. A familiar but slightly distracted voice replied, but there was no picture with it. "Tell the Commissioner to come in, if he can entertain himself for a minute or two."

The secretary was red in the face as he turned to face his former Chief, but Tortha only chuckled. "Sounds as if the Chief has the right spirit. Finish the job, even if the world's about to fall down on your head."

The office hadn't changed much since Tortha Karf last saw it, ten days after leaving it to Verkan Vall. Most of the movable furniture had been Tortha Karf's private property and had gone with him; most of the fixed furniture, except for the horseshoe-shaped desk, was data-processing equipment intended to resist any effort to move it without using chemical explosives.

Verkan Vall was seated at the Chief's desk, apparently watching a screen with one eye and a keyboard with the other. Both arms of the desk had acquired the inevitable litter of papers, photographs, disks, charts, and filmspools. Without raising his eyes from his work, Verkan waved Tortha Karf to a chair that gave the Commissioner a clear view of the whole office and one of the transparent walls.

A luxurious couch squatted by the wall, carved dark wood with leather upholstery and a Fourth Level Europo-American look to it. It was hidden from the outside by an obviously Indo-Turanian ornamental screen of ivory plaques set in lacquered bronze frames.

Another artificial alcove held several overstuffed reclining chairs, probably from Fourth Level Julian-Roman or Macedonian Empire Sector. They looked comfortable, although Tortha Karf wasn't prepared to be as charitable about the colors. Above the chairs several elaborately woven decorative hangings draped a carved wooden screen. He recognized the work of Vall's adopted sister-in-law Zinganna, who'd been raised from Prole to Citizen because of her help in breaking up the Wizard Traders Organization. (Or at least in breaking it up as much as it had been broken up, Tortha Karf added by way of a mental footnote.) She now had a happy marriage to Paratime Police Inspector Kostran Galth and a growing reputation as an artist.

At one end of the screen was a wooden liquor cabinet of the sort that seemed to be universal in every civilization that reached the level of inventing distilling. At the other end was a long case with transparent sides and several glass shelves. Tortha Karf walked over to it and studied the contents, then began to laugh softly.

The rest of the decorating showed the firm hand of Verkan Vall's wife Hadron Dalla. This case was Vall's, the souvenirs from some of his most important outtime cases.

There was the .357 magnum revolver he'd used on an escaped Venusian night-hound. On the second shelf were two thumbscrews from Fourth Level Spanish-Imperial, where Verkan had once rescued a missing Paratimer from the Holy Office of the Inquisition. To the right was an ugly jade idol of a crocodile with wings like a bat and knife blades for a tail from the Crocodile-God Case. On the next shelf were a knife and a more sophisticated solid-projectile pistol Vall had used on a Second Level Akor-Neb time-line, when Dalla (then between marriages to Verkan) got herself into trouble over reincarnation. Trouble was one of Dalla's normal habitats, of course, but that was worse than usual. There were several different models of Paratime Police-issue weapons, two or three more swords, depending on whether one of them was considered a long knife, and a curious back-acting flintlock pistol from Kalvan's time-line.

There was also a lady's handbag, and Tortha Karf remembered rather too well how it had earned its place in the case. Dalla had used it to disarm a would-be assassin from the Organization, saving Vall's life and proving that she had the makings of a good policeman. She'd done well, but she shouldn't have had to do it at all. The Paracops had made more mistakes than Tortha Karf liked to think about in dealing with the Wizard Traders Organization. Even now, after ten years' hard work, mostly Vall's, he wasn't sure if the Organization was dead or just lying quiet until trouble elsewhere diverted police attention.

A polite cough drew Tortha Karf's attention toward the desk and the man now rising from behind a darkened screen. "Welcome home, sir. How are the rabbits in Sicily?"

"Breeding like rabbits, as usual. I've tried everything short of importing cobras, but I can't do that because they'd have no natural enemies on the island. So I suppose I'll just have to be content with exporting what vegetables the rabbits are gracious enough to leave me." He gestured toward the screen. "What had you by the leg there?"

"Somebody on a Fourth Level Alexandrian-Roman time-line has reinvented the steam engine and one of the local kings has decided to conquer the world with a fleet of steamships. He has a nasty habit of burning cities to the ground, and he's on his way toward the island of Crete. Exotic Foods and Beverages has a central conveyor-head there, for their wine imports. It's also a major tourist trap; Dalla spent a ten-day there as a girl. I was trying to get a computer evaluation of the risks of teaching some of our pearl divers from Fourth Level Sino-Polynesia to attach limpet mines to the king's ships. The time-line has gunpowder, so it's only a minor secondary contamination at worst."

"What did the computer say?"

"That it wasn't going to say anything for several hours. I was going to have dinner sent up, and Dalla can join us when she gets back from the Bureau of Archives. She wanted to check their artifact collection on limpet mines so that if we decide in favor of training the divers we can produce a mine that looks as right for that time-line as possible."

"Any other problems?"

"Yes. More trouble on Europo-American."

"I'm not surprised," said Tortha Karf. Europo-American, Hispano-Columbian Subsector, was an area of about ten thousand parayears' depth in which the major civilization had developed on the Major Land Mass and from there spread to the Minor Land Mass, Northern Continent. The Hispano-Columbian Subsector had been very volatile since a major war had been concluded there twenty years ago, when it fractured into half a dozen new belts. Ever since, the major powers (usually two) had been acting like participants in a mutual suicide pact. Since they had nuclear weapons, the subsector had been under observation by a Paratime Policy study-team. The same thing had happened all over most of Third Level, with only a few time-lines escaping nuclear devastation.

There were a near infinity of time-lines, all on the same planet and each needing to be policed. The five primary levels were based on the different outcomes of the Old Martian civilization's attempt to colonize the planet Earth when their own world was dying. On First Level the Martian colony was a complete success, until they followed the path of their parent world too closely and exhausted the Earth's resources.

All that had saved First Level civilization from the same fate as its parent world was the development of Paratemporal Transposition and the discovery of an uncountable number of exploitable time-lines. Ghaldron, working to develop a faster-than-light space drive, and Hesthor, working on linear time travel, combined their research and discovered a means of physical travel to and from a second, lateral time dimension. Once Paratemporal Transposition was discovered, the First Level race began to send its conveyors to these parallel worlds, bringing wealth and resources back to the Home Time-Line.

Over twelve thousand years, First Level civilization developed a parasite culture so nearly perfect that few host worlds ever suspected its existence. There was one vulnerability: the

Paratime Secret. It had to be protected, and this was the Paratime Police's primary duty. If this secret were ever exposed, the very existence of the First Level race would be in danger.

When it didn't interfere with their primary duty, the Paratime Police also tried to prohibit flagrantly immoral conduct by First Level traders, tourists, observers, criminals, and out-and-out fools. It was a difficult job, and it sometimes seemed that the Paracops spent more time covering up dislocations than apprehending and punishing wrongdoers. This was one reason why Chiefs tended to retire early, along with First Level politics and headaches like the one Chief Verkan was facing on Europo-American; Tortha had come close to quarantining that one himself during the last Big War.

Fourth Level was the biggest level. It was here that the original Martian colony had come to such utter and complete disaster that few Fourth Level races had any knowledge of their true origins. Most had founded complete branches of pseudoscience to justify their Earthly origins, on the basis of incomplete primate skeletal remains.

Fourth Level was divided into a number of sector groups, sectors, subsectors, and belts based on where human civilization had first reappeared. There were four major sector groups: Nilo-Mesopotamian, Indus-Ganges-Irriwaddy, Yangtze-Mekong, and Andean-Mississippi-Valley of Mexico. The Nilo-Mesopotamia Sector Group, the largest, was the home of Europo-American, Alexandrian-Roman, Indo-Turanian, Sino-Assyrian, and Macedonian Empire Sectors.

Europo-American was now the home of a brand-new subsector, the Kennedy Subsector, including those time-lines where the major ruler of the Northern Continent had survived an assassination attempt. John F. Kennedy's assassination had left other Hispano-Columbian subsectors moving quickly into instability.

"I'm beginning to think that we're going to have to close the entire Hispano-Columbian Sector," said Verkan. "It's only a matter of time before this new undeclared war on the Major Land Mass has the two major powers in a missile-throwing contest. When that's finished, there won't be much that passes for civilization on that subsector. And this is getting to be a danger with most of Hispano-Columbian, especially those dominated by the Nazi and Communist sects."

"I agree with you totally. I've had my eye on that sector

ever since it had its first Big War to Free the World. I only held back because of pressure from the Paratime Commission. Some of the biggest outtime trading firms—Tharmax Trading, Paratime Petroleum, Consolidated Outtime Foodstuffs—move a lot of product through that sector. Before you do anything, I suggest you talk with Councilman Lovranth Rolk to see what kind of support he can drum up from Management in the Executive Council."

Verkan Vall's face, normally as expressionless as a pistol butt, relaxed visibly. "That's good advice, Commissioner. I'm glad you came in today. I don't want to tell you how to do your new job any more than you want to tell me how to do mine, but I have to say this: I think you may have left for Sicily too fast and stayed too long. Both the Commission and I could have used your advice a few times."

"I'm sure you could have," said Tortha Karf. "That's why I went. I might have yielded to the temptation to give that advice. Then where would we be?" He answered the question with a Sino-Hindic phrase from a time-line extraordinarily rich in scatological allusions.

"It's not just the people who have some real grievance against you, Vall. It's everybody in and out of the Paratime Police who isn't happy with the youngest Chief in five thousand years. One who's appointed his wife as Chief's Special Assistant—" Tortha held up his hand to stop Verkan's objections. "I agree that Dalla was the best-qualified candidate, but not everyone knows her as well as I do.

"Not to mention that you're an aristocrat with a rather peculiar hobby time-line that's also going to make or break the careers of a lot of Dhergabar University professors. I'd rather desecrate a temple of Shpeegar Lord of the Spiders than beard a professor who thinks he's lost a publication opportunity because the Paracops meddled!"

Verkan laughed, but Tortha could hear the strain in it. Guiltily he realized that he'd been doing exactly what he'd left for Sicily to avoid—giving unasked-for advice. He also realized that Vall looked—older? More strained? Tired? None of the words seemed completely wrong, or completely right either; all implied more emotion than Vall was letting show even now. He finally decided that Vall really looked like nothing more than a handsome man just into his second century who also happened to have the most nearly impossible and by far the most thankless job on Home Time-Line.

"Vall, tell the computer and the limpet mines to wait. Or put a limpet mine on the computer for all I care. I'm taking you and Dalla out to dinner at the Constellation House."

"But I can't—"

Tortha Karf drew himself up into a posture of mock attention and saluted with the precision of a new recruit who hadn't learned which superiors insisted on salutes. "Sir, if I can't obtain your cooperation, I'll be obliged to inform Chief's Special Assistant Doctor Hadron Dalla that you have refused."

Verkan pulled his face into a faint look of mock horror. "No, no, anything but that! I'll come along quietly." He emptied his drink and set the glass back on his desk while reaching for his green uniform jacket with the other hand.

II.

Sesklos, Styphon's Voice and Supreme Priest of Styphon's House, sat alone in his private audience chamber, wondering why fate had permitted him to live so long and come so far just to fall so low. He would have cursed the very gods, had he believed in any. Wasn't it bad enough that the Daemon Kalvan had fallen upon them like a blazing rock out of the night sky? Did he need to hear from Archpriest Dracar that Anaxthenes, his most trusted advisor and one he considered as a son, led the conspiracy that had turned priest against Archpriest and deacon against novice? The Great Council of Balph, already halfway through its second moon, seemed as interminable as the winter wind and just about as likely to abate.

Just thinking of the howling wind outside brought a fit of shivering to Sesklo's frail body. He quickly added charcoal to the brazier. The additional heat stopped his shivering, but it seemed that no matter how hot the rest of his body became, his fingers and toes were always chilled. The price of ninety-one winters. Despite any discomfort, Sesklos hoped it would not be his last. The grave would be much colder and much less comfortable.

Sesklos's eyes lovingly caressed each of the treasures that furnished his audience chamber: a rainbow-colored feather tapestry of a plumed serpent from the Empire of Mexicotal, a Thunderbird buffalo skull from the Great Mountains, a twisted ivory narwhale horn from the White Lands beyond farthest Hos-Zygros, a great stone battle-ax from the time of the Ancient Kings, a sacred golden bull of the Western Tribes, a fist-sized jewel-encrusted gold pendant from the throat of a barbarian king in the Sastragath. . . .

Too many priceless objects to count even on a hundred lonely nights, the treasure of kingdoms, yet only the merest fraction of the Temple's great wealth. How could one man, arriving from out of nowhere, throw all of this into jeopardy? Or had he? Was it possible that the golden throne of Styphon rested on sand?

And yet treasure was only one of the Temple's strengths. Styphon's House was as rich as any two Great Kingdoms combined. She ruled the trade in corn, chocolate, cotton, and tobacco, and owned the Five Great Banking Houses. At sea she had two fleets of galleasses and more merchant vessels than a scribe could count beans in a long day. There were granaries filled to bursting, armories stacked with enough pikes, bills, halberds, swords, arquebuses, and muskets to raise a mountain, and magazines filled with thousands of tons of Styphon's Best—perhaps not as good as Hostigos Unconsecrated, but good enough.

In men, Styphon's House could count twenty thousand of Styphon's Own Guard, thirty-five thousand Zarthani Knights, and enough gold and silver to buy every free companion in the Five Kingdoms; Sesklos refused to count Hos-Hostigos as a *true* Kingdom. Plus a horde of rulers, from Great Kings to petty lords, one and all in Styphon's debt.

A sharp rap at the door brought Sesklos out of his musings. "Enter."

Archpriest Anaxthenes came through the door, followed by two of Styphon's Own Guard in their silvered armor with Styphon's design etched in black on the breastplate, matching glaives, and bright red capes.

Sesklos gave a nod of dismissal to the Guardsmen. When they had left, he asked, "What are these rumors I hear about you and the One-Worshippers?"

"Father, they are true, but there is more to be said than you have heard."

Sesklos winced at the First Speaker's use of the term "Father" now, although it was surely true that he was Anaxthenes's father in all save the body. Sesklos had been Father Superior of the Temple Academy in Balph when the eight-year-old Anaxthenes, the only surviving member of a noble family killed in a nomad border raid in Cythlos, was brought to the Academy to be raised one of Styphon's Own. There was little to recall that little tow-headed boy of eight in the broad-shouldered, shaven-headed Archpriest who faced Sesklos now; only the piercing, startlingly blue eyes were the same.

Like that homeless waif of forty years ago, Sesklos too had come a long way. After thirty years as Father Superior of the Temple Academy, few even considered him as a candidate for the Archpriesthood, much less the Inner Circle and finally Styphon's Voice. But he had had the power to mold the minds and hearts of young priests-to-be, and mold them he did. When he had at last entered the Archpriesthood, his rise had been dazzling. Even now over half the Inner Circle were his former charges, and Anaxthenes had been his best and brightest pupil, as well as his most unruly. His body had grown straight and tall, but his mind was as enigmatic as ever.

Anaxthenes, don't fail me now!

He was too old and weighed down with past sorrows to see the son of his heart burned at the stake or buried alive in the catacombs beneath Old Balph. Styphon's House needed all her strong sons now more than ever.

"Father, are you all right?"

Sesklos shook his head to clear it of images of the past. His mind was wandering again. Old age was like a thief, at first stealing those things that were rarely used, then growing bolder and more daring, until nothing was left but oblivion.

"Why, Anaxthenes, in our hour of need have you helped rend the fabric of the Temple?"

"That cloth has already been rent asunder, first by the Usurper Kalvan, then by the traitors Zothnes and Krastokles. The old ways are doomed; our House must rebuild itself or die."

"These are strong words, my son. But there is a new wind in the air, one so strong it shakes the very throne of Styphon. Are the blocks of Roxthar and Cimon strong enough to build a new foundation for his House?"

"I believe so. They are the only clay of this House that does not crumble at the breath of Kalvan. There is too much sand in the clay of Dracar and Timothanes."

"And what about the clay of Sesklos?"

"Like rock, but deeply etched by the winds of time."

Sesklos had to fight to keep a smile from his lips. Anaxthenes always had a way with his old teacher, like a favorite concubine with an old king. "I fear you are right. But the One-Worshippers are like a flame in the breeze. Only Lytris knows which wind will fan them or blow them in your face."

"Yes, but it is also true that only they have roots that dig deep into the soil itself. The others but live on the surface and are buffeted by every zephyr. And it is an ill wind blowing our way."

"What if I agree? What can I do?" asked Sesklos.

"Put your hand upon my hand in the Council."

"Dracar will denounce us both. His lust for my chair blinds him even to the weather."

"Then promise him that which he desires most."

Sesklos felt an invisible hand clutch his heart. "But I have saved that gift for the son who is not of my loins but of my heart. Does he value it so little?"

"Father, as a sign of your love, above all other things. But of what value is a chair when the body lies prostrate and unmoving?"

Sesklos sighed; he was too tired to resist. "I will do as you ask. It is all I have left to give. I only hope that the Temple you build will be stronger than the ruins I leave behind."

THREE

I.

Grunting with effort, two workmen and an under-priest of Dralm pulled the heavy door of the pulping room shut. The noise from the pulping room faded from an ear-battering din to a distant rumble, although Kalvan could still hear the vibration of the horse-powered pulper through the stone floor. The other sounds—the thump of the horses' hooves, the squeal of unoiled chains and green-wood bearings, and the shouts of the foremen as they drove the ex-Temple slaves of the work crew to keep things going—were no longer clearly distinguishable.

Kalvan turned to Brother Mytron. "How are the horses bearing up under this work?"

"Better than men would," Mytron replied. His tone hinted of problems best not discussed here in the open hallway. Had Mytron been listening too long to Duke Skranga, who saw Styphon's spies everywhere? Or was he just being naturally cautious about speaking within the hearing of men he didn't know? Kalvan hoped it was the latter; Skranga's zeal to prove his loyalty to the Great Kingdom (and therefore his innocence of any part in Prince Gormoth's murder) was leading him to see Styphoni lurking under every bed and urge others to do the same.

Meanwhile, Kalvan decided against mentioning his plans to

make most of the paper mill equipment water-powered. Apart from the matter of security, it would involve either moving the mill or a lot of digging of millponds and building of dams and spillways. There was no guarantee the men and money would be available when spring came and the ice melted, and it would be pointless to even make the effort if the winter's work hadn't discovered how to produce usable paper. So far all the mill had produced was mush that smelled like the Altoona drunk tank on the Sunday morning after a particularly lively Saturday night.

"How goes the rag-cutting room?"

"Well enough, Your Majesty, but no one is working there now. We've chopped all the rags as fine as necessary, and no more have come in the last five days."

This was no surprise. There wasn't too much difference between the rags the mill was cutting up for paper and the clothes the poor of Hos-Hostigos were wearing this winter.

"I'll see what the quartermasters can do about providing you with something." The quartermasters would probably say they couldn't do anything, but Kalvan's experience of supply sergeants led him to expect they would be holding back more than they'd admit to just anyone. A platoon sergeant was "just anyone"; the Great King of Hos-Hostigos was somebody more.

Brother Mytron led the way down the hall and through a freshly-painted wooden door into another hall, with log walls and a roughly-planked roof. It was cold enough to make Kalvan wrap his cloak more tightly. Wind blew through chinks between the logs and planks, and dead leaves crunched underfoot. About all that could be said for these hastily-carpentered passageways between the buildings of the mill was that they were better than wading through knee-deep snow in a wind that made five layers of wool seem as inadequate as a stripper's G-string.

Warmth and foul-smelling steam greeted Kalvan and My-tron at the end of the passageway, also flickering torchlight and heartfelt curses in an accent that Kalvan could only tell was from somewhere other than Hos-Hostigos. Beyond a row of shelves holding a fine collection of blackened clay pots, Kalvan saw a muscular man with a blond beard standing stripped to the waist beside a row of pots on a stone-walled bed of hot coals. The smoke from the coals mixed with the steam to make Kalvan swallow a harsh cough. The man wouldn't have heard it in any case; he was too busy thundering at a small boy who was cowering in one corner of the room.

"—and the next time you let the goat fat burn, I'll try to find a coating that calls for boy's fat. *Your* fat, you lazy Dralm-forsaken whore's son—oh, I beg your pardon, Brother My—*Your Majesty*!" The man bowed and started to kneel, but Kalvan waved him to his feet.

"Don't stop your work for me. Just tell me what you have here. It smells like a glueworks."

"Well, maybe that's not so far from what it is," said the bearded man. "You see, Your Majesty said that sometimes animal fat was used to coat the—the *pulp*—to make *paper*. You didn't say what kind or how much, which was a good test, by Dralm, of our wisdom."

It was really a sign that Kalvan didn't know himself; there were times when he would have given a couple of fingers for one college-level chemistry textbook. Not that anybody here would know the scientific names of the essential chemicals for treating wood pulp, but at least the book would help him to recognize them. Right now, he wouldn't have known aluminum chloride if he fell into a vat of it. So they were going to have to make do with clay and animal-fat sizings on the paper, if they ever made *those* work!

"You're trying to find out what kind of animal fat works best?"

"Yes. I've got all these pots lined up and I try a different mix in each one. This first one's goat and sheep, the next is sheep and horse, the third one's pure horse fat. . . ."

The man listed the ingredients of all eight pots with the pride of a father listing his children, but Kalvan only remembered the first three. After that he realized that he was listening to a description of the experimental method—rule of thumb, even crude, but a foundation on which a lot of things this world desperately needed could be built.

"Master—?"

"Ermut, Your Majesty."

"Master Ermut, I'd say you passed Dralm's test very well. Your wisdom will be rewarded by something more than just your freedom."

Ermut bowed. "Thanks be to the Great God and Your Majesty. I'll say this much, though. I'd not cry at being still a slave as long as I was free of Styphon's collar."

Ermut didn't dare turn his back on his Great King, but Kalvan got a look at it on the way out. He'd always wondered what the scars left by those iron-tipped whips they'd found at the Sask Town temple-farm looked like. Now he knew.

II.

Kalvan sipped at his freshly refilled cup of mulled wine and contemplated the logs crackling on the hearth of what had once been the lord's bedchamber. Now Mytron had his bed in one corner of it and used the rest of it for an office and for entertaining junketing Great Kings.

When young Baron Nicomoth rode back from the Battle of Fyk, where he'd fought gallantly, he found his mother dead, his outbuildings burned, most of his hands run off into the Hostigi army or even farther, the crops rotting in the fields, and not two brass coins to rub together to remedy any of it. So he buried his mother, swallowed his pride, sold the family lands to the Great King, then took a commission in the Royal Horse Guards.

Since the qualities of intelligence and adaptability were in as short supply here-and-now as they were otherwhen, Kalvan quickly noted the young man's usefulness and made him his aide-de-camp. In the way that some junior officers will favor a respected senior, Nicomoth had his beard trimmed into a Vandyke similar to Kalvan's. He was even said to walk like the Great King. Nicomoth was on the slim side, but other than that their builds were quite similar, particularly when they were both in armor. Kalvan was sure that one of these days he'd be able to take advantage of having a double.

Nicomoth had left behind a rather good if small wine cellar, which Kalvan and Mytron were now busily depleting. Kalvan emptied his cup, set it down, and decided against another if he wanted to be fit to ride back to Tarr-Hostigos tonight.

"Mytron, I've said I'll see what I can do about more rags. Is there anything else you need?"

Mytron looked into his wine cup, wrapped his ink-stained fingers around it, then shook his head. "The Potters' Guild has promised to deliver what they call 'all the clay they have found fit for the Great King's service.' I will be charitable until I have seen how much or how little that is. It is said that the clay pits have frozen harder than ever before in living memory."

That was probably true, but for the sake of the Potters' Guild Kalvan hoped "all the clay" was "much" rather than "little." Brother Mytron's placid and even-tempered manner was deceptive, and Kalvan himself couldn't endlessly bow to the guilds.

"We have enough old swords to cut all the rags we are likely to see this winter. I have had to be harsh with some of the workers who would take such swords or sell them, in either case to defend against wolves and bandits. Have I done well?"

"Yes." Another of those painful decisions. Respect for the Great King's property had to be enforced—by the headsman, if necessary—no matter how many wolves and bandits were roaming the countryside. Besides, a sword given out for wolf-hunting today could be in a bandit's hands by the end of the moon.

"As to wire—we shall need much more when we know how to make the *paper*. For now, what the Foundry is sending is enough."

The brass wire for the screens on which the rags and wood pulp were supposed to drain into paper pulp was produced by an ancient practice that Kalvan had had to see with his own eyes to believe. One apprentice fed bar stock through a hole of the right gauge cut in an iron or stone plate, while another sat in a suspended chair underneath. The apprentice sitting in the chair gripped the end of the wire with pliers and swung back and forth, so that his weight and movement dragged the bar through the hole and forced it into wire.

Like so many of the here-and-now metalworking techniques, it was fine for high-quality, small-scale production—the beautiful steel springs of the gunlocks, for example. It was hopeless for really large-scale production. For that they'd need horse- or water-powered wire-drawing equipment, something else he'd really needed a month ago at the latest but would be lucky to see before Rylla's child was old enough to walk.

Kalvan wondered if the primitive state of large-scale metallurgy was the result of economics, military tactics, deliberate interference by Styphon's House, or a combination of the three. Certainly the good small arms and poor artillery made for a lot of small political units instead of a few large ones. The large ones could have generated enough revenue to make their rulers independent of Styphon's House, particularly if the economic surplus also supported an educated class, something like the medieval monks. Such a class would be an intolerable threat to the fireseed secret.

If that series of guesses was anywhere near the truth, Kalvan now understood why Styphon's House was rumored to be ready to preach the next thing to a war of extermination against the cult of Dralm. The priests of Dralm would be more than ready to be such an educated class—with a little help that Kalvan I of Hos-Hostigos intended to give them.

Kalvan decided he really didn't want to ride home tonight and poured himself more wine. "Mytron, I meant what I said about rewarding Ermut. I'm going to charter a Royal Guild of Papermakers as soon as there's any paper to make, and he'll be one of the first Masters."

"He deserves the honor, Your Majesty. He's done the same as he did with the animal fats on other work here."

"Then he has the makings of a Scientist."

"A what?"

"A kind of priest in my own land, one who was sworn to seek new knowledge. Ermut has stumbled upon one of their methods. It was called 'Experimenting.'"

"*Experimenting.*" Mytron rolled the word around on his tongue several more times. "And these *Scientists*—priests—what gods did they worship?"

"Seldom the gods of my own land. They were not good gods, and they did not help a man to know much. Although some of the Scientists served in the temples of Atombomb the Destroyer. They were free to choose to worship any god or none at all. Their oaths concerned how they were to do their work and not hide it from others or tell lies about what they had learned.

"Most of them did work in temples called Universities. Some of these were larger than Hostigos Town, that is, the way it used to be before the War with Styphon.''

"The Scientists must have been very rich. Or did your Great King pay them?"

"Some one, some the other." Kalvan put his cup down and lit his pipe. "If Dralm and Galzar give us victory in this coming War of the Great Kings, I mean to found such a University in Hos-Hostigos. There men like Ermut will teach Experimenting and the other arts of the Scientist. Had there been such a University anywhere in the Great Kingdoms long ago, when the lying priests of Styphon proclaimed the fireseed secret, its Scientists could have flung that lie in their teeth.

"Mytron, your work here at the paper mill will end when you have taught all you know and chosen someone fit to replace you. When do you think that will be?"

Mytron frowned. "Not less than another five moons, but not much more than that either."

Kalvan grinned. "Good. I want you to be head of the University. *Rector* would be your title."

Mytron frowned even more deeply, then said carefully, "My first duty is to the Great Father Dralm. I cannot forsake him."

With equal care, Kalvan replied, "I do not know the duties imposed on you by that oath. This is shameful in a Great King, but it is the truth. So I do not know for certain if I am asking you to forsake your service of Dralm. Yet I can say certainly that you will not have to swear any oaths against Dralm, or do anything I know to be unlawful, or to cease to perform the rites of the Great God."

"Then I will not refuse now." The frown faded a little. "I cannot accept without permission from Father Xentos, of course. He is the judge of the oaths of the priests of Dralm in Hos-Hostigos. Also, he would find me hard to replace at the Great Temple."

In fact, Chancellor of the Realm Xentos had already bent Kalvan's ear several times about how he and Brother Mytron were being forced to neglect their duties to Dralm to serve their Great King.

"I will speak to Father Xentos, to learn more about the duties of a priest of Dralm. I still hope that both he and they will permit you to become Rector of the University."

"If it is proper that I serve the Great God by serving Your Majesty in this, I shall do it with all my heart," said Mytron.

This seemed to call for a toast, so Mytron poured out the last of the mulled wine, and they both drank to the University finding favor in the eyes of Dralm.

Kalvan's pipe had gone out; he relit it and sat back to stare into the dying fire. He could see all sorts of church-and-state complications bearing down on him like a runaway truck on an icy mountain road. They would have been likely enough at best; with Xentos they were certain. In spite of his unworldly air, the Chancellor was as tough as a slab of granite and as shrewd a bargainer as an Armenian rug dealer. Anything Kalvan got out of him—particularly the permanent reassignment of his right-hand man (and probably handpicked successor) as Rector of the University—was going to cost.

But Dralm-dammit, he had to make a start somewhere at making sure he wasn't the only man in the world who knew half of what would be needed to bring down Styphon's House! Until he'd at least made that start, everything could fall apart if his horse put a foot in a rabbit hole! Kalvan thought of King Alexander III of Scotland, who'd started three centures of Anglo-Scots wars by riding his horse off a cliff in the dark.

Being the Indispensable Man sounded like fun until you were actually handed the job. Then you realized that the best thing to do with it was to get rid of it as fast as possible.

III.

The job of digging Dalla out of the Archives lasted another round of drinks. When they finally reached her, she told them to go on to Constellation House; she would change at the Archives and meet them there.

Constellation House was perched on top of a mountain a good half hour's air-taxi ride outside Dhergabar City. That gave Verkan Vall plenty of time to bring his old Chief up to date on everything of mutual interest, starting with Kalvan's Time-Line, Styphon's House Subsector, Fourth Level Aryan-Transpacific.

"Everything was going about as well as anyone could hope until winter came. Kalvan had no more internal enemies, Nostor was a shambles, and Sask and Beshta were beaten into submission. Even the Princes who didn't want to join Hos-Hostigos weren't about to make trouble."

"No," said Tortha. "I imagine a lot of them are thinking along the lines of 'The enemy of my enemy is my friend,' and anybody who's as heavy-handed a creditor as Styphon's House is bound to have more than his share of enemies. What about the big council Styphon's House was going to hold in Harphax City?"

"They moved it to Balph. We think it's because of the weather; it's been the worst winter in living memory, and the roads have been completely impassable most of the time. We haven't infiltrated the Great Temple yet, and they're not talking. I suspect they may be waiting to see what happens during the rest of the winter. Not that enough hasn't happened already, of course."

Tortha recognized the signs of coming bad news in Verkan's voice. He wasn't surprised, either. "I can imagine," he said. "My first independent assignment was shepherding a party of tourists fleeing from a sacked city to the nearest operating conveyor-head. It was five days' journey downriver, through country that had been fought over two years running. If we hadn't been able to use boats and travel mostly by night I don't think we'd have made it. At least I didn't have any arguments from the tourists after the first village where we found human bones in the soup pots."

"It hasn't been quite that bad yet in Hos-Hostigos, except in parts of Nostor. They're calling it the Winter of the Wolves, though. Between the wolf packs and the snowdrifts, nobody's going anywhere if they don't have to.

"I haven't been back there myself since I took over as Chief. Dalla went once, to Ulthor. They're not as badly off as the inland people, since they missed the fighting and shipped grain and meat in from the Middle Kingdoms before winter. Dalla still tried to ride to Hostigos and lost two horses and a guard to wolves the first day. After that she decided to stick to interviewing refugees and building our cover. She came back after a ten-day, and it was another ten-day before I could persuade her to eat a proper meal."

They sat in silence as the air-taxi passed out of the rainstorm and Dhergabar together. Ahead the mountains loomed against the clear sky, spangled with the lights of country homes and resorts. A full moon silvered the scattered clouds above and the occasional stream visible through the trees below. From the air it might have been the wilderness of Kalvan's Time-Line; in fact it was a garden planted with trees instead of flowers, like much of Home Time-Line. If the air-taxi let them down in the middle of this forest, they might wander for all of ten minutes before a robot or a Prole gardener found them. The nearest wolf was in Dhergabar Zoological Gardens.

"The University cut back its team to a handful of volunteer observers when travel became impossible. We don't have any work in Kalvan's Time-Line that's really worth sending in people."

Tortha Karf recognized another note in Verkan Vall's voice now, the frustration of a man who has to live in ignorance because he won't send men into danger where he can't go himself just to satisfy his curiosity. It was a frustration he knew his former Special Assistant would become accustomed to as the years passed. If there'd been any chance he couldn't, he'd never have become Chief of Paratime Police.

"Fortunately, Kalvan's still going to have the best army in his world, if not the biggest, when the campaigning season opens. Brother Mytron and Colonel Alkides were experimenting with methods for remixing Styphon's Best to bring it up to the quality of Hostigos Unconsecrated, and Kalvan's integrated the four to five thousand mercenaries he captured as Listra-Mouth and Fyk into a regular royal army."

Tortha Karf said nothing. He'd recognized a third note in his young friend's voice—what on some time-lines was called "whistling in the dark."

Verkan also appeared to be getting too attached to his friend Kalvan; that could prove to be a major problem if push came to shove. After all, Kalvan was still a theoretical danger to the Paratime Secret, the foundation upon which the whole of First Level civilization rested, and if Kalvan became a threat to that secret, Verkan Vall, chief guardian of that civilization, might find himself with a job no man could welcome.

The two men were beginning to look hungrily at the menu by the time Dalla arrived. She made her usual dramatic entrance carrying a medium-size flat package and wearing a blue cloak that covered her from the base of her throat to the floor.

Tortha couldn't help wondering what Dalla had on under the cloak. There'd been a time when the answer to that question would probably have been "little or nothing," but that time was long past—or so he hoped. Dalla was as decorative as she was competent, and this had led to a few episodes that made her first companionate-marriage to Verkan Vall rather hectic.

Both had learned something. Dalla was now much less impulsive and more careful about the company she kept. Vall didn't wear his pride in his sense of duty so openly on his sleeve. They seemed to be settling into the kind of marriage that a Chief of Paratime Police really needed. Either that, or no marriage at all—what Vall and Dalla had the first time around had the vices of both and the virtues of neither. Not to mention what a Chief's political enemies could do to exploit his personal problems!

A few minutes passed in kissing Dalla, ordering dinner, and consuming the first round of drinks and a large plate of appetizers. Dalla's gown was reasonably opaque and not too revealing otherwise, although it did show enough skin to tell the Commissioner that she'd had a deep-layer skin-dye to match her blond hair. Like Vall, her coloring would not attract attention on any Aryan-Transpacific time-line.

Her gown also seemed remarkably precarious in its attachment, and Tortha found he couldn't keep his eyes off the solitary fastening that stood between her and disaster. He noticed he wasn't the only man in the room doing so either. Finally Dalla said in an expressionless voice, "Don't worry about it. I have a laboratory now, and test critical components of my gowns for resistance to fire, acid, mechanical stress, and telekinesis."

Verkan Vall knocked over his glass in trying not to roar with laughter, and this seemed to call for more drinks. While the waiter was bringing them, Dalla unwrapped her package. It was an elegant leather-bound printed book, with a title on it that Tortha Karf didn't know but an author he knew rather too well.

"*Gunpowder Temple*, by Danthor Dras?"

"It's his *Styphon's House: A Study of Techno-Theocracy in Action* retitled," Dalla explained. "The public edition will be out in a few days, but he sent one of the presentation copies to Vulthor Tharn. For the Archives, not as a personal gift," she added, answering the unspoken question of both men. "I wouldn't have asked to borrow it otherwise."

"Is it rewritten as well as just retitled?" asked Verkan.

"I had it computer-scanned and the answer is no. However, there's a new introduction summarizing Kalvan's Time-Line up to the beginning of winter. He also promises a full-scale study of Kalvan's Time-Line and all the Styphon's House time-lines where Hos-Hostigos wound up under the ban, as a companion volume."

"He'll do it, too," said Verkan. "If half of what I've heard about Scholar Danthor is true, he's about as easy to stop as a glacier."

Tortha Karf nodded absently, aware that he'd suddenly lost much of his appetite for dinner. The greatest living expert on Aryan-Transpacific culture did nothing by chance, or at least he hadn't in the last three centuries. If he was bringing out a new edition of his definitive study of Styphon's House at this point, there had to be a reason. Tortha Karf had a number of theories about what that reason might be, none of which made for pleasant dining.

"Has Kalvan's Time-Line been receiving more public attention while I was in Sicily?" he asked.

Both Verkan and Dalla shook their heads. Dalla added, "The time-line's been too dangerous to attract reporters that we and the University people can't protect. The University people have been writing a lot, but all in the scholarly journals. I'd have expected some of them to try a popular article, but none of them have done it so far."

"That sounds like Danthor Dras sitting on them," said Tortha Karf grimly. "He probably wants to be the first to reach a popular audience. Once he's sure of being in the light, Kalvan's Time-Line is going to become everybody's favorite topic of conversation. So will any mistakes the Paratime Police and their Chief make in handling it."

Dalla frowned. "That incident where you found one of Danthor's colleagues was guilty of—something worse than academic fraud? You think he still holds it against the Paratime Police? That was more than a century ago!"

"It was. However, Danthor reminds me of some Fourth Level mountain-tribe chief. Once somebody's done him an injury, he won't die happy until he's paid it back or at least had his sons swear they will do it."

"After not saying a word for a century?" This time it was Verkan sounding skeptical.

Tortha took a firm grip on both his glass and his temper. "By the time he was in a position to fight me again, I was too firmly seated in the Chief's chair. He also had a few enemies of his own at the University. He's not the most lovable man there, even if he is right most of the time."

"That's like saying that Queen Rylla isn't the most even-tempered woman in Hostigos," said Dalla. "But go on."

"Anyway, he seems to have spent the last century outarguing, outwriting, or outliving all his enemies. Now there's a new Chief of the Paratime Police who isn't on quite such a firm footing as old Tortha Karf. Danthor's own flanks and rear are safe, and Kalvan's war against Styphon's House will give him a ready-to-hand audience without his having to do anything except write his fiftieth book. That's a situation a child couldn't fail to notice, and Danthor's forgotten more about strategy than most generals ever learn."

Before either Verkan or Dalla could reply, the waiters arrived with dinner. Tortha had thought his appetite was gone for the evening, but the fish, house sauce, and hot bread smelled irresistible. He let the waiters load his plate. Before long he was picking at the food.

A little later, he noticed that Verkan and Dalla were no longer paying him or their own loaded plates any attention. They were so lost in each other that they didn't even look up when the pattern of projected constellations on the ceiling overhead flared into a supernova. If they'd been fifty years younger, Tortha would have suspected they were holding hands under the table.

The sight restored his good humor. Strictly between him and his conscience, he was willing to admit that Dalla's old hostility toward him had some justification. He had been careless about their first marriage, keeping Verkan grinding away at one job after another.

Well, Dalla had no more worries coming from him. Now she had a much more difficult job: protecting her husband from himself.

FOUR

I.

Balph, the hub of Styphon's House on Earth, lay some forty-five miles downstream on the Argo from Ktemnos City. While nowhere near as large as Ktemnos City with its half a million people, Balph was still large enough to be called a city.

Despite being the fourth largest city in Hos-Ktemnos, its only industry was religion. Old Balph, the original trading settlement, had long ago been encircled by its strange offspring. Someday it too would be leveled for some new edifice to Styphon's glory. Balph proper was already the home of the Great Temple, the largest golden-domed temple in the Five Kingdoms, sixteen minor temples and shrines, the Temple Academy, the Temple Treasury, the Supreme Priest's Palace, and the Great Council Hall of Styphon.

Supreme Priest Sesklos sat at the apex of the Great Council Hall's triangular High Table, with First Speaker Anaxthenes to his right and Archpriest Dracar to his left. Ever since Sesklos's talk with Dracar, opposition to Anaxthenes's coalition had evaporated. With twenty of the thirty-six Archpriests of the Inner Circle behind him, Anaxthenes was now forging a program that would change the course of Styphon's House in ways the others would never even begin to realize until it was too late.

First, all new candidates to the upper priesthood were required to take a test of their faith in Styphon. How smugly the hypocrites—including himself!—had voted for this provision after carefully ensuring they would never have to take such a test themselves. Then they'd passed a resolution to lend one hundred and fifty thousand ounces of gold to King Kaiphranos to hire mercenaries and buy supplies for the war against Hostigos.

Next they'd put together the First Edict of Balph, condemning the Usurper Kalvan and his minions but leaving an escape clause for any whose loyalty was wavering. There was more than one such, according to secret reports from Hostigos, especially as the winter grew harsher.

By Styphon, they would crush this interloper before another winter fell!

As he'd been prompted earlier by Anaxthenes, Archpriest Neamenestros spoke up. "I suggest that we now deal with the rumors that have been spread by the Daemon Kalvan's dupes: that Styphon's House recognizes no other gods but Styphon."

A polite way of saying that what former Highpriest Vyblos of Nostor Town or the dearly departed Krastokles had said in public should have been said only in private, although all of the upper priesthood had been saying it to each other for as long as Anaxthenes could remember. Cimon and Roxthar both squirmed in their seats but kept quiet as they had promised.

"Why should the Council of Balph deny the special divinity of our god, the brightest star in Heaven's sky?" snapped Archpriest Timothanes.

"Because the mercenaries we need to win the war against the Usurper worship Galzar with a fervor our priests lavish only upon the weekly offering bowl," said Anaxthenes. He hoped that would be enough to make Timothanes think twice about further defiance.

"The time for declaring Styphon's sole divinity will come when the Usurper's bones are moldering in their grave cloths. Already some of Galzar's priests openly council their charges to side with the Usurper in the coming war. We must make our peace with Galzar before Kalvan forces an open breach. He who owns the mercenaries, owns the Five Kingdoms."

"Yes," said Archpriest Heraclestros. "And we own most of the gold in the Five Kingdoms."

"Wise words," said Supreme Priest Sesklos. "I call for a vote."

Twenty-four heads nodded, while twelve were still. Dracar and his allies looked like cats passing fish bones.

"The resolution passes. It shall be decreed that Styphon respects the divinity of all sixteen gods, excepting the false god Dralm. We also offer the services of our healers to any and all priests of Galzar engaged in the struggle against the unlawful Usurper who calls himself Great King Kalvan of Hos-Hostigos. Styphon's Will Be Done."

When Styphon's Voice had fallen silent, Anaxthenes added, "The Daemon Kalvan and his minions threaten not only all our lives, but Styphon's House on Earth as well. King Kaiphranos is but a poor weapon to hurl against such as is the armor of Kalvan; a weapon easily broken or turned aside. Should this happen, I fear Kalvan's next march would be upon the Holy City itself!

"We need a sharper and better sword. Why not that of King Cleitharses of Hos-Ktemnos? Let him help lance the boil that is Kalvan on the body of the Five Great Kingdoms. I say we should issue a proclamation, calling forth the Sacred Squares of Hos-Ktemnos to come to the aid of the God of Gods!"

That was the prearranged signal to Archpriest Theomenes, spiritual guardian to Great King Cleitharses, to touch his first two fingers to his mouth. Anaxthenes touched his fingertips to his forehead, granting Theomenes permission to address the Council.

"Great King Cleitharses has found his faith disturbed by the misfortunes brought down upon Styphon's House by the Usurper Kalvan. He will not willingly and of his own free will grant that which is ours to ask, but he will listen to our united voice. While a wise and fair king, Cleitharses has little love for the clamor of battle or the open air."

That brought snickers from the assembled Archpriests. Cleitharses's last campaign was over ten years ago against King Leucadiphon, one of the three petty rulers who claimed suzerainty over the Upper Sastragath. The war had quickly turned into a nightmare of lost skirmishes and misdirected or scanty supplies, until the Army of Hos-Ktemnos had only been saved by the steadfast Sacred Squares, man for man the best fighting force in the Five Kingdoms. Cleitharses's idea of pleasure was reading about sufficiently ancient deeds of glory or adding another scroll to the Royal Library.

"Furthermore, King Cleitharses is worried about a new Great King so close to the borders of Hos-Ktemnos who adds Princedoms like a lodestone pulls iron filings."

"Who will the Great King choose as his Captain-General?" asked one of the Archpriests.

"Duke Mnesiphoklos, Lord High Marshal of Hos-Ktemnos."

"He has seen seventy winters. Isn't it time he hung up his spurs?"

Another Archpriest added, "He is good at fighting barbarians, but will he be able to stop Kalvan?"

A dozen voices tried to answer at once, but Roxthar's voice cut through them like a saw. "The Daemon Kalvan must be stopped. We need a warlord of Styphon."

Supreme Priest Sesklos raised his hand for quiet. "Archpriest Roxthar is right. We need a soldier of the Temple. Someone we can trust to sow the fields of Hos-Hostigos with the corpses and water them with the blood of the Daemon's army. I move that we call upon Grand Master Soton of the Holy Order of Zarthani Knights."

This time the voices were shouting in protest. Soton was known to be as much a servant of Galzar as he was a priest of Styphon, and there were many here who had been cut by his sharp tongue.

"Silence!" roared Sesklos. Anaxthenes stared. He had not thought Sesklos had so much determination left in him. "Grand Master Soton is a man of the battlefield, not some lickspittle underpriest currying favor with his superiors. We shall ask him to bring eight Lances of Knights and offer him an additional three thousand Guardsmen. That should stiffen the Army of Hos-Ktemnos enough for our purposes.

"First Speaker, have a scribe sent to my chambers. I have letters to draft."

II.

King Kalvan reined in his horse and held up a gloved hand as a signal to the riders of his escort. "Hold up there!" he added, in case some hadn't seen the signal.

It was getting dark, the clouds were getting thicker, and while it wasn't snowing—thank Dralm for small mercies!—the wind was blowing the snow already on the ground.

"Your Majesty, should we be stopping here?" Count Phrames's voice came from just behind. "We are too strong to tempt wolves or bandits if we keep moving, but if we stop we may look like easy prey."

"In that case, they're going to get a nasty surprise," said Kalvan as he pulled a pistol out of his boot and checked the load and priming. Then he pulled his mount's head around with one hand, holding the pistol cocked and ready with the other.

As he left the road, Kalvan heard Phrames calling out that the Great King wished to ride apart and pray to the gods of his homeland for guidance. If he'd thought there was anybody to answer, Kalvan wouldn't have minded doing exactly that. However, neither his father's determination that his only son should follow him into the ministry nor here-and-now's crowd of gods and goddesses had altered his basic agnosticism.

What he was actually thinking of doing probably wasn't any more rational than praying, but it seemed to work better for him. He intended to ride up to the four-foot hemlock standing below a little cliff that marked the place where he'd left 1964 Pennsylvania and ended up here-and-now. The hemlock marked the site of the farmhouse where an escaped murderer was holed up. He'd been on his way toward the farmhouse with fellow Pennsylvania State Policemen Steve Kovac and Jack French when he was scooped up by the cross-time flying saucer.

Somehow, returning to the tree and climbing the cliff calmed him down when he needed it, and sometimes gave him an idea for the solution to some particularly knotty problem. He'd been there three times since last autumn; this fourth time he needed a relaxing place to think even more than before.

In the last month, the hunting parties had taken their toll of the wolves, but not all of them came back. A man who didn't kill his wolf with the first shot might find its teeth in his throat before he could reload. Some parties came back short half their strength; tales began to go around that the wolves were demons in animal shape.

Other parties marched off into storms and didn't come back at all. In Nostor, Kalvan finally had to withdraw the hunting parties completely, because they were being ambushed by bandits and starving peasants for their horses and weapons.

Kalvan remembered Duke Chartiphon's speech at the banquet celebrating the beginning of fireseed production in Hostigos. He'd predicted they would make a howling wilderness of Nostor. They had, too, with help from weather, wolves, and the civil war that broke out after Count Pheblon and Duke Skranga had Prince Gormoth assassinated and then put Pheblon on the throne in his place.

Not that anyone missed Gormoth, to be sure. He'd been a bad enemy and would never have been a friend worth having. But as long as a nominally friendly Prince ruled Nostor, the Great King of Hos-Hostigos couldn't simply march in and take charge, even if the place was falling apart. That would make it look as if Great King Kalvan was more concerned with his own power than with the overthrow of Styphon's House, and that reputation would be a real political headache. Not as big a one as a live Gormoth would have been, but a live Gormoth could always have been turned into a dead one. Prince Pheblon would just have to be supported as much as possible, in the hope that he would repay that support by his contribution to the spring campaign.

It was the coming campaign that concerned Kalvan as the riders on the road disappeared behind the trees. This latest inspection tour made it clear that the hunters were finally getting the better of the wolves. Woodcutting parties were going out again, so people weren't freezing to death quite so often, and winter had to be two-thirds gone unless another Ice Age was coming on. However, when spring arrived, so would the next round against Styphon's House.

By the time Kalvan's thoughts had gone that far, the snow was up to his horse's knees and looked as if it would be even deeper farther on. Kalvan guided the horse to the left, down into the bed of the little stream, then stopped as he felt his mount's hooves beginning to slide on the ice.

"Dralm-dammit!"

He could see the hemlock, or one that looked very much like it, in the dusk ahead. He wasn't going to get there unless he dismounted and left his horse, which would make both him and it ridiculously easy prey for wolves. As for the little cliff, it might as well be in Alaska for all his chances of reaching it tonight. Whatever ideas might come there couldn't be worth risking his neck, or even his horse. Good mounts weren't easy to replace in Hostigos, and wouldn't be for quite a while.

Kalvan backed the horse until there was enough room to turn, then rode back downstream. He returned faster than he'd come, because as he turned the horse the howl of a wolf floated down from a nearby hill. The horse whinnied nervously, and Kalvan had to work to keep him from breaking into a trot.

Count Phrames met Kalvan by the road with an I-told-you-so expression on his face. "Your Majesty, I beg you not to ride out again like that while we are in wolf country. On your safety—"

Kalvan broke off his cursing. "Phrames, Queen Rylla has already appointed six nursemaids for our child. I'll recommend you as the seventh if you wish it."

Phrames winced as if he'd been slapped, and Kalvan immediately felt guilty for taking out his frustration with the world in general on the Count. He felt even guiltier for throwing the fact of Rylla's pregnancy in Phrames's face. One of the many little details about Hostigos Kalvan had learned, after the campaigning season ended and there was time to think, was that for years Phrames had been Rylla's intended husband and the prospective heir-matrimonial to Hostigos. To see her married to a total stranger sent by the gods from nowhere couldn't have been pleasant for Phrames, even if the stranger gave her a throne and a crown.

"I am sorry, Phrames. I spoke in anger and haste, and my words were unworthy of a king."

Phrames grinned, white teeth showing above a frost-tinted brown beard. "I spoke without proper respect to you, I admit. But I did speak with proper respect for Queen Rylla, who's the one I'll have to reckon with if I let wolves or bandits take you."

"Then by all means let's both show her respect and turn for home. There seems to be nothing more out here worth seeing or doing tonight. Also, the envoy of Prince Araxes of Phaxos is coming tomorrow, and I want to show him at least the respect of being awake and unfrozen.''

Kalvan holstered his pistol and pounded his gloved left hand gently against his saddlehorn to see if there was any feeling left in the fingers. He'd had one bout of frostbite during the Korean War that had made him more susceptible to a second.

Phrames snorted. "What His Reluctance Prince Araxes needs is a swift kick where he sits down from the Great King's army and everybody else who wants to help. We may have to sell tickets."

Kalvan didn't entirely disagree, after two months of hearing Araxes's excuses for not swearing allegiance to Hos-Hostigos and another of total silence. However, if the man was going to the trouble of sending an envoy over wolf-ridden, snowbound roads, common courtesy required listening to him.

They rode across the little bridge built over the stream last autumn, one of a score or so that Kalvan had ordered built by peasants and prisoners of war to make it easier to move guns and wagons around Hostigos. The beams and planking seemed to be holding up, but one railing was sagging ominously. Kalvan called out to his scribe to make a note of this. He pretended not to hear a petty-captain adding that if the Great King could notice something like that, he would certainly notice a man riding like a sack of cabbages, "so remember that you're on a horse, Niclos, and not on the ridgepole of your father's barn, thank you, or you'll wish you'd never been born . . .''

Two hundred yards up the road, the head of Kalvan's escort overtook a woodcutting party—twenty men and a dozen mules and horses laden with branches and logs—that completely filled the road. Phrames swore like a trooper, several of the woodcutters swore back, and finally Kalvan had to urge his horse through the drifts to restore order. Voices stilled as he approached.

The leader of the woodcutters was the yeoman farmer Vurth, who'd been Kalvan's first host here-and-now. Kalvan had amply repaid the farmer for taking in a stranger who didn't know when or where he was by fighting off a band of Nostori raiders threatening Vurth's homestead. Kalvan didn't believe in omens, but he had to admit that seeing Vurth's homely bearded face grinning up at him made him feel better, even though the wind was still rising.

"The wolves aren't what they were a month ago, Your Majesty," Vurth explained. "It's worth it, to not sit by a cold hearth. So we went out, and what with the frost breaking off the branches, we didn't have to do much cutting."

"Good work, Vurth. We'll buy three mule-loads for the shelter at Hostigos Town. Pick men to take it, and they can ride there with us." Kalvan looked past Vurth to a pair of mules halfway up the train. "I'll pay the bounty on those wolves, too. How many are there?"

"Five and a half-grown cub, Your Majesty."

"I hope you didn't use any of the royal fireseed on them."

"No, no. Styphon's owl dung is good enough for those, and we didn't even have to shoot two of them. My oldest daughter's husband, Xykos—he's as big as a bear and found himself some armor at Fyk—just stands there and lets the wolf bite his armor. Then while the beast's trying to reckon why the man doesn't taste right, he swings the ax. Wolves don't take to being hit on the head with axes, let me tell you!"

"Your son-in-law sounds like a good man. Would he care to join the hunting parties, or take a post with my Lifeguards?"

"I don't think he'd say no if you asked him come spring, Your Majesty. Right now, though, his wife's half a moon from her first. So he'd as soon not be away from home for a spell. I'm sure you understand we mean no disrespect."

"None taken, Vurth. I know a little of what he's going through, and by spring I'll know more. I'll send a gift for the child and speak of this again some other time."

"Dralm bless Your Majesty, and give you and Queen Rylla a son to go on ruling over us as well as you've done," said Vurth. Kalvan heard murmurs of agreement from the other woodcutters. He backed his horse away, thanking Somebody that it was too dark for anyone to see his face turning color.

It helped to hear things like that whenever he had the feeling that maybe he was on the wrong course and should have simply ridden on instead of starting the biggest war this world had known in centuries. If the people who had to pay the price in burned houses and ruined farms, stolen livestock and poisoned wells, dead sons and raped daughters, thought he was ruling well, maybe he was actually doing something right.

"God helps those who help themselves," had been one of

his father's favorite aphorisms. Kalvan wasn't going to place any bets on the source of whatever help he received, with all due respect to the late Reverend Morrison. But certainly Kalvan had never heard of any good coming from just lying down and letting events roll over you like a steamroller.

FIVE

I.

Kalvan sighed happily as Rylla wrapped the freshly heated cloths around his feet. He wasn't worried about frostbite any more, but the warmth seeping through him still felt delicious. The temperature must have been dropping toward zero when he rode into Tarr-Hostigos, and the wind had been blowing half a gale.

"There," Rylla said decisively. "Your toes don't feel quite so much like dried peas." She stood up and took his hands. "Your fingers still feel cold, though." She sat down on the bench beside him and tucked both of his hands inside her chamber robe.

Between the warm fur lining of the robe and the warm Rylla inside it, Kalvan's fingers quickly finished thawing. In a few minutes, he could feel how Rylla's waist was beginning to swell with the child she was carrying.

"Has it moved yet?" he asked.

Rylla's blue eyes clouded for a moment. "No. Amasphalya the chief midwife and Brother Mytron both said that it would not be a good sign if the child moved so soon. When the snow turns to rain is when it should start moving."

"If the snow ever stops! If the winter is at all like this in Grefftscharr, they must be watching for the coming of the frost giants and the last battle of the gods.''

Kalvan tried to keep the fear out of his voice. He doubted he'd succeeded any better than he had all the other times since he learned Rylla was pregnant and what had happened to her mother. Princess Demia had two miscarriages, bore Rylla safely, then died in childbirth trying to give Prince Ptosphes a son. That was one reason why Ptosphes had never remarried; he had a daughter who was as good as any son, and other acceptable heirs beyond her. He would not send another woman to Hadron's realm when he didn't have to.

It didn't help that Kalvan had already done just about everything he could hope to do to improve Rylla's chances. He'd explained antiseptic theory to Mytron and some of the other temple priests of Dralm, as well as to the chief priestess of Yirtta Allmother. He would have taught it directly to the midwives, but they were even fussier about their guild privileges than the blacksmiths, who were still arguing about whether bore-standardization for infantry muskets would infringe on their traditional rights! Taking lessons from a mere Great King was beneath the midwives' dignity.

At least they'd sworn to learn from Mytron and the others. If they didn't, all the guild privileges in the Six Kingdoms wouldn't save them. The midwives who attended Rylla were going to be clean and keep her clean, if Kalvan had to stand over them through the whole birth with a pistol in each hand!

Kalvan pulled his hands out of Rylla's robe and looked at the maps on the wall to the left of the bed. It made him feel better to see something where he had made a difference and would go on making one. He'd not only taught his officers to see maps as an important weapon, he'd established a Royal Cartographic Office that was producing one complete set on deerskin and four smaller sets on parchment every week. The deerskin sets would go to the major castles, while the parchment ones went to the field regiments. With luck, every castle in Hos-Hostigos, every army commander, and most of the regiments would have maps before the campaigning season opened.

The first map was Hostigos—or Old Hostigos, now that it was the senior Princedom of a Great Kingdom—Center County, the southern corner of Clinton County, and all of Lycoming County south of the Bald Eagles. Hostigos Town was on the exact site of otherwhen Bellefonte, with Tarr-Hostigos guarding the pass through the Bald Eagles.

Then Hos-Hostigos, with its seven other Princedoms. Reading in a circle around Old Hostigos, from northeast to south, they were Nostor (a former enemy turned weak ally), Nyklos, Ulthor (with a port on Lake Erie), Sask (another former enemy now turned into the gods-only-knew what kind of ally), Kyblos (with its capital on the site of otherwhen Pittsburgh), Sashta (a new Princedom created originally as part of the alliance against Hostigos, which Kalvan had allowed to remain in existence as a favor to Sask and Beshta), and finally Beshta itself. That was the map Kalvan had studied most closely; he hoped he wouldn't need to do much if any fighting in Old Hostigos itself.

Finally, the map of the Six Kingdoms. From north to south, they ran:

Hos-Zygros—New England and southeastern Canada to Lake Ontario;

Hos-Agrys—New York, western Quebec, and northern New Jersey;

Hos-Harphax, or what was left of it—Eastern Pennsylvania, Delaware, Maryland, and southern New Jersey;

Hos-Ktemnos—Virginia and North Carolina (the richest of the Great Kingdoms); and

Hos-Bletha—From South Carolina to the tip of Florida and west as far as Mobile Bay.

Kalvan didn't spare too much time for the Six Kingdoms map either; he'd long since decided it was a waste of time to worry about grand strategy for the whole war to overthrow Styphon's House. They didn't have enough intelligence about the enemy's plans, potential resources, or high command—which for the time being meant the Inner Circle of Archpriests at Balph.

They might have been better off if the "Council of Trent" Styphon's Voice had called last autumn had been held in Harphax City, as originally planned. Somebody must have realized that Harphax City was close enough to the borders of Hos-Hostigos to be full of Kalvan's spies, or at least people willing to sell him secrets for the right price. So they had moved the Council, Archpriests, bodyguards, baggage trains, old Uncle Tom Cobley and all, to the Great Council Hall of

Styphon at Balph itself. Balph was a one-industry town: Styphon's House. A mouse couldn't get in there without being vouched for by three upperpriests; Styphon's House might not understand the military value of security, but apparently it knew how to practice it.

Without knowing what was happening at Balph, it was impossible to tell if Styphon's House was going to step out from behind the Kings and Princes it had always used as front men and wage this war on its own. There were military advantages to either choice.

Making war by proxy was always risky; the proxies might develop minds of their own, as any number of Italian city-states had discovered with their *condottieri*. In fact, the cult of Galzar the War God encouraged a general brotherhood of all mercenaries, and there was no way Styphon's House could do anything about that without appearing to declare war on Galzar.

Kalvan rather wished they would be that stupid; the war would be over by next winter if Styphon's House made enemies of enough mercenaries. However, he doubted that would happen. Supreme Priest Sesklos might be ninety-one and past being a war leader, but some of the other Archpriests were said to be shrewd enough to head off militarily disastrous decisions.

On the other hand, the Kings and Princes might not be willing to be Styphon's front men anymore. They could now make their own fireseed, raise their own armies, and snatch their neighbors' land without the consent of Styphon's House. They still might need gold and silver to pay mercenaries if they wanted to spare their own subjects the burden of military service. However, other people besides Styphon's House could now provide that; Great King Kalvan I of Hos-Hostigos, for example.

Styphon's House could probably find a respectable force of allies if it were willing to pay enough, in both gold and power. Styphon was not a popular god, at least in the Northern Kingdoms. Few would fight for Styphon's House cheaply. The price of the rulers' aid might bring down Styphon's House as completely as any defeat in battle.

Except that then the countryside might be overrun by mercenaries whose employers could no longer pay them, living off the land, gradually turning into armed mobs and turning that land into a desert. The idea of the whole Atlantic seaboard winding up like Germany toward the end of the Thirty Years' War turned Kalvan's stomach.

He reminded himself sharply that he was speculating much too far ahead of available intelligence and forced the nightmare out of his mind. What about the one man who would certainly fight Hos-Hostigos whether Styphon's House helped him or not?

King Kaiphranos of Hos-Harphax didn't care whether Kalvan worshipped Styphon, Dralm, Galzar, or rattlesnakes like some of the Sastragathi tribes. He did care that Kalvan was in rebellion against him, suborning the loyalty of his sworn Princes and generally committing treason, insurrection, usurpation, riot, robbery, and spitting in the streets. Proper Great Kings put down rebels, and even King Kaiphranos (known to all as Kaiphranos the Timid) considered himself a proper Great King.

What Kaiphranos thought and what he was were two different things. The man was well past seventy, and it was notorious throughout the Great Kingdoms that he'd always wanted to be a flute-maker. He'd never ruled and now barely reigned. At best he drizzled. Left to his own feeble devices, he'd barely be able to rely on more than his own Royal Army of five thousand, less than half of it at all well trained or well armed.

His family was another matter. Kaiphranos had two sons, Philesteus and Selestros. Prince Philesteus, the elder, was a soldier with a reputation for courage, which would be more important than competence in the here-and-now army he was leading. Princes and barons loyal to Kaiphranos or wanting to get rich off the loot of Hos-Hostigos would follow him, and so would enough mercenary captains to make a useful difference.

King Kaiphranos also had a younger half-brother, Grand Duke Lysandros, who was that fortunately rare thing, a publicly devout worshipper of Styphon. If Styphon's House sent gold and men to aid Kaiphranos, Lysandros would do his best to see that neither was wasted. That made it far more likely that Styphon's House *would* send the money and men, and make Hos-Harphax a far more formidable opponent.

Kalvan stood up and started pacing up and down the room below the maps. Rylla, who'd been putting her long blond hair up in a nightcap, looked at him in silence. Then she sighed, handed him his fur-lined slippers, and stood up to join him. He stopped long enough to hold her briefly and kiss her. His list of Reasons Why I Love Rylla would now fill a long parchment scroll. High on the list was the fact that with her he didn't have to pretend to be the sent-by-the-gods Great King Kalvan with answers to everything. He didn't have to be afraid to admit it when he was scared, too tired to sleep, or with no idea at all of what to do next.

"Dralm-dammit! Everything—the survival of Hos-Hostigos, you, the baby—it's all going to depend on whether Styphon's House sends King Kaiphranos against us by himself, or waits to get help from Hos-Ktemnos and Hos-Agrys. If they wait, we could be outnumbered three to one."

"We could be," said Rylla. "On the other hand, time lets us find new allies, too. Also, if what one hears of Prince Philesteus is true, he will be as hard to hold back as a yearling colt. He will attack for the honor of Hos-Harphax, even if he has no hope of victory."

"So it will be a race between Prince Philesteus's sense of honor and Styphon's House offering him enough to make it worth holding back?"

"That's a good way of putting it."

That also should mean a spring campaign against nothing more than a Styphon-reinforced Hos-Harphax. Say, forty-five thousand enemies against forty thousand Hostigi, total strength. Allow five thousand Hostigi left behind in garrisons to defend the Trygathi border, key towns, castles, and depots, assume the Styphoni-Harphaxi alliance would risk throwing all their men forward, and the two field armies came out at forty-five thousand enemies against thirty-five to thirty-six thousand Hostigi.

Not hopeless, but not good either. If all the Hostigi troops were up to the standard of the regiments of the Royal Army of Hos-Hostigos or Ptosphes's Army of Hostigos, and all the artillery were the new mobile four- and eight-pounders, Kalvan would cheerfully have faced two-to-one odds. They weren't, they weren't going to be, and there was nothing to do about that.

He could hire mercenaries, of course. But Styphon's House could easily outbid him, and even if they didn't, the money would be better spent on improving the Royal Army or the Princes' troops. That was another mistake the Italian city-states had made: spending all their money on mercenaries and none on arming and training their own people. The *condottieri* not only hadn't been reliable, they hadn't learned how to fight anybody except one another. When the French invaded in 1494, they rolled up Italy from the Alps to Naples like a rug in a single campaign.

So he had thirty-six thousand men, some of them twice as good as anybody they'd be facing, against possibly as many as fifty thousand of unpredictable quality. Definitely not good. Kalvan doubted he could afford a single major defeat, or even more than a couple of drawn battles or expensive victories. He had to destroy his enemies without losing the ability to protect his friends and allies from the vengeance of King Kaiphranos and Styphon's House. Otherwise those friends and allies would dry up and blow away.

He couldn't afford to hire many mercenaries. Much of the Royal Treasury would have to go to repairing winter damage, purchasing supplies for the coming campaign, and buying more horses and arms. Could he afford to take the offensive, in spite of what the Winter of the Wolves might have done to their food stocks and the draft animals for the wagons and guns?

"We can probably afford it better than anything else—if we can move the guns," Kalvan said out loud. Rylla gave him one of her why-don't-you-talk-to-me-instead-of-just-yourself looks and he explained.

She nodded when he'd finished. "If we can put all of our men into the field, that will lessen the odds against us. Also, if we take the offensive, we can keep all our men together and improve the odds still more. If we wait for the enemy to come to us, there will be calls for a regiment to defend this town and a battery to defend that bridge. If we honor all the requests, we will soon have no army left. If we ignore them, the people will wonder about their safety. Many of the soldiers may desert to defend their homes and families.

"Also, if we keep the army together, it will be easier to send messages. That's almost as good as growing wings on—"

Kalvan interrupted Rylla's dissertation on the principles of war by kissing her again, harder and longer than the first time.

For a moment he was almost sorry that she was pregnant. The spring campaign would be long over before she could be in the saddle again, and she was one of Hostigoş's best generals.

She was also somebody who couldn't stay out of the thick of the fighting once she got within hearing of the gunfire. A recurring nightmare for Kalvan was finding Rylla the way he'd found a Nostori cavalry officer—shot out of the saddle by a charge of case shot, ridden over by his whole troop, then stripped naked by looters and tumbled into a ditch. He hugged and kissed Rylla again until the nightmare went away.

Rylla looked at the map of Hos-Hostigos again. "We can move food and guns down to the castles in southern Beshta as soon as the roads are open. That way, we don't have to move the whole army and everything it needs at once, or as far."

A depot system made sense if they were going to take the offensive. It even made sense if by some miracle the enemy struck first. A few well-gunned, well-supplied forts in the path of Kaiphranos's army could tie down a lot of his strength. If he wasn't brave enough to move until he had Styphon's aid, the forts could support cavalry units to scout and harass him all the way to the walls of Harphax City. Harmakros in particular would just love a chance to take his troopers south and singe King Kaiphranos's beard!

"We'll have to be careful to give them adequate supplies and reliable garrisons," Kalvan said. "It won't do for the main army to march south and be shot at by our guns because the garrisons have been starved out or turned their colors."

"I know the men for the garrisons," said Rylla with an impish grin. "The mercenaries that Balthames's Beshtans rode over at the Battle of Fyk. If there's anybody absolutely sure not to love Beshtans, it's those men."

Kalvan agreed and tried to remember the disposition of those troops in the new Royal Army. He had offered amnesty, land, and a place in the Royal Army of Hos-Hostigos to the mercenaries who had been captured during the wars with Nostor and Sask; a majority had signed on.

Now he recalled where the mercenaries were. "They're with the Third and Fourth Regiments of Horse. We can send them to Beshta as part of an observation force under Captain-General Harmakros."

Before Rylla could reply, Kalvan realized that he might

finally be tired enough to go to sleep and draped an arm over her shoulder. "Let's go to bed."

He wasn't quite as tired as he'd thought, but it didn't take long for the warmth of the bed and Rylla's steady soft breathing to put him under. The last thing he remembered thinking before dropping off was that despite all his problems, he was still a lucky man to be here with Rylla as Great King Kalvan instead of merely Corporal Calvin Morrison of the Pennsylvania State Police.

Six

I.

Outside the shuttered windows of the great hall of Tarr-Hostigos, Kalvan knew that it was a dazzling bright winter day, without a breath of wind disturbing last night's freshly fallen snow. It was also cold enough to perform a traditional form of surgery on brass monkeys.

Inside the great hall, both fireplaces were blazing and charcoal braziers stood in every corner and on either side of the two thrones. Candles and rush tapers also added their bit to both the heat and the light. It was still nothing that Kalvan would have called "warm" in either English or Zarthani, but at least he could hope to refrain from undignified gestures such as stamping his feet or blowing on his fingers.

The royal herald at the head of the stairs blew on his trumpet with more enthusiasm than talent. His companion, carrying the double-headed copper poleaxe that accompanied each Great King at official functions, raised his voice.

"Baron Menephranos, envoy of Prince Araxes of Phaxos, craves audience with the Great King of Hos-Hostigos."

Baron Menephranos stepped into the great hall, followed by an attendant carrying four scrolls on a silver tray and flanked by two efficient-looking bodyguards in the black and green livery of Phaxos. The guards fell back as the baron strode forward, stopping halfway to the throne to bow until Kalvan waved him forward.

58

Menephranos was a tall, gangling young man who was almost certainly older than he looked, which was about eighteen. Kalvan found it harder than ever to be optimistic about Prince Araxes's allegiance; this wasn't the sort of negotiator he would have sent on serious business.

Menephranos approached the royal throne, bowed again, and handed the first scroll to Kalvan. He inspected it to make certain that Chancellor Xentos's seal was on it along with Prince Araxes's, signifying that it had been read by the Chancellor and found satisfactory. Then he handed the credentials to Rylla.

Normally he would have handed them to Xentos himself, but the old highpriest of Dralm was in bed with a nasty cold that might turn into pneumonia if neglected. Kalvan and Rylla had forbidden him to attend the audience; Rylla had added that if he went on arguing, she would tie him to the bed, put sleeping draughts in his wine, and if all else failed, shoot him in the foot. The last threat was probably a joke, but with Rylla you could never be sure.

"Baron Menephranos," said Kalvan. "It is Our understanding that your lord, Prince Araxes of Phaxos, has some considerable matter he wishes to lay before Us. Let Us hope that it is one which will lead to good relations between the Great Crown of Hos-Hostigos and him. We have suffered no injury at his hands, nor have We given him any that We are aware of." Araxes's example had undoubtedly encouraged other Princely waverers to refuse their allegiance to Kalvan, which counted as an injury on anybody's books, but why not be tactful?

"The Great King speaks the truth," said Menephranos. His voice was also older than his face, a fine baritone that seemed too strong to come from such a narrow chest. "It is my lord's message that he must refuse his allegiance to the Throne of Hos-Hostigos, and that he does this out of no enmity to the man proclaimed Great King Kalvan the First, but out of a greater concern for his own nobles and people."

Menephranos picked up the second parchment, ignoring the general hostile muttering that had begun when he used the word "proclaimed." He went down on both knees to Kalvan, who saw that the parchment was sealed with both Araxes's seal and that of the High Chancery at Balph, seat of Styphon's Voice and of the Great Council.

Kalvan described the seals, waited for the new muttering to die down, then said, "We have long been curious as to what plots against the true gods and those who honor them the arch-deceivers of false Styphon hatched in their sty at Balph. Now, perhaps, We shall know more than We have. If so, Prince Araxes *may* have Our gratitude, though We do not have his allegiance."

Kalvan drew his dagger and slit the seals. The scroll had two sheets. One was a short letter from Araxes that restated in more flowery language what Menephranos had already said about the Prince's refusal of allegiance. The second was headed *First Edict of Balph*. Kalvan skimmed the Edict, heard Rylla muttering under her breath, and realized that his face must be showing too much. He pulled it straight, finished reading the Edict, then cleared his throat and began reading it aloud.

FIRST EDICT OF BALPH

SESKLOS, *Supreme Priest and Styphon's Voice*
  to:
THE LAWFUL KINGS AND PRINCES OF THE KNOWN WORLD
Greetings:
Be it known, that:
  Throughout all the years since the great Revelation of the fireseed mystery given us by Styphon, God of Gods, that secret has been guarded by Styphon's House.
  Throughout all the years in which that secret has been guarded, it has been guarded not in hopes of temporal power or wealth.

This time harsh laughter joined the muttering. Kalvan waited for silence and went on.

  It has been guarded in the hope that by moderating the power of the Kings and Princes to make war at their whim, the lands of the Known World might remain unravaged by war and their people secure in their lives and wealth.
  Now the godless usurper and ally of demons calling himself Kalvan—

Kalvan waved the hall into silence; if they started cursing at every insult to him, they'd be here all day.

Now the godless usurper and ally of demons calling himself Kalvan has revealed Styphon's holy secret to all men. He has given to Kings and Princes the power to unleash the scourge of war upon the land whenever they wish, without let or hindrance save from their own wills.

He has so greatly deceived and led astray certain Princes that they have sworn impious oaths to join him in his rebellion against Styphon's House and the God of Gods.

As all may bear witness, Styphon and the true gods have now visited their curse upon the land for the crimes of the usurper and ally of demons Kalvan. Not in the memory of man has war wrought such havoc, nor has the winter been so fierce, nor have demons in the shape of wolves ravaged the land so freely.

It is proper and lawful that Styphon's House endeavor to lift the curse from the land by all means in its power, so that the innocent will not suffer along with the guilty.

To this end we proclaim:

That no oath sworn to the usurper and ally of demons Kalvan is binding in any way whatsoever upon any man.

That Styphon's House will freely give the secret of fireseed to any King or Prince who has sworn no false oaths to the usurper and ally of demons Kalvan, and that this fireseed shall be free of demons and all other unclean beings which abound in Kalvan's foul and impious substance.

That such Kings and Princes who receive the secret of lawful fireseed shall admit into their councils such consecrated priests of Styphon as may be necessary to guard the fireseed against the influence of demons, and that these priests shall be allowed all that they deem necessary to preserve the cleanliness of the fireseed and the true worship of Styphon God of Gods.

That against such Kings and Princes as have made unlawful oaths, produced unclean fireseed, or despitefully used the priests of Styphon, Styphon's House may proclaim all measures it deems fit, even unto Holy War, save that these Kings and Princes abjure their crimes and make full and fit restitution and repentance.

Done in the Great Council of Balph, this twenty-sixth day of the Moon of the Long Darkness in the four hundred and eighty-second year of Styphon's Revelation.

SESKLOS

Kalvan was too angry to sit still. He jumped up from the throne, snatched the third parchment from the tray, and tore it open. This document renounced the words of the traitorous dupes of the Usurper Kalvan, the so-called Archpriests Zothnes and Krastokles, who had fraudulently disparaged the other true gods except for the false Dralm, god of bilge-cleaners and latrine-diggers. Kalvan was glad Xentos wasn't there when he read *that* aloud, to an accompanying chorus of "Down Styphon!" and "Death to Sesklos!"

"I know it stinks," said Kalvan when he could make himself heard. "But consider where it comes from. Would anything from the Lord of the Flies and his servants *not* stink?" That drew laughter, reminding the hall of the endless peasant jokes made to explain why the priests of Styphon's House were always demanding more manure for their saltpeter mills.

Kalvan was privately sorry to see that someone at Balph had the sense to see what the result of a One-God, One-Way schism might be here-and-now, especially considering all the mercenaries who took the worship of Galzar Wolfshead as seriously as the Roman Legionnaires took the cult of Mithras. There went the Holy Crusade against Styphon, at least for now.

When he opened the fourth parchment, Kalvan began to laugh. "Sesklos seems to think he has some hope of proving his case, and encloses what seems to be a great many empty words on demons, oaths, prophecies, divinations, and such matters."

Kalvan sat back down and looked at Menephranos. "Nonsense does not become less nonsensical by being repeated in more flowery language, or did no one ever teach Sesklos that?"

Menephranos seemed to feel that he had to reply. "I cannot judge the thoughts of Styphon's Voice. Yet I know that Prince Araxes is greatly concerned not only for his own lords and people, but for others who have been—whom Styphon's House sees as having been led astray by the proclaimed Great King Kalvan. Surely even Your Majesty must see—"

"Little man," said Rylla in a voice that lowered the temperature of the hall about ten degrees. "The word 'must' is not used to Great Kings." Rylla's hand was very close to the hilt of her dagger, and Kalvan didn't like the expression on her face. The last time he'd seen one like it, she'd thrown the lid of a stone chamberpot at him and would have thrown the pot itself if he hadn't made a strategic retreat in the face of overwhelming bad temper.

Kalvan decided the situation needed defusing before some hothead took his cue from Rylla and turned the audience into a brawl or worse. Kalvan did not care to be known as a ruler who could not keep order in his own court, or worse still, allowed the envoys of allegedly friendly Princes to be lynched before his eyes.

He stood up, ostentatiously wiped his hands on his breeches, then drew his own dagger and thrust it through one corner of the Edict of Balph. "Will someone please summon the Steward of the Privies?" he called. "Have him bring one of his buckets. I think he is the man among us most skilled at dealing with filth."

Several people promptly dashed for the door, and even the green-and-maroon-uniformed Lifeguardsmen burst out laughing. Menephranos tried to join in the laughter but wasn't very successful, since his face was turning the color of the coals in the braziers.

When he could make himself heard without shouting, Kalvan went on. "Baron Menephranos. Like a good dog, you have barked as your master taught you. It is not your fault that you bore a shameful message that does your master no honor. Therefore we will not violate the laws of hospitality sacred to Father Dralm and Yirtta Allmother by bidding you leave Hostigos at once. However, we would consider it a courtesy if tomorrow's sunset did not find you within the bounds of Old Hostigos."

"As Your—Your Majesty commands," said Menephranos. His face was still flushed, but his voice was almost steady, and he bowed himself out with as much dignity as anyone could reasonably expect under the circumstances.

"Someone ought to make that little cockerel a capon before he gets too fond of crowing," said Rylla to nobody in particular. Kalvan hoped nobody at all had heard. Otherwise he might wind up like Henry II, who'd lost his temper in the presence of some of his more hotheaded knights and wound up being held responsible for the murder of Thomas à Becket in his own cathedral.

"Baron Klestreus!" he called.

"Your Majesty?" The retired mercenary general who was now Chief of Intelligence lumbered over.

"Do any of your people have old friends among Menephranos's retinue?"

"Not that I know of. Why?"

"It doesn't matter. Send some of your most trustworthy men around to Menephranos's lodgings tonight with enough money to make new friends. Men who can hold their wine and keep their eyes and ears open."

Klestreus nodded and lowered his voice nearly to a whisper. "Not friends of Skranga, either."

"No." He stopped Klestreus as the man backed away. "Before you go, Baron. That Edict of Balph, and that other proclamation denouncing Baron Zothnes, doesn't sound like the work of Sesklos—or at least not the Sesklos I thought I knew. Do you have any idea who might be behind this?"

"Hmmmmm. It could be the work of Archpriest Anaxthenes, First Speaker of the Inner Circle. I've only met him once, at the court of Hos-Ktemnos. I was impressed by his mother wit; some call him the *mouth* behind Styphon's Voice."

"Dig up whatever you can on him and anyone else who might be behind this resurgence of the House of Styphon, and make me a report. And by Dralm, get someone into Balph if you have to bankrupt the Treasury! If you don't have any news within a moon, I'll have Skranga stick his nose in."

"Yes, Your Majesty." Klestreus's voice was a little shaken.

"Now put your men on to Menephranos." Klestreus withdrew, calling for his messengers. Anyone the Chief of Intelligence sent out tonight could be trusted to remember anything Menephranos's men spilled, not sell it to the highest bidder, and guard Menephranos himself from any Hostigi hotheads. Kalvan wasn't prepared to trust Duke Skranga's Secret Servicemen that far, although the former horse trader was a natural intelligence officer. Unfortunately, Skranga was so crooked that he probably saw playing both ends against the middle as a sort of indoor sport to keep the winter from getting too dull, like Ping-Pong or gin rummy.

He hoped Klestreus wouldn't call his bluff and force him to use Skranga to crack Balph. It was good strategy to keep both intelligence agencies mistrusting each other; he paid a price, however, when it interfered with their real work.

Kalvan turned to the advisers nearest the throne. "I want a message taken to Chancellor Xentos that the Great King and Queen would like to wait on him and seek his advice about holding a Great Council of the Realm."

Everyone of suitable rank within hearing immediately started arguing about who should have the honor of doing the Great King's bidding. Kalvan sighed and slipped an arm around Rylla's waist, although it felt like embracing a suit of heavy-cavalry armor. The Zarthani were a long way from the "I say to one, come, and he cometh; I say to another, go, and he goeth," of the Roman Legions. In the Great Kingdoms at least, they tended to regard that sort of obedience as fit only for serfs, barbarians, and the Middle Kingdoms of the Mississippi Valley.

"Why must we take council with Xentos?" asked Rylla, but apparently at the world in general and Styphon's House in particular rather than at him.

"I want to hold a Great Council for the same reason we held one before the Battle of Fyk. Styphon's House has stolen a march on us, we may have to move fast to catch up, and I don't want everybody and his uncle complaining they weren't consulted."

"Yes, but it will take the better part of a moon to have all the Princes of Hos-Hostigos brought here. Can we give Styphon's House a gift that big?"

"We can't and we won't," said Kalvan. "What I want to find out is how much I can safely do by way of appointing men to represent each Prince and telling the Princes themselves afterward. Also, if I can do that at all, Xentos may have good advice about which men we can trust. Finally, all the priests of Dralm in the Great Kingdom look up to him, and many of the other priests as well. If we have his support for what we do in advance, we'll be more likely to have the priests on our side if any Princes make a fuss."

Rylla giggled. "You have a devious mind, Kalvan. A wise one, though. If you were not a prince in your own land, you should have been."

Kalvan tightened his grip on her waist and felt some of the stiffness go out of her spine. Devious? Maybe he looked that way, and if it made his job easier, he didn't mind. What he really wanted to be was intelligently cautious about this business of setting up a Great Kingdom to make war on Styphon's House, while learning how to rule it as he went along.

Maybe he did have some natural talent for ruling. Right now, though, it looked as if it would be mostly on-the-job training that would make the difference between keeping or losing both his throne and his head.

II.

Kalvan sighed wearily as he hitched his shoulders and pulled the neck ruff up over his head. The neck ruff was four hundred years out of fashion otherwhen; here-and-now it was the latest fashion from Hos-Agrys—all the Great Kings and Princes wore them, or so Rylla claimed. As far as he was concerned, it was far worse than a necktie or even a clerical collar. For at least the five hundredth time, he reflected that there was more to the business of being a Great King than leading armies and taking Great Queens to bed!

At least his afternoon audiences were over. The first had been a group of Nostori merchants all the way from Nostor Town to tell him that this was a bad winter. Ouch! What did they expect him to do—raise his arms, mumble abracadabra, and send the storm clouds fleeing? The sad part was that this was exactly what seemed to be expected from Great King Kalvan, Sent by Dralm to Save the People of Hos-Hostigos from the Hosts of Styphon.

Next he'd heard from a delegation of the Fletchers' Guild with a list of complaints, chief of which was a strongly worded query as to why the new Royal Army of Hos-Hostigos wasn't using any archers. When he'd suggested that they consider joining the new Gunsmiths' Guild, they'd reacted as if he'd asked them all to undergo a voluntary orchidectomy.

Kalvan sat down at his desk. He'd made that himself, because nobody in the Fitters' and Joiners' Guild would be responsible for such an abomination. Furniture-making, like so many other crafts he'd once taken for granted, had a long way to go here-and-now. Nearly the only furniture was tables, chests, benches, and things that looked like an old-fashioned upright cupboard, for holding valuables. Chairs were brand new and all the rage but hardly found outside palaces and the homes of the wealthiest merchants. Kalvan would have given a couple of regiments for a padded armchair with a foot rest!

The top of Kalvan's desk was made from the bole of an oak tree that had been young when Leif Ericson sailed to Vineland, and it was covered with scrolls, maps, and parchments weighted down by one of the new rifled pistols he'd had made up. The workmanship of the pistol was magnificent: mother-of-pearl inlay in dark walnut wood, worked and etched silver facings, and an ivory butt with a carved representation of Galzar. It must have taken someone all of three or four months to handcraft it for the King. Three or four months in which the craftsman could have turned out a dozen utilitarian pistols, or even three or four muskets.

Now that the immediate crisis was over, everyone—well, almost everyone—seemed to want to return to the old ways of Before Kalvan. Output at the rifle shop had dropped from fifteen rifles a day to six. Part of that slowdown was due to the harsh weather, but what was really going on was that the shop could turn out five smoothbores for each rifled musket it produced. Despite the fact that the Royal Treasury was paying them five times as much for each rifle, every time they thought Kalvan wasn't looking, they went and stepped up the production of smoothbores. The only reason they were still making even six rifles a day was because their Great King had threatened to mount a few heads on the palisade of Tarr-Hostigos if production dropped any lower.

Cannon production had dropped to almost nothing because they'd run out of brass. Last month he'd had them melt down every brass chamberpot, utensil, and ornamental vase in Hostigos Town and the outlying villages. Result: one cast-brass sixteen-pounder, three eight-pounders, and one four-pounder.

Note: find local source of copper, thought Kalvan.

Kalvan could well appreciate the love for handcrafted quality goods; after all, wasn't he from the land of Maytag, Ford, Westinghouse, and General Electric? The real problem here-and-now wasn't one of aesthetics, though, but of survival. How could he get that across to the provincial-minded guilds and mercantile associations?

Not that there weren't successes. His army reforms had gone over well throughout Hos-Hostigos, especially standardization of regiments and ranks, primarily because the career army officers loved them. There were now three new grades between captain and captain-general where before there'd been only grand captain. All of this meant promotions and pay raises—in peacetime, too! They weren't so happy about the new Royal Army; perhaps they'd caught a glimpse of the future to come. In return for the promotions and raises, they'd still swallowed it and helped quell their Princes' objections.

Kalvan looked down at the mountain of parchment and vellum piled on his desk and wondered if he wasn't making a big mistake, reinventing paper. He was sure that legions of his descendants would curse him for it. That is, if the paper-makers ever produced anything better than the soggy throw rug they'd brought him this morning. At least it didn't smell as bad as the last batch. He never remembered paper smelling at all, much less like rotten eggs. It was the sulphuric acid that was causing the smell, but they had to use *something* to bleach the pulp after it was pounded and beaten.

Maybe he was going in the wrong direction. It was becoming obvious that the acid, even in mild solution, was destroying the fiber. Why not try a completely differently bleaching agent? What about lye or slaked lime? It would certainly bleach the fibers, most probably without the smell. Maybe he was on to something? As soon as he finished with today's paperwork, he'd visit Ermut and tell him to try a lye solution. He'd leave it to the papermaker to discover the right strength.

It was nice to have people around he could depend on, even if he could count their number on the fingers of his two hands. Now back to work.

He picked up the top parchment; it was a plea from Ryx, a small town thirty miles north of Hostigos Town, for a party of hunters to track down a wolf pack. Kalvan made a note to speak to Colonel Hestophes, the hero of Narza Gap, whom Kalvan had put in charge of Hos-Hostigos internal security, which right now meant wolf- and bandit-hunting.

Good officers were another thing in short supply; Chartiphon had politely refused to leave the Army of Hostigos for the Royal Army. That was just as well, as Kalvan didn't want Ptosphes to lose all his best officers. Harmakros had become a

Captain-General in the new Royal Army, and Colonel Alkides of the Army of Hostigos was now Brigadier-general Alkides in command of the Royal Artillery. Hestophes was a proven fighter, and Kalvan was grooming him for higher rank.

There were other requests—some of them desperate—for hunters, trappers, food, and fireseed; there was even one ludicrous request for two hogsheads of winter wine! The last request was the easiest to take care of; he placed the parchment into a basket for scraping and reusing. The only groups in Hostigos that this ill winter wind had blown good seemed to be the innkeepers and the royal scribes.

Kalvan kept at his work until he could see the grain of his desk top, then rang for his servant to bring him some hot carob. It was a poor substitute for coffee, but. . . .

Arriving along with the steaming carob was Chancellor Xentos, wearing his blue robe and cowl with the eight-pointed star of Dralm on the breast. He had a ruddy, kindly face that looked young in spite of the wrinkles and snow-white hair; perhaps it was his perpetual alertness and the twinkling blue eyes. His nose was still red and dripping from the end of his cold, but otherwise he looked far better than when Kalvan and Rylla had waited on him three days ago.

"It appears I arrived at just the right time, Your Majesty."

Kalvan nodded and motioned Xentos to take a chair. "Cleon, bring the Chancellor some hot carob."

When Cleon returned, Xentos took a sip, then said, "Ah, this *is* good. I seem to feel the cold in my joints more with each passing year."

Kalvan laughed. "You've got lots of company this year, young and old."

"That is the truth, Your Majesty. This is a winter to stay close to the hearth if there ever was one. Which reminds me of one reason for my visit. I just left the royal chambers, and Brother Mytron was threatening to chain Rylla to the bed if he caught her riding bareback again. In her condition and with her mother's example, Dralm be merciful!" Xentos struck his forehead with the palm of his hand.

Kalvan had to swallow a fist-sized lump before he could trust himself to speak. "Dralm-blast it! I've told her— ayyyyyy! Oh well, I'd have easier luck talking to a hurricane. Sometimes it's as if I was married to an elemental force of nature instead of a woman. I'm just glad she's in Brother

Mytron's hands; Prince Ptosphes and I . . ." Kalvan made a washing motion with his hands.

"She's been like that ever since she began to crawl," said Xentos with a smile. "And the cries she could make! I love her like a daughter, but I wish Father Dralm in his wisdom had seen fit to mix a little caution into that bundle of fireseed. At least now that she's with child, we won't have to worry about her riding off into battle."

Kalvan felt pretty good about that. Rylla's pregnancy had turned out to be one of his best-executed plans, even if it had cost him one of his best generals. Also a plan in which he'd enjoyed the campaign even more than the victory. Now if only the spring campaign against King Kaiphranos ran half as well. . . .

"Xentos, have you heard anything from the Harphaxi priesthood about King Kaiphranos's plans?"

"We have seen few messengers from as far as Hos-Harphax this winter. The only information we have received about King Kaiphranos has come from a brother who just arrived from Arklos. He has heard that King Kaiphranos has sent requests to all his Princes and nobles for troops to prepare for war against Hos-Hostigos. Few have thus far reached Harphax City. It is said that many of the royal heralds have not yet returned, which may be due either to storms or to those who would rather not hear their messages."

That was about what Kalvan had expected. Some of Kaiphranos's nobles would use the winter as an excuse for not preparing for a war they did not intend to fight. Others would heed their liege lord's call. The fewer the better for Hos-Hostigos; unfortunately, the winter worked as much against Kalvan's sending out antiwar propaganda as it did against Kaiphranos's calling up his levy.

"Xentos, I have long wanted to discuss with you the founding of a University in Hostigos."

"A *University*?" said Xentos, his forehead wrinkling. Kalvan understood the Chancellor's perplexity. There were no institutions of higher or even lower learning in the Great Kingdoms. The nobility was taught by tutors; everyone else picked up what he could at home or served an apprenticeship in one of the guilds. Only priests attended anything even remotely like schools.

"A University is like a school for priests, only instead of

just teaching religion it teaches everything.''

''Everything?''

''Astronomy, alchemy, agriculture, medicine, law, even the arts.''

Xentos shook his head. ''Dralm be praised! Your Majesty never ceases to keep this old man in befuddlement. These things are not mysteries, but common matters learned at any man's hand. Why should they be taught at schools?''

Kalvan spent the next half hour explaining the Enlightenment view of classical education to Xentos. He stopped when the old man sighed in resignation.

''Yes, yes, let us start our own University! How else can so much knowledge be packed into one man's head? Dralm in all his wisdom has given Hostigos far more than a simple warlord in you, Your Majesty. Sometimes I wonder if you have come from a land far more distant than the ends of this earth.''

To head Xentos off from this line of conversation, Kalvan added, ''I have decided on a Rector to head the University, but I need your permission.''

''My permission?''

''Yes. He's one of your priests. Brother Mytron.''

''Brother Mytron!''

''Yes. Besides being a fine surgeon, he knows herbs, the weather, history, and many other things.''

''You are right in this. His wisdom and great piety are why the Temple of Dralm values Brother Mytron so highly, especially in our struggle against the false god Styphon.''

''I know you value him highly. Is there something I could give you in exchange?''

Xentos turned away for a moment, then looked back into Kalvan's face. ''Because of the abominable Edict of Balph, the priests of Dralm have decided to call a Great Council of our own to determine our strategy against Styphon's House. It will be held in Agrys City in summer. I would like Your Majesty's permission to attend.''

Kalvan could smell the way this wind was blowing: no Great Council, no Brother Mytron. If he let the priest attend the Council, Xentos wouldn't be here for advice and consultation when he would be most needed, during the war with Hos-Harphax. On the other hand, if he could get the University established, then all his work would not be in vain if something happened to him. Generals who led from in front were poor insurance risks; look at Gustavus Adolphus or Turenne.

There would also be no end to the mischief that the priests of Dralm could cook up at their Great Council. But they wouldn't need Xentos's help for that, and in fact there was a real need for the voice of Hostigos to be heard in Agrys City. If only he could be sure just which way Xentos might pull if it came to a tug-of-war between church and state!

It occurred to him that perhaps it didn't really matter. Even if Xentos's loyalties were divided, more good than harm might come from this Great Council. The Council could rally all the people whose religious beliefs were mortally offended by the unmitigated gall of Styphon's House in actually daring to demote a god! Not just any god, either, but Dralm the Father God, the Great God, the foremost figure in the Zarthani pantheon. One did not have to be particularly devout in one's worship of Dralm to believe that no good could come of men presuming to cast down gods.

Kalvan felt like laughing, but he knew it would have offended Xentos by seeming irreverent. If the battle between him and Styphon's House had come down to a straightforward question of who had the biggest army and the longest purse, the victor would certainly have been Styphon's House. As it was, a serious religious offense had been committed, and might decide the outcome of a war between a lifelong agnostic and a Temple run mostly by men who worshipped only their own wealth and power!

God or the gods, if any, must have a rather sardonic sense of humor.

Kalvan nodded graciously.

"You have Our permission to attend the Council."

"Thank you, Your Majesty. I hope the University prospers under its new Rector."

"I think it will. Of course, having Brother Mytron at the University will give Dralm a voice and an ear in its affairs."

"So I had assumed, Your Majesty."

Kalvan resisted the urge to grind his teeth. "Now that this is settled, what are your recommendations for the Great Council of Hos-Hostigos?"

"After asking guidance from Dralm, I have reached my decision."

Xentos's decision was that it would be worth the delay for Kalvan to secure the presence of all the Princes or at least their lawfully appointed envoys. To be sure, a Great King did have the power that Kalvan was proposing to exercise, but was it wise to exercise it so early in the history of the first new Great Kingdom? Xentos gave, at great length, a good many reasons why it was not, but added that only Dralm could judge for certain.

"If Xentos really left as many things up to Dralm's judgment as he wants people to think he does, he'd be a doddering old fool," Kalvan told Rylla afterward. "However, that's one of the few things I'm *not* worried about. Xentos may be as determined as a Sastragathi chief to win his feud with Styphon's House before he dies, but he's no kind of a fool."

"Nor as old as he looks," said Rylla with a broad wink. "I've heard it said that Xentos uses a special bleach to get his hair and beard so white. But—will you take his advice?"

Kalvan shrugged. "It's good advice, and I'm not sure I'd have a choice even if it wasn't. After all, I publicly asked for it in the hearing of the full court."

"You will be honored for your respect for the Great God, as indeed you ought to be."

"Thank you, darling," said Kalvan. He hoped he was keeping the sarcasm out of his voice. Respect for the local gods was one thing if it stayed at the level of politicians kissing babies and putting on Indian headdresses. It was something else if it meant dividing authority in Hos-Hostigos between himself and Xentos. Not that the priest wasn't competent, but he had always been and would stay incredibly stubborn, and church-state conflicts (more shades of Henry II, as well as the later Henry with all the wives) were exactly what Kalvan didn't need as long as he had Styphon's House on his hands.

SEVEN

I.

Xentos was shrewd enough to realize that he should do something in return for Kalvan's cooperation, such as help assemble the Council. Sending word of the Council and copies of the Edict of Balph to all the Princes used up horses at a rate that made Harmakros wince when he contemplated mounting his cavalry for the spring. It also used up a few of the messengers; the wolves were fewer now, but the weather was only slightly warmer, and a two-day blizzard swept across the Great Kingdom while half the riders were still on the road. Xentos dipped into the Treasury of Dralm to replace the horses and help the families of the dead.

On the twelfth day of the Red Moon the Great Council of Hos-Hostigos met in the great hall of Tarr-Hostigos. Prince Sarrask of Sask and his silver-armored bodyguard were the first to arrive. When not drinking beer at the Crossed Halberds tavern, he was in Hostigos Town square watching the Royal troops at drill and on parade.

Prince Balthames arrived three days after his father-in-law. Before the evening was through, he tried to seduce one of the royal pages. This earned him a ruined nose that kept Brother Mytron up all night trying to repair. His older brother, Prince Balthar of Beshta, arrived the next day in a mail-armored wagon with an escort of fifty cavalry and never left his room until the day of the Council.

Prince Pheblon, the new ruler of wartorn Nostor, was the next to arrive. He had salt-and-pepper hair worn down to his shoulders, a black goatee, and an understandably harassed expression. Prince Armanes of Nyklos not only came himself, he brought two thousand ounces of silver to contribute to the Royal Treasury. Kalvan made a mental note to find out whose confiscated estate had produced the silver. More work for Klestreus and/or Skranga. Prince Tythanes of Kyblos was the last to arrive.

Prince Kestophes of Ulthor did not come himself, but he sent a large embassy. The head of it, a Count Euphrades, assured Kalvan that he also bore what might be called a watching brief for several Princes of Hos-Agrys who had ties of blood or friendship to Prince Kestophes. Kalvan made another mental note to see if anyone in Euphrades's retinue could be persuaded to tell who these mysterious Princes were. He had no objection to Princes who wanted to join Hos-Hostigos learning the secrets of its Councils; he did object violently to those who might simply want to know which way to jump when the spring campaign opened.

However, a limited gain in military security was not enough reason to mortally insult Prince Kestophes by refusing to seat his ambassador. So far, Ulthor was Hos-Hostigos's only port on the Great Lakes, which meant the only route to the Middle Kingdoms and the West, particularly Grefftscharr. Prince Kestophes was going to have to do something much worse than send an unduly inquisitive ambassador before Kalvan would take notice of it. Official notice, that is. . . .

Kalvan's modified enthusiasm for Chancellor Xentos underwent a further modification when the Council assembled and Xentos walked in with Baron Zothnes, the former Archpriest of Styphon's House. The hisses of indrawn breath made the great hall sound like feeding time in a snakepit, and Kalvan heard mutterings about "Styphon's spies." Rylla's father, Prince Ptosphes, went as far as grasping the hilt of his ceremonial dagger. Kalvan made another mental note to sit down with—or if necessary, *on*—Xentos until he explained why he'd brought the defecting Archpriest into the Council without a word of warning. Meanwhile, he had to stand behind his Chancellor or look like an even bigger fool than he already was. Which would make the Council a waste of time, and the Princes would not take kindly to that. Not at all. . . .

Kalvan rose and rapped the table with the ceremonial mace he was using for a gavel. "Peace, my lord Princes. Baron Zothnes is high in Our confidence. He has foresworn the service of false Styphon by oaths to which most of you were witnesses. Will you deny this, so denying hope of reward to those who see the truth about Styphon and repent of their sins and errors? Will you be harsher in your judgments than the Great God Dralm himself?"

As he sat down in the face of a temporarily subdued Council hall, Kalvan reflected that there was something to be said for being the son of a minister with a fine line in hellfire-and-damnation sermons.

Zothnes, whalelike in his fur robes, was abject in his thanks. Personally, Kalvan would much rather have had the other defecting Archpriest, Krastokles. He'd been one of Sesklos's handpicked troubleshooters, and it wasn't really his fault that the trouble shot first. However, only Dralm could get the benefit of former Archpriest Krastokles's repentance now. He'd died early in January, so suddenly that there was talk of poison, although Kalvan personally suspected appendicitis.

As it turned out, Zothnes was the most useful member of the Council. Everyone had read the Edict of Balph, everyone knew that Styphon's House was sharpening axes for them, and everyone knew that there was only so much they could do without knowing more about the Inner Circle of Styphon's House than they did.

Unlike Krastokles, Zothnes had never been an Archpriest of the Inner Circle. He was essentially a manager, but one of his managerial skills was a very good memory for useful facts about everyone who might help or hurt him. As Zothnes delivered his rambling briefing on the Inner Circle, Kalvan realized that if Zothnes ever rode one of those cross-time flying saucers to a world with gossip columnists, he'd make his fortune overnight.

The names of highpriests and Archpriests and upperpriests swirled past Kalvan until he felt as if he were reading a long Russian novel without a cast of characters to help him keep track of who was doing what to whom. He made yet another mental note, this one for at least the twentieth time: get the scribes together and work out a system of Zarthani shorthand.

One of these days something vital was going to be forgotten because everybody thought it was somebody else's job to remember it.

Gradually five names came to the front: Sesklos, Supreme Priest and Styphon's Voice; Archpriest Anaxthenes, First Speaker of the Inner Circle; Archpriest Roxthar, Keeper of the Sacred Flame and political infighter *par excellence*; Archpriest Dracar, second in line behind Anaxthenes for Sesklos's chair and not at all happy about it; Archpriest Cimon, the painfully honest and reform-minded "Peasant Priest."

Remembering the Cluniac order and the Franciscans, Kalvan suspected Cimon might prove the most dangerous. A serious reform movement within Styphon's House was something they needed like more wolves.

"There have been First Speakers of the Inner Circle who achieved the title only by outliving all their rivals," Zothnes emphasized. "Anaxthenes is not one of them. No man knows his mind, and few have learned of his plans for them until he has executed them, for better or for worse. Sesklos loves him like a son but is often child to Anaxthenes's plans. Should he thwart them now, he might die clutching the viper to his chest. More than one of Anaxthenes's opponents has died thus."

"Let us not be among them," said Rylla.

Note, thought Kalvan. *Royal food-tasters, yesterday at the latest.*

"Bless Your Majesty, and with Dralm's help may it never be so," said Zothnes. There was a chorus of agreement from the Princes.

"Anaxthenes is no believer in Styphon," continued Zothnes. "Indeed, it is said that he believes in nothing save his own ability to outwit all his enemies. Nor is Archpriest Dracar. Cimon is useful for public appearances and talking with the local priests, while Roxthar wears his piety like a shroud and his ambition like a dagger. There are so many tales about Archpriest Euriphocles and Archpriest Heraclestros, highpriest of the Great Temple of Agrys City, being true believers, it is hard not to wonder."

Zothnes dabbed at rheumy eyes with a handkerchief that must have been stolen from a chimney sweep. "A strange, sad fate for Styphon's House—that men subject to all the weaknesses of believers should be among those to control its destinies. Indeed, Dralm works in mysterious ways."

Sarrask of Sask howled with laughter, and everyone else except Prince Balthar of Beshta at least chuckled. Kalvan and Rylla looked at each other but stifled their own laughter at the expression on Xentos's face. To hear even a former priest say that it was a sad fate for a temple to be run by those who believed in its god was clearly something he had never believed he would hear and very much wanted to believe he hadn't heard now.

Zothnes's supply of gossip eventually ran dry, but before it did, the Council knew they had a better idea of who and even what they were facing. The Edict of Balph and the leading personalities of the Inner Circle pointed only one way.

Prince Ptosphes stood and summarized. "Styphon's House will not fail to send gold and fireseed to King Kaiphranos. They may even place a portion of the men in their own pay under Harphaxi command. Most certainly, though, such men will shake off Kaiphranos's authority like a dog shaking itself dry the moment Styphon's House gives the order."

"I almost feel sorry for Kaiphranos," said Prince Tythanes of Kyblos. "He won't know which way to look for enemies."

Sarrask snorted like a boar interrupted at feeding. "I'll feel a damned sight sorrier for him once his head's on display outside Harphax City."

In order not to appear to be dominating the Council, on the second day Kalvan let Ptosphes continue with the military briefing he'd worked out in advance with Rylla, the First Prince, and Duke Chartiphon. Before long they were all standing in front of the big deerskin map of the Five Kingdoms, while Ptosphes used a poker borrowed from the fireplace as a pointer.

Hos-Zygros was neutral, at least for now. Great King Sopharar was known to be a dedicated follower of Dralm yet was far enough away from Styphon's House center of influence to sit out the coming storm. They would make trouble for anyone who made trouble for them, and for the time being nobody else. Even if they wanted to raise an army to intervene in the war, their population was small—Hos-Zygros was the second least populous Great Kingdom after Hos-Bletha—scattered, and by all reports hard hit by the Winter of the Wolves.

Hos-Bletha, at the other end of the Eastern seaboard, was nominally neutral but would probably interpret its neutrality in ways friendly to Styphon's House if they had a chance. "I say 'if' because the nomads and wild tribes from the Valley of the Great River are said to be stirring, even moving eastward. Small blame to them, if it's true that the Mexicotal are moving north on Xiphlon."

"Small blame indeed," said Rylla.

The Mexicotal held here-and-now Mexico as far as Yucatán and bore a grisly resemblance to the Aztecs, complete with a fondness for human sacrifice. The semidesert country of northern Mexico and Texas and its savage tribes had kept the Mexicotal away from the Kingdom of Xiphlon, in here-and-now Louisiana, Mississippi, and east Texas—at least until now.

"That may also keep the Zarthani Knights at home," added Ptosphes. "I will count it a gift from Dralm if it happens."

The Holy Order of the Zarthani Knights were here-and-now cousins of the old crusading orders, and had protected the eastern frontiers of Hos-Bletha and Hos-Ktemnos from Sastragathi nomads and tribal uprisings for centuries. Kalvan didn't know a great deal about them, but as heavy cavalry they might be a little handicapped in broken country, particularly against Hostigi pikemen and mobile artillery.

What Hos-Ktemnos would send depended on the tribes and on whether the Knights came north. King Cleitharses would at least send mercenaries in his pay and money to the Harphaxi Princes he trusted to hire more.

"If Cleitharses can find any who are fools enough to trust *him*," put in Sarrask.

"They'd be no greater fools than you, willing to fight Kalvan for a pittance and the chance to marry off your daughter," said Prince Balthames, referring to the origins of his arranged marriage with Sarrask's daughter.

For a moment it looked as if Sarrask was going to reply by drawing his sword. Kalvan made another mental note: find out what's got those two behaving like the Kilkenny cats, and sit on Princess Amnita if she's behind it. A quarrel between Sarrask and his son-in-law would inevitably involve Beshta, which was beginning to look like the key Princedom in the coming campaign.

"If he feels safe enough, King Cleitharses may even send some of the Sacred Squares of Ktemnos," said Prince Tythanes of Kyblos. His Princedom was the southernmost in

Hos-Hostigos and therefore the nearest to Hos-Ktemnos. "Some of us will be greeting Hadron in Regwarn, Cavern of the Dead, if that happens."

Kalvan saw no reason to disagree, even to cheer up all the glum faces around the table. The Sacred Squares of Hos-Ktemnos were universally regarded as the finest infantry in the world. They reminded him of the old Spanish *tercios*, but with better firearms they didn't need the sword-and-buckler men, so a Sacred Square was four hundred musketeers and four hundred billmen. They even had something like a divisional system, with a Great Square of three Sacred Squares, five hundred cavalry, and anywhere from four to ten light guns.

As far as Kalvan was concerned, the Sacred Squares of Hos-Ktemnos could stay at home with his blessing as well as Dralm's!

Hos-Agrys was the biggest and most dangerous question mark. It was the closest, it could do the most damage if it chose to intervene, and in Ptosphes's and Kalvan's opinion it probably would.

To be sure, the evidence was conflicting. On the one hand, no fanatically pro-Styphon monarch would be letting the priests of Dralm hold a Great Council in his capital city. On the other hand, Great King Demistophon was the heir to the long tradition of Agrysi hostility to Hos-Zygros; it was possible he would be unfriendly to Hos-Hostigos merely because King Sopharar was not. Personally, Demistophon was hot-tempered and prone to strong, even insulting language; he was also not prone to hold grudges and preferred to be on good terms with everyone. When that wasn't possible, he would choose what looked like the winning side.

"To anyone not knowing that we have Kalvan's wisdom and Dralm's blessing fighting for us, that must look like Styphon's House," said Ptosphes. "Demistophon has an army twice that of Kaiphranos the Timid and the wealth to hire as many mercenaries as Styphon's House will let any one man contribute to their cause."

That was a point Kalvan wanted driven home. Styphon's House might do battle mostly by proxy, careful not to alarm the Kings and Princes too much. They'd be even more careful not to let any one ally claim too large a share of the victory. The Archpriests weren't about to defeat Kalvan only to make one of the other Great Kings an equally dangerous enemy.

So it would be a complicated and uneasy alliance marching against Hos-Hostigos, with even troop deployments likely to be affected by politics. That was fine with Kalvan. Hadn't Napoleon himself once said he preferred to make war against allies?

Of course, there was one way of taking Hos-Agrys out of the picture. If those unknown western Princes were really interested in revolting, and a little help could tip them over the edge, King Demistophon's temper might do the rest. Of course, Demistophon might eventually want to take vengeance on Hos-Hostigos, but "eventually" might not mean this year. Also, if by some chance King Sopharar of Hos-Zygros could be persuaded that Demistophon's army moving so far west to suppress the rebels was somehow a threat to him. . . .

Very neat. Except that some of the western Princes of Hos-Agrys had claims on Zygrosi lands, or at least said they had. If they seized those lands, and even worse, if they insisted that Hos-Hostigos recognize the seizure in return for their support against Styphon's House, then King Sopharar would be persuaded that it was Hos-Hostigos threatening him. If that happened. . . .

Too many "ifs," Kalvan decided, and too little solid evidence. Not even the names of those Princes! File the whole question of raising a rebellion against Demistophon and get back to the business at hand.

Kalvan discovered that while he'd been speculating, the discussion had turned to the best strategy. Ptosphes was arguing for the southern strategy for meeting what was coming at them that Kalvan and Rylla had worked out in their bedroom.

"An army in Beshta is close to Harphax City, which is the best way of making Kaiphranos fidget. It will be on the flank of any army coming through Arklos or Dazour. If our cavalry knows its business, we'll have warning in time to cut off either advance."

And if the cavalry didn't know its business, they were all dead—much deader than Lee's hopes of victory at Gettysburg, killed because Jeb Stuart forgot he was supposed to scout before anything else.

"What about two advances, one along each possible route?" asked Prince Balthar of Beshta, his cadaverous face growing even longer. Balthar wore a food-stained black robe and wooden peasant clogs. He looked exactly like what he

was: the Ebenezer Scrooge of the here-and-now Princes, and
the butt of ribald songs and jokes throughout the Great Kingdoms. He'd been happy enough last year to loot the vaults of
Styphon's temples in Beshta but was now beginning to regret
letting greed overcome his usual foot-dragging paranoia.

"Then each force will be weaker than our united army,"
replied Ptosphes. "We will fight them one at a time and smash
them both."

"And if they come through Nostor?" Balthar squeaked.
"Or what if the army of Hos-Agrys marches far to the west,
then moves south? What of Nyklos and Sask then?"

Sarrask of Sask snorted. "If they come through Nostor,
half of them will starve, and Prince Pheblon can knock the
rest on the head. Sorry, Pheblon, but from what I've heard a
mule crossing Nostor would starve unless he carried his own
rations."

Pheblon's bleak expression was all the answer anybody
needed.

"As for an advance all around Yirtta's potato patch to
come from the west—Balthar, do you think we're fighting
fools who'll try to reach a man's brain by way of his arse-
hole?"

The only man who didn't laugh was Balthar, and Kalvan
didn't entirely blame him for not seeing the humor of the situation. In last year's wars, his lands had escaped most of the
fighting. This year, no matter how he wriggled, they seemed
destined to be the main battleground.

They didn't discuss taking the offensive, but Kalvan didn't
worry. An army in the south with good scouting on either
flank could be as offensive as it wanted to be against what had
to be the objective: the Styphoni armies. An offensive before
the enemy's plans became clear could only be aimed at real
estate, and there was only one piece of real estate around
whose capture could be decisive, Harphax City itself. Unfortunately, there was no way the Hostigi were going to be equipped to besiege and storm a city of two hundred thousand people, with enemies still able to operate in their rear.

They did discuss garrisoning the forts in Beshta and southeastern Sask, so the Hostigi could start raiding and scouting as
soon as the roads dried. Balthar's face grew even longer, but
he'd noticed Rylla's eye on him and kept his mouth shut. That

was a further reason for putting reliable garrisons into Beshta as soon as possible—to keep an eye on Balthar. There were rumors (*note: have Skranga and Klestreus investigate, independently*) that Beshta had been buying grain in Hos-Harphax. If Balthar had been paying for it in information. . . .

The Council ended by appointing Count Harmakros Captain-General of the Army of Observation, as they christened the garrisons. Then it turned into a party, with only tough venison, potatoes, salt pork, and rabbit stew, but plenty of wine.

Kalvan kept wishing for bourbon but also held his cup out every time a servant passed by, and they came every time they saw it empty. He was in the middle of his tenth cup and a long dissertation on the difference between an enemy's capabilities and his intentions, when Rylla squeezed his hand.

"Kalvan, I think it's time we were in bed," she whispered into his ear.

"Bed?" He realized he'd spoken louder than he'd intended and tried unsuccessfully to lower his voice. "I'm not sleepy, but—"

"I know that, you idiot! Do you think I'd ask you to come to bed if I thought you wanted to *sleep*?" She pinched him on the ear and kissed the side of his neck. Kalvan felt his face turning the same color as the wine and started to swear, then heard the stifled laughter all around him and saw Ptosphes nodding slowly to Rylla.

Kalvan kissed Rylla, then led her toward the door. Not-quite-so-stifled laughter followed them out.

Score one for Rylla! In a week it would be all over the Great Kingdom that the King and Queen were still like lovers on their wedding night. Who couldn't think that was a good omen and proof that there was nothing to worry about in the spring campaign?

On-the-job training in kingship might be hard on the king's subjects. With teachers like Rylla, it wasn't so bad for the king.

II.

Danar Sirna felt as nervous as a first-year student attending orientation as she entered the University Presentation Hall. The Chancellor of Dhergabar University, in his usual natty charcoal-gray tunic, stood to one side. Half a dozen news service personalities, including Yandar Yadd and several she didn't recognize, fussed at the technicians working the lights and sensors. She searched for the distinctive profile of Danthor Dras, Scholar Emeritus, Chairman of the University Department of Outtime History, and supreme authority on Fourth Level Aryan-Transpacific, Styphon's House Subsector, but he was nowhere in sight.

No doubt the time for a properly dramatic entrance hadn't arrived. Sirna's former husband had taught her about those, even if he'd only called himself a politician. . . .

Enough of that, she told herself firmly as she tried to find a seat as close to the front as possible. After twelve years in the Outtime History Department, she'd never once seen the legendary Scholar Danthor. She wouldn't have had the opportunity now except for her surprise appointment to the Second Kalvan Study-Team. Or at least it had been a surprise, until she talked with Hadron Tharn, her former husband's chief. Now she knew that it was an assignment both dangerous and exciting, probably enough of both to take her mind off her failed marriage.

She sat down next to a striking woman with unusually blond hair. She wondered if the woman was an adopted Prole until she turned, then Sirna recognized the familiar profile of Baltov Eldra, the First Kalvan Study-Team's historian and the leader of the Second Team.

While she was debating whether or not to strike up a conversation, Eldra said, "Hello. My name is Eldra. What's yours?"

"D—Danar Sirna." They touched hands in greeting.

"You must be a member of the Second Team."

"I am. How did you know?"

Eldra laughed, a pleasant chiming. "You're one of the few around here who doesn't look like a stuffed shirt."

"A what?"

"Colloquial expression from a semicivilized Fourth Level

time-line. It means someone who's overflowing with himself, or stuffed into his shirt."

"Oh. I should have guessed. What was it like on Kalvan's Time-Line?"

"Fascinating—if you don't mind no hot and cold running water, no decent heating, food that's either underdone or burned—"

"I have that every time I try to cook for myself," said Sirna. They both laughed. "What about King Kalvan? What's he really like?"

Eldra sighed. "He's handsome, regal, charismatic, brilliant—just about everything you could want in a man."

"It sounds as if you got to—know him rather well . . ."

Eldra shook her head. "Not that I didn't want to, but Queen Rylla's a she-wolf in human shape. Besides, Kalvan's World is like most Aryan descendant cultures—a strong paternalistic moral tradition, with Virgin icons and sublegal houses of prostitution. Any woman with healthy, natural urges who doesn't sublimate them to marriage and motherhood is considered a harlot. Unless you find a lover on the team—and I wouldn't recommend that—be prepared for a long, lonely two years."

"It wouldn't be the first time," said Sirna. She hadn't had a real relationship with a man since her marriage foundered.

The sudden appearance of Danthor Dras ended their conversation. He had a broad, leonine face framed by long silver locks combed dramatically back in great waves and white eyebrows leaping like wings from his craggy brow. As he greeted acquaintances among the newscasters, his voice was low and gravelly, never missing a dramatic emphasis or pause.

After an overlong introduction by the University Chancellor, the Scholar strode to the podium. "Usually my lectures are not so well attended, at least by nonstudents not seeking credit." He paused for the expected wave of laughter, then continued. "After several centuries of promoting outtime historical studies, I am gratified by this sudden surge of public interest—even if it was brought about by the bungling of the Paratime Police!" Both the newscasters and the University people applauded.

"As most of you know, Kalvan's Time-Line is of special importance to Paratemporal Studies because we can pinpoint the precise moment the Kalvan Subsector split off from the parent

Styphon's House Subsector. Usually we do not spot the crea-tion of a new subsector for months, years, or even decades. The discovery of the Kalvan Subsector is a unique event in Home Time-Line history.

"What makes Kalvan's Subsector even more important is that it is limited to a single time-line. This means that the University can place the subsector under detailed surveillance, comparing any changes that take place with five control time-lines directly adjacent.

"I do not believe it is possible to overstate the importance of this discovery. At the least, it should revolutionize our under-standing of Paratemporal processes and social change. If the Kalvan Effect makes long-term social and technological changes on the Kalvan Subsector, we will be very close to the day when we can prune, graft, and trim outtime societies to our own specifications by the selective introduction of gifted individuals. The end result will be an increase in outtime resources that can safely be brought to Home Time-Line and our Fifth Level Industrial and Service Sectors, as well as greater protection for the Paratime Secret itself."

To say nothing of giving the University historians and sociologists more control over outtime activities, thought Sirna. They'd been fighting the Paratime Police over that for millennia. Remembering some of the faculty meetings and dinners she had attended, Sirna wondered if the academics would do as well as the Paratime Police had done over the past ten thousand years.

She frowned. That was a heretical thought for a future faculty member and supporter of the Opposition Party! Maybe her bad marriage had soured more than just her out-look on men; it was probably just as well that she would soon be too busy to worry about such things.

Danthor Dras went on to explain how he'd become an authority on Fourth Level Aryan-Transpacific, Styphon's House Subsector. Three hundred years ago he'd been involved in a survey of Fourth Level Aryan Studies when he happened upon Styphon's House Subsector, at that time virgin territory. Danthor had spent about a third of his time since then either on Styphon's House Subsector studies or outtime; twenty of the outtime years had been spent as an upperpriest at Balph.

At the Great Library of Balph Danthor had discovered scrolls chronicling the Zarthani migrations from the west coast of the Minor Land Mass to the east coast. The roots of this migration began in Grefftscharr over fifteen hundred years before, when the Great Lakes iron-ore deposits were discovered. Until that time, trade between the iron-poor city-states of the Pacific coast and the Middle Kingdoms was sporadic and of no great importance. A hundred years later the Iron Trail was blazed and huge caravans from Grefftscharr were making the transcontinental trek for California gold. The Grefftscharri kings made treaties with some of the barbarian tribes, conquered or exterminated others, and paid tribute only when necessary.

Trade with the Middle Kingdoms brought increased wealth and power to the west coast and aggravated tensions between the northern Kingdom of Echanistra and the city-states of the south. This rivalry broke out into open warfare when the southern city-states allied against the northern kingdom, and ended only when a southern land and sea force sacked the great city of Echanistra.

Another four hundred years of periodic warfare depleted the treasuries of the southern city-states and lead to the deforestation of much of the Pacific Northwest, which had been supplying the lumber for uncountable warships and stockades. With the trees cleared, the land changed from forests to meadow and pasturelands, and the population continued to grow. When there was no longer enough land, they began to move south. The southern city-states saw these northerners as barbarians with uncouth ways and a corrupt tongue, and went on the offensive.

Meanwhile, Grefftscharr, much richer from its sales of arms and iron, began to expand into the Ohio River Valley. Here they collided with the newly formed Iroquois Confederacy, the fiercest and most organized Amerind resistance the Zarthani had faced. King Childorec the Red of Grefftscharr knew full well that he didn't have the manpower necessary to defeat the Iroquois while simultaneously containing the Crow and Shawnee to the south. He invited the northern Zarthani of the Pacific coast to migrate to the Atlantic seaboard. They came over the Iron Trail in families, clans, tribes, and nations.

The Zarthani immigrants quickly became embroiled in the long and bitter war against the Iroquois. The Zarthani had the advantage of better arms and armor, as well as Grefftscharri military aid. The Iroquois were fighting for their homeland, their families, and their lives. It was a savage war with no quarter given or asked. After almost a century of warfare, the Zarthani armies under the command of Erasthames the Great defeated the last major Iroquois army at the Battle of Sestra. Within fifty years the victorious Zarthani had scourged the native Amerinds from every valley and mountain in their domain.

The last migratory wave came after the entire Pacific Northwest was subjugated by the south. The new Zarthani refugees found the lands of the Northeast already occupied or wartorn, so they moved down the Potomac River into Maryland and Virginia. Here, aided by adventurers and experienced fighters from the north, they built a line of forts and proceeded to subdue the Tuscarora, Powhatan, and other local tribes. In the south, intertribal mistrust and conflict made the Amerind resistance less determined than in the north. Many fled west or were assimilated. Within a few decades there were hundreds of small towns and villages dotting the lush southern tidal lands.

"We now come to a day about thirty years after the founding of Ktemnos City," said Danthor Dras, with a toss of his head that made his silver hair ripple and catch the lights. "A village highpriest of the minor healer god Styphon, experimenting with various medicinal compounds, mixed together a batch of saltpeter, sulfur, and charcoal. The results were explosive but fortunately not fatal. Once the formula was perfected, it didn't take very long for the hierarchy of Styphon's House to see the military and political potential of this miraculous explosive they named 'fireseed.' "

With an ironic raising of his eyebrows he added, "In the beginning, their motives for guarding the secret of gunpowder may have been the noble desire of the followers of a healer god to protect their world from the ultimate weapon. Whatever they were we shall never know. We can be sure they are the basest of motives now." A picture of a Styphon's House temple-farm appeared on the screen behind Danthor's head, displaying a priest in black robes lashing at several temple slaves with an iron-tipped whip.

Sirna heard gasps of horror and disgust around her. Religion and other pseudophilosophies hadn't flourished on Home Time-Line for at least ten thousand years; many at the University felt that First Level culture and psychohygiene should be spread among less enlightened time-lines as a matter of duty. That they were successully opposed at every point by the Paratime Police and their supporters had fueled the fierce hatred of the guardians of the Paratime Secret among University faculty and leaders of the Opposition Party. Weren't the Paracops just as callous and self-serving as the outtime primitives who subjugated and enslaved their fellow beings? Or so the argument ran.

Sirna had never been able to answer it satisfactorily. No wonder Hadron Tharn wanted inside information on Kalvan's Time-Line. If Kalvan single-handedly tamed this barbarous time-line, the Opposition would have a potent counterargument to the Paratime Police's hands-off policy.

When his audience had quieted down, Danthor Dras continued. "It took Styphon's House less than two centuries to thoroughly dominate the Kingdoms of Hos-Ktemnos and Hos-Bletha. The Northern Kingdoms, however, were far more resistant. Their long struggle against the Amerinds had made them more independent and warlike than their southern cousins, but their population was less and their geographical isolation greater.

"Styphon's House's recent aggression against the Princedom of Hostigos was a small move in a greater plan to consolidate their power over the western Princedoms of Hos-Harphax. They opened with their time-tested method: divide, bribe, and plunder. It worked as well as usual on every time-line but one."

On the screen appeared a picture of Tarr-Hostigos, flying a blue halberd head on a red field, the flag of Hostigos. The next picture showed the same castle in ruins, now flying the black and orange banner of Nostor. There was a burst of questions from the newscasters, but Danthor's voice beat them down. Next came a picture of Danthor Dras himself, wearing an orange robe, the vestments of a Styphon's House upperpriest, outside the same ruined castle.

"I recently returned from Time-Line IV-1-8674-52-483-189762493, one of the Kalvan control time-lines. This is what I found in the Princedom—or should I say ex-Princedom?—of Hostigos. It is divided between Nostor and Sask, with Nostor having the greater share. The ruling family has been exterminated along with most of the nobility and landed gentry. Of course there exists no new Great Kingdom comparable to the one founded by Kalvan on time-line IV-1-8674-52-484-1.

"This Kalvan has managed to alter the history of his time-line to that degree. I suspect, however, that he will personally not last more than another year once Styphon's House has mobilized its full strength against his new Kingdom of Hos-Hostigos. There is no denying that the loss of the fireseed secret was a great blow to Styphon's House and their control over the ruling class of the Five Kingdoms. I also know that the Temple's resources are much greater than our Fourth Level Europo-American policeman has yet realized.

"Much of the Five Kingdoms' capital is tied up either in the Temple's Treasuries or the vaults of Styphon's Great Banking Houses. Then there are the Styphoni military orders, the Zarthani Knights and Styphon's Own Guard. Wholesale trade monopolies on cotton, chocolate, tobacco, and corn. The Great Fleets. Millions of believers.

"Yet win or lose, there will be change. Styphon's House has thrown technological development throughout Styphon's House Subsector into an artificial stasis field by absorbing capital and by encouraging small political units separated by trade barriers, each with an inadequate revenue basis for generating investment research and development. Even if Kalvan loses, much capital is going to pour out of Styphon's treasury into the hands of kings, princes, artisans, and mercenaries. They can win the war with Kalvan but may lose to technological progress in a few generations. Put into circulation, capital will inevitably have effects.

"This is what makes Kalvan's new subsector so important, *whatever* happens to Kalvan. We now have an opportunity to better understand and control the processes of outtime history like nothing we have had before and like nothing we can hope to see again in our lifetimes."

The lights on the recording equipment went out, and the technician at the portable control panel waved both clenched fists over his head to signal that he'd caught everything. Danthor Dras grinned. "Now, does anyone have any comments or questions?" He pointed to Baltov Eldra, who had her fingertips at her temples in the interrogative mode.

"Isn't it possible that you might be underestimating Great King Kalvan's intelligence and resourcefulness? I have been on Kalvan's Time-Line and seen him at work. He struck me as a man of intelligence, leadership, and adaptability. I also suspect that you overestimate Styphon's House."

"Perhaps I do," said Scholar Danthor with an affability that Sirna was quite sure was assumed. "But why should I rule out the possiblility that Kalvan is simply a second-class man up against what until now has been third-class opposition? It seems to me that would be rejecting a tenable hypothesis merely to curry favor with the faction that seems to have taken to worshipping Kalvan. I've never been in the habit of abandoning scholarly ethics that thoroughly."

Sirna bit her lip to keep from laughing at the blandness in the Scholar's voice. For two centuries he'd been in the habit of finding just how close he could come to the limits of scholarly ethics in the interests of winning an audience, and everybody at the University assumed that there were a few carefully suppressed incidents where he'd gone over. However, he was still making a valid point. Just how good *was* Calvin Morrison?

"I admit the question should be left open," said Professor Baltov in a voice that made it clear she admitted nothing of the kind. "Particularly since in this situation, Kalvan needs both creative intelligence *and* the kind of intelligence to take advantage of other people's mistakes. I do have some hypotheses of my own on this matter, though."

"I wouldn't expect it to be otherwise," said Danthor. "Only please don't expect me to take sides with you if Kalthar Morth decides you've become a supporter of the Great Man Theory of History and turns his heavy artillery on you. I have to fight Scholar Kalthar on my own account often enough not to want to fight him on other people's."

There was a sprinkling of laughter among the audience. Danthor's debates with Kalthar were well known for both their exuberance and their acerbity.

"I understand, Scholar Danthor," said Eldra, both her words and tone noncommittal. Her clenched jaw told another story.

Eldra was obviously more than just a strong supporter of Great King Kalvan. Sirna wondered if the same were true of the rest of the University people who'd witnessed Kalvan at work. If it were, she could see trouble looming ahead for her. She was going outtime as part of the University's reinforcements partly to finish work on her doctorate, partly to see what the Paratime Police were doing or leaving undone on Kalvan's Time-Line. That second job came straight from Hadron Tharn.

Of course she'd been the logical candidate for the job. Her parents were both consultants to Hadron when he needed expert opinions on medicine or geology, and her ex-husband had actually been Hadron's office manager. Why not use somebody whose reasons for being in Kalvan's world were as legitimate as anyone up to Verkan Vall himself could ask?

Why not indeed, except for the problem of what it might do by way of sowing factions in a University team that might be facing real danger in the Great Kings' War. No, *would* be, unless Kalvan was able to smash all his enemies on their own territory. Sirna was no military expert, but she'd read enough to know that that would take a miracle; it was not doubting Kalvan's intelligence to doubt that he could produce miracles to order.

Assuming that the University team would be dodging bullets, then what should she do? If the fighting was heavy enough, she'd have a perfect excuse for doing nothing except research, keeping up her cover, and staying alive. If it didn't get that bad. . . .

The problem was, Baltov Eldra wasn't the only person who seemed to think highly of Kalvan, and even people who didn't care much about him wanted to see Styphon's House destroyed. To a culture of atheists like Home Time-Line, religious tyrannies were never popular. If all she found the Paracops doing was giving Kalvan noncontaminating assistance, the less she said about it the better. She wasn't at all sure what Hadron Tharn would do with the information she gave him.

The only thing she knew for certain was that if the Paracops learned of even the most innocuous spying job—well, when it came to being caught in crossfires she'd take any of Kalvan's battles in preference!

Even worse, there wasn't anyone she could ask for advice or information. Baltov Eldra? She hardly knew the Professor, and her bias was obvious. Hadron Tharn? He might give useful advice, but it might not be the best for her. He would also tell her parents, and they'd take her doubts as one more sign of the rebellion that began when she left Ulvarn Rarth.

As Sirna rose from her seat and turned toward the door, she

even allowed herself the heretical thought that Hadron Tharn might be a little more like her former husband than was altogether good. He certainly had the same weakness for theories that ignored what Danthor Dras had called "the irremediable perversity of individual human beings," although perhaps it didn't affect Hadron's personal life as badly as it had Rarth's. Nor did it make much difference; Sirna was looking for a mentor, not a bed partner.

She decided that she was probably looking for something she wasn't going to find. She would just have to grit her teeth, learn all she could about Kalvan's Time-Line, and then hope she went outtime soon enough to be fully oriented before the shooting started.

Eight

I.

"Way! Way, there! Way for the Great King of Hos-Hostigos!"

The leading riders of Kalvan's escort were shouting at the wagon train ahead loudly enough to make the draft oxen look up dubiously. Kalvan suspected they were also shouting loudly enough so that any hostile ears within half a mile would know who was riding along this muddy Beshtan road with only sixty-odd men for escort. He remembered that Rylla hadn't liked his coming south on this tour of inspection. Her asking *him* to stay out of danger was a real turnaround, but she did have a point. Was he doing anything useful other than indulging a Great King's power to get rid of a bad case of cabin fever?

It didn't matter now; he was less than four miles from Harmakros's headquarters at Tarr-Perca. He could dine and sleep at the castle tonight, then consult with Harmakros and Count Phrames on the situation of the Army of Observation. Maybe they could tell him what he needed to know, and they probably couldn't spare enough men to safely escort him any farther south. If so, he'd head north again.

At least Kalvan had accomplished one major thing during the harsh winter months: he had created an independent Royal Army of Hos-Hostigos. It was necessarily a compromise force, since Kalvan had no hereditary lands to supply troops. He would become Prince of Hostigos on Ptosphes's death, of course, but he hoped that event was decades away.

When last fall's invasion of Sask ended in Sarrask's surrender, there'd been seven to eight thousand mercenaries, hired by Gormoth and Sarrask for the war against Hostigos, with no place to go. Styphon's House considered them Kalvan's troops since they hadn't fought to the death, and King Kaiphranos considered them generally untrustworthy.

Kalvan made them an offer, with the blessing of Prince Ptosphes and the grudging agreement of Prince Pheblon of Nostor and Prince Balthames of Sashta: twenty acres of land and ten newly minted gold crowns for each enlisted man; a hundred acres and a team of oxen for each petty-captain; and a small barony and a thousand crowns for each captain in selected regions of war-ravaged northern Hostigos, Nostor, and Sashta. Almost two thirds of the unemployed mercenaries had taken Kalvan up on his offer.

Kalvan organized these volunteers into four infantry regiments of five hundred men, eight cavalry regiments of two hundred and sixty men, and an additional Mobile Force of six hundred mounted pikemen and musketeers, two hundred of the musketeers with rifled weapons. The new Royal Army and the tried and true Army of Hostigos would form the anchor for the Great Army of Hos-Hostigos. He would have liked a better ratio of foot to horse in the Royal Army, but here-and-now mercenaries were predominantly cavalry. They reminded him most closely of the German Reiters, sixteenth-century mercenary pistol-wielding heavy cavalry who'd dominated the battlefields of France during the wars of Religion.

His next step had been to reform army organization without turning it on its head, starting with the new Royal Army and ending with all the Princely armies of the Great Kingdom of Hos-Hostigos. Standard organization had been companies, bands, and blocks of varying size, sometimes in the same army. The whole system wasn't much advanced over the three medieval battles: Vanward, Center, and Rearward.

Kalvan retained the companies, made them 110 men strong under a petty-captain, put two companies into a battalion, and made a regiment under the command of a colonel out of three battalions, one a headquarters outfit with 60 officers and halberdiers. With the cavalary, it was troops, squadrons, and regiments.

Kalvan sent a third of the army to their new homes and quartered the rest in Hostigos Town and Tarr-Hostigos for drill and training in his new tactics. This had put a real strain on the capital's housing, despite some hastily built barracks. Nor had the citizens been happy about competing with the new Royal Army for rations. . . .

The hill the road climbed ahead was higher than the one his troop had just descended. As they left the shelter of the valley, Kalvan felt the chilly wind on his back and his horse whickered irritably. At least the wind was only chilly, not cold, and the hard blue sky overhead now shed freezing rain instead of snow. The mud of the road had turned rubbery everywhere, and in a few places it had thawed enough to be sticky. It wasn't spring yet, but the Winter of the Wolves was definitely behind them.

Toward the middle of the wagon train Kalvan came to a big long-hauling wagon, two sets of wheels connected by a long beam and drawn by eight oxen. Tied to the beam was a massive canvas-wrapped bundle; on either side of it were two iron-rimmed gun wheels. Another eight-pounder was on its way to the Army of Observation, disassembled for easier travel. The carriage, trail, tools, and harness would be back somewhere in the train. When the whole piece was assembled at Tarr-Locra, one more Beshtan gun could go into the shop to be modernized with trunions and a proper carriage.

The head of the wagon train his troop was passing reached the crest of the hill before Kalvan came up with it. He saw the train's captain rein in abruptly and throw up his left hand in a signal to halt. Kalvan rode up to him as he drew a pistol from his saddle holster; Kalvan and his troopers did the same.

The far slope of the hill was steep enough so that the road made a wide bend halfway down, where a small village straggled along the bend. Smoke billowed from three or four houses, too much for any chimney, and mounted men were riding up and down the road in front of it, shooting randomly into the windows of the unburned wattle and daub huts.

Farther down the road, half a dozen troopers were driving a miscellaneous gaggle of livestock, with dead fowl hanging from their saddles. The Harphaxi colors of yellow and red fluttered from lance tips and on a banner held by a dismounted man standing over a dead horse.

"Move out!" shouted Kalvan, drawing his sword. Major

Nicomoth, commanding the escort, drew his and held it out with the flat of the blade across the chest of Kalvan's horse.

"Drop back to the rear, Your Majesty, I beg you!" he cried. It still sounded more like an order than a loyal subject's humble request.

Kalvan controlled an impulse to tell his aide-de-camp to perform unnatural acts upon himself and let the escort pass on either side. Charging down that hill at the head of the troop, he'd be in as much danger of being unhorsed and trampled as of being shot by the enemy.

All along the train, teamsters were running to the heads of their teams, while guards checked the priming of their weapons and took position. Some perched on the wagon seats to keep a lookout; others crawled under the wagons to fire from cover. Then Nicomoth shouted "Charge!," the one order no cavalry outfit in any land at any time ever needed to hear twice.

Kalvan's escort, a troop of the First Royal Horse Guards, were all experienced soldiers and expert riders; they didn't bunch up as they plunged down the hill. Halfway to the village, the hillside's boulders and scrub gave way to cultivated fields. Some of the riders took their horses over the ditch beside the road and into the fields, taking a shortcut toward the cattle thieves.

The Harphaxi raiders weren't beginners, either. They dug in their spurs and rode for their lives, except for two who were picked off by wild pistol shots at miraculously long ranges. Another stayed behind to give the banner-bearer a hand up onto his own mount.

Three pistols and a musketoon banged, and both the helpful rider and his mount screamed and went down kicking. The banner-bearer knelt, holding the banner out before him like a pike with one hand and drawing a pistol with the other. He fired as Nicomoth charged him, but the bullet went wild. In the next moment, Nicomoth's sword came down, splitting the man's face. The Guardsman behind Nicomoth drew rein, leaned out of the saddle, and picked up the fallen banner on the tip of his sword. Kalvan joined in the cheering.

As if the cheering had frightened them from their cover, six mounted men rode out of the rear of the village. Kalvan noted that several wore three-quarter armor and each had a heavy-barreled musketoon slung across his back as well as pistols.

Their horses also looked bigger than the Harphaxi ones. Whatever or whoever they were, it wasn't friendly. One threw a lighted torch onto the thatch of a hut as he passed, then all six were riding hell-for-leather across the hillside fields toward the far end of the hill.

"After them!" shouted Nicomoth. The squad chasing the cattle thieves had already anticipated the order; they were pounding across ditches, walls, fences, and last year's stubble, the few who still had loaded pistols firing as they rode. An unarmored rider dropped out of his saddle, and one of the armored knights reined in and turned back to help him. It was a gallant but futile gesture. Two of the Hostigi lost their seats jumping a fence, but others quickly came up with the fallen rider and his comrade. Two war cries, a quick flurry of swords, and another Hostigi and the knight were down.

That was all Kalvan saw before he rode into the village at the rear of Nicomoth's second charge. Houses and barns narrowed his view as the Hostigi thundered through the village, turkeys and geese overlooked by the raiders flapping frantically in their path. Doors and shutters slammed hastily as villagers who'd been coming out to greet their rescuers ducked back into their houses.

By the time Nicomoth and Kalvan passed the dead raiders, their surviving comrades were out of sight around the far end of the hill. Kalvan rode with the Guardsmen that far, then reined in. The raiders had obviously followed a track that ran straight as an arrow between two farms, then climbed a hillside into second-growth forest. A hundred yards beyond the village, horsemen would have had to go single file, within pistol shot of the trees. A better place for five men to ambush fifty couldn't have been found within miles.

"Your Majesty!" Major Nicomoth was dismounted now, kneeling beside the two dead men. "This one is a Zarthani Knight, I swear it. See where the Tarr-Ceros proof mark has been removed." He was holding up the dead Knight's helm as Kalvan rode up.

It certainly did look as if a proof mark on the helm had been effaced with a heavy file. Kalvan looked down at the other dead man. He was dressed in deerskin from head to foot and had long black hair bound up under a simple iron cap. If Kalvan had seen a face like that in Pennsylvania, he would have said the man had a good dose of American Indian blood in

him. The resemblance was increased by the iron-headed toma-
hawk trailing from his outflung wrist on a braided leather
thong.

"He must be the Knight's oath-brother," said Nicomoth,
kneeling and pulling the dead man's cap over his face.

"He doesn't look Zarthani," said Kalvan.

"He is probably from one of the Ruthani tribes who live by
hunting and fishing in the swamps of Hos-Bletha," said
Nicomoth. "Some of them have turned to the worship of the
true gods, and their warriors often serve the Zarthani Knights
as scouts. Then they may swear oath-brotherhood with a
Knight and he with them. To abandon an oath-brother is a
crime no Zarthani Knight's honor would ever let him think of
committing."

Counting the possible Zarthani Knight and his oath-brother, the raiders had lost seven dead and one badly wounded
prisoner, in return for two Hostigi dead and one wounded plus
two horses dead and four hurt. Allowing for what losses the
village might have suffered, the day seemed to have gone to
the Hostigi. Kalvan felt good about that.

He felt almost as good about the simple chance to be in action again, able to fight his enemies with a sword and pistol instead of parchment, pen, and sealing wax. A Great King had
to use more of the second than of the first, of course, but
Kalvan knew he wasn't going to be happy doing all of his
leading from behind a desk.

By the time Kalvan's men had policed up the bodies, the
wagon train was up to the village and Count Phrames himself
had ridden in from the opposite direction—regular Hostigi
cavalry, mercenaries, and a handful of tattooed Sastragathi on
horses that looked more fit for the soup pot than for the field.
Kalvan made a mental note to ask where the Sastragathi had
come from, then a more urgent note to get at least some of the
mounted men out of the village. The villagers' defenders now
considerably outnumbered the villagers themselves; they were
in almost as much danger of being trampled by their friends as
they'd ever been in from their hit-and-run enemies.

Kalvan gave the order to clear the streets of villagers, then
rode over to ask Phrames for an escort.

"By all means, Your Majesty," replied Phrames. "I'll send
twenty of my men with your Guardsmen, and you can all ride
on to Tarr-Locra in time for dinner. I'll follow as soon as I've

heard the villagers on what they've lost and told off some men to help them rebuild.''

Phrames raised his voice. ''We can't give back everything they've lost, but we can add it to the debt the Harphaxi are going to pay when we come to grips with them.''

A lot of cheering followed that last sentence. Kalvan turned his horse, leaving Phrames to ride over to the largest unburned house and knock on the door with his pistol butt. With Phrames on the scene, there was nothing more to worry about.

Correction. There was nothing more to worry about in this village, or today. There was a Styphon's Own lot to worry about if Zarthani Knights were coming north so soon. Six might just be scouts, learning the countryside and Hostigi tactics, but what would they be scouting for except a larger body of the Knights, and where were they?

Kalvan racked his brains all the way to Tarr-Locra without coming up with a reassuring answer to that question.

II.

Captain-General Harmakros's page poured more wine into both men's cups, bowed, and stepped back. Kalvan sipped at his, trying to keep his face straight; the wine apparently couldn't make up its mind whether or not to turn into vinegar.

''Where did those odds-and-sods with Phrames and down in the barracks come from, by the way?'' asked Kalvan.

''The mercenaries are mostly men we were going to settle in Sashta, who couldn't find free land.'' Kalvan looked steadily at him. Harmakros sighed. ''Or who didn't want to settle down and become farmers at all.''

''I thought so. And the Sastragathi? They're a little far from home.''

''A couple of small tribes forced off their land, and some chief's younger sons.''

"No outlaws?"

"None that I know of."

For once, Kalvan's attention to Xentos's rambling lectures paid off. "They wouldn't admit it if they were. But if the Sastragathi learned we were accepting their outlaws and forcing lawful warriors to serve beside them, the whole Sastragath would think twice before giving us aid. Not to mention the problems of keeping the outlaws from making off with everything that isn't tied, nailed, or boarded down."

Harmakros grinned. "Remember those gallows on the hill across the stream that feeds the moat?"

"They did look new."

"They were busy, too, at least for the first half moon. After that, I think the survivors had learned their lesson. Besides, we're feeding them much better than they ever ate at home."

He lowered his voice, although the boy was standing discreetly out of hearing at the far end of the chamber. "There *is* more food in Beshta than I'd expected. They must have been trading across the border into Hos-Harphax, just as we suspected. Paying only in silver, as far as I can tell, but there are a few merchants and court officials I wouldn't mind questioning rigorously for a day or two."

"You haven't arrested anyone?"

"I couldn't touch anyone important enough to know anything without Balthar's throwing a tantrum. I wasn't going to do that without asking you. I just informed some of the merchants that the Great King might forgive their treasonable trade if they would sell their grain to his loyal soldiers at the same price that they paid for it. I wasn't going to make Beshtan grain merchants rich just to feed a few hundred Sastragathi, I swear to Dralm!"

Kalvan laughed. "I didn't expect you would." Apart from the initial act of hiring soldiers without proper authorization from his commander-in-chief, Harmakros had handled the situation well. However. . . .

"I'll forgive you this time, Harmakros. Only don't do it again. If you do, I'll have to dismiss you or be accused of letting my favorites assemble private armies." Kalvan had to force himself to continue, ignoring Harmakros's crestfallen expression. "I don't want to lose your services or disgrace you, but on the other hand I don't want people like Skranga thinking *they* can go off to the Sastragath and bring back a private regiment of storm troopers!

"Furthermore, you were lucky this time. What if you hadn't found the Beshtan grain hoard? We don't want to hire more men than we can feed with what we have on hand. They'll turn to looting our allies, then when the war starts, live off our enemies."

"As Your Majesty wishes." His Great King was speaking and Harmakros would obey, although he obviously found it hard to believe there was anything wrong with living off your opponent's land. That didn't bother Kalvan; Harmakros was intelligent enough to realize sooner or later that in a war where the real enemy was Styphon's House, every bit of unnecessary damage done to the land of a potentially friendly or neutral ruler was bad strategy even if it might look like good tactics.

Harmakros emptied his wine cup, set it on the table, then made a gesture to the page. He went out, closing and latching the door behind him.

"You have him well trained, I see. Now all he needs is a pistol so that he can shoot Prince Balthames if the man comes too close."

Harmakros turned red and swore. "If that Sashtan son of a diseased sow comes within ten yards of the boy, I'll geld him myself with a dull knife!" He looked down at the table. "The boy is my son."

Kalvan mentally reviewed what he knew about Harmakros's career, which wasn't as much as a commander-in-chief ought to know about one of his corps commanders.

"A bastard?"

"Yes. His mother was the daughter of one of the Beshtan grain merchants. She's dead now, but his grandfather is a good man. Raised him, then told me about him when I visited him about a moon ago. The boy was already so well trained for service that I knew I could take him with me and nobody would ask questions. He takes after his mother more than me."

"I would never have guessed he was yours if you hadn't told me."

"Good. The problem is, I have no legitimate children. Empedila—my first wife, a cousin of Phrames—was killed in a riding accident. We'd been married only a year and a half. I was about to contract a betrothal to the daughter of Baron Euripigon in Nostor when all at once Hostigos and Nostor were deadly enemies. I don't even know if Jomesthna is still alive."

"So young . . ."

"Aspasthar."

"So Aspasthar is the last of your house."

Kalvan wished he'd learned more about Zarthani inheritance laws and customs. One of these days, if he lived long enough, he would be more of a Supreme Court justice than a commander-in-chief, and the more he learned about the laws he would be interpreting before that day arrived, the better for both him and Hos-Hostigos. Meanwhile, there was a solution that didn't require admitting his ignorance of the law.

"I think I can see my way to making him a royal ward, with some sort of palace post suitable to his rank," said Kalvan. "We can call him the orphan of someone who has deserved well of the Great Kingdom and leave it at that. We can even provide him with an estate, so that you can marry again without your wife having to worry about any of her dowry going to enrich your bastard." That problem had caused a good many miserably unhappy marriages and more than a few wars in the Middle Ages, if Kalvan recalled correctly. He saw no reason to suspect that human nature was much different here-and-now.

"Thank you, Your Majesty," said Harmakros. He was looking down at the table even more intently, and Kalvan decided to look away until the Captain-General had regained control of his face. "Thank you. That is one less thing to worry about if Galzar's judgment goes against me in this year's war."

III.

A freezing drizzle was making the courtyard into a skating rink when Count Phrames rode in just before nightfall. The three men dined in Harmakros's chambers on a tough old turkey, succotash, and bread that could have been chopped up and used for case shot. Kalvan chewed the bread cautiously, dipping it into the succotash from time to time. He had a full set of sound teeth and wanted to keep it that way; here-and-now dentistry would have satisfied any Constitutional lawyer's definition of "cruel and unusual punishment."

Phrames ate little but drank a lot of wine from a barrel that was at least one grade better than that which Harmakros and Kalvan had drunk earlier. "If I had just one wish," he said after the fifth cup, "I would ask to be left alone with Balthar's chief tax gatherer for an hour. I wouldn't even ask for weapons. Bare hands would be enough." He gripped the silver wine cup as if it were the tax gatherer's throat.

"Better yet, what about an hour in Balthar's treasure room with a large sack?" asked Harmakros. "You could probably pay for the whole Army of Observation for a year with what you collected."

"Or I could pay Prince Araxes's debts to his nobles," said Phrames. "He'd probably name me heir to Phaxos in return."

All three laughed. A little investigation by Klestreus had provided an adequate explanation of why Prince Araxes was becoming the Great King of Fence-Sitters. He'd stayed out of debt to Styphon's House—give him that—but only at the price of going heavily into debt to eight of his richest nobles. That gave them a veto over everything Araxes did beyond choosing the menu for dinner; they were exercising it now on his foreign policy. They didn't want him to join a Great Kingdom where the Great King rode his nobles with a very tight rein. On the other hand, they didn't want him to risk the Great King's wrath by enlisting under Styphon's banner.

"Not that our wrath would be much to fear," said Kalvan. "At least not for now. We have all the enemies we can handle already. But Araxes doesn't know that, and *I'm* not going to tell him. If Styphon's House had the wits to pay Araxes's debts, they could probably win him over, but right now I don't think they would agree to do that even if they could agree on any policy at all about Araxes. It's pretty obvious that Araxes let the Edict of Balph out of the bag at least a moon before Styphon's House wanted anybody outside the Temple to know about it. That gave us time."

Time that had been put to good use, too. Kalvan was able to bring the others up to date over the next round of wine. The three Agrysi Princes hadn't sworn allegiance or even revealed their identities, but they had not only pledged but paid enough silver to hire three thousand mercenaries.

Count Euphrades rode in as escort for the silver, with two hundred and fifty men of his own, well mounted, well equipped, and apparently well trained. He looked as if he intended to stay for the duration and maybe pick up one of the bumper crop of vacant Princedoms the war was expected to produce. Kalvan wasn't so sure about that and was determined to prevent it if he could, but he also wasn't going to turn away willing recruits.

So Kalvan was hiring mercenaries after all. He was also improving the weaponry of his own soldiers, since both the Hostigos rifle shop and the musket foundry were working full blast. The output of the Hostigos cannon foundry was up now that the weather allowed some transportation over the roads of Hos-Hostigos; brass and iron were once again arriving. Not to mention the regiments of pikemen who were training on every day weather let them, and all the captured and repaired obsolete weapons that were going into the hands of the militia. . . .

To oppose all this, Styphon's House was issuing unconvincing denials of designs on *any* true King's or Prince's lands or wealth. "At least they haven't convinced those Princes who see that the demon-exorcising priests would simply be spies and paymasters for pro-Styphon factions," Kalvan added. "That seems to include a good many of the Zygrosi, including King Sopharar. He sent Rylla a beautiful set of silvered armor, with a helmet plumed in snow owl feathers. She says she'll wear it when we storm Balph."

"How is Rylla?" asked Phrames. A little wistfully, Kalvan thought.

"She says she's well. Mytron and the midwives say she's well. Ptosphes says she's well. She looks well to me. And there are so many prayers going up to Yirtta Allmother that she must be clapping her hands over her ears."

He didn't want to mention his fears and how he sometimes woke up in a cold sweat from nightmares about Rylla's dying like her mother, at least not in Phrames's presence. He doubted that if he'd been in Phrames's place he would have taken things half so well, even if it were a god-sent hero who won his intended bride. It was his fortune and that of Hos-

Hostigos that Phrames was a here-and-now Sir Galahad.

"I just wish we knew what was being hatched at Balph," said Harmakros, trying to steer them on to safer ground.

Of course, Styphon's House was like an iceberg; the important seven eighths of it were out of sight. A lot of things that would eventually be dangerous to Hos-Hostigos were doubtless being hatched down there. For the moment, it didn't look as if Styphon's House would be able to convert itself into a proper Pentagon in time for this year's campaign. At best, Hos-Hostigos would face not just an alliance, but an alliance run by a committee.

"There is an animal in my homeland called a camel," said Kalvan. "We have a legend about it." He described a camel, then told them about a camel's being a horse designed by a committee.

"Here's to Styphon's plans having humps, bad breath, and a foul temper," said Harmakros. They drank to that, then Harmakros added, "Although the worst plans can still bring victory if there are good men to fight for them." He didn't need to say "Zarthani Knights."

The Knights themselves were no secret. Their plans for this year's war were, and were likely to stay that way. "I asked the villagers if they'd seen men like the dead Knight," said Kalvan. "A few said they had, but only six or a dozen at most."

"Any House Master has sixty Knights at his personal command," Harmakros put in. "I suspect Soton has sent one of his trusted comrades north to find out what's going on. Soton's not the sort of man to take the word of Styphon's House on something that could draw in two thirds of his men."

"I suppose not," said Kalvan. "But he's a consecrated Archpriest of Styphon's House. I suppose the Knights also take vows of some sort. Can they refuse obedience to Styphon's Voice?"

"Not if Sesklos gives them a simple order to come north and wage Holy War against us. But if Soton receives no such order—well, he's not only an Archpriest of Styphon, he's also the Prince of more land than some Great Kings—Kaiphranos, for one—and never mind what the law says! If those lands were in danger, Soton could behave like their Prince if Sesklos will let him. He may, too."

Harmakros walked over to the deerskin map hung on the wall, drew his sword, and ran the point along the western borders of Hos-Bletha and Hos-Ktemnos. "Our friend Soton wears three helmets. One is Grand Master of the Holy Order of the Zarthani Knights. Another is Archpriest of Styphon's House. Last, he's a general in the armies of Hos-Bletha and Hos-Ktemnos. The Knights are the principal weapon against the tribes and nomads of the Lower Sastragath. The Great Kings neither have to spend a single piece of silver to keep it, nor worry about Princes winning battles and becoming ambitious.

"If Styphon's House wants to take away that weapon and use it somewhere else, they're going to have to persuade the Great Kings of the south that it's a good idea. If the nomads are on the move, that may take a while. It may not even happen at all. Hos-Hostigos may be a headache to Ktemnos and Bletha, but a nomad invasion could be more like a kick in the belly!"

Harmakros's explanation made sense to Kalvan, even if it probably erred on the side of optimism. No point in raising that objection now, when they knew so little.

Put Klestreus on to interrogating everybody who'd ever been near the Sastragath. Talk to Colonel Verkan when he returned from Grefftscharr, and see if he would discreetly question his fellow free-traders. They got around, and usually kept their eyes open. They kept their mouths shut too, but gold, silver, and trading privileges (or losing them) could do something about that.

Kalvan poured himself some more wine and relaxed. The Zarthani Knights were good, but they were also widely scattered, and no cavalryman is much good on a half-starved horse. They couldn't even begin their move north until they could cut green fodder on the way; cavalry mounts couldn't maintain their strength by grazing.

Spring was coming late even in the south. It would be another month before there was any chance of bringing thousands of heavy cavalry and all their support troops north. The Sacred Squares of Hos-Ktemnos would be even harder to recruit for a blitzkrieg, since they would have to walk and be fed while they did, although their rations could be carried in wagons whose oxen could graze. . . .

Kalvan wasn't going to object if Dralm did decide to

swallow up the Zarthani Knights in Chesapeake Bay. Gods or
no gods, it was best to be prepared for the worst, and there
was a good deal that could be done along those lines right
now.

Let Harmakros buy fodder as well as rations; five hundred
well-fed horses were better than two thousand starving ones.
Another shop to make field carriages for artillery; the Hostigos foundry would scream if it had to give up more of its
trained people, but he'd see if Verkan could recruit replace-
ments in Zygros City. Bring a squadron of the Mounted Rifles
south to add to the Army of Observation; he'd been holding
off on that, to keep the Harphaxi from learning about rifles,
but they wouldn't be a secret much longer. Meanwhile, a few
points of Zarthani Knights ambushed at three times the range
they were used to might encourage the others to stay. . . .

Kalvan refilled his wine cup and carried it with him as he
went to stand beside Harmakros and Phrames at the map.

NINE

I.

Phidestros, Captain of the Iron Company, strode into the alley as if he were walking into his favorite tavern. Behind him Zelos imitated his captain's manner. It would be hard for them to avoid being seen sooner or later. As long as no one saw them behaving as if they didn't have a perfect right to be in this dark, smelly alley behind the Drunken Harlot, their chances for success were much greater.

Phidestros checked his pistols, then watched while Zelos did the same. They both had two, while Phidestros also carried a sword and a double-barreled pocket pistol. The smaller pistol was no good against an armored man or even an unarmored one at much more than arm's reach, but within those limits it had provided nasty surprises to several of Phidestros's late enemies.

Zelos started to roll an empty barrel toward the rear door of the Drunken Harlot. Phidestros clutched the man's shoulder and shook his head emphatically. Zelos looked confused, but obeyed. There was no point in explaining to Zelos again how Lamochares's men were *supposed* to come out, if he didn't yet understand. Zelos had the strength of two men but only half a man's wits; neither was going to change tonight.

Phidestros put his ear against the rear door to listen for signs that the brief rattling of the barrel had been heard. All he could hear was the tinker shop rattle of pots and plates in the kitchen and beyond it the rumble of the crowd in the front rooms. There was too much noise to let anyone inside hear street noises easily, and even if someone did, he would probably not be suspicious. By law, Harphax City had a curfew and a watch to enforce it, although ever since the mercenaries started swarming into the city for the coming war of the Great Kings, the watch had found it wiser to look the other way at armed men on the prowl after dark.

This, thought Phidestros, was only just. The mercenaries might occasionally brawl and rape, but they'd driven the common thieves and footpads of the nighttime streets to skulking in dark corners like rats—those who had learned in time that mercenaries were well armed, deadly opponents.

Phidestros was about to back away from the door when he heard shouts rising above the usual crowd noises. One was unmistakably a woman's voice, shouting a stream of obscene accusations against the men of Lamochares's company. He didn't need to hear the actual words to know what was being said; he'd rehearsed Clina in her part often enough. He'd also been impressed by her quick memory and her insistence on being paid half the money in advance, but then he hadn't been looking for a common whore when he found her. He'd been on the lookout for someone intelligent enough to learn quickly how to act like a common whore and in the meantime keep her mouth shut, without being so intelligent that she'd realize what her chances were of living after she'd done her job.

Now chairs were going over backward and tables were scraping as Lamochare's men rose in outrage at the woman's slurs on their bedroom manners and willingness to pay for what they'd made her do. Phidestros stepped back from the door, then moved to the left. Now anyone coming out would be illuminated by the light from the second-floor bedroom window just above the door, while Phidestros would be as invisible as one of Styphon's fireseed demons.

A sudden explosion of howls and curses told Phidestros that somebody had knocked down the torches in the front rooms. With darkness to hide them, his men could now go to work. He had too much respect for Galzar to ask him for aid in this plot; instead he made a Sastragathi gesture of aversion against snakebite.

Two pistols went off practically together, then a third, then two more. Chairs stopped going over and started smashing as men fell over them or picked them up for use as weapons. More women screamed—the girls of the house, who hadn't expected the war to start in their own backyard.

Phidestros let Zelos wrestle the barrel into the middle of the alley, where it wouldn't block the door but could confuse anyone bolting into the alley. He heard no more pistol shots, but an appalling amount of every other kind of noise. It reminded Phidestros of the bear pit in the Royal Menagerie of Hos-Zygros.

Without any warning the door flew open, crashing against the wall so hard that loosened chunks of brick splashed into the mud. Five men burst out, followed by a thick cloud of greasy smoke and the heartfelt curses of the Drunken Harlot's cook. Four of the men were soldiers, two each from Lamochares's and Phidestros's companies.

The fifth was Petty-Captain Ephentros, the only man fit to keep Lamochares's company together now that the captain himself was too fever-stricken to command it in the field. Phidestros would not have wasted time in prayers of thanks even if he'd known where to send them. He drew his pocket pistol and shot Ephentros through the head.

In his fall, Ephentros knocked over the barrel. Between the pistol shot and the clatter of the barrel, the other four men seemed to think they'd run into a thieves' ambush. Three of them dashed madly for one end of the alley, while the fourth headed in the opposite direction at a slighly more dignified pace. Halfway to the street he raised his pistol, saw Zelos trying to set the barrel upright again, and shot him.

Zelos gave a horrible gurgling scream as he fell. The inhuman sound frightened the people in the second-floor bedroom into putting out their light, throwing the alley into complete darkness. It also made the man who'd shot Zelos stop at the mouth of the alley. The faint moonlight reflected off the man's armor told Phidestros two things: first, that he wasn't a member of the Iron Company; and second, that he was a fool not to darken his armor so that it wouldn't reflect the treacherous moonlight. Phidestros fired, and was raising the other pistol when the man collapsed with a groan and lay kicking in the mud.

Zelos was dead. As he made certain of this and reloaded his pistols, Phidestros heard the thump of a bar dropping into place and the scrape of furniture being pushed against the kitchen door of the Drunken Harlot. Whoever or whatever was screaming and shooting off pistols in the alley, the people inside wanted to keep it outside.

Phidestros hurried toward the south end of the alley, stopping briefly to see if the man he'd shot needed finishing off. While he wasn't completely dead yet, he was bleeding so badly that nothing short of Styphon's Blessing would save him or even let him speak before he died. Phidestros stepped out into the street just as a party of the watch rounded the corner at a brisk trot, more than a dozen men as well as a few boys carrying torches.

Phidestros holstered his pistol and strode toward the approaching watchmen, half of whom kept straight on and vanished in the direction of the Drunken Harlot's front door. His troopers in the front rooms would do what they could to prove their innocence, but he would have to do most of the work, both tonight and during the next few days. The stakes were high; he could end up with authority over Lamochares's company, a hundred and sixteen good men less the two he'd just shot and two guns. He could also end up facing the axe as a traitor, or the noose as a common murderer.

At least he would not be breaking one of his ironbound rules. He would not be risking his authority over the Iron Company by wantonly expending them to advance himself. If he lost this gamble, the goodwill of the Iron Company toward a man under sentence of death would hardly matter all that much.

A torchboy and two of the watch approached Phidestros, their hands on the hilt of their swords.

"Greetings, Captain," he said to the man who was obviously in charge, wearing a plate back-and-breast instead of a leather jack. "Forgive me, but I am somewhat uneasy for my men."

"They will be dealt with according to the laws of Harphax and the will of His Majesty King Kaiphranos," said the watch captain. "Now come along with us and the others." He pointed to a group of men being led out of the Drunken Harlot by the other half of the watch.

One of Phidestros's men tripped and was promptly smashed across the back by the flat of a halberd head. Phidestros clenched his fists, holding them low so the watch wouldn't see, swallowed curses, and fell in behind the watch captain.

II.

The rabbit peered impudently from underneath the gnarled surface root of a lemon tree just downhill from Tortha Karf. Tortha could have sworn it also wiggled its ears at him.

Tortha reached for his gun, then remembered that he was unarmed except for the muzzle-loader from Kalvan's time-line he'd brought out to try on the range after lunch. It was primed and loaded, and maybe he could hit the rabbit with it; on the other hand, he hadn't had much practice. If the bullet kept going, it might reach the workers in the nearest grove before it fell to the ground. Solid-projectile weapons weren't like needlers or other beam weapons; those solid projectiles could bounce.

The workers would probably forgive him for accidentally shooting one of them, or maybe even doing it on purpose. They didn't think of Tortha Karf as quite a god, perhaps, but certainly as the sort of hero entitled to a whim or two now and then. Considering their history, this wasn't altogether surprising. The Yaltides were descended from a Madagascar tribe on the Afro-Sinic Sector of the Yangtze-Mekong Basic Sector Grouping. Tortha Karf's father had found them suffering not only from famine but from slave raiders let loose by a civil war in China that kept the Chinese Imperial Fleet's patrolling squadrons at home. Bringing them to Fifth Level as a work force for the Tortha family estate had earned their enduring if not necessarily eternal gratitude.

That was all the more reason for being careful with his shooting. An early lesson for any Paracop was not to take advantage of people's hospitality, women, or superstitions for his own pleasure. You seldom knew when their patience was going to run out until it was much too late. Even if you escaped the people you abused, you were apt to become careless, then some other outtimer would save the Paratime Police Bureau of Internal Control the trouble of bringing you up on charges.

Tortha Karf firmly put away both temptation and the pistol, then noticed he'd forgotten to turn off the taped message playing on the portable screen perched on top of the picnic basket. He ran it back and listened to Verkan Vall's description of the latest crisis on Fourth Level Europo-America, where a number of penetrated subsectors were getting thoroughly embroiled in the war in a place locally called "Vietnam." A map showed it as part of a peninsula in the southeastern corner of the Major Northern Land Mass.

"The situation has grown worse since our last conversation, increasing the possibility that this war could finally trigger a full-scale nuclear exchange. Even if this doesn't happen, suspicion of anything unusual will increase, and internal surveillance has become much more efficient throughout these subsectors since the Second Global War. There are also authors making small fortunes with stories of aliens from space dropping in unannounced and spying on the world. All we need is for the KGB or the FBI or the Vatican to start taking them seriously.

"The odds definitely favor our having to pull out of other Fourth Level Europo-American, Hispano-Columbian subsectors as well. The commercial interests that opposed you twenty years ago are going to make an even bigger stink now, so I'm not going to rush into things. I'm going to recommend that the Paratime Commission appoint a Study Group to analyze the whole Europo-American situation, with representatives from everybody who thinks they have something useful to say.

"That will make it a committee much too big to do anything except talk, of course. However, nobody will be able to claim that he didn't get a chance to be heard. Also, if we keep an eye on them, we may learn who are the real idiots and who can be trusted. I'm going to give Dalla the main responsibility for watching the Study Group. I'm afraid that means she and I won't be going outtime together this year, but she sees why." Tortha Karf hoped Vall was right; a discontented Dalla could give the new Chief a full-time job he didn't need.

"I have to be in a position to spend at least the first two months of the campaign in Kalvan's Time-Line. Otherwise, I'll seem to be a man who ran out on his friends when they were in danger. Even if somebody doesn't shoot me for that, I'll certainly lose command of the Mounted Rifles and access to Kalvan."

The screen flickered into a map of the theater of the coming Great Kings' War. There were two red blobs, one in northern Hos-Ktemnos and one around Harphax City, facing one large blue blob in southern Hos-Hostigos and a number of blue spots echeloned all the way back to Hostigos Town. About forty thousand men for Kalvan, slightly less than thirty for Kaiphranos, and about the same for the Styphoni army in Hos-Ktemnos. With three opponents to every two of his own men, the odds didn't look good for Kalvan, although he'd defeated worse in the war against Nostor.

Suddenly a blue line looped out from Beshta almost to Harphax City and then back again. Vall's voice explained:

"The armies would already be moving if they were of normal size, which on Kalvan's Time-Line would mean at most ten to fifteen thousand men on a side. However, there still isn't enough green forage to support either army advancing as a single body. That's one advantage Kalvan has. With his better discipline and staff work he can probably maneuver two armies independently without losing touch with each other. That is, when he learns about the army in Hos-Ktemnos. I've already figured out a way of leaking the information without letting anyone know it's coming from me."

Tortha Karf winced. It was one minus already just for a Paratime Police Chief to have an outtime "friend," but it was something else again to aid that friend with supplies—which Verkan was already doing—or intelligence. At the moment it didn't add up to a violation of the Paratemporal Code, but it skirted the line too close for Tortha's peace of mind, besides providing useful ammunition for the new Chief's enemies—who would multiply geometrically the moment he closed Fourth Level Europo-American.

Verkan's voice continued. "However, the roads are now dry enough so that cavalry carrying their own rations can move fast. So Kalvan had Harmakros send two thousand Mobile Force cavalry under Phrames into Hos-Harphax. They were to loot and burn anything belonging to King Kaiphranos or Styphon's House, scout out the land, fight only if they had to, and above all *keep moving*.

"Phrames did a good job. He stayed out seven days, because he overran a supply dump and the band of Harphaxi cavalry holding it. With the extra supplies he was able to swing west, outrun two Lances of Zarthani Knights, and make it back losing only a hundred men and two hundred horses. He seems to have raised the very Styphon on the way; our people in Hos-Harphax said you could see the smoke of his fires from the walls of the city.

"This should tickle up something in Hos-Harphax, but it's too soon to say exactly what. We are definitely having a problem getting intelligence from our people there. Grand Master Soton is there trying to whip the Harphaxi Army into shape, and is also instilling some rudimentary notions of security; he's the one who came up with the secret mobilization in Ktemnos. We wouldn't have known about that one ourselves if we hadn't just managed to get a man into Balph.

"We have two of our people working in Harphax City taverns frequented by mercenaries, and two more passing themselves off as sutlers. The second pair will move out with the army, when and if. We're not getting much information from the University people; most of them are up to their eyebrows in work at the foundry. The only two who aren't are Professor Baltov Eldra and Director Talgran Dreth, who are back on Home Time-Line assembling this year's team of scholars.

"So I'm going to send out Inspector Ranthar Jard to join both the foundry and the Mounted Rifles as a Zygrosi friend of mine. I'm sure I don't need to tell you that he can still keep his eyes and ears open and his mouth shut better than most. He's also remarkably hard to kill.

"He'll reach Hostigos Town in about a ten-day, with some Grefftscharri gold and a message from me. I'll follow in less than a moon, with a full-scale caravan of food and military stores from one of our control time-lines. That should land me in Hostigos before the shooting really starts, but after Ranthar Jard's had time to look around and ask a few questions.

"I hope he doesn't find anything that requires official action. Apart from the problem of dividing the University team when they'll need to be guarding each other's backs, Danthor Dras could easily make something out of any hint of scandal. He's going to be broadcasting a series of lectures on the Styphon's House Subsector and Kalvan's Time-Line, using all his favorite visual effects. Anything he says about the Paracops will have an audience of several hundred million, and we can just as well do without that, thank you . . ."

III.

Grand Master Soton signed his name at the bottom of the parchment with less than his usual flourish. The scroll contained a requisition to the royal granaries of Hos-Harphax for enough food and fodder for three Lances of Knights and their horses. It was the least he could do, having signed their death warrant by bringing them to this dreary and inhospitable land. He'd spent the two weeks since he'd arrived from Ktemnos City by galleass inspecting King Kaiphranos's excuse for an army. It was even worse than First Speaker Anaxthenes had feared, and Anaxthenes was not known for his optimism. Anaxthenes had been right to send him here to reconnoiter the Army of Hos-Harphax, and now he even understood why he'd been ordered to bring the Lances with him.

Yet to send so many Brethren to almost certain death stuck in his throat like a chicken bone. If there was one thing certain, by Ormaz, it was that he'd never make a statesman—good or otherwise.

King Kaiphranos's Royal Horse Guard wasn't up to muster, and singularly ill equipped—a polite phrase for bridles that fell apart in your hands and pistols whose hammers were frozen with rust. The fifteen hundred Royal Lancers led by Prince Philesteus were if anything overequipped; the silvered or gilded armor could blind friends as well as opponents on a sunlit battlefield. They were also composed of younger sons of the nobility and wealthy merchants, and were hard to control unless used wisely. And who in Styphon's name could do that? Kaiphranos, so old he couldn't mount a horse without help? Prince Philesteus, as rash as he was courageous? Duke Aesthes, a commander who'd never won a battle though he'd fought three, and owed his present rank of Captain-General of Hos-Harphax to the fact that he could listen to Kaiphranos's endless monologues about the best kind of reeds for flutes? Only in the Harphaxi Army. . . .

There were some good mercenary troops, but they were of little use unless competently led. The Hos-Harphax levy were the dregs of the Five Kingdoms: gallows-fruit, bastards, imbeciles, and the scourings of every prison in the twelve Princedoms of Hos-Harphax. And their mounts! Never in his whole life had he seen such an assortment of bags of bones. The entire lot wasn't worth the shot it would cost Kalvan to bring them down.

The Knight doing steward's duty entered and said, "A Captain Phidestros to see you, Master."

"Bid him enter."

As a mercenary, Phidestros had appealed to the Knights' justice rather than the Great King's, a wise choice as more than one mercenary commander had been hanged to appease the local citizens. Soton wondered what Phidestros would have done if he'd known that the Grand Master was satisfied that the captain had plotted and committed cold-blooded murder to place the Blue Company of Captain Lamochares under his own banner.

Personally, Soton also thought that the young blackguard should be drawn and quartered. However, the Holy War was much more important than any murder or any ambitions of a mercenary captain. Unless he could prompt a full confession, which he rather doubted, he would have to find a lesser punishment. Otherwise Phidestros's death would seem arbitrary, offend the mercenaries, and make for bad blood between them and the Knights.

There was also no doubt that Phidestros had shown initiative and cool courage, two things in desperately short supply in the Army of Hos-Harphax. If all else failed, Kalvan's army would soon dispatch Phidestros to Regwarn, Cavern of the Dead, the final resting place for those without honor or belief in the gods.

When Captain Phidestros entered, Soton with a silent gesture sent the steward Knight out for wine. Then he leaned back in his chair as best he could and contemplated the man standing before him on the far side of the table.

It was a contemplation that would have been easier if Phidestros had been somewhat shorter. Then he would not have made Soton more conscious than usual of his own lack of height, and of how oversized this chair borrowed from the palace was for him. The next time he traveled north he would bring one of his own chairs from Tarr-Ceros.

Meanwhile there was no purpose in letting himself be distracted from great matters by trying to dominate in small ones.

"Sit down, Captain Phidestros, and tell me why you think you and your men should not be punished for the work at the Drunken Harlot three nights ago."

Phidestros sat down with an almost contemptuous grace of movement that told Soton very clearly that the man knew why he was being told to sit. Either he was very sure his case was fireproof, or he was playing some deep game without much caring whether he won or lost. Soton decided to assume the first, since the second was too disquieting to even contemplate without evidence.

Soton also had no evidence for the story that Phidestros was the bastard of someone too highly placed to acknowledge him but too fond of him not to advance his education and career whenever this could be done quietly. No evidence—yet Soton's belly told him that no other explanation made sense any longer (although he still would not wager on which of the half-score men named as Phidestros's sire might be the one).

"I do not think that I and my men were without blame, Grand Master," said Phidestros. "Indeed, I think that some among Lamochares's men suffered quite innocently, and I would see to making provision for their kin. I know that Ephentros left a widow and two daughters, for example. Also, the owner of the Drunken Harlot has the right to the price of replacing his furniture. At the moment he has nothing but a lavish supply of kindling wood."

In spite of himself, Soton smiled, then hardened his face. Undoubtedly Phidestros could pay enough to quiet a great many tongues; the Iron Company had left the field of Fyk last autumn not only in good order, but thoroughly looted the baggage train of Sarrask afterward. There were Princes with smaller war chests than Phidestros, but there was no chance of Phidestros being accepted into the service of Hos-Hostigos as long as Sarrask of Sask was alive. The one neatly balanced the other, depriving Phidestros of one major weapon in an ambitious mercenary captain's arsenal: the ability to switch sides whenever he found a pretext plausible enough to satisfy the scruples of the more devout Galzar-worshippers among his men.

"I will pay whatever you think is fair, in return for a grant of the right to take Lamochares's men into the Iron Company. Ephentros was the only man fit to command them as an in-

dependent company. The other petty-captains are not bad
men, but they lack experience. Also, there is bad blood between some of them."

Soton clenched his fists; this man had as much gall as the so-
called Great King of Hos-Hostigos. "I have heard as much.
But aren't you burying Lamochares without bothering to find
out if he's dead?"

"I am far from burying the worthy Lamochares, Grand
Master. I wish him long years and an honorable career. However, all my wishes will not drive out the marsh fever in time to
let him take the field this summer. If Lamochares's company
is not put in the hands of some captain, it will be lost to
Styphon's service this year."

That was true enough, particularly since one of the few
things Soton did know was that Lamochares had become careless about the pay and equipment of his men as the fever grew
on him. The late Petty-Captain Ephentros had done his best,
but that hadn't been good enough. Lamochares's men would
need a good deal of discipline hammered into them and silver
spent on them before they were any fitter to take the field than
their captain.

They would probably also follow the man who gave them
what they needed like lost sheep following a shepherd. And
almost certainly if the man had the reputation and—Hadron
take the man, but there was no denying it!—the commanding
presence of Phidestros.

"How will you heal the bad blood between your men and
Lamochares's if I do give them to you?"

Phidestros's answer showed that he had been doing a good
deal of thinking on the matter. Too much thinking, in fact.
Soton began to have the feeling that he was listening to a
superb actor playing a part in one of the Mystery Plays. However, it was not the sort of feeling that Soton was prepared to
let carry him away when plain facts were shouting in his ear.

Fact: Lamochares's men would indeed be leaderless if they
weren't put under some other captain.

Fact: If they were left leaderless, they would not be taking
the field this summer when every man would be needed to
crush Kalvan, even if they were nothing more than cannon
fodder. The company would be left behind, idle, unpaid, and
a menace to the lawful citizens of Harphax City, whose fond-

ness for mercenaries would doubtless run out when the mercenaries' purses did.

Fact: Phidestros could undoubtedly give Lamochares's company everything they needed. That would save a hundred and fourteen men and two good guns to the service of Styphon—an addition not to be despised.

Fact: Under Phidestros, the men would also be under a captain loyal to Styphon's House—or at least as loyal to it as any mercenary captain ever could be. They would not be under Prince Philesteus and Duke Aesthes, or obeying Styphon's House through Grand Duke Lysandros. Soton knew enough about those men to trust the first two hardly at all and Lysandros only as long as his ambitions for the crown of Hos-Harphax were not threatened.

Fact: Phidestros's Iron Company strength was now one hundred and thirty-seven men. With Lamochares's Blue Company, Phidestros could have a double company with over two hundred and fifty men.

Phidestros's claim to Lamochares's company was worth granting—at a price.

"Captain Phidestros, I shall not render a final judgment today, because I have only your word for some of the important matters on which we have spoken."

"So be it, Grand Master. My men and I have little to fear, for Styphon will guide you to the truth."

Soton had to force back the laughter that threatened his poise. It did not seem to the purpose to reveal his suspicions so blatantly, however. Another time would serve better to politely warn Phidestros against sticking that long nose of his into places where people might be tempted to cut it off.

"I would add that if I do find you fit to take command of Lamochares's men, I will request one further thing of you."

"Ask, and if it is lawful in the sight of the God of Gods and Galzar Wolfshead, it shall be granted."

"It is lawful," said Soton tightly. He badly wanted to say, "Oh, demons fly away with your piety and drop it in Kalvan's chamberpot." Prudence silenced him. "It is certainly lawful to ask you to have Lamochares's guns fitted with trunnions and the new-style carriages at your expense."

Soton again wanted to laugh; Phidestros was finally looking unsettled. "Fitting the twelve-pounder they call the Fat

Duchess will take some time, Grand Master. Also a good deal of silver.''

"Nonetheless, I must be satisfied that you will take proper care of weapons entrusted to you before I raise you higher among the captains serving Styphon's House. Is this not also lawful?''

Soton was reasonably sure that Phidestros's mutter was a "Yes." He kept a grin off his face until the captain had departed, then drained an entire goblet of wine without taking it from his lips and hooted with laughter.

Add a heavy fine for the brawl at the Drunken Harlot to the cost of refitting the two guns, and even the Saski loot would be stretched thin. Then Phidestros could perhaps be encouraged to give up his intrigues and ambitions and settle down to doing the work he knew so well. Styphon's House had plenty of ambitious would-be allies; it had rather fewer reliable captains of mercenaries.

TEN

I.

It wasn't until Soton entered King Kaiphranos's audience hall that he finally began to understand why Kalvan had been so successful so quickly. The Grand Hall was low-ceilinged and shadowed, like most of the rooms in Tarr-Harphax. One window worthy of the name had been laboriously carved through the wall, but otherwise the only outside light and air came through firing slits. When they built the keep of Tarr-Harphax, petty Princedoms were fighting almost yearly over the lands left vacant by the destruction of the last Ruthani tribes. Princes and Kings who wanted to sleep peacefully at nights built for defense, not comfort.

At least Kaiphranos had beeswax candles to light the hall, not the grease-soaked tapers used elsewhere in the castle that gave very little light and a great deal of smoke and stink. Most of the hangings and tapestries were faded, some ripped or frayed at the ends. Even the gilded leather throne of King Kaiphranos IV was cracked and peeling. Soton had seen better furnishings in the longhouses of Sastragathi headmen.

Kaiphranos himself seemed hardly more than another shadow. He was bent and crooked, and his wispy white hair splayed out of his crown like an unruly bird's nest. Even from a distance, his red velvet robe showed dark purple wine stains.

Flanking Kaiphranos in lesser chairs of state were his eldest son and heir, Prince Philesteus, and the white-bearded Captain-General of Hos-Harphax, Duke Aesthes. Philesteus wore armor under his robes and was eccentric enough to go clean-shaven, which left his thick neck and double chin exposed to all. Duke Aesthes could hardly carry himself at all; at seventy he was past active campaigning. During the thirty years when Hos-Harphax didn't need to take war and armies seriously, this wouldn't have mattered. Now, however. . . .

Across the table from Kaiphranos sat his younger half-brother, Grand Duke Lysandros, a slender, fine-featured man of middle age whose mink-lined, gold-filigreed robe was worth more than the entire contents of the hall. Out of all of Kaiphranos's advisers, he was the closest to Styphon's House and the fittest general. For once, Soton wished he had a purseful of the First Speaker's little vials, so that he could put the scales of Hos-Harphax back into balance.

As he sat down next to Lysandros, Soton wished even more that he had a drink in his hand, preferably good winter wine. From the look on Lysandros's face, he knew this was going to be an ordeal. He leaned over and whispered to Lysandros, "Where's Prince Selestros?"

The Grand Duke answered in a voice loud enough to startle Kaiphranos. "Selestros is out wallowing with some he, she, or it."

Kaiphranos cleared his throat. Quite unnecessarily, Prince Philesteus barked, "Give ear to the Great King!"

The chamber was so silent that Soton could hear the creaking of joints as Kaiphranos straightened in his chair.

"Grand Master Soton," said Kaiphranos. His whining voice reminded Soton of a befuddled old tutor who'd roamed the streets of Geas, the village where he'd grown up, then left as soon as the first whiskers graced Soton's chin.

"Yes, Your Majesty."

"Is it true what I've heard, that you plan to leave Us with tomorrow evening's tide?"

"Yes, it is true. I have been called by Styphon's Voice to lead the Great Squares of Hos-Ktemnos against the Usurper."

Kaiphranos's face crumpled like that of an infant about to start squalling. "What have I done to bring this plague upon our land? I have worshipped all the true gods and paid Styphon's offerings. I have given my people peace and the gods send me demons! And now the Grand Master prepares to steal away in the night, to leave my Kingdom to death and ruin."

Soton made an effort to keep his expression neutral. He glanced over at Lysandros and saw him roll his eyes.

"I am not deserting anyone. I told Captain-General Aesthes days ago that I would be leaving soon. I was not sent here to command the Army of Hos-Harphax but to see that it was fit for battle." Soton raised his voice. "This I have done. Styphon's treasure has armed and refitted the Royal Army you have so long neglected, bought you twelve thousand mercenaries, and provided you with three Lances of the Holy Order. Your army has a commander, two, perhaps three. You don't need me."

"Grand Master Soton is correct, Your Majesty," said Archpriest Phyllos, highpriest of Styphon's Great Temple of Harphax City. "Furthermore, I have just received word that a convoy is on its way from Balph with a hundred tons of Styphon's Best and three thousand of Styphon's Own Guard. There is also another convoy leaving Agrys City with eight thousand more mercenaries and ten thousand ounces of gold for the war against the Usurper."

Soton's head reeled. He would have to completely rethink the war against Hostigos. Why hadn't he been informed of all this, or were there yet more surprises hidden in the sleeves of Anaxthenes's robe?

"I want the Grand Master to lead Our Army! He will bring us Styphon's Own Blessing."

Soton stamped on his anger until his voice came out in a deadly monotone. "If you had kept your own house in order, there would be no need for Styphon's troops and Styphon's gold to give you back the Kingdom *you* have lost. We are not here at your pleasure but at Styphon's will. What has been given can just as easily be taken away."

As Soton had expected, King Kaiphranos's cloak of anger fell away. Left behind were a frightened old man and a son who'd never grown up puffing himself up in anger. To defuse the situation, Soton added, "Let your son reunite his future Kingdom and earn his spurs. Even in far-off Bletha we have heard of the fame of the Harphaxi Royal Lancers." It was so easy to salvage Philesteus's pride, yet it went against Soton's heart. Let Anaxthenes do this double-tongued work!

"Yes, Father," said Philesteus. "The Grand Master is right. With our great host will we skin the snake in its own den."

Kaiphranos waved away his son's words. "I want to know more about this army you plan to lead from Hos-Ktemnos. Why do they not open the battle against the Daemon Kalvan?"

"I am not at liberty to speak about their plans. We have learned that in Harphax City even stone walls have ears."

"Are you accusing me of harboring traitors and spies?" The old King was beginning to get his color back.

"Of course not. But is it not true that a highpriest of the false god Dralm passes through these halls?"

Kaiphranos averted his gaze and stared at the floor. A moment later a servant entered bearing goblets of wine on a tray. Soton was shocked when he took one and saw the green corrosion on what appeared to be a golden stem.

"Highpriest Socratos is an old friend and trusted advisor, and I could not believe he would violate Our trust. Nor is this what we have come here at this Council of War to discuss." The old King brightened as though struck by inspiration. "I now want to annouce Our decision in the matter of a proper reply to the godless attack by the hosts of the traitor, rebel, and servant of demons Kalvan on the land of Harphax ten days ago. We have in this matter sought the advice of our councillors and captains and the wisdom sent only by the gods."

Soton steeled himself for the worst; he was fairly sure that the bit about seeking advice was pure diplomacy, meant to placate Syphon's House. Styphon's House had eyes and ears in enough places in Harphax City to have known if Kaiphranos had consulted with any significant number of his "councillors and captains." No, whatever was about to come out would most likely be the old man's decision—or whim. Considering that Kaiphranos's last major decision had been to appoint Lysandros Captain-Governor of Harphax City, which meant that the only competent general of the royal house of Harphax would not be taking the field during this campaign, Soton was not optimistic that what he was about to hear would contain any great amount of wisdom.

"It is Our will that the Royal Treasury be called on to ease the suffering of those who have lost homes, herds, and kin to the hosts of the traitor, rebel, and servant of demons Kalvan.

"It is Our will that the Count Phrames and all other men who may be proved to have followed him into Harphax to the destruction and wasting of Our land shall be under the same ban as the traitor, rebel, and servant of demons Kalvan, and shall suffer the same penalties at the hands of Our justice.

"It is Our will that Duke Aesthes shall take his seat at Tarr-Argros and shall from there command a force of horse to watch a line from Tarr-Argros south and west to Tarr-Kelos, that no further invaders may cross it without warning.

"It is Our will that no man who has sworn oath to the Great Crown of Hos-Harphax shall pass forward of this line without Our express command, given under Our hand and seal.

"It is Our will that the hosts of Harphax be readied with the greatest despatch to march and utterly crush the traitor, rebel, and servant of demons Kalvan, at such time as Our noble and loyal allies may be able to give of their strength to this purpose.

"This is Our will in this matter, proclaimed this eleventh day of the Month of the Tall Grass in Our seat of Tarr-Harphax."

Soton was suddenly glad he hadn't been smoking a pipe. If he had, it would have clattered to the table, betraying to all his gaping mouth. As it was, he was able to compose his features before anyone noticed, although safely out of sight under the table, his hands were clenching into fists.

Kaiphranos's strategy was simple: to lie down and let the Hostigi do what they pleased—as long as they did it only along the frontier. Aesthes's patrols would detect any enemy attacks penetrating deep into Harphaxi territory, Soton supposed, but they would be unable to scout out such an attack before it was launched. Add to this lack of warning Duke Aesthes's past performance and Prince Philesteus's rashness, and what might the Hostigi do before the Harphaxi met them in battle, assuming now that Kaiphranos really meant to array his army so that it was fit to do so?

Lysandros's face gave away no more than usual. The Captain-General's face was too swathed in white, tobacco-stained whiskers to reveal much expression. Philesteus had neither whiskers nor any reason to hide his countenance. He looked horror-struck and gobbled like a turkey for a moment before he found his voice, while his face turned the color of a turkey's wattles.

"Fa—Your Majesty! This—the honor of Hos-Harphax demands—we shall seem. . . !"

Kaiphranos looked mildly at his heir until he could be sure that the Prince had lost his voice again. Then he said more firmly than Soton would have expected, "I am the judge of the honor of Harphax and what it demands. What it demands now is that we not expose any more Harphaxi to attacks—from which we cannot defend them—by provoking the Hostigi further. With the help of the true gods and our friends and allies, this will not always be the case, but most surely it is so now."

Soton looked at Captain-General Aesthes, hoping to hear him deny that his men were as helpless as that. When he saw the Duke slowly nodding his head like a bear just waked from sleep, Soton's stomach turned to cold iron. There would be no opposition to Kaiphranos's witless demonstration of spite against Styphon's House, as well as fear of the strength of Hos-Hostigos, unless one wished to intrigue it into existence by dealing directly with some of the captains or even Lysandros. Such dangerous games Soton would leave to highpriest Phyllos, who would never have to deal with the Captain-General on the field of battle in the face of a deadly enemy.

"Your Majesty," said Grand Duke Lysandros. "It seems to me that we provoke the servant of demons Kalvan by our very existence, or at least by our refusal to let an enemy of the true gods proclaim himself Great King and rule over our lands and subjects ny time it pleases him! Unless we are to cravenly submit our-elves to—"

"It is not well done to call your Great King and elder brothur a coward," said Kaiphranos.

From the battle running across Lysandros's face, it was easy to see that he held neither respect nor affection for Kaiphranos. But with two healthy heirs between him and the crown he so obviously lusted after, there was little he could do but swallow his bile. "Forgive me," Lysandros finally choked out. "I do not wish to go beyond calling Your Majesty's attention to facts that your advisers have not, perhaps, brought to your notice."

"This wish does you credit, so I will assume your indiscretion arises from your eagerness to defend the honor of Harphax. We will speak of this no further, Duke Lysandros. I will take your advice under consideration."

Lysandros now looked as though he'd swallowed not only his bile but his tongue as well. It occurred to Soton that perhaps there was method in the apparent madness of keeping Lysandros out of the field during this campaign. A major victory to his credit, or more likely an honorable part in a defeat, would give him allies among the nobles and mercenary captains who could only feed his ambitions.

It also occurred to Soton that very probably Styphon's House would not be losing so greatly by Lysandros's remaining safely behind the walls of Harphax City. Barring the direct intervention of Styphon and Galzar on the side of Harphax, Kalvan was going to eat Kaiphranos's army for breakfast and pick his teeth with their bones. Lysandros was as brave as he was able; he might not wish to survive such a defeat, and if he were in the forefront of the battle, he might not survive whether he wished to or not. Some men could do Styphon's House as much service dead as alive; Lysandros was not one of them.

King Kaiphranos continued. "Prince Philesteus, it is Our wish that you may lead such of your Royal Lancers as you wish into the field to form part of Our strength watching the hosts of the traitor, rebel, and servant of demons Kalvan. You and they are to obey the orders of the Captain-General in all matters where his authority runs."

Both Aesthes and Philesteus started to reply, then both seemed to think better of it. For the first time in several minutes Soton felt like smiling. Duke Aesthes was clearly none too happy about having under his authority a Prince notoriously hotheaded enough for three captains half his age. Philesteus was just as clearly torn among joy at going into the field at the head of his Lancers, frustration at being under the Captain-General's orders, and reluctance to leave Harphax City and a chance to intrigue with captains of his own faction against Kaiphranos's policy.

From the bland way Kaiphranos was looking at his two companions, Soton was quite sure he was reading their thoughts just as clearly. Had the servants of Styphon underestimated the wits remaining to Kaiphranos? If so, he would have to discuss the matter with First Speaker Anaxthenes when he returned to Balph.

"My Knights and I must take counsel as to how we may best obey the will of the Great King. I must say that I think he has been given advice by men not knowing the true strength that Styphon's House may bring to the aid of his allies. Yet it is no shame to them not to know the secrets of the God of Gods."

"Will you be taking your Lances of Knights away from the host of Harphax?" asked Duke Aesthes. His rheumy eyes remained aimed like twin cannon mouths at Soton, ignoring the glare from Philesteus and the cough from Kaiphranos.

"As I said, I must take counsel with my Knights. I can say, however, that there seems small need for that at present."

Which means, old man, that my eighteen hundred Brethren will be within reach of your orders if you need to rein in that spirited stallion Philesteus the Bold and find no one else to help you because they're all afraid of offending their next ruler. But Styphon have mercy on you should you make ill use of them, for I shall have none!

Gods, let me escape from this snakepit and I will do anything you ask of me, even sacrifice captives to you like the Mexicotal!

Highpriest Phyllos moved for the first time, and Soton found himself looking into eyes that made him think of a whole battery, loaded and with the matches smoking in the gunners' hands. So perhaps he'd just knocked on the head a plan to move Styphon's Own Guard out of Harphaxi reach? Certainly Styphon's House could not afford to leave the Knights alone in supporting Harphax against Kalvan. Too many Harphaxi nobles would never forget or forgive if they did that, and Lysandros's devotion to the God of Gods would become even more of a black mark against him.

Too bad for Anaxthenes's cat's paw if this was another of the First Speaker's grand schemes. Archpriests were going to have to learn the difference between cavalry and infantry just like everybody else if they wanted to stop Kalvan before grass grew on the ruins of Styphon's temples!

II.

Master Gunner Thalmoth finished winding his slowmatch around the eight-foot linstock, then held the lighted end up to his lips and blew on it until Kalvan was afraid the man's beard would catch fire.

"Everybody back!" Thalmoth shouted. The other gunners and Foundry workers backed away from the gun-testing pit, leaving Thalmoth standing alone with the smoldering match poised over the touchhole of the new sixteen-pounder inside. "Farther!" he shouted as a few of the younger workers showed signs of wanting to stay close enough to see what happened.

The workers kept backing, and somehow in the process Kalvan had to join the retreat to avoid being jostled in a manner not befitting a Great King's dignity. He grinned, wondering if Thalmoth had planned this to avoid having to publicly give orders to his sovereign.

Suddenly the linstock dipped, the priming powder puffed, and the sixteen-pounder spewed flame and white smoke. Double-charged for the proof firing, it reared halfway out of the testing pit on its oak beam, then thumped back into place. From where Kalvan stood, it looked completely intact.

Half a dozen picked men ran forward with sponges to cool the barrel, rammers, and tools, and to measure any deformation of barrel or bore. As the light breeze blew away the smoke and dust, they leaped down into the pit, leaving Thalmoth posing dramatically on the rim with the linstock over his shoulder.

Kalvan didn't begrudge the old man his moment of glory; he'd come out of retirement to take charge of the testing program for the Royal Hostigos Arsenal and was clearly worth any two other gunners in Hostigi service except Alkides. Although a native of Hostigos, Thalmoth had spent twenty of his younger years as a mercenary, and he'd handled guns in more battles than he had fingers and toes.

Finally Thalmoth turned to the spectators and gave the thumbs-up signal for success that Kalvan had introduced. The next step would be firing a proof charge with the breech dug in to give the gun maximum elevation. Then a field carriage—and thank Galzar or Somebody that the gunsmiths, regular smiths, and carpenters had finally stopped arguing about who should be in charge of the carriage shop!—and last of all a naming ceremony, with Uncle Wolf Tharses presiding over the gun's acceptance into the Royal Artillery.

That would be about the last such ceremony for a while, though. No more bronze for the Foundry, or at least not much; Kalvan doubted if there was a brass chamberpot left in the entire Great Kingdom! Hooped wrought iron would do for the four- and eight-pounders, but Hostigos already had about as many of those as there'd be horses to draw. What was needed was the heavies, the sixteen-pounders and those thirty-two-pound siege guns he'd been dreaming of since last fall. Made of bronze and firing either solid shot or cast-iron shells—he'd seen the first experimental shells last week—the heavies would pry open any castle he'd seen like a sardine can. Made of hooped wrought iron, those brutes would simply be too heavy to move over here-and-now roads without slaughtering draft animals like hoof-and-mouth disease.

Wait a minute! If he couldn't make siege guns with hooped wrought iron, what about siege *mortars*? They could be made large enough to lob a really destructive shell a few hundred yards, and have a high trajectory that would carry it over any walls. Solid shot, too. If castles couldn't be battered open, perhaps they could be hammered flat from above, or at least made uninhabitable, and if the shells could be filled with some sort of incendiary compound. . . .

Of course, the mortars would have to be very short-ranged in order to be light enough to move easily. Four or five hundred yards would probably be the limit. However, they could easily be dug into pits like the one being used for gun testing. It would require some fancy shooting to hit them, and a few dozen riflemen in other pits close to the walls could discourage enemy gunners from standing in the open long enough for that.

Mortars might be a poor man's weapon, but Kalvan had been on the wrong end of enough Chinese mortar barrages to have a lively respect for them. Besides, anything that impressed upon castle-holders that a siege was no longer something to sneer at would be an asset to the Great Kingdom.

Kalvan sent a page off to his tent for a piece of the thin-cut pine he used in place of notepads and some charcoal. For at least the fiftieth time he cursed the slowness of the paper project, which had worked up only as far as a high grade of mush. For the fortieth time, he realized that Brother Mytron was doing the best he could with the knowledge and tools available, not to mention the time he could spare for the paper project.

Mytron in fact now wore three hats. He was Royal Papermaker of Hos-Hostigos, Surgeon General to the Royal Army, and Rector of the Royal University. Unofficially, he was also chief Rylla-watcher, a job in which Ptosphes and Kalvan gave him all the help their military duties allowed. That wasn't much, with the campaigning season getting nearer each day. As soon as the streams and river shrank a bit. . . .

Unfortunately, the warmer weather had only given Rylla her own bad case of cabin fever. She felt fine and was firmly convinced that keeping her shut up like the crown jewels was good for neither her nor the baby. She argued the point with her husband, with her father, with Mytron, and even with Amasphalya, who as a girl of fifteen had helped her grandmother bring Ptosphes into the world.

Maybe Rylla had a point. Certainly there were plenty of "good breeders" (as Amasphalya put it) among the women on both sides of her family. Maybe Princess Demia's troubles hadn't been passed on to her daughter? Maybe any baby who didn't miscarry from its mother's temper tantrums could easily survive mere cannon shot? Maybe Kalvan was being a little selfish, keeping Rylla shut up just to save himself one more worry?

Maybe, and he wasn't going to change his mind now, either. If Rylla sailed through the last month of her pregnancy as well as she had the first eight, she could have her next baby in a trench at the siege of Balph if she wanted to. But for this one, she stayed put!

The page returned with the pine and charcoal. Kalvan realized he was hungry, and sent the boy off to the gunners' mess to scrounge some food and wine. Rylla claimed that he didn't keep enough ceremony with his meals, but he'd be damned if he was going to take up time for that sort of thing now. With a twenty-nine-hour day and no need for sleep, he just might get done half of the things that needed doing no more than a moon or two late.

III.

Kalvan was finishing his sketch of an eight-inch mortar and the wing of a rather tough goose when he heard one of the pages clearing his throat.

"Your Majesty, Duke Chartiphon wishes audience."

Kalvan tossed the goose bones aside, wiped his hands on his breeches, and stood to greet Chartiphon. Despite his new titles and responsibilities, the old Captain-General of Hostigos appeared much the same as he had when Kalvan had first entered Tarr-Hostigos. He was a big man with a gray-streaked golden beard and rugged features, still wearing the same battered and lead-splotched breastplate and two-handed sword.

Chartiphon bowed, then motioned to a man standing behind him to come forward. "Your Majesty, this is Ranthar, a free-trader come from Grefftscharr. He bears a message from Colonel Verkan."

Ranthar was a tough-looking young man with sandy hair and a bristling beard. He wore well-made but well-worn leather riding clothes and looked to be well under thirty until you saw his eyes. Kalvan hoped he would have a chance to hear from Ranthar the stories of some of what those eyes had seen.

More immediatley to the point was the signet ring on Ranthar's left middle finger. It was Zygrosi work, plain bronze, and there were only four rings like that in the whole world. None of them would likely be in the possession of someone Colonel Verkan didn't trust.

"You've assured yourself of a warm welcome already, Trader Ranthar. How is Verkan?"

Trader Ranthar bowed gracefully, as though meeting Great

Kings was an everyday event for him, then smiled. "Colonel Verkan was well the last time I saw him. Also very busy, putting together a shipment of food and weapons for your use. He sent me on ahead overland with a pack train while he followed with the ships across the Saltless Seas to Ulthor. If you send men to Ulthor now, they should be just in time to meet him and unload his cargoes swiftly."

Ranthar handed Kalvan a leather-wrapped wooden tablet listing what Verkan was sending. It was quite an impressive list, with its most notable entries a thousand stand of muskets, five tons of Kalvan-formula fireseed, six hundred sets of pikeman's weapons and armor, and a hundred tons of grain and salt meat. Also nine hundred ounces of silver and three hundred ounces of gold riding on Ranthar's pack animals along with a miscellany of gunlocks and other lightweight gear.

"Well done," said Kalvan. "Take twenty ounces of the gold for yourself before you turn the rest over to the treasury. I'll tell Colonel Verkan that he's chosen a good messenger." Not that this was any surprise; a free-trader who didn't learn to pick good subordinates probably wouldn't live to wear out his first hunting knife.

"I thank your Majesty," said Ranthar. "Colonel Verkan says he wishes he could have sent more sooner. However, the nomads of the plains are on the move. King Theovacar would let neither food nor arms nor fireseed leave his realm until he was sure the nomads were not turning north at once. Even then, Colonel Verkan had to pledge all he owned and all he could borrow from his fellow traders in payment."

"He will be repaid in full, if not before the campaign, then afterward."

"At Styphon's expense?"

"Exactly."

Ranthar's report confirmed others, both about the nomads and about Theovacar's character. Theovacar was only about twenty-five and definitely ambitious to expand his kingdom, but equally determined not to risk what he already had. Not a bad man to do business with if you had something he valued—and Kalvan realized that if he offered to show Theovacar the way to the copper and iron deposits around Lake Superior, he'd have something the man should jump at. Also a permanent solution to any shortage of metal for cannon.

He'd have to talk with Verkan when the man came in, to be sure he wasn't planning to sell King Theovaçar knowledge he already had. Even if the deposits were known, of course, that didn't mean they couldn't use a better way of getting the metal from the shores of Lake Superior down the lakes to Greffa. Kalvan knew only a little more about mining than he knew about papermaking, but if it could also solve his shortage of artillery. . . .

He'd have to work mostly through Verkan, of course. That might mean turning the man from Colonel of the Mounted Rifles into here-and-now's first copper magnate, which would be a pity; the man was too good a combat officer to be spared easily. However, it was also probably necessary; one of these days Kalvan might stop having to make ten men do the work of fifty, but he suspected he'd be a grandfather before that day was even in sight.

Ranthar was now fumbling something out of his belt pouch. "This is not from Colonel Verkan, but it was from a man who thought someone trusted by the colonel would be the best way of sending it to Your Majesty secretly. As you will surely see, it would be the end of him if any of Styphon's minions were to find his trail. I can tell you that the man was on his way from Agrys City, but I would rather not tell any more."

He handed Kalvan a piece of parchment, folded in four and with the badge of the Inner Circle of Styphon's House stamped into the sealing wax. It directed a certain Captain Xantythros to transport two thousand mercenaries in Agrysi pay southward in his ships to the mouth of the Potomac River. He was to return with a full Lance of Zarthani Knights, landing them at Harphax City no later than a date eighteen days from now.

The meaning of the date was obvious; it was about when the Harphaxi were supposed to march. That in itself was useful to know, although Kalvan had never had any intention of waiting more than another half moon. But why this shuffling around of the Knights, particularly when the Harphaxi Army would need a lot more than one additional Lance to make a difference? They had only three Lances of Knights with them already, and they would need five or six more to stiffen the well-born nitwits and mercenaries of their cavalry enough to face the Hostigi.

Unless the Inner Circle *wasn't* planning to stiffen the Harphaxi with their best troops! There'd been rumors of bad blood between the Harphaxi and the Styphoni, who were mostly Knights and Styphon's Own Guard. Had the Inner Circle now decided to fight its own war and strengthen the Harphaxi just enough to make them a better grade of cannon fodder? If that could be proved and a word whispered into King Kaiphranos's ear by a well-placed and reliable secret agent, if there were such a thing. . . . He'd have to talk with Klestreus and Xentos; this was much too hot for Skranga.

One thing was certain. This wasn't something he could decide all by himself. "Chartiphon, send out messengers. We're going to hold a small Council of War at Tarr-Hostigos. Count Phrames should be arriving from Beshta sometime tomorrow. We'll set it for tomorrow night. I want Ptosphes, Klestreus, Xentos, Rylla, and Mytron."

"Good news?"

Kalvan shook his head. "I'm afraid not. Styphon's House is up to more of their shenanigans. Here, take this message to Prince Ptosphes and have him read it to you."

Chartiphon nodded and left. Like most men who weren't scribes or priests, Chartiphon felt no shame at not being able to read, although he was good at recognizing map symbols. Fortunately most of the upper nobility and merchants knew how to read and write the runic Zarthani alphabet, but Chartiphon had begun his career as a simple trooper and owed his rank both to his abilities and to Ptosphes's eye for talent.

Kalvan turned to Trader Ranthar. "I'm afraid you'll have to stay in protective custody for a while. It's not that we don't trust you, it's that I don't trust Styphon's House not to have spies around here. If they learned what you've done, the first news I might have for Verkan is that you'd been kidnapped and probably tortured to death for what you might know about his plans. That would be poor payment to him and even worse to you."

Ranthar laughed. "Thank you, Your Majesty. I hope you're not allowing the Styphoni more common sense than they have."

"I'd rather give them credit for too much than for too little."

Ranthar nodded, and at Kalvan's gesture of dismissal bowed himself away. He suspected that Ranthar would visit the nearest tavern, probably the Crossed Halberds, and have a drink or two before surrendering himself to protective custody.

Left alone except for the pages and bodyguards watching from a discreet distance, Kalvan began to pace up and down. If Styphon's House was shaping its strategy as the letter implied, Hostigos was faced with something more like a war on two fronts than a single attack with two prongs. That would throw all his strategic plans into the melting pot, and mean some pretty damned large-scale changes at the last minute. Of course it would mean the same for the Harphaxi, but they were so much less likely to be able to cope with the job, that things might just balance out.

Kalvan decided to stop worrying about troop movements until he had a map in front of him and some reliable advice in his ear. One thing was certain: the University's next job after developing paper was going to be inventing a semaphore system. Relay riders would have to do for this campaign, but he'd need something faster if he was going to have to make a habit of coordinating two or three armies spread over two or three hundred miles of real estate. Napoleon's campaign in Russia had fallen apart as much because of lack of staff and communications as because of supply problems.

Also, a system of codes—nothing fancy, simple substitution would do. Styphon's House was said to have ciphers for the most secret work of the Inner Circle; they obviously weren't using them for regular military communications, although they'd managed to keep their southern mobilization awfully quiet.

Finally, do something about the Styphon's House command of the sea. They hadn't done much with it this time; until now most of the troops moving into Harphax City from the south and from Hos-Agrys had marched overland, supplied out of the Temple warehouses when they couldn't buy or forage locally. This might be about to change; one of Xentos's friends who had already reached Agrys City had written to him reporting many laden merchant vessels sailing up the Hudson and returning empty. *Put Klestreus and Skranga on that.*

This war would still be decided on land. Some other time, Styphon's ships might do a lot more damage, and Kalvan had no desire to play the role of the French in some here-and-now future Mahan's *Influence of Seapower on the Wars Against Styphon's House.*

Royal Navy of Hos-Hostigos: put on the list of long-term projects. Note: Need seaport. They had one on the Great Lakes—Ulthor; now they needed one on the Atlantic. This might mean rolling up more of Hos-Harphax than he'd planned. But that would have to wait; this coming campaign would be for survival and more time. Time, the one thing Styphon's House seemed determined to deny him.

ELEVEN

I.

The sunset light reddened the walls of First Speaker Anaxthenes's chamber and the smoke curling up from Soton's pipe. After his disastrous meeting with King Kaiphranos, Soton had left Harphax City at the next high tide. The wine in his cup was already red; he sipped at it and tried to shut out Archpriest Roxthar's voice breathing fire and slaughter against Prince Philesteus.

It was not wise to ignore Roxthar completely even when he was apparently talking for the sheer pleasure of relieving his feelings or hearing the sound of his own voice. The tall, dour Archpriest made a dangerous enemy, and a quarrel with him would put Soton at the mercy of Anaxthenes, who was a good deal less bloodthirsty but considerably more skilled at taking advantage of another's mistakes. Great Styphon, what wouldn't he give for a stout Lance of Knights and a band of Sastragathi berserkers to fight!

Eventually Roxthar went off the boil and bubbled into silence. Anaxthenes refilled everybody's cups and appeared to lose himself in contemplating the sunset. From outside they could hear muffled sounds of clanking armor and boisterous cries that signaled the changing of the watch in Balph.

"What are we to do, then, now that King Kaiphranos seems to have lost what wits he had?" asked Anaxthenes. "Roxthar, we know your advice is to deprive Kaiphranos of Philesteus's support by charging the Prince with heresy. With no other captain fit to command the hosts of Harphax against Kalvan, Kaiphranos will either have to send Lysandros into the field or turn to Styphon's House. Either way, both Harphax and Ktemnos will march at our command. What say you, Master Soton?"

What Soton would have liked to express was his desire to spend about five minutes taking his war hammer to Kaiphranos, Philesteus, and Duke Aesthes. However, that course had even more disadvantages than Roxthar's, or any other course that would be seen as moving directly against Great Kings or important Princes. Styphon's House had to show itself loyal to those rulers who at least did not lift a hand against it or else mold the bullet for Kalvan to fire into its head.

"We have to leave Philesteus to his own devices. He is the only man fit to lead the Royal Army of Hos-Harphax." Roxthar looked as if he wanted to spit at those last words. "I know they're hardly worth their rations and fireseed, but we can't afford to lose them entirely. If nothing else, they are five thousand more bodies to take Kalvan's shot.

"Also, Philesteus is popular with no small number of mercenary captains and certain of the Harphaxi Princes who are leading their own levies." No need to add that many of those were also men who had no wish to see Roxthar's beloved Grand Duke Lysandros on the throne of Hos-Harphax. "I should say that harsh dealing with Philesteus might cost us the goodwill of men who lead ten thousand soldiers and thirty guns."

"That seems likely enough," said Anaxthenes. "That also doesn't make it any easier for us to march with Philesteus, if his father ever lets him march." From Anaxthenes's tone, the First Speaker obviously expected the Harphaxi to sit in their camps until Styphon's Second Revelation.

"There is no need for us to do likewise," said Soton. "In the field or in their camps the Harphaxi will draw on themselves a substantial portion of Kalvan's forces. At Tarr-Thebra, I already have five of the Sacred Squares, the Royal Square of Hos-Ktemnos, three thousand of the royal cavalry, including the knights of the Royal Guard, eight Lances of Knights and four thousand of the Order's foot, and five thousand mercenaries with another two thousand on the way. Another Square and several thousand Holy Warriors are on the march to me. Let me stay where I am, give me sufficient stores and fireseed, and I can march north to challenge Kalvan without one word to Philesteus.''

"Will the captains of Hos-Ktemnos follow you in this?''

"They are likely to shoot me if I *don't* lead them north. Cleitharses has left his best Captain-Generals in the western marshes to guard against the Upper Sastragathi war bands. Some of these eastern Squares haven't fought a pitched battle for generations. This is their chance for glory and honor, and they will let none stand between them and it.''

It took some time for Soton to explain what he proposed to do with a host swollen to more than twenty-five thousand men. It would have been easier with a map, of course. Soton reminded himself to make sure that any of Kalvan's map-makers who were captured were brought straight to him. If the arts by which Kalvan made maps increase like rabbits were not demonic, they would be worth learning.

"If the Harphaxi move at all, Kalvan will have to pit much of his strength against them. He cannot throw it all to the east, because he will not want to leave himself open to an advance through Sask.''

"And if the Harphaxi do not march?''

"Your Eminence, when one fights the nomads, one quickly learns to spy out the land ahead as one marches. Either that, or one dies young. I will have a day's warning or more of the approach of any host large enough to destroy mine, if indeed even a servant of demons can conjure up such a thing.''

Roxthar's face was working. "And if our weakness toward the cowardly Harphaxi's defiance of the God of Gods makes them abandon our cause altogether?''

"Then there will be civil war in Hos-Harphax, because not all the Harphaxi are cowards, and they will not sit quietly to be called such!'' Soton knew his face must have turned the color of the sunset, and he had to take several deep breaths before he would trust his voice again.

"To guard against this, another Lance is on its way north to join the three already there. That will bring the strength of Styphon's armed servants in Harphax to over five thousand, and if all else fails, they can fight their way to safety.''

With an extra Lance, the Knights in the north would also be

equal in fighting power to the bands of Styphon's Own Guard. Their Commander would thus have an equal voice with the Guard's captain. That was worth giving up a Lance from the southern host, where the knights of the Royal Guard could do everything except scout nearly as well as the Order's Knights.

"Is this a real possibility?" asked Anaxthenes.

Soton nodded. "Yes, Your Eminence. Would it be possible to anchor some ships in the Bay of Argros? I can arrange signals and notify my Commander."

Anaxthenes shrugged. "It seems unlikely that the ships at Agrys City and Percotro will have much more work before the war begins. We can send them south."

Soton suppressed a grin of triumph at wresting a secret out of the Inner Circle. The ships that had taken supplies to the mercenaries of Hos-Agrys had been waiting to bring mercenaries or princely levies south from Hos-Zygros. It had been clear for two moons that Great King Sopharar of Hos-Zygros would not send any of his own troops. Now it seemed that he was not even encouraging his subjects to aid the God of Gods! There would have to be a reckoning for that, one day—much later than Roxthar would like, of course, but much sooner than the Zygrosi expected.

Soton poured more wine, and they drank toasts to Kalvan's downfall, the vengeance of the true gods on false Dralm, and proper rule for Hos-Harphax. And one to victory in the north. Soton also drank a silent toast to a swift journey south or to Galzar's Hall for the Knights he had abandoned to the Harphaxi.

TWELVE

I.

They held the Council of War in the royal bedchamber.

"You—people—will do anything to keep me walled up," Rylla protested, only half joking. Even Rylla admitted, however, that her bedroom was the most secure room in Tarr-Hostigos that was also large enough to hold the whole Council and the necessary maps. Tarr-Hostigos was no longer crammed to the rafters the way it had been five days ago, when a draft of six hundred new recruits for the pike companies was camping in the courtyard because every other place it was physically possible to quarter them was already full. It was still too crowded to make certain that everybody there was on legitimate business, or that eavesdroppers could always be kept at a safe distance from important meetings.

Kalvan hoped this informal Council wouldn't have to do more than act as a meeting of minds among the "Inner Circle" of the Hostigi High Command. There were going to be a good many captains among the forces of Hostigos who would take umbrage at not being able to put in their half-crown's worth at a more formal Council. Some of them might even think of taking their men out of the campaign.

Hoping was the best Kalvan could do. It seemed far more likely that this was as much of a Council as this campaign

would have. The army would have to be on the march before
all the Princes and captains could be gathered in one place.
Napoleon had said, "Ask me for anything but time," and now
the internal feud between the Styphoni and the Harphaxi had
given the Hostigi a large and unasked-for gift of it. Kalvan
wasn't about to give it back just to soothe a few too-easily-
ruffled feathers.

Correction: the *armies* would have to be on the march fairly
soon. It was obvious even to Klestreus when they studied the
map that the informal division of Hostigi forces was going to
have to be formalized. The odds were that for most of the
campaign the army moving against Harphax would be out of
supporting distance and even out of easy communication with
the army facing the Ktemnoi and the Zarthani Knights.

Kalvan called for suggestions for names for the armies.

The one he would be leading personally against Harphax
wound up the Army of the Harph; the one Ptosphes and Chartiphon would lead in the west was christened the Army of the
Besh. Once they knew what to call the two armies, they got
down to the more serious business of what troops should be
assigned to which one.

"We can't do too much shuffling," Kalvan emphasized.
"Moving infantry exhausts them and takes time. Moving
cavalry around takes less time, but it wears out horses and uses
up forage. As for moving artillery, forget it. Also, we don't
want to take anybody away from Harmakros's Army of
Observation. They all know the territory they'll be fighting
over like their fathers' backyards by now. Out west they'll be
much less useful."

"That is true only up to a point, Your Majesty," said Chartiphon. Kalvan suppressed a sigh. The Duke only became
formal when he was going to be stubborn, and when he was
stubborn he made mules look docile. "Harmakros also has the
best-trained scouts in all the strength of Hostigos, and the
Army of the Besh will need every one of those to be sure of
even *finding* our enemies. Remember what Klestreus has said
about how good the Knights are at concealing their
movements."

Kalvan couldn't recall when or even whether Klestreus had
said that, but it certainly agreed with everything he'd heard or
guessed about the Knights. Ptosphes was nodding, obviously
in agreement with his Captain-General and old friend;

Klestreus was as close to looking embarrassed as Kalvan had seen him. Obviously he wasn't accustomed to being dragged into this kind of high-level argument over strategy, which wasn't really his fault, of course; here-and-now warfare had been much simpler when he was learning it.

Count Phrames, travel-stained and weary from his three-day ride, frowned and bent over the map. He was looking at the squares of red parchment centered around Thebra City, the here-and-now equivalent of Fredericksburg, Virginia, and the northernmost major fortress of Hos-Ktemnos.

"If I were Soton, I really wouldn't be considering any other way north except the Pirsystros Valley." He drew a finger from Thebra City to the here-and-now Shenandoah Valley, then north up the valley to where it ended in the Princedom of Syriphlon. "The valley has good roads, good forage, plenty of water, and mountains on either side to guard the flanks of the army."

"We're not planning to move south and attack them on the march," said Ptosphes dubiously. "Why should they worry about their flanks?"

"They don't know what our plans are," said Kalvan. "But Soton does know that we *could* do it. Which means that if he's half the general he's supposed to be, he'll be taking precautions against it."

"*If* Soton is in command," added Chartiphon.

Klestreus grinned with what looked remarkably like triumph. "I won't say that everybody in the Army of Hos-Ktemnos will be jumping when Soton says 'frog.' I do say that everybody will be listening to him, and not doing anything he doesn't like without a very damned good reason for it. The Lord High Marshal Duke Mnesiphoklos and Princes Anaxagron and Anaxephon all know and trust Soton, and are interested in maintaining the military reputation of the Great Crown of Hos-Ktemnos. The only chief captain I've heard of who might balk is Prince Leonnestros of the Princedom of Lantos, who wants a military reputation of his own so he can succeed Mnesiphoklos as Lord High Marshal.

"Even he won't defy Soton openly. He'll be outwardly obedient, then try to claim his share of the glory afterward by spreading rumors about how he advised Soton. If anything goes wrong, he'll claim he saw it coming but didn't want to go against the Grand Master."

Not for the first time, Kalvan thought that Niccolò Machiavelli would have felt right at home here-and-now.

"Besides, the Pirsystros Valley makes sense even to someone less shrewd than Soton," put in Rylla. "If they move much farther east, they might have to fight with their backs to the Enetriba—"the Potomac"—or even with half their army on one side and half on the other. Also, they'll be close enough to our Army of the Harph so that if the Harphaxi don't move, Kalvan will be able to turn west faster than we've planned and strike at the Ktemnoi.

"If they move any farther west, they'll be in the Trygath. They'll never be able to move artillery and wagons on its roads. I'd like to think our enemies are big enough fools to try, but I don't think Dralm has addled their wits that badly.

"No, Father, you can wait for them around here—"she tapped the map west of South Mountain, near Gettysburg "—and be fairly sure they'll come close enough to be found easily. That's in hostile Syriphlon, so you can forage to the south, but it's also only four days' march from our supply depots in Sask. You can leave the country behind you intact, so that if you do find some reason to retreat in a hurry, you can just go back the way you came. In fact, you can even—"

Ptosphes burst out laughing, then looked at the ceiling in mock anguish. "Dralm, Yirtta, Appalon, Galzar—you told me to raise my daughter as a warrior, and look what comes of it. She flouts her own father at his own Council!" Rylla giggled and Ptosphes laughed again, more gently. "I sometimes wish I hadn't had to do it, little one. You didn't have much of a girlhood."

Rylla shrugged inside her tentlike chamber robe. "Hostigos was a poor Princedom then, Father. A girlhood for me was something we couldn't afford. Now that I'm a woman, I have everything anyone could ask for." She threw Kalvan a look that would have made him blush if there'd been anybody except old friends present.

Joking aside, even those who wanted to couldn't find a flaw in Phrames's and Rylla's logic. Since Ptosphes no longer had a case for a cavalry-heavy army, that made the job of dividing the Hostigi forces a few minutes' work with soapstone tablets and pineboard notepads.

The Army of the Harph would have most of the Royal Army's "regulars," Prince Armanes commanding both his own Nyklosi army and the contingents from Kyblos and Ulthor, and an impressive quantity of mercenaries. Kalvan would command the army in person, with Harmakros, Phrames, Armanes, and Hestophes as his subordinates.

The Army of the Besh would have an even more impressive quantity of mercenaries, half the army of Old Hostigos, and the Princely armies of Nostor, Beshta, Sashta, and Sask. Ptosphes would be commander-in-chief, with Captain-General Chartiphon, Prince Pheblon, and what everybody hoped would be more help than hindrance from Balthar of Beshta and Sarrask of Sask.

Each army would have a reinforced company of Mounted Rifles and a few hundred of Harmakros's now almost-tame Sastragathi. The grand total Kingdom strength would be somewhere around twenty-six thousand men for Kalvan and twenty-four thousand five hundred for Ptosphes. Kalvan would have about one-third cavalry, Ptosphes about two fifths but not as good, and each would have roughly half the sixty-odd available field guns, some of them much odder than Kalvan would have cared to depend on, but Great Kings with their backs to the wall can't be choosy.

Since this arrangement meant an absolute minimum of troop-reshuffling, both armies could be on the march within ten days, their advanced guards even sooner—with a little help from Galzar and more than a little from Lytris the weather goddess. The two army commanders would probably find it prudent to hold their own Councils of War before they moved, but even these shouldn't take too much time. The strategy of the campaign was being kept as simple as possible—partly because nothing complicated was necessary, partly because Kalvan didn't entirely trust Ptosphes and Chartiphon to get grand strategy right the first time they ever tried it.

The Army of the Harph would move southeast by whatever route offered the easiest going for the heavy equipment and also let it rest its right flank on the Harph itself, for protection and fresh water. It would advance straight at Harphax City until the Harphaxi army marched out to be fought and smashed. Not just defeated, but smashed, routed, driven back to the walls of the city and made useless for the rest of this year and maybe the next.

Meanwhile, Ptosphes would wait by South Mountain, keeping track of the whereabouts of the Ktemnoi, discouraging their scouts and foragers as vigorously as possible, destroying any unsupported detachments he could find, but above all keeping his army intact, united, and between the Ktemnoi and the heartland of Hos-Hostigos.

"Are we supposed never to face up to them in battle?" growled Chartiphon.

Kalvan would have liked to say "No, not until I come to join you," but he knew that would be such an insult to both Ptosphes and Chartiphon, not to mention their Princely lieutenants, that he'd have real trouble getting their cooperation. If only this war could have been postponed.until he'd finished training his subordinates! The political quarrels in the enemy's camp had given him a few badly needed weeks, but he needed *years!*

"Not unless you're fairly sure of winning or at least of not losing too many men," said Kalvan. "Remember, you're defeating them every day your army is there in front of them, ready to block their advance or strike them in the rear if they turn against me. The Harphaxi are the easy ones to reach, push into a fight, and knock right out of the war. The Ktemnoi have plenty of room to maneuver, they're not defending home territory, and they can be reinforced as long as King Cleitharses can hold Styphon's House up to ransom in return for more help in the Holy War."

In fact, the situation of Hos-Hostigos was beginning to smell a lot like that of Germany in World War I. They were facing a war on two fronts, one against an opponent who could be smashed quickly, the other against an opponent with staying power. Of course, in this case the opponent with staying power also had the better army, and there were enough other differences to discourage Kalvan from using the example in his arguments with the Council.

Not to mention the fact that if he described World War I, he would also have to describe how it came out.

Once the Harphaxi were smashed, Kalvan would take the Army of the Harph across the river, establish communications with Ptosphes, and coordinate an attack on the Ktemnoi from both front and rear, with at least a three-to-two advantage in numbers to the Hostigi. The Ktemnoi should certainly be badly mauled, and King Cleitharses taught an expensive lesson about the cost of making war on behalf of Styphon's House. The invaders might even be destroyed outright—

"—and if that is the case, we may have peace as a naming-day gift for Rylla's child," said Ptosphes, nodding slowly in approval as he lit his pipe. "Hos-Bletha has always been a moon late and a crown short in northern wars. Hos-Ktemnos and Hos-Harphax will have precious little left to fight with. Hos-Agrys will be more concerned with guarding its back against the Zygrosi and scooping up loot from the ruins of Harphax. We could really have peace with everybody except Styphon's House itself, and the gods know that would be no bad thing."

"Amen," said Kalvan as heartily as his father had ever ended a prayer. "Now the only thing left to discuss is how to provision two armies instead of one."

Logistics had been the bane of most pike-and-shot armies back otherwhen, and things were obviously no easier here-and-now. As Napoleon once said, "An army marches on its stomach." Armies of more than twenty thousand men had large stomachs indeed.

Standard fare for each soldier was about two pounds of bread or biscuit a day, supplemented by about a pound of meat, beans, or some other protein-rich food. For a force of twenty-five thousand, this meant thirty-seven *tons* of victuals a day.

Nor did this include oats and barley for the horses, who could eat eight times as much as a man. Each army had about ten thousand cavalry and artillery horses, including remounts, and about four thousand more horses and six hundred teams of oxen to pull its three thousand or so carts and wagons. Even if each man carried four days' rations on his back or his mount, Kalvan's most optimistic estimate only gave the armies twelve to fourteen days' supplies.

They were going to have to find a way to supplement those rations without making bitter foes out of their present enemies and future neighbors. At least they would be an army on the move; a stationary army in a primitive society had a choice between dying of starvation or dying of disease. Kalvan remembered the case of Louis the Fourteenth and his armed party of three thousand, who'd had to delay their departure for Luxembourg for two weeks because the main French army had exhausted all food and forage along their intended route.

Here-and-now armies supplied themselves by the time-honored method of stealing anything that wasn't nailed down.

This was cost-effective but otherwise undesirable, since it turned soldiers into bandits and caused public relations problems that more than once had led to the independent discovery of guerrilla warfare. Probably the most successful pre-Napoleonic system of logistics had been Albrecht von Wallenstein's system of "contributions," a polite way of extorting money from enemy civilians to pay for an army's supplies with the promise of eventual restitution—but only if the attacking army won, which gave the noncombatants some really mixed emotions!

"Brother Mytron, I want you to take your men off the paper project and have them make some wooden chips about the size of a Hostigos crown."

Everyone looked at Kalvan curiously, waiting for him to once again pull the rabbit out of his hat. One of these days he was going to reach into that hat and dismay everybody including himself by finding it empty. But thank Dralm, that hadn't happened yet!

"We will use these wooden 'crowns' to represent real gold crowns."

Xentos looked scandalized and Ptosphes's lower jaw was about to scrape the floor. Kalvan knew he'd just introduced a form of paper money into a world where it had been hard currency or nothing. He had a feeling that his great-grandchildren were going to hate him for this.

"Chartiphon, I want you to set up a Quartermaster battalion for the Army of the Besh. Phrames, you do the same for the Army of the Harph. I want both battalions to carry at least one wagonload of the wooden crowns. After entering enemy territory, the Quartermasters will be responsible for circulating letters to every town, village, and hamlet under our control. These letters will ask the council, mayor, or headman for a monetary contribution for the Royal Army of Hos-Hostigos.

Chartiphon looked appalled. "Were I to hear of a man bringing such a letter into Hostigos, I would have him hanged and set the rope myself."

More harshly than he'd intended, Kalvan snapped, "Would you rather have your soldiers running wild all over the countryside, robbing and looting isolated farms for their own benefit?"

Chartiphon looked sheepish. "No, Your Majesty. It's—it's

just hard for me to see how any reasonable man could take such a letter seriously."

Kalvan's smile was so grim even Rylla stared. "You're wrong there, Chartiphon. The letters will also threaten death by hanging to anyone who doesn't comply. We will send out squads of cavalry to gather the contributions. In any village or town that refuses, the leading men will be executed and their houses looted and burned. I suspect we'll only need three or four examples like that before our letters are taken very seriously indeed."

Rylla was looking at him as though he'd just turned into one of Styphon's demons.

Hestophes was the first to smile. "I think it will work."

"So do I," said Phrames. "At least it will work if we can keep people from making false tokens and passing them off to us as real ones."

"We'll burn the keystone of Hos-Hostigos onto each token," said Kalvan. "We'll also keep records of how many tokens went to each place. If they turn in three times that many after the war—well, the hangmen will have some more business. Also, the next time we have to do this we can have the tokens made out of brass or iron."

The rest of the military men were now nodding in agreement. Xentos and Mytron refused to meet Kalvan's eyes. He mentally crossed his fingers that they would come around in time, then concluded.

"We'll give them the tokens in return for gold, silver, jewelry, and food. They can redeem them after the war for gold crowns, courtesy of Styphon's House. Then we'll use the money to buy supplies from local merchants and farmers. With the magazines we've already established in Sask and Beshta, we should have enough supplies to let us engage both hostile armies. Now all we have to do is win the war!"

11.

Rylla didn't look up from her loom as Kalvan entered the whitewashed room. It was the first time he'd ever seen her at a loom, so she must have just started and needed to concentrate on her work.

She'd also put on old clothes for her weaving. In fact, her gray dress was almost a rag, with rents here and there showing the bare skin underneath. It was dirty, too. That bothered him. Rylla took great pains to keep herself and her garments clean.

The dress was cut off just below the knees, and there was an iron ring around one ankle that was attached to a chain ending at another ring set in the wall, a ring that looked heavy enough to hold a full-grown bull. Above the ring hung a tapestry showing Styphon hurling fire down on a writhing, armor-clad figure surrounded by cringing, flaming demons.

Kalvan gasped, and Rylla turned, showing a lip freshly cut, a burn on her chin, a left eye blackened and swollen almost shut. He suddenly realized that the skin under the iron ring was raw and—

"Nooooo!"

Half gasp, half shout, Kalvan's cry woke him up while he still had enough self-control not to cry out again once he realized he was awake. He was sweating as if he'd just stepped out of a Turkish bath, and for a long moment he was afraid he was going to lose his dinner.

He didn't—not quite. Instead he forced himself to lie still and breathe steadily while he tried to drive the latest nightmare out of his mind. Seeing Rylla dead in battle or during childbirth was bad enough. Seeing Rylla a brutally mistreated slave in Balph was indescribable.

After a little while Kalvan realized he wasn't going to get back to sleep. If he lay tossing and turning half the night—well, the nightmare might be indescribable, but if Rylla woke up and saw him, he was going to have to describe it. Either that, or pretend nothing was wrong, and he knew that his chances of getting away with that were about the same as his chances of storming Harphax City single-handed.

It wouldn't help Rylla to either know what was on his mind

or know that she was being lied to. For the first time since she was a girl, she was afraid for herself, not for her father or her soldiers or Hostigos or her husband, but for herself and the baby she carried. Out of that fierce pride Kalvan knew almost too well, she was trying to hide it, but sometimes when she thought no one was looking she dropped her guard.

Kalvan knew that nothing short of canceling the war so he could be home when the baby came would really help Rylla. But he could at least make sure she could wrestle with her own demons without having to worry about his as well.

Kalvan swung his feet out of the bed, listened to Rylla's breathing again, then tiptoed to the wardrobe and pulled on the first clothes that came to hand. He would probably look like a scarecrow, but this wouldn't be the first time he'd spent a sleepless night prowling Tarr-Hostigos. It was beginning to be said that this was another ritual he used for communicating with the gods of his own people.

It was a bright moonlit night, and Kalvan was recognized the moment he stepped outside the keep. Since he wore both his sword and a short-barreled artilleryman's pistol thrust into his belt, the guards made less fuss than usual about letting him move around on his own. He knew there would always be half a dozen pairs of eyes watching him, but as long as they kept their distance and the mouths attached to those eyes stayed closed, everybody would be as happy as could be expected under the circumstances. Kalvan checked the priming and load in the pistol, then started walking.

The night breeze blew past him, drying the sweat on his skin and bringing the familiar smells of Tarr-Hostigos: mold, stone, stables, close-packed and seldom-bathed humanity, and the ghosts of burned grease and roast meat. From beyond the walls of the castle, the wind brought the smell of smoke from the nearest campfires, as well as the sound of singing. Kalvan stopped to listen and made out a new version of an old song:

> "Hurrah! Hurrah! We'll burn the bastards out!
> "Hurrah! Hurrah! We'll put them all to rout!
> "We'll steal their pigs and cattle, and we'll dump their
>   sauerkraut,
> As we go marching through Harphax!"

From the parapet, the campfires dotted the slopes of the

Bald Eagles on either side of the Gap down to Hostigos Town. Around the town itself, lights glowed from the doors and windows of new barracks and from establishments catering to the less authorized needs of the royal soldiers. Out beyond the town, the brightest glow of all told Kalvan that the main Foundry was still hard at work. No more artillery for now, but there were fifty other kinds of metalwork any army needed, and never enough of any of them. Brass was still unavailable at any price, but pig iron was pouring in from Kyblos. The highly valued Arklos plate was under the Ban of Styphon, but Pennsylvania had always been iron rich, and someone in Hos-Hostigos would soon be making comparable armor. *Note: Design a working blast furnace and send a model to Prince Tythanes.*

For a good blast furnace, they'd need a better source of heat than wood. *Coal mine: Start as soon as war ends.* There was coal all through the Appalachians; they even knew about it here-and-now, although they used it as a medicine.

Many of the campsites were on wooded land, since Kalvan discouraged pitching tents in the fields of working farms. Every acre sown and harvested was a minor victory after the Winter of the Wolves, and the farmers were ready to defend their crops as fiercely as their wives and daughters. Kalvan made a mental note to draw up fire-safety regulations to prevent forest fires, then remembered that there'd been plenty of rain the past two weeks. No danger of setting the woods on fire for a while.

He also remembered that some of those campsites were on land that had been wooded until war, the Winter of the Wolves, barracks-building, and the foundries all made their claims on the trees. The farmers would be getting a lot of newly cleared land if this went on; he and Ptosphes would have to set up some regular method of awarding claims to avoid bloodshed and even feuds. He'd also have to do something to make sure the new land didn't erode with its top cover gone, and in the long run he'd have to encourage using less wood for fuel. Heating and fuel, another reason for mining coal. Maybe he could even tinker up a steam engine for the paper mill?

Maybe, if he not only won but survived the war. There was also nothing he could do to be sure of that—or at least nothing he hadn't done already—except see about getting as much sleep as he could without the nightmares. Not that there was much he could do about his dreams. He would just have to depend on Dralm or luck for that help and hope he got it. A Great King who was so tired he could barely sit in his saddle was not doing his job in war or peace.

Kalvan was making his fourth circuit of the walls of Tarr-Hostigos when he happened to look down into the courtyard. The two men whose movement drew his eye were in the shadow of the wall for about twenty paces, but something in the way they walked. . . .

Then they came out into the moonlight, and Kalvan laughed softly. Down below were Ptosphes and Phrames, neither of them talking. Phrames looked like a man suffering from acute indigestion; Ptosphes looked more like a man facing hanging at sunrise.

It was some consolation to know that he wasn't the only leader of the Hostigi who was spending a sleepless night.

It was also some consolation to remember that if he, Phrames, and Ptosphes were all spending sleepless nights, they had more respectable reasons for doing so than Prince Balthames of Sashta. He was said to be pacing his castle's halls over the fact that Princess Amnita was pregnant with a child who couldn't possibly be his.

That would be enough to irritate even a prince like Balthames, whose moral fiber had the consistency of wet Kleenex. What added insult to injury (or so Klestreus had reported) was Balthames's near certainty that Amnita had got herself pregnant by systematically seducing her husband's boyfriends, and his suspicion that she'd been put up to it by her father, Sarrask of Sask!

Definitely a consolation to have only minor matters like life and death to worry about!

In fact, it was enough of a consolation that by the time Kalvan had finished his fifth circuit of Tarr-Hostigos his eyelids and feet were becoming remarkably heavy. By the time he'd finished the sixth, he felt as if he needed to prop his eyes open with his fingers and lift his feet with a block and tackle.

He didn't even contemplate making a seventh circuit. Instead he stumbled up the stairs to the keep, then on to the bed-chamber. He was just awake enough by the time he reached the bed to notice that Rylla was still asleep, and to remember not to undo his night's work by falling into bed with all his clothes on.

Then Kalvan collapsed peacefully, and only woke up well after dawn to the sound of Rylla's singing. He listened for a moment, so happy to find her in good spirits that he could even ignore the fact that she couldn't carry a tune in a saddle-bag. He sat up and stretched.

"Welcome back from the dead, Your Majesty," she said.

"Thank you. I hope our child doesn't have much of an ear for music."

"Why?"

"Because if he does and you sing him lullabies, he's going to wind up absolutely *hating* his mother."

"You—!" She got as far as throwing the nearest pillow at him before she broke into laughter.

THIRTEEN

I.

Baltov Eldra rose from behind her desk as Danar Sirna entered her office.

"Welcome back," said the professor. "How was Greffa?"

"I'd expected more impressive ruins. After all, when the Iron Route was open, Greffa had about half a million people. Now it has only about half that many. I suppose the Grefftscharri were thrifty and used the abandoned temples and merchants' palaces for building stone."

"Exactly. Would you like a drink? Don't be ashamed to ask for something civilized, either."

Sirna blushed, remembering Eldra's lecture the day she'd let slip a remark about "her last chance for a civilized drink for quite a while." That sort of remark, Eldra had said eloquently and at some length, could put her or indeed the whole University Team in danger. At best it could force the Paratime Police to kill or at least alter the memories of some innocent person.

"It will be even worse in Kalvan's Time-Line," she'd concluded. "There a remark like that could reach Kalvan's own ears. He already knows too damned much about the Paratime Secret for everybody's comfort. If he's given a clue that paratemporal travelers are *in* Hostigos, watching him—well, it will be an open-and-shut case for killing him.

"Colonel—I mean, Chief Verkan will do his duty, but he

won't thank the people who made it necessary. The University Team will probably be shut down regardless of what happens after Kalvan's death, and as for the person responsible—if she ever goes outtime again, it will be over a lot of people's dead bodies. Mine included. Please remember that," she added with a jab of her pipestem that made Sirna feel a pistol was being pointed at her.

"Ale, thank you," said Sirna, bringing her mind back to the present.

"Ah, a proper lady's drink," said Eldra as she punched in the order on her desk keyboard. "However, if you want to be sure of being taken for a proper lady, I'd suggest leaving that gown behind."

"Oh. Is it dressing—above my station?"

"Not really. It's just a little too revealing, particularly with your height and figure. It doesn't quite suggest the degree of propriety I think you want to maintain, unless you can persuade one of the Team to play a legitimate male protector."

"I thought Zarthani laws and customs didn't absolutely require that I have one."

"The laws and customs don't. The University does, for the time being. Kalvan's Time-Line is in the middle of a war, and there are lots of rough types running around who might try to get away with more than they normally would with an unprotected woman. Also, there are bound to be ordinarily quite decent men who think that tomorrow they may die, so why not have a little fun tonight? We don't want to have to kill too many of either kind. It offends comrades and kin and generally attracts the sort of notice we'd rather avoid."

"Suppose I dealt with the man myself?"

"You could. As a free-trader's daughter, they'd expect you to be handy with firearms. I don't recommend it, though. You're not a noblewoman, and even if you didn't start a feud, you could end up on the wrong end of a breach-of-promise suit. We don't want the University Teams dragged into court, either, if we can avoid it."

"So I should keep my head bowed, my mouth shut, my neckline high, and my skirts low?"

"Until you have the feel of the time-line, that's the safest course. Once the war's over, Hostigos may be a better place for women than the rest of Kalvan's Time-Line, but that will be at least a year."

"Is that from Rylla's example?"

"Yes."

"How could Ptosphes have raised her any other way, if she was going to be heiress to Hostigos?"

"Very easily, my dear, or do you still have a touching faith in male decency at your age?" The tone was light, but Sirna detected barbs and bitterness underlying it. She remembered the stock University phrase for Professor Baltov's four noisy companionate marriages: "the victory of optimism over experience."

"No. I suppose another Ptosphes could have adopted a male heir and then married Rylla off to him as soon as she was of age."

"Yes. One we know of on another time-line did just that, Styphon take him. Rylla was about fourteen, and the adopted heir combined the worst features of Gormoth of Nostor and Balthar of Beshta. *Our* Rylla was raised to do what she wanted, then landed herself a first-class husband on top of it. Oh well, if we start moaning about how unequally the luck of the universe is divided up, we'll never get anything done."

A robot rolled in with Sirna's ale and winter wine for the professor, and conversation took a back seat for a moment. While they drank, Sirna pulled out a list of equipment she'd selected from the terminal's surprisingly well-stocked storerooms. She'd known that the Fifth Level Kalvan Project Terminal had been expanding as the Project grew, but she hadn't expected storerooms that looked big enough to supply all the paratimers of a large subsector. She deleted the questionable gown, replaced it with another she knew had a neckline up somewhere around her chin, then skimmed the rest of the list and handed it to Eldra.

The professor's eyebrows rose. "That's a pretty big medkit you're taking, isn't it?"

"Yes. I was surprised to find some of the things in stock."

"We've been unloading new shipments every couple of days while you were in Greffa. Things are about to get very lively on Kalvan's Time-Line, and we don't want to have to spend time sending requisitions all the way back to First Level where the clerks can lose them. The Kalvan Project has a Grade Two priority, but you know how much that means. Our request for a hundred needler charges will still be kicked down to below some associate's request for a new rug."

Sirna knew that. She also knew that a stockpile of equipment here on Fifth Level would be out of sight of the Executive Council, reporters, or the people who were waiting for her reports. It would not be out of reach of the University people —or the Paratime Police, starting with Verkan Vall.

To turn the conversation away from this potentially dangerous territory, Sirna shifted into Zarthani and told her story of how her father, the free-trader Charthar of Greffa, had been gifted by the gods with some skill as a healer, had learned healing arts wherever he went and practiced them when trade was poor, and finally taught much of what he knew to his daughter before he died.

Eldra was smiling by the time Sirna finished. "I'm impressed. You have the Grefftscharri accent better than any of us except Verkan Vall."

"Thank you. Is there anything in the kit I should have left out, or anything missing I could safely have put in? I was thinking of antiseptics—"

Eldra shook her head. "Kalvan was drumming antiseptics into Brother Mytron's ear five minutes after he learned Rylla was pregnant. That we know. The knowledge hasn't spread generally. There not being any distilling to produce high-proof ethanol doesn't help either.

"Also, we have to reckon with the possibility of Styphon's House declaring any of Kalvan's nonmilitary inventions to be of demonic origin. They won't dare outlaw his fireseed formula or rifling because they'd lose too many allies, but something that doesn't kill people—"

"That doesn't make any sense!"

"It makes enough sense for the people of Kalvan's Time-Line, and their opinion is the one that will matter once you're out there among them. Remember that, and face the fact that one day you may have to let an outtimer you've come to care about die of blood poisoning because you can't use outlawed or contaminating medical knowledge to save him. You'll find such an outtimer, too. Maybe not in Kalvan's Time-Line, but much sooner than you expected."

Sirna wanted to express grave doubts that she would ever care for someone so barbaric as to fight and die for a religion, but something in Eldra's face and voice stopped her. A story that the most scurrilous University gossip had never hinted at but which had obviously left something sunk very deep in the professor.

"I'll remember," Sirna said and covered her uneasiness

with another drink. Eldra sat looking into space or maybe into the past for a moment, then keyed the big screen on the wall behind her desk to life. A map of the current theater of action in Kalvan's Time-Line sprang into sight.

"As you can see, things are building up rather quickly to as nice a pair of pitched battles as you ever wanted to be a long way from. Ptosphes has moved down to what Kalvan would call Chambersburg, Pennsylvania—Tenabra in Kalvan's Time-Line. The vanguard of the Knights and the Ktemnoi is up to Tarr-Corria—Hagerstown, Maryland. Ptosphes may be about to decide to give battle, because as far as he can see, the enemy has only about seventeen thousand men assembled at Tarr-Corria. He knows the rest have to be catching up sooner or later, but he doesn't think they've done so."

"Do we know differently?"

"We suspect Soton either knows something we don't or is just confident that he can fight and win against three-to-two odds. We don't have anybody on the ground with Soton, and we've done all the air reconnaissance we can do without risking giving a portent. We don't want that, not when we don't know to whom we'd be giving it!"

Sirna looked at the map again. "Wasn't there a battle in the American Civil War on Kalvan's home time-line fought near Tarr-Corria?"

"Yes. Antietem, I think. That was the Northern victory that ended the war and made General McClellan the President after Lincoln. No, wait a minute. That was another Europo-American subsector, not Kalvan's. Have you been reading up on his home time-line?"

Sirna nodded. "Mostly American history, but some European. Genghis Khan is fascinating in a horrid sort of way. Hitler is just plain horrid."

"Wait until you've talked to a few people who've been out-time on lines where the Third Reich won." Eldra took a long pull at her drink. "Some of them make Aryan-Transpacific, Styphon's House Subsector look pleasant!"

"So Ptosphes and Soton will probably be going at it within the next few days?" asked Sirna.

"It looks that way. Kalvan has moved down to within three days' march of Harphax City itself without meeting any serious opposition. He's slowed his advance now to give Philesteus and Duke Aesthes a chance to bring the Harphaxi Army out into the open field to meet him.''

"Why doesn't he just march on Harphax City?"

"No siege guns and too few men to blockade the city. Also, he'd run into supply problems. The country between where he is now and the city will be foraged bare in another week.''

"So what are the Harphaxi waiting for?"

"Philesteus and Aesthes are waiting for another shipment of Styphon's muskets and fireseed to rearm the city militia and reequip some of the worst-off mercenaries. If they marched now, almost a quarter of their army would be Styphon's House troops, the Guards and the Knights. Philesteus doesn't know whether he'd rather be called a coward or give Styphon's House a chance to claim credit for victory.''

"He sounds like a fool," said Sirna.

"He isn't, really. He's an acceptable cavalry commander, but high-level politics and grand strategy are over his head. The same goes for most of the other Harphaxi. Which is why Kalvan is going to stamp them into the mud of the Harph when the shooting starts." There was no mistaking the positively bloodthirsty note of anticipation in Eldra's voice.

"Anyway, the shooting is going to start within a ten-day at most. I want to take you and the other new recruits for the Second Study-Team to Kalvan's Time-Line in time to at least catch the aftermath."

"Isn't that going to cut short our field orientation on Kalvan Control One?" Sirna was annoyed. She'd been looking forward to a month or so in the next-door time-line the University used for orienting the Kalvan's Time-Line Team members to what Styphon's House Subsector of Fourth Level Aryan-Transpacific looked, sounded, and smelled like.

"There isn't any more Kalvan Control One," said Eldra grimly.

"But—I thought that was the safe one, where Gormoth of Nostor fell off his horse at Marax Ford and—"

"—dashed out the brains none of us thought he had? Yes. Unfortunately, somebody with even fewer brains forgot to check out the other changes between Kalvan's Time-Line and Kalvan Control One. One of them was a very good mercenary captain named Strothos. The other was Sarrask of Sask—much abler and thoroughly vicious. Hostigos had a one-year reprieve, then Sarrask and Strothos led twenty thousand men against it."

The screen shifted to show blue and red arrows writhing all

over a map of what was now Hos-Hostigos, until the blue arrows shrank out of existence. The screen shifted again to show a night aerial view of a burning town.

"That was Hostigos Town from as close as we dared to come after we got all but two of our people out." Another shift. "Afterward we were able to send in a few people disguised as traveling harness-makers. Men only."

Sirna recognized Bear Creek Bridge on the west side of Hostigos Town, or at least where the bridge had been. Now its stone abutments stood smoke-blackened on either side of a stream fouled with ashes, burned timbers, and some floating —things—Sirna was very glad she didn't have to smell.

Shift. The Street of the Coopers, formerly hard-packed earth lined with the kind of solid wood-and-plaster houses skilled craftsmen could afford under the peaceful rule of a good Prince. Now the street was churned into mud and littered with corpses and horse droppings. A few scavenger dogs gnawed at the corpses, and from the ashes of the houses chimneys rose like monuments to the dead.

Shift. The road up to Tarr-Hostigos, lined with gallows and with a corpse dangling from each one. Carrion birds were pecking at some of the bodies. Others had already reached a point where not even a bird would approach them.

Shift. The gateway of Tarr-Hostigos, the gates themselves gone, the hinges pried loose by looters, smoke-blackened stones, dark bloodstains on the flags of the courtyard, and over the gateway a row of spikes—

"No!"

Sirna's stomach twitched, then heaved. She was equally afraid of losing her lunch in Eldra's presence and of not having her stomach empty before she saw anything worse. She closed her eyes briefly, swallowed, and decided that she could live with the sight of the heads decorating those spikes. Harmakros, she noted, had his skull split from forehead to left ear. They must have taken his head when they picked up his body on the battlefield. Some of the others—Ptosphes and Chartiphon at least—must have suffered the same fate.

There was also one empty spike.

"What happened to—Rylla?"

Eldra swallowed. "You don't want to know the details. As to what happened to her head—somebody lifted it off the spike one night. Probably took it away for a decent burial, or at least that's what Sarrask thought. He retaliated by herding two hundred Hostigi hostages into the local temple of Dralm, setting it on fire, and having musketeers shoot down anybody who tried to get out.''

Eldra silently punched in an order for more drinks, then made an elaborate business of relighting her pipe. When it was drawing well and there was a thick veil of smoke over her head, she spoke again.

"So Kalvan Control One is gone, and we haven't really staffed the other Control Time-Lines for full-scale orientation. You could learn something on one of them, but not enough in time to go out with me to Kalvan's Time-Line this summer.

"You could also go out with me to Kalvan's Time-Line with nothing but the hypno-mech orientation. You already have the language down very well, and Greffa has at least some of the right flavor, so you wouldn't be completely a lost lamb. Normally I'm as strict about the 'No field orientation, no go' rule as anyone, but a time always comes to bend the rules. If you're willing, I'll make this one of the times.''

If Sirna had thought any of the Zarthani gods existed to hear a prayer of thanks, she would have sent one that she hadn't lost control of her stomach. Those pictures of sacked and ruined Kalvan Control One must have been a test, one she'd apparently passed—at least to the point of being given another test.

Spend a safe summer of orientation in an unmolested but badly equipped Control Time-Line, or plunge headfirst into Kalvan's Time-Line in the middle of a major war with nothing but her hypnotic learning and experience in Greffa to arm her against what she might be facing.

She knew how she should analyze the situation before making her decision, as both a proper student and First Level Citizen. She also knew that only one factor really made a difference, and that was the knowledge that if she didn't go to Kalvan's Time-Line with Eldra, she'd never be sure of her own courage again.

Her ex-husband would doubtless have called that attitude a relic of barbarism, along with physical courage itself. He might even have called it a sign of reverting to her Prole ancestry; that had been something he threw at her often enough when they were alone and he didn't have to be con-

cerned about his image as an enlightened man utterly opposed
to all class or race considerations.

"I'll go," said Sirna. Her ex-husband didn't matter. All
that mattered suddenly was Baltov Eldra's triumphant grin
as she raised her drink to toast Kalvan's victory. Sirna felt
slightly guilty at that grin—after all, she was taking advantage
of Eldra's kindness to spy on her—but not guilty enough to
change her mind.

She raised her own cup. "Then—down Styphon!"

FOURTEEN

I.

The Heights of Chothros were blocking the view to the northwest by the time Captain Phidestros reached the van. He could have reached it sooner if he hadn't wanted to spare his horse and inspect his columns. This was the first time that the Iron Company had been the advance guard for the left flank of the Army of Hos-Harphax, and Phidestros knew that his men were on display even if they didn't.

So far he'd seen nothing to concern him, or at least nothing that couldn't be handled by petty-captains—loose saddle girths, frayed musketoon slings, and the like. Even had these minor flaws been ten times as common as they were, the Iron Company would still have made much of the rest of the Army of Harphax look like rabble. That would not have kept the other captains from trying to advance themselves or at least conceal their own ineptness by pointing out Phidestros's minor lapses.

Phidestros spurred his horse at a trot along the Great Harph Road until he was fifty paces ahead of the lead horseman of his center column. He would have given his next ten years' honors and booty for the Iron Company's horses to grow wings so that they might fly across the Harph and join Soton's Army of the Pirsystros, also known as the Holy Host of Styphon.

In the eight days since the Harphaxi chose to march against

Kalvan, it was possible that there were mistakes they had not made, but Phidestros was not prepared to wager more than the price of a cup of bad wine on it. He feared that the Army of Harphax was a sinking ship—a ship sinking, moreover, through the fault of its builders and crew—and unfortunately it would be some time before the Iron Company could safely imitate rats.

Phidestros topped a little rise and looked back at the Iron Company. At least the Harphaxi would have their scouting done well today. The center column was mostly Lamochares's men, armed with pistols and swords, ready to come to the aid of the flankers and meanwhile under Phidestros's eye. The left and right columns were the old Iron Company with musketoons, horse pistols, and swords. The left was nearly invisible in the brush and small trees toward the Harph; the right was on more open ground that stretched toward the wooded base of the Heights of Chothros.

Phidestros cantered down the far side of the rise, opening the distance to the men behind him another twenty paces. It felt good to be out in the fresh air, not breathing the dust and sweat and dung smells of even his own men, let alone ten thousand more.

He'd have to drop back into the center column before long, though. The Great Harph Road ran through the West Chothros Gap just ahead, with the Heights to the right and rugged, wooded country running down to the Harph on the left. The Hostigi had been foraging on this side of the gap; too many abandoned farms had been stripped bare to let Phidestros believe otherwise. Even without the signs of the foragers, the West, Middle, and East Gaps were places no one but fools like Philesteus and Aesthes would fail to picket. No point in riding into an ambush, and being the Harphaxi's first—

Four smoke puffs rose from behind a stone wall lying across the path of the Iron Company's right column. Before Phidestros heard the distant *pop* of the discharges, he saw two riders and one horse at the head of the column go down. He measured the distance from the wall to the targets with his eyes and whistled.

Three hits out of four shots at six hundred paces!

To Phidestros, that also smelled of those new far-shooting muskets—"rifles"—that King Kalvan had introduced for the scouts of the Hostigi Army.

Four more smoke puffs rose from behind trees on the near side of the wall, and two men nearly eight hundred paces away dropped from their saddles. That settled the matter for Phidestros. Few infantry weapons could reach that far, and those that could did well to hit a fair-sized barn at extreme range. Hostigi riflemen, for certain.

The rightward column was bunching up, whether to help their comrades or organize for a charge Phidestros wasn't sure. He was sure that he didn't want them to present such a fine target while they made up their minds.

He cantered back to the center column, shouting orders the moment he had their attention. Two men rode off to the leftward column to warn Petty-Captain Kylannos of what was going on. Two others rode back along the column to order the gun team to bring up the four-pounder. He'd had to sell Lamochares's twelve-pounder to the man who ran the foundry to make him hurry with the field carriage for the lighter gun. It was a good deal handier for this kind of work anyway, so for now that did no harm.

A dozen troopers gathered around Phidestros himself and followed him off the Great Harph Road along a glorified track that led across two farms toward the right flank. Phidestros was working up to a canter when he came to a narrow but steep-banked stream cutting between the two fields. He trotted onto the rough log bridge that carried the track across the stream, and was halfway across when he heard wood creak and begin to crack underneath.

Suddenly the whole floor of the bridge tilted to the right, spilling Phidestros and his mount into the stream.

Phidestros was kicking his feet free of the stirrups from the first cracking sound, so he and Snowdrift parted company in midair. Somehow the horse landed on his feet, to come up snorting and dripping foul-smelling mud but undamaged except for temper.

Phidestros wasn't quite so lucky. Most of him landed in the muck, but his right knee met a stone that felt like a blacksmith's hammer. He could raise his face and upper body out of the mud, but for a terrifyingly long moment he couldn't move his legs.

Then four or five of his men were dismounting and half scrambling, half falling down the bank of the stream to him. With their help, he found that he could stand, although his right knee was throbbing and sending red-hot jabs of pain up and down his leg. That he could feel and move it suggested nothing was broken, but the pain warned him to plan on spending the rest of the battle in the saddle and pray that nothing happened to Snowdrift. He'd have prayed for that anyway; tractable mounts who could carry his weight for long weren't easy to come by and cost the Treasury of Balph when you found one.

The rapid popping of musketoons suggested that at least some of the right-flankers were wisely dismounting to shoot at the Hostigi rather than charging headlong. Two grunting men hoisted Phidestros on their shoulders and let him take a look over the bank of the stream, which confirmed it. He also saw about twenty of the right-flankers riding toward a small orchard that ran to within three hundred paces of the Hostigi position. There they just possibly might be able to hit the Hostigi instead of just slightly interfering with their marksmanship.

Another of the Iron Company's mounted men went down as Phidestros watched, then he turned at a shout from one of his men who'd been examining the wrecked bridge.

"Captain, look! The Ormaz-forsaken timbers were sawed through, or pretty damned near."

Someone had indeed sawed halfway through each of the main timbers supporting the floor of the bridge so that it would look sound until an unsuspecting passerby put weight on it. Phidestros looked again, then clawed muck out of his beard and grinned.

"We'll burn three candles for Galzar tonight! Whoever sawed the timbers went too far, so the bridge gave way under a horseman's weight. Suppose it had held until we tried to take the four-pounder across? We'd have had to send back to Harphax City for one of the dockside cranes to fish her out!"

By the time the mounted flankers had reached the orchard, they'd lost four men, and the rest of the Iron Company's right-flankers had lost three. Phidestros saw some movement behind the wall that looked suspiciously like horsehandlers bringing forward the riflemen's mounts so they could withdraw. He cursed the Hostigi, but not too loudly, because he had to respect what those eight men had in them to make them willing to stand up to odds of thirty-to-one even if they did have half-magical weapons.

Magical or not, those rifles were going to have to be thought about. A man armed with one of them would be worth three or four ordinary musketeers; a larger force—well, Phidestros was glad he didn't have to solve the problem of fighting one today. He hoped that whatever knowledge went into making those rifles was not demonic, or rather would not be *called* demonic by Styphon's House. Phidestros had his own opinions on the existence of demons, whether allied with King Kalvan or anyone else.

Meanwhile, those riflemen meant that Kalvan was close at hand; the Mounted Rifles of Hostigos were the crack troops of his Mobile Force. And the Mobile Force, in turn, would not be far from the main body of the Army of Hos-Hostigos. Battle was possible today, certainly no later than tomorrow—unless Kalvan *did* have demons at his command and chose a night attack, in which case there'd be nothing to do but keep a sharp lookout, load weapons, and pray to Galzar.

Assuming that Kalvan had merely a human captain's resources, however—

"Yoooo!" Phidestros called up to the mounted men on the bank. "Six of you, ride back to Prince Philesteus. Report that we have found the Mounted Rifles of Hostigos scouting for Kalvan's main body three miles south of Chothros West Gap. We expect the Mobile Force is close enough to us that we will need reinforcements as fast as they can be sent up." That was as much as he could be sure was the truth, and perhaps more than was tactful to say to Philesteus, but to Regwarn with tact, he had his men to consider!

Not to mention the possibility of a small victory of his own.

The mounted men started arguing among themselves as to who should beard Philesteus. Phidestros gripped Snowdrift's saddle with one hand and drew his pocket pistol with the other, then followed his men downstream until the banks were low enough to let everyone climb out. As he moved, he was aware again of the sharp pains in his knee and also of the fresh mud oozing into his boots, not to mention the drying muck on his arms, clothes, and skin that was beginning to ripen in the hot morning sun.

11.

Kalvan was on the bank of the Harph, inspecting the night's haul by the Ulthori levies, when the messenger rode up to tell him that the scouts were in contact with the Harphaxi vanguard. A good quarter of Prince Kestophes's men were former fishermen, and Kalvan had been sending them across the Harph each night to bring back anything and everything that could float to the east bank. Kalvan had no intention of leaving his river flank vulnerable in case the Harphaxi had a captain with the brains to think of an amphibious landing; he had every intention of being in a position to conduct one himself.

After a couple of days of Ulthori piracy, the local citizens who hadn't taken to their heels or their boats formed the habit of hauling their watercraft up on shore and hiding them. The Ulthori search parties wandered farther and farther inland, usually burning the boats and making off with everything portable worth the trouble to carry it down to the Harph. So far they hadn't started burning houses or assaulting civilians, and one reason for the morning's inspection was to make very clear to them exactly what would happen to them if they did and how little they would like it.

The messenger's report was not the clearest that Kalvan had ever heard, even here-and-now, but it was plain that the Heights of Chothros was the key point in the coming battle. Kalvan, Major Nicomoth, and the escort of Royal Horse Guards mounted up and rode east. They could have covered the eight miles to the West Gap in half the time it took, but Nicomoth sent scouts ahead to smoke out ambushes each time the trees crept within musket shot of the road, which was more often than not.

Kalvan consoled himself by thinking that this pace at least spared the horses, but he was not in good temper by the time they reached the West Gap, about where New Providence would have been back home. He nearly lost his remaining patience when he saw the entire High Command of the Army of the Harph, with the exception of Verkan, waiting for him. With nobody sure just where the enemy was or how strong, this looked like a good way to lose not only the battle but the war if hostile cavalry suddenly galloped up the Great Harph Road.

Second thoughts and a second look kept Kalvan's temper under control. Without radio, the corps and regimental commanders had no way to coordinate tactics or pass intelligence except for mounted messengers, who would be even more likely snapped up by prowling enemy cavalry.

Also, this Forward Command Post wasn't exactly undefended. Harmakros's Sastragathi were lurking behind every tree, the personal staffs of most of the commanders were still mounted and armed, and a glint of armor around the flank of a low rise hinted at a cavalry regiment or better within easy reach. Kalvan's Horse Guards had joined the staffs by the time he dismounted, and Harmakros's aide had unrolled a map and was pointing out who was where, or at least seemed to be, when he joined the generals.

The Harphaxi advancing toward the West Gap were almost certainly the whole left-flank column of the enemy, possibly fifteen thousand strong. The rest of the Harphaxi should be off farther to the northeast, probably making for the East Gap north of the village that occupied the site of Christiana.

"At least that's our best guess at the moment," said Hestophes. "Colonel Verkan has picketed the Heights, and we expect messengers from him within the hour. The other column can't be out of sight from the Heights without being as good as out of today's fighting."

In this kind of country that was probably the case, particularly for an army with inadequate transport and communications, as well as discipline that hardly deserved the name. In fact, it was possible that the two Harphaxi columns were completely out of supporting distance of each other. Did this give the Hostigi a chance to smash the left column before the right could come to its support?

A look at the map told Kalvan there was a chance, but not a particularly good one. At the moment the Harphaxi probably had more men close to the West Gap than the Hostigi, if estimates of the Harphaxi columns' strength were accurate. The Hostigi army was echeloned back as far as Millersville and down to the Harph, at the Ulthori camp somewhere just below the site of Safe Harbor Dam. To concentrate his troops before the Harphaxi could seize the West Gap would mean grinding, foot-blistering, horse-wearing marches. It also meant a good chance of having to open the battle with a frontal assault on the West Gap, which didn't appeal to Kalvan even if he did have the edge in numbers and many of the Harphaxi were the scourings of every tavern and poorhouse in Hos-Harphax and Hos-Agrys.

Not to mention that the currently unlocated or at least out-of-sight Harphaxi right probably contained Styphon's House troops—the fanatical infantry of Styphon's Own Guard, who had not won the name of Styphon's Red Hand for their good deeds—and the cavalry of the Zarthani Knights. Everybody else he was facing, except probably the Harphaxi Royal Army, could be fooled or frightened away. The Styphoni would have to be *fought*, whenever and wherever they turned up.

So much for what he shouldn't do. Now for the hard part. What should he do, other than wait for the Harphaxi to make the first move and then react to it? While that wouldn't necessarily cost him the battle, it would probably lose him the chance to make it decisive enough.

Kalvan lit one of his special stogies with his gold tinderbox, a gift from Rylla, and squatted by the map again, careful not to drop ashes on it. He was mentally composing orders for bringing up the rest of the army when galloping hooves drew him to his feet. A Mobile Force officer on a thoroughly lathered horse pounded up and hurled himself out of the saddle before his mount had come to a complete stop.

"Message from Colonel Verkan, Your Majesty. The right column is making for the Middle Gap. The Zarthani Knights are with it. One of our patrols has also seen enemy reinforcements moving from the left column to the right."

"How many?"

The officer paused to catch his breath before continuing. "The patrol said at least four thousand, mostly cavalry."

Kalvan's eyebrows rose. He ignored the fact that his cigar had gone out and bent over the map again. The Middle Gap was north of—what was its name otherwhen? Georgetown?—and the road through it followed roughly State Highway 896 to Strasburg—Mrathos, here-and-now.

If the estimate of four thousand reinforcements to the column headed for the Middle Gap was correct, that was now the main enemy thrust. For a moment, Kalvan wanted to curse in frustration at the ancient commander's dilemma: can you trust the people you need to send you intelligence when you can't go see for yourself?

Kalvan decided to trust the report. Dralm-dammit, if he couldn't trust somebody who was probably handpicked by Verkan, whom he did trust, he might as well turn around and march home right now!

Harmakros traced the Middle Gap road over the Heights with his sword point. "It looks as if somebody in Harphax has heard of flanks, other than horse's or women's."

Kalvan nodded, then stood up grinning. What he was about to do was a gamble, but less of one than he'd faced last year, and this time he was using his own dice.

"Hestophes. How many men do you have ready to march for the West Gap?"

It turned out that Hestophes had about five thousand: the four Royal regiments of foot—The King's Lifeguard, Queen Rylla's Foot, and the First and Second Regiments of Foot; the infantry veterans of Old Hostigos; and several companies of first-grade mercenaries.

"I'll give you a thousand cavalry and twelve guns to add to that. Take the whole force to the West Gap, find the most defensible position that blocks it, and defend it."

"For how long?" Hestophes didn't look perturbed; his long scarred face was as expressionless as a stiff-upper-lip Englishman's. He still obviously wanted any suicide missions to be clearly labeled as such.

"Until you've drawn the main weight of the Harphaxi left into trying to push through you," said Kalvan. "Or until there's danger of your retreat being cut off, if that happens first."

"Done, Your Majesty." Hestophes pulled on his gloves and turned to Harmakros. "Count, if you can give me an escort from your guards, men who were down this way on the spring raids, I'll ride on ahead and have the ground all picked out while the men are coming up."

"Will twenty be enough?"

"That should do, if they all have eyes in the backs of their heads."

Even if they did, Hestophes was going to have his hands full if the enemy came up in force before his men did. Kalvan tried not to think of losing the man who'd stood off a Nostori force ten times his own strength at Narza Gap last year, or of what all the widows and orphans in Hostigos would say if it turned out that he was sending Hestophes's six thousand to their deaths. That was not likely, though. Man for man they were probably the best infantry force ever seen here-and-now, and they weren't supposed to defeat the Harphaxi left outright, just keep its attention while the rest of the Hostigi plan unfolded. . . .

Harmakros's five thousand cavalry, mostly veterans of the Royal Mobile Force and the Army of Observation, would be stationed on the open ground north of the Heights to watch the Middle Gap and hold it as long as possible. Kalvan would give them a thousand infantry and four guns; the infantry should mostly go up the Heights to reinforce Colonel Verkan.

"If we can make them think the Heights are held in force, so much the better." Harmakros was looking moderately unhappy, and Kalvan knew why. "Don't worry. I know your troopers are spoiling for a fight. They'll get one sooner or later, and if it's sooner, it will probably be against the Zarthani Knights. If that's not a big enough fight, I don't know what I can do for them!

"Prince Armanes, you will remain here"—Kalvan tapped a point on the Great Harph Road about three miles north of Hestophes's most likely position—"and be prepared to move to support either Hestophes or Harmakros at their request. Any request for help from them shall be treated as if it came from me personally."

"As Your Majesty commands." Prince Armanes was very much a book soldier, but he wouldn't do anything dangerously stupid as long as you handled him right. His twenty-four hundred Nyklosi were also about the best of the Princely armies.

That took care of somewhat more than half the Army of the Harph, but it tied up the whole enemy army one way or another for long enough to let Kalvan move his remaining eight thousand more or less where they would do the most good—or the most damage, depending on whose viewpoint you took. Meanwhile, the rough wooded ground between the West Gap and the Harph would hide the eight thousand from any scouts less determined than the Zarthani Knights, who would have to fight their way past Harmakros before they could do any good.

What was George Patton's description of a certain maneuver—"We're going to hold on to them by the nose while we kick them in the pants"? The first pants to be kicked would probably be the Harphaxi left's, already somewhat out at the seat after several hours of frontal assaults on Hestophes. After that, Kalvan intended to play the battle very much by ear, but he would have a good chance to get into the rear of the enemy's main column on the right, and they'd have next to no chance of getting into *his* rear.

The thought of rears gave Kalvan a final idea. One of the things the Ulthori had been looting across the Harph was clothing. They'd been mustered into service in what they'd owned as civilians; even when that had been half decent it had been a bit threadbare, and now most of it looked like rags destined for the bins of the paper mill. Half of the men now looked like Ulthori peasants, except for their Hostigi red scarves and sashes.

Why not put a few hundred Ulthori in the captured boats and send them downriver into the Harphaxi rear? Let them loot to their hearts' content, looking as much as possible like a peasant uprising. Maybe they could spark a real one if he gave them orders to turn captured weapons over to any local peasants who seemed anti-Styphon enough. Maybe, but that would be getting into delicate territory politically; enough for now that they just pretend to be a peasant army and scare the whey out of Philesteus.

Kalvan tried to think if there was anything more that didn't have to be left to the chance of battle, and decided there wasn't. One of his history professor's favorite remarks came to mind, a quotation from some Army manual: "No battle plan ever survives contact with the enemy."

This Battle of the Heights of Chothros would be no exception. The number of things that could still go wrong was rather appalling. The best Kalvan could honestly say was that he'd disaster-proofed the Army of the Harph, given it a damned good chance of victory, and would have to leave the rest to Galzar, Duke Aesthes, Prince Philesteus, and plain old-fashioned luck.

"Very well, gentlemen. I think it's time we stopped talking and prepared to start shooting. Oh, Harmakros!"

"Your Majesty?"

"If any of your tame Sastragathi take Prince Philesteus's scalp, don't let them bring it to me!"

FIFTEEN

I.

"Here they come again," said Hestophes. He wasn't quite as calm as he was pretending to be; Kalvan noticed that the pipe in his mouth was not only unlit but upside down.

The new Harphaxi attack seemed to be aimed at what Hestophes called Barn Hill, at the northern end of his position. Six guns and a thousand infantry held the slopes around the half-ruined barn; three thousand more and the cavalry held the saddle stretching diagonally from northwest to southeast. The southeastern anchor of Hestophes's position, where Kalvan now sat on his horse, was referred to as Tavern Hill, for the stone-walled inn that crowned it. Another thousand infantry and the other six guns held the slopes of Tavern Hill or crouched behind loopholes knocked in the walls of the tavern itself. The ones in the upper-floor windows and on the roof had an excellent view of the lower slopes of Tavern Hill, strewn with the dead and dying from the first two Harphaxi attacks.

The third attack looked like about five hundred cavalry and a thousand infantry, wearing yellow sashes and plumes and carrying the flag of Hos-Harphax, a gold double-headed ax surrounded by a circle of nineteen stars on a red field. Most of the infantry were arquebusiers and assorted skirmishers with halberds and bills sticking up at random intervals. They were marching raggedly enough, but they were also marching out of range of the guns on Tavern Hill, with the additional shelter of a fold in the ground topped by a low stone wall.

Out of the dust behind the cavalry came three gun teams, turning toward the wall with the gunners jumping down from the horses or running up behind. The guns looked to be eight- or ten-pounders, great clumsy things that probably weighed more than a Hostigi sixteen-pounder and once off their traveling carriages would be about as mobile as the Rock of Gibralter. However, they could reach the pikemen in Hestophes's center, who would have to stand there in massed formation and take it or risk inviting a cavalry charge.

Correction: they would have had to stand there and take it, except that when Kalvan came up to visit Hestophes he also brought a thirteenth gun. It was the newest of the sixteen-pounders, which Uncle Wolf Tharses had honored with the name *Galzar's Teeth*.

"May they be sharp," said Hestophes, looking back at the gunners digging the big piece into position.

Kalvan grinned. "I've heard that thirteen people at one table is unlucky. I've never heard that thirteen guns on one position is."

"If so, it will only be unlucky for the Harphaxi."

From behind came a shout, a gunner trying to be respectful to his superiors even when they insisted on standing in his line of fire. The generals and their escorts shifted twenty yards to the left, then another twenty as the gunner shouted even louder. Finally there was a thunderous roar as *Galzar's Teeth* fired its first shot in action.

Here-and-now gunners hadn't had good enough field guns to learn the trick of aiming short and letting the shot ricochet into its target. Even if they had, the soft ground at the foot of the rise might have defeated them, the way it had Napoleon's gunners at Waterloo. However, the slight downgrade helped. The sixteen-pound ball fell short but kept rolling fast enough to smash through the stone wall to the right of the enemy guns.

Stone dust and bits flew. The enemy gunners didn't even bother to look up. Mercenaries, undoubtedly—the Harphaxi artillery was even more of a joke than the rest of their army—but a good grade of mercenary. Kalvan mentally noted a need to find out their names and, if they were captured, to try and recruit them.

The artillery duel went on for a good ten minutes with a minimum of damage on either side. Several Harphaxi shot flew over the mercenary arquebusiers to the left of the First Foot and rolled back down into their ranks. Kalvan saw one damned fool of a new recruit stick out a foot to try stopping one of the rolling shot; a moment later he was on the ground with his foot missing, screaming loudly enough to make his comrades back away. Hestophes looked back at the crew of Galzar's Teeth with a get-your-act-together-*now* expression on his face.

Whether inspired or intimidated, the gunners succeeded. Their next shot fell close to the leftward enemy gun and must have done some damage, because the next time it fired the carriage split apart. With their own piece useless, its crew shifted to the other two guns, increasing their rate of fire. A couple of stone balls landed among Queen Rylla's Foot. Unlike the mercenaries, they held steady until the wounded were carried away, then closed their ranks. Kalvan mentally noted down their Colonel for a commendation. *Time for something like the Presidential Unit Citation for regiments that did particularly well.*

In the next moment Galzar's Teeth slammed a roundshot squarely into the muzzle of the enemy's left-hand gun. It burst apart like an exploding boiler, and something hot must have fallen into an open fireseed barrel, because there was a crashing roar and a tremendous cloud of white smoke. When the smoke cleared away, both guns were wrecked and most of their gunners were down; Kalvan saw riders in the cavalry of the attacking column struggling to control their spooked mounts.

"Good shooting!" said Hestophes. "One could wish they'd been that good sooner, but guns are like women. They need careful handling and long familiarity before you can be sure they'll do what you want them to do." The last remark was made in such an austere tone of voice that Kalvan couldn't help wondering if Hestophes was speaking from personal experience or not.

Kalvan rode over to the gun to praise the shooting and to give the gunners ten crowns with which to celebrate after the battle, while Hestophes organized his counterattack by the four Royal regiments. By the time Kalvan returned, three regiments were on their way downhill in alternating companies of pike and musket. Queen Rylla's Foot formed a column on the left and a forlorn hope of three mercenary arquebusier companies was out in front.

"The wall ends on the left and the ground is firmer there," said Hestophes. "Any cavalry charge will come in there. I'm going to take the First and Second Regiment of Horse down to where they can support Queen Rylla's Foot, and meanwhile stiffen those mercenaries who don't like cannonballs."

Major Nicomoth suddenly seemed to have developed an exceptionally severe case of the lice that had infested everybody in the last few days. Kalvan and Hestophes exchanged looks, then Kalvan smiled. "All right, Major. You may take thirty of the Royal Horse Guards and ride with Hestophes, as long as you swear to obey him as you would me."

"With my life, Your Majesty."

Kalvan watched the cavalry forming up with the thought that Nicomoth was the classic well-born young cavalry officer who knew to perfection two of the operations of war: charging gallantly and dying gallantly. Kalvan still liked the man, but he would have cheerfully traded twenty of him for one more professional soldier like Harmakros, Hestophes, or Count Phrames—who were about all he had, as a matter of fact. A pity that none of them had the rank to command the Army of the Besh, particularly Hestophes, who wasn't even a noble, just the grandson of a mercenary whose widow had married a Hostigi merchant.

That, at least, could be remedied. It would *have* to be remedied, in fact; Hestophes had been a colonel-equivalent at Narza Gap, but now he was a brigadier-general doing a major-general's job, and there'd been some grumbling about a commoner holding such an honorable post. Well, if Hestophes finished off today's assignment and was still alive, he'd be a Baron. That would solve the problem of having him obeyed; Chartiphon had started from a lot farther down and nobody had questioned his orders since Ptosphes ennobled him.

Handing out goodies to men who'd done well was one of the

rewards of being Great King, a reward that sometimes almost made up for the headaches.

Nicomoth's yearning for a cavalry charge went unsatisfied. The Hostigi regiments stopped short of the soft ground, and the arquebusiers and musketeers of the three in line let fly almost seven hundred strong. Two more volleys and a couple of shots from Galzar's Teeth, and the Harphaxi were edging away toward Barn Hill and into range of *its* guns. Two salvos from those, and the Harphaxi infantry didn't even wait for the mercenaries on the hill to start toward them. They retreated, not quite as a rabble but certainly as a unit with most of the pepper and a couple of hundred men knocked out of it.

The Harphaxi mercenary cavalry made a brief feint toward the left of the Hostigi force, but the arquebusiers let fly, emptying a good many saddles. Then the pikemen and halberdiers covered their comrades, everybody moving so precisely that it was hard to believe they'd only been drilling since last fall, and then not continuously.

Hestophes and his two regiments rode forward ready to break the enemy to pieces, and Kalvan led the rest of the Royal Horse Guards down to stiffen the mercenaries, but neither of them had any work to do. The enemy cavalry sheered off, picked up the surviving artillerymen, and departed as fast as the stableful of glue-factory rejects they were riding could carry them.

"Don't worry, Major," said Kalvan as the Hostigi returned to their positions. "You'll be able to charge all you want before the day's over."

"Sooner than that if Your Majesty is planning to remain here," said Hestophes. "The lookouts on the tavern roof have sighted a new Harphaxi column approaching. They say it may number six thousand men, and the Royal Banner of Hos-Harphax is at its head."

Six thousand wasn't too many men for Hestophes to handle from his present position, unless the Harphaxi suddenly developed the ability to launch a coordinated attack, and if they did that, Prince Armanes was on call with more than two thousand completely fresh troops. It was definitely enough to surround the position and make it completely useless as a command post for Great King Kalvan.

"What will you need to meet them?"

"More fireseed, and soon. Also, some cavalry to take our prisoners from the first attacks to the rear." He did not add, "And for the Great King to take his royal arse with them so I won't have to worry about it!" but thought it very loudly.

"We'll send you the fireseed before the next attack, or in the first lull after it," Kalvan said. "As for the prisoners, my guards and I can escort them back as far as Armanes's position." Kalvan managed to keep from laughing out loud at Hestophes's efforts to suppress a sigh of relief.

II.

The scene at the south end of the Middle Gap over the Heights of Chothros reminded Phidestros of the struggles of a farmer he'd once seen, trying to get five pigs into a cart that anyone could have told him would hold three at most. The farmer had finally admitted defeat only after the cart collapsed and the ox hauling it broke loose and ran off, followed by four of the pigs.

Prince Philesteus and Duke Aesthes, it seemed to Phidestros, were much like the farmer. They had dimly grasped the notion that the way to win a battle was to get around the enemy's flank. They had not grasped in the least how to *find* that flank. Still less did they seem to know what to do with much of their army while they were searching.

So something like a third of the Harphaxi army was either through the Middle Gap or on the way; the Iron Company would have been among that nine thousand if Duke Aesthes hadn't given them a rest as reward for their good scouting. Phidestros had taken the reward gladly, although he'd been surprised to discover that Aesthes could tell good scouting from bad.

The pace of the advance through the Gap made turtles look fleet-footed, when everything wasn't at a halt due to a gun losing a wheel or two sets of wagon traces getting tangled. Not to mention the places where the road's incline required eight animals to do the work of four. Phidestros recalled seeing one entire team lying in the traces, dead from a futile attempt to pull an Agrysi nine-pounder back on the road.

After an eighth of a day of this, Phidestros realized that there was no reason for him to ride about in the confusion, trying to see what most likely wasn't there to be seen. He sent Banner-Captain Geblon and six of his toughest veterans over the Gap to scout, then rode back downhill.

He'd just reached the Iron Company's temporary camp when he heard peculiarly deep-toned trumpets blaring to the west. He hurriedly turned off the road and watched from the fields as a Lance of Zarthani Knights cantered past.

The Holy Order of the Zarthani Knights had been formed three hundred and fifty years before, when the civilized Ruthani of the Lower Sastragath tried to drive out the Zarthani settlers encroaching on their tribal homelands. The Knights had broken the Ruthani alliance and afterward become the defenders of the southern Great Kingdoms against the barbarians of the Lower Sastragath and farther west. The Knights were also a priestly order of Styphon's House, and had helped spread Styphon's worship throughout Hos-Beletha and parts of the Sastragath.

As always, the Knights were marching in the formation in which they expected to fight. At the head of the Lance went the flag of the Order, a large white banner bearing a black, broken sun-wheel with curved arms. They rode in a wedge-shaped formation, with the oath-brothers riding ahead as skirmishers, and the fully armored Brethren forming the tip. The hundred Brother Knights had black armor with white and black plumes on their helms, and carried a heavy lance, a brace of pistols, and a sword. Behind the Brethren were two hundred Confrère Knights in three-quarter black armor with lance and pistols, followed by two hundred sergeants in back-and-breast with pistols and sword. A hundred horse-archer auxiliaries and as many mounted arquebusiers brought up the rear.

A third Lance added to the other two that had already gone up the Gap would make more than two thousand of the Order's cavalry ready for Aesthes's hand. Phidestros had the liveliest doubts that the Captain-General would know what to do with them, and hoped their own Knight Commander would be able to find something on his own.

The dust from the Knights' passage was barely starting to settle when Phidestros saw bright flashes of metal, then a solid mass of red emerging from a cloud of dust. A Temple Band of Styphon's Own Guard swung by, glaives shouldered, musketoons slung across their silvered breastplates, and most of them singing a hymn to Styphon in voices that would have knocked dead from the sky any birds who hadn't long since fled the battlefield.

Phidestros backed his horse still farther into the field as Styphon's Red Hand marched by, and did not return to the road until he could no longer hear their singing. He badly wanted to find out what might be going on toward the west, where he'd seen a good deal of smoke and heard more than a good deal of firing, including artillery. He did not want it badly enough to call himself to the notice of a Temple Band whose grand-captain might have the ear of the Inner Circle.

Phidestros snatched a quick meal of bread, cheese, and sausage washed down with warm flat ale, while the baggage boy changed the wet cloths bound around his injured knee. He no longer had to stifle a gasp when he put his weight on the leg, but he knew he'd best plan on running no footraces for a while and spending that day either lying, sitting, or riding.

Several messengers rode by while he was eating. Two coming from the west stopped and accepted a few coins in return for their messages, but neither was able to tell him anything about the battle in the West Gap. The Hostigi seemed to be making a stand with a good part of their army, at least; certainly nobody had been able to push through the West Gap to find the rest. They had not attacked, either. The second messenger added that the Royal troops of Hos-Harphax were coming up and seemed to regard this as good news, but then he spoke with a Harphaxi accent. Doubtless he found it prudent to at least pretend ignorance of the true value of Kaiphranos's men.

Phidestros realized that if the Iron Company were to be thrown into the battle at the West Gap, their approach to it would be over open ground; he could at least send more scouts ahead to find what was going on when he needed to know. Of course this might leave him short of trustworthy petty-captains. . . .

Phidestros was just emptying the mug of ale when Geblon returned. Geblon's normally round face looked pale with dust and something more that made Phidestros sit up and motion Geblon to his side so that no one could overhear the Banner-Captain's message.

"The Hostigi barely tried to hold the far end of the Gap, let alone the crest. Their—*riflemen*—did some damage, their Sastragathi bandits a little more, but that was all. They're holding Mrathos with hardly more than a thousand men, but in trenches with artillery. Everybody thinks there must be more Hostigi, and half of them are scattered all over Yirtta's potato patch trying to find them."

"Isn't Aesthes trying to rein them in?"

"He's determined to reduce Mrathos before he moves a yard farther. He *may* do that before nightfall. I couldn't get close enough to the lines around the town to ask him or anybody else who might know."

So if the Iron Company crossed the Middle Gap, it would find itself on a field where the enemy might or might not be present, and if present, in unknown strength. Certainly a Captain-General who did not know his business would be present, and so would thousands of Styphon's finest troops. Not just on the field, but perhaps behind the Iron Company—and Styphon's Red Hand, at least, had a reputation for killing even allied troops, not just to keep them from retreating but to force them to stand and die to the last man.

"Did anyone recognize you or name the Iron Company in your hearing?"

Geblon shook his head. "Not that I remember."

"You're sure?"

"Almost sure."

"Sure enough to swear an oath?"

Geblon opened his mouth, obviously to ask what kind of an oath, then shut it again. He knew of the reputation of Styphon's Red Hand, and he'd been a mercenary long enough to know that no one could be punished for not obeying an order he hadn't received. The less he knew about what was in his captain's mind, the less danger he'd be in if by chance Styphon's House or the Harphaxi wanted a convenient scapegoat.

If the example was to come from the Iron Company, Phidestros was determined that it should be from him. He owed them that much—that, and not leading them into a battle on the ground of a lackwit's choosing. Not if he could avoid it, by Galzar!

SIXTEEN

I.

"Remember, at all costs keep five hundred paces between you and Eurysthes's column. If the cavalry can't fit into a gap that big, I'll have them all sent to one of Yirtta's temple-houses for the blind!"

"It shall be done, Your Majesty," said Baron Euklestes with a grin. "That should also let both us and Eurysthes shoot at any Harphaxi unwise enough to ride into the gap, without fear of hitting each other. Am I right?" Kalvan nodded. "Then—when do we march?"

Kalvan hesitated a moment over his answer. Great Kings weren't supposed to admit to being at the mercy of their subordinates, even when the subordinates were as good as Harmakros. On the other hand, Euklestes seemed intelligent enough to benefit from a short lesson in generalship.

"As soon as I receive the next message from Count Harmakros on how the battle around Mrathos is going." They both looked at the blue eastern sky above the treetops and at the towering plume of black smoke trailing across the blue.

It bothered Kalvan that Harmakros had brought about a major fight at Mrathos. Mrathos was the here-and-now site of Strasburg, where two years before he met the flying saucer, he'd lost a good friend. Sergeant Joe Bonnetti, Calvin Morrison's mentor his first two years as a Pennsylvania State

Trooper, had been run off a wet road and killed by a drunken driver, a drunken driver with so many political connections that he'd got off with a slap on the wrist. There was no way to talk about this memory, either; even if there'd been anyone around cleared for the "secret" of his origins, they might call it an evil omen.

What was even more annoying, Kalvan wasn't entirely sure they'd be completely wrong. Was living among people who took gods and demons and sorcery for granted making him superstitious?

And wasn't this a hell of a thing to be worrying about as the biggest battle of his life approached its climax?

Kalvan turned his mind to a more practical question. What should he do about Harmakros, who'd shown initiative— Dralm-dammit, nearly disobedience!—by holding Mrathos instead of the Middle Gap, and holding back four fifths of his men while the garrison of Mrathos drew most of the Harphaxi right on to itself? Certainly he'd infected Captain-General Aesthes with an obsessive desire to reduce the town—to rubble and ashes, if nothing more—before moving on, or even bothering to control the rest of his troops. Some French general whose name Kalvan couldn't recall had got the same bee in his bonnet at Waterloo and spent the whole battle attacking the Chateau of Hougmont, leaving the rest of Wellington's right flank completely alone. The garrison at Mrathos didn't need to do nearly as much, and it looked as if they might have already done it.

More of Kalvan's friends might die today at Mrathos, but so would a lot of his enemies. He spurred his horse back toward the rear of the units lined up for the counterattack. He'd be riding back there, along with the artillery and the counterattack's own private cavalry reserve, the Second Royal Horse Guards and the First Dragoons. Kalvan might be commanding, but the counterattack would actually be led into action by Phrames.

This was unorthodox but made sense for several reasons, one of which was that Phrames knew his business. Another was the superior quality of the cavalry, mostly Royal regulars and several squadrons of the Ulthori Household Guard. They were better able to take or deliver the first shock as long as they could be kept from charging massed infantry. The infantry of the counterattack included too many small mercen-

ary companies plus Euklestes's column of two—call them
"regiments" to avoid being insulting—of Hostigi foot militia.
They were the survivors of last year's battles who could be
spared for field service; while they'd smelled powder, they'd
hardly done a day's training between last fall and the day the
Army of the Harph marched east.

In the rear, Kalvan would have the infantry under his eye.
He'd also be clear of the scrimmage up ahead, able to move
his reserves where they were most needed—or even move them
to another part of the battlefield entirely. He might have to do
that if Aesthes pushed past Harmakros's Mobile Force and
Armanes needed help—and where the Styphon *was* Harmakros's messenger, and what should he do to the Count that
would persuade him not to do this sort of thing again, without
making him afraid to blow his nose without an order?

Another universal commander's problem: how to encourage initiative without losing control of your subordinates.
Kalvan reflected morosely that the problem had probably first
presented itself to some Neanderthal chieftain leading a raid
on a neighbor's cave.

II.

A shift in the breeze suddenly thinned the smoke
pouring up from the farmhouse. It hadn't been much smoke,
compared to what was pouring up from Mrathos two miles to
the east, but it had been enough to screen Verkan's patrol of
the Mounted Rifles from what lay beyond the hedges border-
ing the farmyard. Now the screen was gone, and Verkan was
staring at more than a hundred of Styphon's Red Hand, and
particularly at a mounted officer who was staring back as
though he'd just seen one of Styphon's fireseed demons
materialize out of the haze.

Verkan was the first to break away. His pistol shot missed
the officer but nicked his horse, which kept the officer busy

long enough for Verkan to shout, "No dismounting! We had orders to find the Styphoni and we've done it! Pull back!"

By the time the Styphoni officer had his mount under control and was sending his men through the gate in the hedge, Verkan's twenty-five Riflemen were trotting away across the farmer's now well-trodden barley. They were on the far side of the field and approaching the boundary with the next farm before the Red Hand opened fire, at long range for their musketoons.

Long range, but not impossible, with fifty men volleying at a single target. Verkan Vall had just enough time to realize that he was the single target, when his horse screamed and reared violently, something went *wheeet* past his ear, and something else went *whnnnnngggg* off his breastplate. Verkan flung himself to the left to avoid falling under his horse, smashed into something solid and hard enough to knock the wind out of him, then found himself suspended clear of the ground with what seemed to be blunt knives digging into his ribs.

He gulped in air, shook his head, and discovered he was caught in the half-rotted framework of an overturned farm wagon. He must have been right on top of it when the Styphoni killed his horse, then smashed most of the way through when he leaped clear. For a long moment he wriggled like a child in the arms of a determined mother, then the rest of the framework gave way and he dropped through to the ground.

The timbers of the bed of the wagon were less rotted, a piece of good luck for Verkan. Bullets *thunked* into the wood as the Styphoni blazed away with more enthusiasm than accuracy. The sound of incoming fire didn't drown out Ranthar's orders to dismount and return fire. The Mounted Rifles were falling into fours with the ease of long practice—three to open fire and one to hold the horses. Ranthar himself was staying mounted, his rifle still slung across his back.

Verkan couldn't see all his men, but from the sudden burst of rifle fire he knew everyone but the horse-holders must have let fly. Two more volleys were punctuated by a cry of pain and several gleefully triumphant shouts, then the volleys gave way to individual fire. The *thunking* of bullets into the wagon bed became less frequent as the Styphoni found it prudent to keep their heads out of the sights of rifles, even rifles in the hands of despised heretics and demon-worshippers.

Then Ranthar was riding toward Verkan and extending a hand down from the saddle. "This is a lousy place for a vacation, Colonel. The roof leaks, the plumbing's blocked up, and the neighborhood's too noisy." A Styphoni bullet kicked up dust between his horse's hind legs, and another drove splinters into Verkan's left hand hard enough to draw blood.

"That's what comes of taking advice from tavern friends," said Verkan. He took the hand, gripped the saddlebow with the other, and swung himself up onto the neck of Ranthar's bay. A few more bullets whistled by, then they were out of range and behind the team of Riflemen who took their Colonel's rescue as the signal to start mounting up.

They'd only lost one man, and from the back of the dead man's horse Verkan looked toward the Styphoni position. It was now decorated with a score of red-clad corpses and the body of the Styphoni officer's horse. A few of the Red Hand were keeping up a sporadic fire, while the rest seemed to be either lying low or holding their glaives, ready to stand off the Mounted Rifles' charge.

Verkan hoped they'd have a long, hot, thirsty wait, and a royal reaming-out from the next Hostigi detachment to come along. He glanced back at his dead mount. It was a pity he couldn't retrieve the saddlebags, but everything compromising in it was in one simulated-leather pouch equipped with a dead-man timer and a charge nobody on Fourth Level Aryan-Transpacific could find, let alone disarm. When the timer ran out, the charge would give a remarkably good impression of a demonic visitation to anyone far enough away to survive.

The timer and charge weren't the safest things to ride around with in the middle of a battle, but every Paracop accepted the possibility of being blown to bits by his own security devices every day he spent outtime, from oath-taking to retirement. It was a much quicker death than some that Paratime Policemen had suffered in defense of the Paratime Secret.

Meanwhile, in spite of his own embarrassingly minor role in the skirmish, the patrol had done its job. It had found Styphoni so far west of Mrathos that it was obvious they'd be able to meet Harmakros's attack in force if he delayed it much longer. The advantage Harmakros had won from the stand at Mrathos and Captain-General Aesthes's lack of control over his wing of the Harphaxi could be lost—if not completely, enough to make the next stage of the battle on the Hostigi left a lot bloodier than it would be otherwise.

Then Harmakros might lose some of his reputation, and either try something foolish to restore it and get killed, or be shoved aside by rivals who also had a claim on Great King Kalvan. Either way, Kalvan would be losing one of his best field commanders, which would be the equivalent of losing a fair-sized battle.

To prevent that, Verkan Vall would have steered much closer to the line between contamination and noncontamination than he would have to now. After all, he was a trusted field officer reporting to the general who'd ordered him out on a scouting mission; he would be expected to offer advice. The rest could almost certainly be left to Harmakros's wits.

Nobody who knew anything about war could call that contamination. Of course, not everybody knew anything about war, a fact that Verkan Vall would have been resigned to as long as the ignorant didn't rise to high rank in the Paratime Police, Paratime Commission, Executive Council, or outtime trade. As things really were. . . .

The thought of how things really were made him dig his spurs into his horse's flanks, pushing it from a trot into a canter.

SEVENTEEN

I.

When Captain Phidestros heard the sudden increase in firing from the far side of the Heights, he ordered the Iron Company to make ready to mount. The most likely explanation for the new uproar was a Hostigi attack, and he wanted to be able to move out as quickly as possible through the Middle Gap to reinforce Captain-General Aesthes. Surely Aesthes, having through no gift of his own found the long-sought Hostigi flank, would not hesitate to call up every man within reach of his messengers to attack it.

Instead the battle roar continued to mount, and white powder smoke climbed the sky above the Heights to join the black murk from burning Mrathos. Still no orders came from the Captain-General or anybody else, and no more messengers came along the road from the west. The battle there was still going on, which suggested that the Hostigi at the West Gap must have either been much stronger than anyone had suspected or else been reinforced since the fighting opened some four hours ago. There could be no other natural explanation for their holding so long, and Phidestros would believe other kinds of explanation when he saw evidence for them.

Without his injured knee, Phidestros would have dismounted and walked off his growing ill temper, striding up and down in front of the Iron Company until either orders

came or he felt better. With his knee still sore, all he could do
was sit on his horse until Snowdrift sensed his rider's uneasiness enough to grow jittery, then dismount and sit on a stump
high enough to be clear of the rank grass and horse droppings.

It didn't help that the muck from the creek now reeked like
a midden, and what had found its way through the chinks in
his armor to creep next his skin itched like all the fleas in Harphax City amusing themselves at once. Men who had business
with him carefully stayed upwind, Phidestros noticed. He also
realized he could do nothing about this until he could strip off
his armor, boil his clothes, and have a thorough bath—
preferably in a proper Zygrosi bathhouse, with clouds of
steam rising around him and a comely wench to ply him with a
soap, scraper, cloths, oil, winter wine, sweet cakes, a mas-
sage. . . .

Phidestros ruthlessly kept his imagination from going any
farther. Instead he decided to light his pipe, only to discover
that he had no more tobacco. He sent his baggage boy to find
some, and also to summon Geblon and Kylannos. If the Iron
Company was to sit around until it perished of boredom, it
might at least sit somewhere there was water and shade.

The nearest place to provide both turned out to be a chest-
nut grove already occupied by a gaggle of stragglers, deserters,
servants, and camp followers, as well as a few genuine suf-
ferers from fever, flux, or the heat. The Iron Company routed
the able-bodied out of the grove at the point of sword and
pistol, took the casualties under their protection, and settled
down to wait with as much patience as they could muster. Phidestros finally managed to find some tobacco and was just getting his pipe drawing nicely when a shout came from the
lookout he'd posted in the upper branches of a tall hemlock at
the west end of the grove.

"Captain! There's fighting south of the West Gap! I can
see a lot of dust and some cavalry at the gallop!"

Phidestros cursed his injured knee, which would keep him
from climbing the tree to take a look for himself. "Can you
see the cavalry's colors?"

"No, there's too much dust and smoke. I can see the Royal
Lancers, though. They're well to this side of the new fighting."

"You've used your eyes well," said Phidestros, reaching
into his purse for coins and with the other hand for a branch

to pull himself to his feet. Fighting south of the West Gap and cavalry at that could hardly mean anything but another Hostigi attack. He didn't know who commanded the Harphaxi there—probably Prince Philesteus himself if the Royal Lancers were present—but it would certainly be someone with enough rank to give weight to any praise he gave the Iron Company. It seemed to Phidestros that the West Gap was more than ever the place for his men now, and any messengers with orders to the contrary who might be on the way could break their necks for all he cared!

"Sound 'Mount'!" he shouted to the nearest trumpeter as his groom moved to Snowdrift's head. Harness jingled and leather thumped as the men around him obeyed their captain's shout even before the trumpet blew. Phidestros swung into the saddle and considered his best line of march to the West Gap.

Straight down the road would bring him in sight of the Harphaxi royal troops and their captain; that would mean attacking with friends at his back and flanks. Not the best of friends, though, except in sheer numbers; the well-born heavy cavalry of Harphax were barely polite to mercenaries and were none too wise in the new kind of warfare that Kalvan was going to teach everybody whether they liked it or not.

No, the Iron Company would swing to the south of the road and move cautiously toward the fighting, with scouts well out in front. Phidestros was even prepared to lead himself, in order to be the first to see how the battle was going. Once again, if the Iron Company retreated without need and there was an example to be made, he would be the one to provide it. But, on the other hand, if there was a need for retreat—well, the Iron Company would have a clear road to Harphax City or even across the Harph.

"Phidestros!" someone shouted, and the Iron Company took up the cry. Snowdrift began to prance, and his rider didn't even try to gentle him. One way or another, the frustration of sitting by the road while the battle was mismanaged all around him was about to end, Galzar be thanked!

11.

The Harphaxi gun bellowed and the twelve-pound
ball thumped twenty yards to Kalvan's right, crashed through
what was left of the fence behind him, and rolled away out of
sight without hitting anything.

"That's the last one!" Kalvan shouted. "Trumpeters,
sound the 'Charge'!"

To their credit, the Royal Horse Guards actually waited
until they heard the trumpeters before they dug in their spurs.
Kalvan knew the efforts they'd make to protect him if he rode
too far ahead and the time this would expend. He reined in his
horse until Major Nicomoth and the first two squads were out
ahead, then urged his own mount up to a canter.

The four Harphaxi guns across the field would take at least
five minutes to reload, and Kalvan's cavalry could be on them
before they were halfway done. Kalvan wasn't sure what
business a Great King had leading regiment-strength cavalry
charges, but when the regiment was the only part of his army
within reach and there was an enemy within striking distance,
he couldn't think of anything better to do.

Dust billowed behind the Hostigi as they rode, horse pistols
drawn, silvered armor gleaming in the hot sun, Kalvan's personal banner of a red keystone on a green field leading the
way. Through the smoke ahead Kalvan could already see some
of the gunners running for the shelter of the trees behind their
position. That would slow down the reloading even more.
Kalvan drew his sword and shouted:

"Down Styphon!"

The Hostigi counterattack had started well enough. Kalvan
had finally led out his force of two thousand horse, fifteen
hundred foot, and four guns without waiting for Harmakros's
message about the situation in front of Mrathos. It was a
gamble, but one that had paid off.

When Harmakros's messenger, on a half-dead horse, finally
caught up with his Great King, he reported that Harmakros
was launching his own attack with all his men. Colonel Verkan
had reported that several bands of Styphon's Red Hand were
moving west, and it seemed wisest to attack Captain-General

Aesthes before the Styphoni could strengthen his position.

Kalvan had rewarded the good-news bearer, sent him off to rest his horse, and rode on in a much better mood. Harmakros could clearly be trusted to use his initiative wisely, even if he did give his Great King ulcers in the process. He had a good sense of timing and eye for terrain, and he also knew enough to concentrate his forces. He was even honest enough to give credit to his subordinates when they deserved it, and Napoleon himself headed a long list of generals who'd lacked that virtue.

More immediately, it meant Kalvan's counterattack would not have to swing far to the west in order to avoid Harphaxi patrols coming from Mrathos. They would all be much too busy with Harmakros. This would save a good deal of time, and the sooner the pressure on Hestophes was relieved, the better. From the amount of firing around his position, he was still holding on, but he hadn't sent a messenger in over an hour—which said things Kalvan didn't like to hear.

Kalvan delivered his first attack on time and in more or less the intended place. Several thousand Harphaxi, including some of the Royal Pistoleers, died, ran off, or surrendered with gratifying speed. In the process a lot of fast-moving horses and rapidly fired guns generated an appalling amount of dust and smoke. When some of the farms and orchards started burning, Kalvan began to feel that he was back on the fog-shrouded battlefield of Fyk.

By the time Kalvan sighted the four Harphaxi bombards, he had under his personal command only a squadron of his Horse Guards—about a hundred and thirty men—and slightly more than a hundred Ulthori heavy horse. With a little persuading, the Ulthori dropped back to guard the rear while Kalvan led his better-disciplined Hostigi out to draw the gunners' fire, then charge. The Harphaxi artillery was notoriously slow to reload; it was safe to use against them tactics that would have been suicidal against Hostigi field guns. Besides, Kalvan knew the only chance of keeping the initiative he'd taken with the counterattack was to hit the enemy wherever and whenever he popped up. The Hostigi couldn't lose this battle, Kalvan suspected, but he was damned sure the Harphaxi could get too many of their men away if given a chance.

These memories took Kalvan halfway to the guns. At that point a light piece banged off on the left; the trooper riding beside Major Nicomoth suddenly had no head, and Nicomoth had most of the trooper's brains spattered all over his armor. The Major shouted "Down Styphon!" again and put his horse up to a gallop.

Several pistols and arquebuses went off among the Harphaxi guns. One gunner jumped onto the breech of his piece to rally his comrades and was promptly shot down. Then Nicomoth, who had drawn half a dozen horse lengths in front of Kalvan, was in among the gunners; he timed his reining-in so well that he sabered two of them before they realized he was within striking distance.

Kalvan swung wide to the left; Nicomoth was one of the best swordsmen in Hostigos and would need no help from his King. Somewhat to Kalvan's surprise, the smoke and dust weren't so thick here, and he found himself with a clear shot at a cluster of frantic gunners. He aimed a pistol at the man holding the rammer and fired. Not entirely to Kalvan's surprise, the gunner went down. Hostigi horse pistols had barrels nearly two feet long, and with rifling added they were more accurate than the Police .38s and Army .45s that Kalvan had used back home.

Kalvan emptied another pistol, then decided to cease fire and reload. There were no more targets anyway; the Guardsmen were all around the guns, taking surrender oaths from the surviving gunners. Nicomoth was ordering latecomers to search for the gun teams, and a troop of the First Dragoons had ridden up from somewhere and was awaiting orders.

Kalvan told them to dismount and send patrols through the tree line behind the guns to see what lay on the other side. It probably wasn't a canyon a mile deep, but Kalvan couldn't see or hear anything to prove otherwise.

The appearance of Hostigi dragoons on the other side was greeted with a burst of musketry. Kalvan's men were closing up when two dragoons staggered back through the trees, holding a wounded comrade between them and gasping, "Harphaxi! The Household Guard and the Royal Lancers!"

"Any of their chief captains—?" Kalvan was asking, when another burst of musketry sounded, then went on to become the steady hammering of massed infantry fire. Kalvan backed his horse away from the trees in case the Harphaxi were launching an attack and would suddenly burst into the open at point-blank range, then suddenly grinned and relaxed. In between the bursts of firing he could hear unmistakable cries of "Down Styphon!"

Kalvan dismounted half the Horse Guards to support the dragoons and led the rest toward the left in search of a way through the trees. A cluster of mounted men materialized out of the dust ahead. Kalvan had his pistol drawn before he recognized Hestophes. The general was splattered with blood and his sword was caked with it; its edge looked as if he'd used it to chop wood. His face was covered with a dried reddish mud of blood and dust, but from the way he was grinning Kalvan doubted he was wounded.

"Your Majesty! It had come down to cold steel in the last attack, when you hit the Harphaxi from the rear. The attack on Tavern Hill died out, which was just as well. Some of the mercenaries found the wine cellar, and I wasn't sure if they could tell friend from foe—or hit anyone if they could. We used the cavalry to clean out the center and Barn Hill, and by then their horses were too blown to charge again. So I left them and the mercenaries on our old position and marched the infantry to where I thought we might meet you."

"Good work," said Kalvan. "Hestophes, try not to get killed in the rest of the battle. I'm going to make you a Baron if it's the last edict I ever sign."

Hestophes's grin turned into a gape of surprise. After he regained his composure he said, "Well, then I'll have to keep Your Majesty alive as well. So if you will—"

"Hestophes, if you start playing mother hen, I'll write out the edict here and now and give it to someone to take to Rylla. That way it won't matter if I survive or not."

Kalvan could make out the blush on Hestophes's face even through the grime. "Very well, Your Majesty. I also picked up the Hostigi militia regiments somewhere off there," he added, with a wave toward the northwest. "Euklestes met the wrong end of a halberd, and I didn't want to leave them alone."

"Damn," said Kalvan. Euklestes hadn't been any military genius, but he'd been intelligent enough to learn. He'd also known that his cousin Baron Sthentros was likely to do something stupid or even treasonable out of his hatred for Kalvan. Euklestes had kept an eye on Sthentros without Kalvan, Skranga, or Klestreus having to do anything that would ruffle the feathers of the Hostigi nobility.

This was no time to think about politics, not in the middle

of a battle, even if he was Great King and politics was part of the job. Kalvan listened to the noise of the fight on the other side of the trees and discovered that both the firing and the shouts of "Down Styphon!" were dying away.

"Let's join the infantry."

By the time they'd done that, the Hostigi were no longer entirely infantry; a troop of the Second Horse Guards and most of the First Dragoons had joined in the final stages of the fight. Soon afterward, the last of the Harphaxi infantry died or surrendered; the halberdiers of the Royal Household Guard mostly died. A few surviving infantrymen were running off to the south, and Kalvan had to hold Nicomoth from turning his troopers loose on them.

"From the dust clouds, I'd say the Harphaxi rear guard is somewhere off there." It struck Kalvan that this battle might be known forever after to its veterans as the Battle of Somewhere Off There. "Besides, I think we're going to have visitors here in a little while." He pointed to a glittering mass of heavy cavalry on a hillside about a mile to the east. On this side of the copse the fields hadn't yet been scoured bare by the marching armies and the dust was less choking. "That must be the Royal Lancers of Hos-Harphax. Their honor won't let them leave the field without charging us."

Nicomoth's reply was a blissful smile. The idea of crossing swords with the highest nobility of a Great Kingdom was irresistible. Not even the Treasure of Balph could have tempted him into riding off the field now.

Not that it would take some lobster-headed notion of honor to produce an attack on the Hostigi. As far as Prince Philesteus would be able to see, Kalvan's force of infantry was the main obstacle to the retreat of thousands of Harphaxi to the north and east, not to mention being no match for a charge by heavy cavalry. Kalvan wished he had about a thousand more cavalry of his own, preferably under Phrames—and where was the Count, anyway?

At least he could hope that knightly quarrels over precedence would delay the Harphaxi charge until he was ready to receive it. Certainly Hestophes was trying to be in three places at once, organizing the position with five four-pounders and the Hostigi militia on the right, five regiments and ten to twelve mercenary companies in the center, and Kalvan with the Horse Guards and Dragoons on the left by the trees. The infantry were arranged in a line of staggered squares of pikemen and musketeers, with the halberdiers in among the musketeers.

Damn the smiths for dragging their feet on bore-standardization so that proper socket bayonets were years away! Maybe plug bayonets would be worthwhile after all; every infantryman carried a knife of some sort. . . .

Distant trumpets sounded and sunlight flamed on dancing lance tips and silvered and gilded armor suddenly on the move. The Royal Lancers were charging. Behind them came five squadrons of the Royal Pistoleers, each with a red-bordered yellow sash and an armored gauntlet holding a pistol, and about a thousand mercenary cavalry, half with lance and half with pistol or musketoon. The total was about three thousand heavy cavalry, most of it the cream of the Harphaxi army.

The front rank of the Harphaxi line was a riot of color; each lance had its own pennon, and anyone of the rank of baron or above had his own personal banner carried by a man-at-arms. Kalvan imagined that the Harphaxi line looked very much like that of the French at Crécy or Agincourt before the English bowmen went to work.

Hestophes had taken a position among the guns on the left. When the Lancers were eight hundred yards away, his sword flashed down and all five guns let fly at once. Long range for case shot, Kalvan thought—then saw Harphaxi chargers going down in a way that told him they were firing round shot. Hestophes must have been gambling on the four-pounders' rate of fire to let him get off a few salvos of round shot before the Harphaxi rode close enough to use case. Kalvan only hoped the gunners could do the job.

Hestophes hit the Lancers with two salvos of round shot before switching to case. Between the roar of the cannon Kalvan could hear the screams of wounded men and horses. The Lancers left at least fifty men and horses behind, and briefly spread out to avoid trampling their casualties. The more optimistic among them couched their lances.

Kalvan hoped Hestophes hadn't accidentally scared them into dispersing so much they'd make a less vulnerable target, then saw he needn't have worried. The first two ranks were thickening up again into a solid wall of flesh and armor

decorated with crests and coats of arms. Every noble house in
Hos-Harphax must have a son or nephew in the charge, and
every house must want its banner first into the Hostigi lines.

Five hundred yards, four hundred—Kalvan saw that the
Lancers wore complete armor, like fifteenth-century knights.
They were magnificent; any back-home museum director
would have died of joy at the sight of all that armor.

The Lancers themselves were about to die of something
else—being four hundred years out of date for a charge
against massed, disciplined infantry with muskets and pikes.

Three hundred yards, two hundred—

"Down Styphon!"

The four-pounders crashed. Sunlight blazed into Kalvan's
eyes from pike points and halberd heads swinging into fighting
position. Then a thousand muskets and five hundred arquebuses let fly so nearly at once that the sound hammered at
Kalvan's ears like a single gigantic discharge.

The Harphaxi line was a target a blind man couldn't have
missed, so densely packed it not only couldn't evade but
blocked the riders behind it when it went down. The whole
leading third of the Lancers fell into a hideous tangle of men
and horses, mostly fallen, many writhing and screaming, a few
already silently being crushed into pulp under flailing hooves
and rolling bodies. A suit of plate armor was little protection
if a one-ton horse mad with pain rolled over it.

The Harphaxi left tried to wheel and face the guns. They
took another salvo of case shot at no more than three hundred
yards while they were wheeling, but the survivors did charge
the guns. By then the rightmost infantry regiment, Queen
Rylla's Foot, was moving forward to support the artillery and
stiffen the militia. *That regiment is definitely going to get
some kind of unit citation.* Its muskets tore at the Harphaxi
flank while the artillery hammered them in front, and the attack melted away.

This left a bend that was almost a gap in the Hostigi line,
and Kalvan saw Hestophes riding back and forth, shifting the
King's Lifeguards to cover the gap. For about three minutes
only three of the five regiments were firing into the main body
of the Harphaxi. Kalvan drew his sword, ready to lead the
cavalry down to the aid of the infantry if the Harphaxi got to
close quarters. Not all the dismounted men were dead or even

disabled, and they were marching forward with a determination that would have been magnificent if it hadn't been so completely suicidal.

Kalvan quickly saw that the infantry didn't need help. The halberdiers of the King's Lifeguards were moving out into the open, swinging their weapons enthusiastically. This kept the ranked musketeers of the Lifeguards from shooting, but not the marksmen in each company. They dropped back and opened aimed fire on any Harphaxi who wasn't being engaged by a halberdier.

Meanwhile, the hammering of the Harphaxi continued, with the artillery on their flank and the musketeers to their front. Kalvan saw one splendidly armored knight lose an arm to case shot, have a leg crushed under his horse, crawl out to be hit in the face by a musket ball and blinded, and be finished off by a halberd blow that split both his helmet and his head.

Kalvan thought of five generations of Hapsburg and Burgundian knights dying miserably under the pikes and halberds of the Swiss. He hoped it wouldn't take the heavy cavalry that long here-and-now, even if their stupidity might make his job easier. He did not want to watch too many more battles like this one.

The Royal Lancers had lost too many of their captains to let them organize for another charge, but their honor wouldn't let them retreat. The Royal Pistoleers and most of the mercenary cavalry weren't so badly hit, although too far out of effective range to do much harm with their pistols and musketoons. Kalvan saw several of their captains organizing a charge, using the Lancers as a shield to cover their movement. He ordered the Horse Guards to mount up.

The cannon were firing independently now, and Kalvan saw Hestophes order them to prepare a salvo. He hoped their fireseed was holding out.

As the Pistoleers and mercenaries worked their way forward, they began to add surviving Lancers to their strength. They were moving slowly, but the carnage around them and the surviving Lancers absorbed most of the Hostigi firepower. Kalvan saw Hestophes signaling frantically to the trumpeters to sound the recall, so they could pull the battle-maddened halberdiers out of the line of fire.

The Lifeguards, closest to the trumpeters, responded first and quickly withdrew. Many of the others couldn't or didn't want to hear; they died in the first salvo. For once the Harphaxi got off lightly. Kalvan saw now that they were pressing home their charge at his center. Hestophes hadn't been sitting on his hands; the pikemen stood in ranks four deep with the musketeers and arquebusiers in the rear. Hestophes's cannon fired a last ragged salvo; the Harphaxi line shuddered briefly, then crashed into the Hostigi pikes.

The pike line wavered, buckled for a moment in the center, then stiffened as the rear ranks reformed. The musketeers were useless now, and the artillery didn't dare fire for fear of hitting friend as well as foe. A few halberdiers were fighting in the front ranks, but too many had been killed when they refused to withdraw. Only the King's Lifeguards had enough halberdiers left, but they were pinned down on the right, keeping the Harphaxi from taking Hestophes's four-pounders and turning them on the Hostigi center.

The entire Hostigi center was being pushed into a giant crescent as the men in the middle slowly gave way before the point-blank fire of the Royal Pistoleers. Some of the musketeers were picking up fallen pikes or using their swords like Spanish sword-and-buckler men but not nearly as successfully. It said a lot for their esprit de corps and Hestophes's ability as a commander, but Kalvan could see it wasn't going to hold the Harphaxi charge.

Kalvan wished fervently that Count Phrames or *somebody* would come charging through the trees like the U.S. Cavalry, but he knew it wasn't going to happen. It was up to him with his little cavalry force to turn the battle or face the first major defeat of the day. He didn't need to remind himself how little Hostigos could afford that.

Kalvan now commanded about two hundred of the Second Royal Horse Guards as well as the First Dragoons with nearly their full strength of two hundred mounted pikemen and two hundred mounted musketeers, and the surviving Ulthori. He divided the Dragoons, sending the pikemen behind the Hostigi lines to reinforce the center and leaving two thirds of the musketeers to remain behind and hold the present position. The fifty best riders among the musketeers were about to become temporary light cavalry. Kalvan convinced the Horse Guards to give up their extra pistols by giving the musketeers' captain the two from his boot tops.

In the few minutes it took to give the orders and mount up,

the Hostigi center had begun to look like a classic double envelopment. It would have been one, too, if the pike line hadn't been in so much danger of breaking. With reinforcements in the right places and Kalvan's small cavalry force to close the noose, they might just pull it off.

If they didn't—well, he hoped that Harmakros and Phrames had learned their lessons well. Rylla's and his unborn child's life depended on it.

For his big roll of the dice, Kalvan decided to ignore Nicomoth's protests and lead the charge himself. The sudden appearance of Great King Kalvan—or the Daemon Kalvan, as the Styphoni called him—just might give the Hostigi a certain psychological edge. Dralm only knew, they needed any and every kind of edge they could get now!

He raised his saber in one hand and a rifled pistol in the other.

"Down Styphon!"

Thunderous shouts of "Kalvan!" and "Hostigos!" rose behind him, then the even more thunderous sound of hundreds of horses on the move.

The Hostigi and their horses were both comparatively fresh; they hit the Harphaxi rear like a blacksmith's hammer striking soft steel. The Harphaxi line gave and buckled as horse-pinned troopers tried to turn their mounts. For a moment Kalvan's worst fear was that the Hostigi would push the Harphaxi right through the weakening pike line, then he saw the Harphaxi rear going from tightly packed to crushed. The pikes were holding; the jaws of the double envelopment were closing.

The first four men Kalvan killed didn't even know he was behind them. Others knew but had no room to fight and no place to run. It was like one of the old buffalo hunts, with the buffalo hunters circling the herd and slaughtering them with Sharps rifles. The Harphaxi stayed in their saddles and kept firing until they were shot down into the writhing or still bodies on the bloody, churned ground.

At some point Hestophes ordered the halberdiers of the King's Lifeguards into the press. A few of the mercenaries surrendered, but most couldn't make themselves heard through the screams of men and horses. What remained of the Lancers and the Pistoleers refused to surrender; some cut down any mercenary within reach who dared to make Galzar's Oath.

Since they wouldn't surrender and couldn't attack, they did the only thing they could do—they died.

Hestophes rode up to Kalvan as the battle was grinding down to a close. He was no longer grinning; in fact, his face looked as if a grin would crack it. He shook his head slowly.

"I feel like a boy drowning kittens," he said. Then he added, "We do have a few prisoners. Two of them have said they saw Prince Philesteus go down after a halberd struck him on the head."

"We'll want to make a search for his body," said Kalvan. He was thinking of Charles the Bold of Burgundy, who'd died in a similar fashion from a Swiss halberd at the Battle of Nancy. He also didn't want a generation of pretenders claiming to be the heir to Hos-Harphax raising armies or at least making trouble.

"If we find it, I want it sent back to King Kaiphranos with all due honor." No need to tell an old soldier like Hestophes that Prince Philesteus might be a little hard to recognize after being hacked down and trampled. At least the Prince had died the way he would have wanted to, and wouldn't have to live to mull over what an idiot he'd been.

III.

Except for the search party, Kalvan and Hestophes kept their men in formation. This provoked some grumbling; not even the most disciplined new-style infantryman could remain untempted by the awe-inspiring amount of loot the dead Lancers and Pistoleers represented. The grumbling ceased when a cloud of dust from the north signaled the approach of another large mounted force. Everyone was tired and thirsty, and the musketeers were down to about five rounds apiece, so if this was a fresh enemy force. . . .

It turned out to be Prince Armanes with his Nyklosi heavy

cavalry and a thousand mercenaries. Phrames was with him; he'd had his horse shot out from under him early in the counterattack and sprained a wrist as well, making it hard for him to catch another one.

Phrames's arrival also solved the problem of what to do with Prince Armanes. The Prince had advanced to join Kalvan without waiting for orders from Harmakros or even bothering to find out if Harmakros needed his help more than Kalvan. Apparently he'd thought that once Hestophes no longer needed his rear protected and Harmakros had attacked, he could go to the most "honorable" part of the battlefield— under the eye of his Great King.

What Kalvan had here was a problem not of tactics but of diplomacy. It was a problem that he would rather have put off until the shooting stopped, but there was no way to do that—and no easy solution, either.

Sending Prince Armanes back in disgrace without his cavalry would be an impossible insult. Sending his cavalry back with him would simply keep them marching for another hour, wearing out their horses without meeting an enemy. Keeping him here would leave Harmakros with no one guarding his back except for the reserves, who didn't have a first-class commander.

However, Kalvan now had one to spare. "Count Phrames, will you ride back north and take command of the reserves, under Harmakros? He will be facing the Zarthani Knights before long, if he isn't already, so keep your men together and take them all."

"Except for enough to guard the baggage."

"Of course," said Kalvan. Great Dralm, he must be getting tired to forget that! Sarrask of Sask had never stopped complaining about the looting of his baggage by some mercenary company at the Battle of Fyk.

"Spare mercenaries—we take their oaths to Galzar. Regular Harphaxi troops are to be guarded closely. The Harphaxi levies—frankly, I think the best thing to do is strip them of arms and armor and send them home."

Phrames grimaced as if he smelled something bad. "That will be turning them loose on their own people."

"Not without weapons, it won't be. Besides, better them looting Harphaxi farms than eating our rations." He doubted that many would ever see their homes again; those that weren't shot by farmers would either die of starvation or at the hands of bands of thieves and bandits. There would be little peace in Hos-Harphax this fall.

"Very true, Your Majesty."

Phrames turned away; Kalvan almost called him back to remind him to leave some men holding the West Gap to maintain communication between the two now widely separated wings of the Army of the Harph. Then he sighed and tried to spit in an unsuccessful effort to get the dust out of his throat. A quick pull from his jack of wine helped more. If Harmakros and Phrames didn't know enough by now to do that without being ordered, then he was completely wrong about both of them.

Right now, what he wanted was to sit down in some shade on soft grass and drink water until he could feel it slosh inside him. He looked past the acres of Harphaxi corpses to the hillside beyond. The grass looked nice and green there, and there were trees around an abandoned farmhouse that would surely have a well. . . .

EIGHTEEN

I.

"The ford is picketed, Captain."

"Styphoni?"

"None that I can see on either bank, sir. In fact, there's nobody at all on the far bank; on our side there's just a half company of Harphax City militia."

Captain Phidestros felt that he had cause to sigh with relief. With nothing but fifty or so clerks and stableboys to bar the passage of the Iron Company and no sign of rain, the way across the Harph was as sure as a captain could hope.

Phidestros spurred Snowdrift down the road toward the riverbank, Geblon and his six guards falling in behind. He made no effort at silence or concealment; against these bumblers either would be more likely to get him taken for an enemy.

"Ho! Who—who is it?" came from the cluster of figures on the bank. Several of them were wearing surcoats with the Harphax City coat of arms, a black portcullis, but most of them wore leather jacks or peasants' garb. They looked like a flimsy collection of scarecrows who'd have a hard time not being blown away in the first stiff breeze.

"The Iron Company of Captain Phidestros. Let us pass."

This exchange took Phidestros over the best part of the remaining distance to the riverbank, where two men stepped out into the road. One carried an antique arquebus, the other wore a rusty back-and-breast and carried a drawn sword.

"I am Captain Habros of the Cordwainer's Guild Arquebusiers. What is your business here?" said the swordsman. He was looking beyond Phidestros as he spoke, at the head of the Iron Company now in sight on the road.

"To cross the Harph."

Habros took a deep breath. "I have orders to let no one pass without permission."

"Whose permission?" If Habros took too many deep breaths, Phidestros was going to demonstrate how meaningless permission was by shooting him dead where he stood. "Nobody is giving or withholding permission for anything. At least I haven't heard that anybody who could is still alive and free." It began to dawn on him that these people might not have heard the full tale of the day's fighting and the utter overthrow of the Harphaxi army.

So he told it briefly, without going into detail or venting his rage at the follies he'd seen, such as the advance through the Middle Gap and the charge of the Royal Lancers. He did not even mention that Prince Philesteus was known to be dead and Duke Aesthes a Hostigi prisoner, merely saying that he had not been easy in his mind about the safety and freedom of either for some time.

By the time Phidestros was finished, Captain Habros was noticeably paler, even in the fading light. "I—we had not heard such . . ." He swallowed. "We had heard that the battle was not going well from some of the City companies retreating, about two hours ago. They said they'd gone far enough to see Styphon's Own Guard retreating or falling back before the Hostigi, but no other friendly troops. We also heard tales of the peasants being up in arms against us."

The "City companies" must be part of the five thousand or so of the Harphaxi rear guard who'd turned around and started back toward the city without firing a shot, even in support of the Styphoni. They certainly wouldn't have seen enough of the battle to describe it clearly. Those Harphaxi who'd not only survived but escaped from the north could tell the whole tale, but they'd be moving farther inland rather than toward the Harph where they risked being swept up by the Hostigi cavalry.

As for the peasant uprising, there at least Phidestros could do these poor wretches a good turn. "We took two of those 'peasants' ourselves and questioned them, then hanged them. They're not even Harphaxi! They're Ulthori fishermen, little better than bandits, that King Kalvan sent downriver to make as much mischief as they could. Guard your horses and weapons, but don't fear the peasants."

At least not until word of this day's work spreads. Even Great Kings have been overthrown by peasant uprisings after disasters like this.

"Thank you. But—how am I to let you pass. . . ?" Habros's voice trailed off as Phidestros drew his pistol and cocked it.

"By standing aside, and letting us do so."

Even a blind man could have counted the odds against the picket by listening to the stamping of horses and cocking of pistols all around the post.

"Pass, friend. May Galzar and Tranth be with you," Habros said with as much dignity as he could muster, then waved his men out of the road with his sword. A dozen Iron Company troopers rode down to the bank and dismounted. Those not told off for horse-holders began uncoiling ropes from their saddlebags and tying them into a single long line to be stretched across the Harph as a guide.

Phidestros would have given a good deal to be one of the line-stretchers. Not only would it be a good example for the Company, it would give him the closest thing to a bath he could expect for some days. His knee would not let him do heavy work in the chest-deep water of the swift-flowing Harph, and that was the end of it.

Thank Galzar, there was also an end in sight to the Iron Company's ordeal. By the time night was halfway through they would be on the west bank of the river, free to ride anywhere their horses would take them—and with no Hostigi following behind.

That had been Phidestros's only goal since he'd ridden away from the crossroads where the Royal Lancers had died almost to a man. His company had been among the mercenaries who had followed the Royal Pistoleers over the ruins of the Lancers in their futile attack against the Hostigi pike line. Kalvan's ruse had been perfect; the Hostigi line gave way until the Harphaxi were almost surrounded, then he drew the noose tight! If the Iron Company hadn't been to the left of Kalvan's charge, they would be feeding the carrion birds right now. Instead Phidestros had seen what was about to happen and escaped with about two hundred mercenaries, but he'd still left thirty good men behind, and some of Lamochares's men had simply deserted.

He'd made up for all the losses, with a whole new company and fifty-odd men who'd ridden in by twos and threes, all looking for a leader who would take them to safety and was not disposed to ask too many questions. He'd entered the battle with three hundred men and a gun; he'd be leaving it with no gun but four hundred men, reasonably well armed and well mounted, and above all ready to follow him anywhere. The question now was—where?

The only friendly army within reach was Soton's Army of the Pirsystros or Holy Host of Styphon, and they were a five-days' ride across doubtfully friendly country. Yet Phidestros was not ready to turn bandit and see his command fall apart. He saw no hope of safety in Hos-Harphax itself. It would be a notable gift from the gods if the Harphaxi got back from to-day's battle a single gun or more than one man in three. It was enough to make a man begin to *believe* in demons!

There was nothing and nobody left to keep Kalvan from marching up to the walls of Harphax City and summoning Kaiphranos the Timid (probably destined to be known as Kaiphranos the Witless after today) to give him terms. Nor would there be a thing Kaiphranos could do but hide under his wife's bed.

Before that happened, Phidestros wanted to be well away from anyplace to be covered by Kalvan's terms. He hadn't heard that Prince Sarrask of Sask rode with the Great King's host, but he knew that the Prince had a long memory and an unforgiving temper. The Great King was a man for rewarding his friends, and if Sarrask asked as a reward the head of one Phidestros, who'd looted his baggage train at the Battle of Fyk. . . .

"Captain! The first man's across!"

Phidestros strained his eyes into the darkness and saw a dim figure on the far bank shaking himself like a dog as he waved his arms. The Iron Company sent up a cheer until Phidestros and the petty-captains shouted them into silence for fear of attracting unwanted attention.

II.

"That's all of them?" Kalvan asked. He'd counted no more than a couple of hundred men in the line of bedraggled and mud-smeared Harphaxi prisoners standing in the torchlight.

"All the ones we fished out, Your Majesty," said the mercenary captain. "I think some of the Mobile Force picked up more somewhere off there." A callused hand pointed off into the darkness. "There's a lot more out in the swamp, but Hadron's Undercaverns have them now." Which was a polite way of saying that even Great King Kalvan would be wasting his breath if he ordered the mercenaries any farther into the swamp.

Kalvan wasn't going to order anything of the kind; it must be nearly midnight, and from the way he felt himself he was surprised anyone in the Hostigi army was still on his feet or even awake. The heavy fighting had ended about three o'clock in the afternoon, except against the Zarthani Knights in the north; the mopping-up and pursuit had gone on until well after dark.

At least it had gone on in the south, against the left flank of the Harphaxi. In the north, the Zarthani Knights and Styphon's Own Guard had died nearly to the last man, but in the process they'd fought Harmakros and Phrames to a standstill. Most of the Harphaxi right who hadn't been bagged already had escaped through the Middle Gap, at least five thousand men. Not a single gun, though, and Harmakros's messenger reported that the Gap was choked with abandoned wagons and discarded weapons and armor. It was a rabble, not an army, that was fleeing toward Harphax City from the Heights.

The one part of the Harphaxi left that got away did so in better order. Four or five thousand of the rear guard had been sighted on the Great Harph Road shortly after Phrames rode north. Before Kalvan could deploy to receive them, he had to finish the Slaughter at Ryklos Farm, the name now given to the massacre of Prince Philesteus's cavalry force. The only survivors of that engagement were a band of mercenaries led by a big man on a white charger. He seemed to enjoy a

charmed life, until he'd finally pulled his men out ju
Kalvan struck the Harphaxi rear.

By the time the massacre was complete, the Harphaxi r
guard had been warned of its danger. They'd turned ar
departed with more haste than dignity, although they didn
disintegrate into a rabble, thanks to a Temple Band of
Styphon's Own Guard who stood and died to a man. By the
time they'd finished dying, Kalvan's cavalry were too blown
for rapid pursuit, his infantry were nearly out of ammunition,
and there were too many miscellaneous groups of fugitives
roaming about who needed rounding up.

One of the largest bands of Harphaxi survivors had decided
that the dry weather of the past week had made it safe to try
wading the swamp on either side of Hogwallow Creek. The
ones who'd lived to learn they were wrong were now being
fished out by the Hostigi and packed off to an improvised
POW compound where Kalvan had captured the four bombards.

Kalvan intended to carry out his original plan of releasing
most of the disarmed prisoners tomorrow, after the Hostigi
had brought up supplies, tended their wounded, and policed
up the battlefield. Right now it was littered with discarded
weapons, which might tempt a disarmed Harphaxi to rearm
himself and make trouble, if not for the Hostigi at least for his
own people. Phrames was right; there was no point in making
the lot of the losing civilians any more miserable than it would
be already.

Kalvan sat on his horse as the mercenaries bound their
prisoners. Even allowing for their bedraggled condition, they
were like too many of the Harphaxi troops Kalvan had seen
this day: ". . . discarded unjust serving-men, younger sons to
younger brothers, revolted tapsters and ostlers trade fall'n; the
cankers of a calm world and a long peace; ten times more
dishonorable ragged than an old-faced ancient." There'd been
plenty of those all right, as well as a few boys not much older
than Harmakros's son. Like Falstaff before them, the Harphaxi captains could say, "If I be not ashamed of my soldiers
I am a soused gurnet. I have misused the king's press damn-
ably"—not to mention losing the Great King's battle. Kalvan
didn't recall what a gurnet was, but he certainly recalled seeing
some of the Harphaxi captains properly soused. Not just the
captains, either; he'd helped round up about a hundred

naries who'd found a wagonload of beer and drunk until
could barely stand, let alone fight.

hat was one of the few times Kalvan had to keep his men
m killing prisoners—when they discovered that the beer
as all gone!

III.

It took Kalvan nearly an hour to grope his way
through the aftermath of the Battle of the Heights of
Chothros to HQ. By the time he saw its fires in the distance, he
knew that either he was getting a second wind or he was too
tired to sleep. Just as well—it never hurt royal dignity to stay
awake until your generals had finished reporting.

HQ proper had been moved into the cellar of a Tudor-style
manor house, once a fine, fortified dwelling but now little
more than a ruin above ground. It stood in a patch of second-
growth timber, and so many Hostigi had pitched tents and lit
campfires in and around the trees that Kalvan had to dismount
and lead his horse the last hundred yards for fear of treading
on a sleeping soldier.

He groped his way down the dark stairs to the torchlit War
Room and was pulling off his gloves when he noticed a pile of
bloodstained bandages on the corner of the map table, and
under it a pair of boots that had obviously been cut off somebody's feet. A policeman's instinct for something being
wrong, as well as a soldier's, had him uneasy before he saw the
faces of the men in the room. The generals were all there except Hestophes, which was strange in itself considering how
badly they must need sleep, and—

"What's wrong?"

Everyone looked at everyone else, waiting for someone to
speak out. About the time the silence was beginning to grow
uncomfortable, Count Phrames stepped forward. "We've just

had a dispatch from the Army of the Besh.''

Kalvan took a close look at the grim faces surrounding him and sat down.

"It's from Prince Ptosphes."

Kalvan sighed. That was a relief; at least he wouldn't have to tell his wife her father was dead or mortally wounded. Phrames looked as shaken as if he'd been facing a band of Styphon's Red Hand by himself. "Out with it, man!" Kalvan said, much louder than he'd intended.

"Ptosphes lost a battle to the Styphoni at Tenabra." Now that it was finally out in the open, Phrames looked as if he'd just cast off a hundred-pound pack.

"It was no shame to him," said Harmakros hastily.

"Of course not," said Kalvan, moving his hand through the air as if to push the words away.

"There was treachery," Harmakros continued. "Balthar the Black of Beshta broke our left flank and Soton saw the gap." Then they were all trying to talk at once, until Kalvan had to shout for silence. They looked at him with widened eyes, and he realized for the first time that his royal anger had the power to reduce these tough generals and noblemen to guilty schoolboys. It wasn't a pleasant feeling, still less so on top of the bad news.

"I think one of us should speak for us all," said Prince Armanes. He had a bloody bandage around his right ear, and the hair on that temple had been roughly hacked off. "I will yield the honor to Count Harmakros."

Kalvan threw the Prince a grateful look for his tact and nodded to Harmakros.

"As I said, Balthar's treachery left a gap in our right. The first troops Grand Master Soton sent through were his mercenary cavalry, but they held it open while he brought up the Knights. Meanwhile, Chartiphon and Sarrask of Sask drove back the Styphoni right under Lord High Marshal Mnesiphoklos. When the Zarthani Knights attacked, our left disintegrated, and Mnesiphoklos was able to rally his Ktemnoi Squares against Chartiphon. Ptosphes ordered the infantry in the center to hold on to the death. They did. Meanwhile, he pulled our right back and gathered in the survivors from the left, then ordered a retreat.''

"Who brought the news?''

"One of Uncle Wolf Tharses's priests with an escort. They stole fresh horses as their own died and lost three men. The priest himself was wounded. He also brought the dispatch from Ptosphes."

"Has anyone read it?"

"No." Harmakros held the parchment gingerly as though it were hot. "It was for you."

Kalvan mentally counted to ten, and when that didn't work, to twenty. "The next time Ptosphes sends a letter with bad news, anybody who may need to know it can read it. That means all of you. Please don't ever again wait for me when an hour can make the difference between victory and defeat." The schoolboy expression was back on their faces as he picked up the square of parchment with Ptosphes's seal on it. "And wake up Hestophes. I'm afraid we'll need a Council of War." He drew his knife and cut through the yellow wax seal with Ptosphes's crossed halberds stamped in it.

The letter told the same story as Harmakros, but in more detail. It struck Kalvan as odd to be reading the tale of a disaster in Ptosphes's usual firm, neat writing; horror stories ought to be scrawled and scribbled. It was a horror story, too, even if it seemed a little less horrible toward the end—

—the good service of Sarrask of Sask. He fought most valiantly on the field, and has done further good work since. Thanks to him, several Saski castles will be properly garrisoned and fit to receive our wounded and defend them. Without his labors, we would be in danger of having to abandon more than three thousand of our wounded, including Prince Pheblon of Nostor.

I have with me, fit for battle, not more than ten thousand men, the greater part of them cavalry. Four fifths of our infantry, apart from the loss of Prince Balthar's two thousand men, is taken or slain. We have only six guns left. However, some three thousand mercenary cavalry have fled; some may return to their duty before we have crossed Sask. Also, Sarrask's plans to defend several Saski castles will force Soton to slow his advance, to blockade them, storm them, or even besiege them, a task for which he has as yet no proper artillery train. Prisoners say that one may be among the reinforcements he is ex-

pected to receive in the next few days, but they are not sure.

"They usually aren't," muttered Kalvan, then apologized when he realized he'd spoken out loud.

I fear that Sask and southern Hostigos will still lie open to the cavalry of the Holy Host, particularly the Zarthani Knights under Grand Master Soton. Both, I must admit, have lived up to their reputation. Therefore, I can see no hope for anything but a prompt retreat to Hostigos to prepare for a stand there. With the garrison troops and the reserve militia to add to my strength, I may be able to meet Soton and Mnesiphoklos with not less than fifteen thousand men, but it is clearly urgent that we receive additional strength from the Army of the Harph as soon as possible.

"He'll receive the whole damned army," said Kalvan, then scanned the last paragraph.

I have prepared a list of men who have done particularly good service in this battle, so that they or their families may be rewarded by the Great Crown of Hos-Hostigos. That list I am sending north at once with a messenger who will entrust it to Rylla for safeguarding if I do not survive the retreat.

With most earnest hopes for Your Majesty's continued good health and good fortune, I am.

> *Your Obedient Servant*
> *Ptosphes*
> *First Prince of Hos-Hostigos*
> *Prince of Old Hostigos*
> *Commander, Army of the Besh*

"Here," Kalvan said, handing the letter to Harmakros. "Actually, it's not as bad as I'd expected." This didn't seem to console anybody, but they all took turns with the letter while Kalvan tried to organize his thoughts so that when he had to speak he could give a convincing imitation of a man who knew what he was talking about.

One decision he'd already taken: all future operations

against the Harphaxi were going to have to be canceled. That was irritating, to say the least, since that killed the best chance he'd ever have of making peace with Kaiphranos. With his elder son dead, his younger son fit only to be a king of the brothels, his Captain-General a prisoner, and his brother a scheming son of fifty fathers, not to mention an army either nonexistent or useless, Kaiphranos might actually be brought to make peace with Hos-Hostigos. A precarious peace, to be sure—it would last just as long as Kaiphranos did, and he could die literally any day. Still, any peace was better than a war on two fronts—and now it was impossible.

"What I want to know is," said Harmakros, "who is this Sarrask of Sask that Prince Ptosphes praises so highly? Was this the son-of-a-she-wolf who was promising to put Ptosphes's and Rylla's heads on pikes outside Tarr-Hostigos?"

"Right," echoed Phrames.

The Reverend Morrison would have said Sarrask had been touched by the Spirit of the Lord. Any number of English teachers or psychiatrists would have called it "Identification with the Aggressor." Kalvan thought it was most likely the case of the schoolyard bully, who after being thoroughly beaten up becomes the best friend of the boy who whipped him. Whatever the reason, it was good to know that Sarrask could now be trusted, even if the price for this information seemed a little steep!

By the time everybody had finished the letter, Hestophes arrived, looking like a cross between a hibernating bear and a candidate for a vagrancy arrest. Since Hestophes couldn't read anything other than map symbols and tavern signs, Kalvan read Ptosphes's letter to him. *Note: Find a way to get Hestophes to read without damaging his pride.* Kalvan couldn't afford to allow one of his most valuable generals to remain illiterate.

When Kalvan was finished briefing Hestophes he said, "I'd like to spend a day or two here. That would make the Harphaxi panic, sure we were going to march on Harphax City. Unfortunately, we don't have any time to spend just frightening the Styphon out of the Harphaxi. So we're going to stay here just long enough to pick our march routes, collect the wounded, and see what we can do about the captured Harphaxi guns. We've collected something like seventy, and

Ptosphes just lost thirty. If we can bring back even a score, it will help.''

"We're going to need more horses for the gun-teams," said Alkides.

Hestophes was nodding slowly, either in agreement or because he was about to fall asleep again. "I'll see what I can do, Alkides. I *think* we have more horses than we need to cover our own losses.''

"Good." Kalvan rose cautiously to his feet and bent over the map table. For a second he had to brace himself firmly on both legs and with both arms to avoid knocking over the table and setting HQ on fire with the lighted candles. "We'll have to use a march route well to the north of our old one anyway. I doubt there's enough forage left along that route to feed a scrawny pair of oxen. Not being able to go through southern Beshta isn't going to hurt much. I swear on Dralm's Sacred Staff that Balthar's turn will come as soon as the Styphoni have been pushed back to Hos-Ktemnos." Then he thought of Harmakros's son. If the Beshtans found out who the boy was and found Tarr-Locra weakly defended—

"Harmakros, you can send two squadrons of horse under a trusted captain to scout southern Beshta. Find out what the people think. Somewhere around here." Harmakros looked at the map, then started as he saw where Kalvan's dagger-point rested.

"Thank you, Your Majesty." Harmakros couldn't turn his back on his King, so Kalvan looked away briefly by turning to Alkides and asking if there was enough powder to blow up the Harphaxi guns they couldn't haul away.

"We've got twelve wagons of Styphon's Best, most not worth the horsepower to haul it away.''

"Good. We're short on Hostigos Unconsecrated, so use it sparingly.

"Phrames, I want you to take two thousand of your best mounted men and four guns and do a repeat performance of your spring raid. Only this time you'll swing northeast, toward the Agrysi border. Make enough of a mess to start the Agrysi worrying and tie down their garrisons, then swing back and rejoin Harmakros after—oh, no more than five days. Seven, if you can live off the land.''

He might hear something from Xentos if the raid provoked King Demistophon into action against the Great Council of

Dralm. Xentos would also hear something from his Great King if he expected the Great King to run military risks in order to let priests argue.

Phrames nodded. His powder-blackened face set in the mask that meant he didn't like making war on civilians but would obey his Great King to the death. Phrames, Kalvan decided, was almost too good a man for here-and-now; he really belonged at King's Arthur's Round Table.

"We can't stay here before Harphax City long enough to make Soton worry about our crossing the Harph and hitting him from the rear. But we can help Ptosphes by scaring the Agrysi badly enough that all the Princes and merchants will scream if Great King Demistophon sends one more mercenary or one more pound of fireseed against Hostigos."

The general staff either understood or didn't have the strength left to argue. Kalvan realized that if they didn't all get some sleep, the HQ of the Army of the Balph were going to be as useless as the beer-sodden mercenaries.

"Now, if you don't all want to be accused of attempted regicide, will one of you get me some food and wine? Also a bed, if there's any straw left within a day's ride."

He was too tired to eat the bread and cheese when it came, but not to drink the wine or even notice that it was pretty awful. After the wine, he wasn't surprised to find himself falling asleep easily, but he was pleasantly surprised not to have any nightmares.

Apparently, "great murthering battles" were good for *something*.

NINETEEN

I.

The conveyor-head rotunda that provided the direct paratemporal link with Fourth Level Aryan-Transpacific, Kalvan Subsector, was as large as many commercial depots that Sirna had seen. Inside the rotunda were five domes of metallic mesh, containing two thirty-foot conveyors, two fifty-foot conveyors, and one hundred-footer, the standard for commercial or passenger transport. Baltov Eldra was standing in front of one of the fifty-footers, giving the Second Kalvan Study-Team its final briefing while the University technicians prepared the conveyor for paratemporal transposition.

"So Kalvan had to retreat, with twenty-two captured guns and a lot of other miscellaneous booty, including several thousand ounces of silver. Before he started back to Hos-Hostigos, he released Captain-General Duke Aesthes, with only a token ransom, to escort Prince Philesteus's body back to Harphax City."

"Of course," interrupted Gorath Tran, a tall man with spider-thin limbs. "Kalvan couldn't release Aesthes without any ransom at all because that would be an insult, implying that the Duke was so incompetent that his services were of no value at all."

"They were," said Eldra. Sirna thought she spoke somewhat brusquely. Eldra didn't like being interrupted by pointless displays of erudition in her own field. Nor did she appear to like spindly University administrators who took up valuable space that could better be used by historians or other trained scholars.

"Now Kalvan was free to start for home." With the point of her dagger, Eldra traced the lines of Kalvan's homeward march on the map. "He didn't need to worry about the Harphaxi, but he took precautions against any moves by the Agrysi and the Beshtans.

"To frighten the Agrysi—" A series of clunks and clanks followed by a burst of electronic beeps and whistles interrupted her. She thrust her dagger clear through the map into the wooden tabletop. "Can't you work more quietly?"

"Professor, do you want to leave today or don't you?" came the reply from inside the metallic dome. "Besides, that was the next to last test. One more, and either this old lady will be ready to go or else you'll have to find another conveyor."

Eldra frowned, and Sirna didn't blame her. Styphon's Holy Host was rapidly approaching the borders of Hostigos, and the Hostigi were digging in for a last-ditch stand. Any more delays, and the University's new team might find themselves in the middle of a battle, or at least in a country overrun with cavalry patrols from both sides inclined to shoot first and ask questions later. A day more or less wouldn't have made any difference on a Styphon's House time-line where war was being conducted in the old leisurely pre-Kalvan way, but Kalvan's Time-Line seemed to have discovered the—what was the Europe-American word for it?—the "blitzkreek."

Nor was it helping Eldra's mood that the maintenance technician insisted she use a paper map; a screen display would affect his tests. He'd tried to explain why and Eldra seemed to be convinced, but Sirna didn't understand more than one word in three. She understood the theory of the Ghaldron-Hesthor Paratemporal Field and the workings of a conveyor well enough to pass her Safety & Emergency Procedures tests, but anything more she knew would always remain arcane knowledge beyond her grasp, rather like Hadron Tharn's financial backing.

"But why did Kalvan send Count Phrames to the north?" asked Scholar Varnath, an expert on Preindustrial Sociology. She was a member of the University's Faculty Council and the oldest person on either Kalvan Study-Team.

"As I was about to say, Kalvan sent Phrames with a raiding

force to frighten the Agrysi and keep them neutral. He did a good job, as far as we can tell. He blew up bridges and minor forts in Thapigos, looted a Styphon's House temple-farm of four thousand ounces of gold and ten thousand of silver, freed and armed its slaves, and finally met the Household Guards of Thapigos under the Prince himself in a pitched battle just short of the border of Phaxos. The Thapigi lost about eight hundred men to Phrames's two hundred, and Prince Acestocleus himself was badly wounded. If he dies, that will be as good as winning another battle for Kalvan.

"Acestocleus is the son of a man who usurped the Princedom of Thapigos twenty years ago. The old Princely house was either executed or driven into exile in Hos-Agrys. They have about five candidates for the throne, two of them with marriage ties to the Agrysi royal house, which has always wanted to add Thapigos to Hos-Agrys. So if Acestocleus dies, there may be civil war cutting the land route between Hos-Harphax and Hos-Agrys, and possibly even war between the two Great Kingdoms.

"This won't be the only case of this kind of trouble in Harphax, either. It's been thirty years since anybody took King Kaiphranos seriously, and the Princes have fallen into the habit of doing more or less as they pleased."

"I still feel sorry for Kaiphranos," said Doctor Sankar Trav, the Team's medical man and Psychist. "His favorite son's dead, his kingdom's falling apart—"

"And it's all his own Dralm-damned fault, so don't waste any tears on him," said Aranth Saln. With his waxed mustache and shaved head, he was so at odds with his companions' appearance that he could have easily been mistaken for an outtimer or a Paratime Policeman on assignment. His only concession to Kalvan's Time-Line was that he was to wear a wig, although he refused to have it bonded to his scalp until they arrived. His specialty was Preindustrial Military Science.

"Besides," Aranth added, "Philesteus knew how to lead a cavalry charge and nothing else. He couldn't have undone the mess his father left behind in a hundred years, even without the Styphon's House-Kalvan war."

"Well, Kaiphranos doesn't exert much influence on events now. There's a rumor that he's so grief-striken he's confined to his bed. There's a nastier rumor that a Styphon's House agent has poisoned him.

"But enough of rumors," Eldra went on. "Count Phrames

then moved still farther north, through Phaxos. Prince Araxes wouldn't provide him with supplies, but he was able to buy some with the temple-farm loot. Next he crossed into Nostor, joined up with the reinforcements Prince Pheblon's Captain-General was sending, and is now nearly back in Hostigos.''

Eldra's dagger traced out another line of march, this one across the Harph into southern Beshta, up the west bank of the Harph, and across the Besh into Hostigos. "That was a regiment sent by Harmakros. They stopped for a day at Tarr-Locra, but otherwise kept moving. They lived off the land, since Beshta is now enemy territory, and I imagine Prince Balthar will be wanting to ride home and defend his lands.''

"Will they let him?'' asked Sankar Trav.

"My guess would be that Balthar will be expected to stay with his new allies and prove himself in one more battle," put in Aranth Saln. "Grand Master Soton is a professional soldier and isn't going to give up nearly two thousand men to soothe a traitorous Prince's nerves. High Marshal Mnesiphoklos might be more considerate of Balthar's desire to defend his lands, but he's from Hos-Ktemnos, where the Princes know their place in the scheme of things. I doubt if he will go strongly against Soton in this matter.''

"That should keep Prince Balthames of Sashta faithful to Kalvan,'' said Sirna.

"Absolutely,'' said Eldra. "Balthames hates his brother so much he'd swear black with white to annoy him. Also, he may have some hope of being proclaimed Prince of Beshta when Balthar is deposed and executed, which he certainly will be if Kalvan wins.''

Eldra was discussing how Kalvan had sent Harmakros back to Hostigos with the Mobile Force to reinforce Prince Ptosphes, when the maintenance tech let out a whoop of triumph.

"Done, citizens! As soon as I call the operators in, you'll be ready to go.''

Under his breath, but loud enough so that everyone could hear, Lathor Karv said, "I doubt if Verkan Vall or his errand boy Ranthar Jard have to wait three hours for an obsolete conveyor to be brought on-line.''

Sirna noted that Aranth Saln showed the only sign of open disagreement among the knowing smiles and nodding heads of the Team. Eldra acted as if she hadn't heard Lathor's com-

ment, and Sirna wondered just how Eldra viewed the Paracops and Home Time-Line politics in general.

The Professor certainly seemed too much the maverick to be
a Management Party supporter, with their devotion to the
status quo and complete support of Paratime Police policy.
For the same reason, one wouldn't expect her to be a member
of the Opposition Party, who were as predictable and rigid in
their resistance to the Paratime Police as Management was in
its support. At a guess, she probably leaned toward the Right
Moderates, with their theme of "the appeal to reason."

By the time the two conveyor operators had taken their seats
at the controls, Sirna and her teammates were strapped into
the passenger couches. Sirna looked up at the metal-mesh
dome overhead that would soon disappear into the indescribable flickering of a paratemporal transposition field. Then she
looked at Eldra.

The Professor's long fingers were twined around the stem of
a pipe she didn't dare smoke during a transposition, twisting
and untwisting themselves into knots like a nest of snakes.
Sirna rubbed her left leg where the top of her riding boot
chafed it and grinned. It was nice to know that she wasn't the
only nervous member of this team.

II.

Kalvan decided to call a halt for a meal in another
half hour. His detachment was getting close to home, but not
so close that he felt like riding all the way on an empty
stomach even if it would save time. They could eat—what to
call it? As the first meal of the day, it should be breakfast;
measured by how long they'd been on the road it should be
lunch, even if it wasn't yet midmorning. Anyway, they could
eat and rest the horses before pushing on to Tarr-Hostigos,
and Kalvan could close his ears to the well-bred grumbling
about Great Kings who insisted on rising before dawn.

He was no longer afraid of what he might finally see when he rode into view of the heartland of Hostigos. Even before the Mobile Force arrived, Soton's cavalry hadn't pushed more than a few raids and a lot of patrols into Hostigos, and now that Harmakros and Phrames had reinforced Ptosphes, they weren't even doing that. The Holy Host of Styphon was camped in Sashta, laying it to waste as they foraged for the supplies they'd need before they could fight another pitched battle.

That was hard on Prince Balthames and his people, but it was an undisguised blessing for Kalvan and the Princedom of Hostigos. The way Soton and Mnesiphoklos drove their men after Ptosphes had been a little frightening even for Kalvan, reading it second-hand in Ptosphes's letters. If Ptosphes hadn't fought the Battle of Tenabra within reach of his supply magazines—so that for the first week he could retreat fast enough to break contact with the Holy Host—he might have been brought to battle and smashed before he could regroup. Kalvan wouldn't have been prepared to believe that here-and-now heavy cavalry could fight that well or infantry march that fast, but when you were dealing with the Zarthani Knights and the Sacred Squares, you had to be prepared to believe quite a lot that didn't apply elsewhere.

As it was, Ptosphes had done damned well to bring ten thousand men in fighting condition out of Sask! The Styphoni were on his heels all the way, scouting and raiding far into his rear, snapping up stragglers, and every so often sending a weak van into an apparently vulnerable position to tempt him to turn and attack.

That was a trick that couldn't work twice—not with Ptosphes. He kept retreating, ignoring the curses and the occasional desertions by men who thought more of vengeance or an honorable death than of the best way to win this war. Kalvan suspected that those curses hurt Ptosphes more than the careful phrases of his letters would ever show, but he knew that his father-in-law would sacrifice even his honor to bring his army back, a loss that would hurt worse than merely losing his life.

The Styphoni paid the price for a swift advance across a countryside whose major fortresses and walled towns were held against them. By the time they'd reached Sashta they'd marched the shoes off their horses' hooves and the soles out of their soldiers' boots, and left behind most of their artillery because their half-starved teams couldn't haul it. They might still have won a battle against Ptosphes alone by sheer weight of numbers but for the arrival of Harmakros and the Mobile Force.

There was nothing for the Styphoni to do after that but forage in Sashta for what supplies that Princedom could provide, and hope the Saski garrisons wouldn't send out too many raiding parties against the convoys coming up from the south.

It was a race between Hostigi reinforcements and Styphoni supplies, and at the moment the race was pretty nearly even. Anything that gave one side or the other a major lead during the next week or two was likely to be political rather than military.

Politics was Kalvan's main reason for riding on ahead of his army. There were too many things he needed to know that couldn't safely be put in letters even by the people who could tell them. What was this League of Dralm that Xentos had mentioned in his first letter from Agrys City after his arrival at the Great Council of Dralm? Would it affect Mytron's work as Rector of the University of Hostigos, and particularly his willingness to see the University fortified and defended? What had Phrames heard or seen in Phaxos that might tell Kalvan which way Prince Araxes was likely to jump—and when? What did the people in Beshta think of their Prince's treachery, and could any of them be persuaded to rebel against him so that he would be worrying about his back while the Army of Hostigos fought him in front? How was the loyalty of Sarrask's garrisons going to be guaranteed, assuming it could be? A dozen other questions, each defining a potential Great King's headache, none of them likely to be answered until Kalvan rode up to Tarr-Hostigos.

They were cantering up a slight rise when the Horse Guards who'd already reached the crest shouted warning of a party of horsemen on the road ahead, coming fast. Kalvan reined in and drew his sword. The Holy Host wasn't supposed to be raiding this far north any more, but if it was—

The leading horseman, wearing a welcome red sash, was Prince Ptosphes. Kalvan sheathed his sword and rode to meet his father-in-law, not quite wishing he had a Styphoni patrol to fight instead but very much aware that too many eyes and ears would be taking in everything he said or left unsaid. It was part of the job of being a Great King, he told himself firmly as he reined in and waited for Ptosphes to ride within conversational distance.

Ptosphes wore his well-battered combat armor and the expression of a man who's mortally ill but trying to hide it from his family. The dead eyes and all the new gray in the bushy brown beard spoiled the act for Kalvan.

"Your Majesty," began Ptosphes. "I have failed you and the Realm of Hos-Hostigos. It is within your right—"

Kalvan's determination to choose his words carefully vanished, and he said the first thing that came to mind. "I have the right to tell you not to talk nonsense, Father. You didn't fail me or anybody or anything. You just had the bad luck to be up against Styphon's varsity."

Ptosphes looked blankly at him, and Kalvan realized that he must have been even more shaken by Ptosphes's appearance than he'd realized. For the first time in months, he'd spoken in English.

"The varsity—it's a word in the language of my homeland. It means men who have sold themselves to evil demons in return for great skill in war or athletic games."

"Ah. Well, that is certainly one way of—explaining—the Zarthani Knights. We had all heard tales of their battles, but facing them . . ." His voice trailed off, but some of the deadness was gone from his eyes.

Kalvan gripped his father-in-law by both shoulders. "We'll talk later. Thank you for coming out to meet me." He didn't know what Ptosphes had come out to offer, although he could guess, and hoped nobody else would ever raise the matter again.

Ptosphes managed a thin smile and turned his horse. Kalvan was about to do the same when he heard a familiar voice saying cheerfully, "Welcome home, Your Majesty. Now we can really start kicking those Styphoni dogs back to their kennels."

The voice was Prince Sarrask of Sask's, except that it seemed to be coming out of thin air, because there was nobody in sight who looked like Sarrask, except—

"Great Dralm!"

The gilded armor was scraped and hacked almost down to bare steel, the ruddy face was tanned and lined, and the jowls were barely respectable ghosts of their former selves. Kalvan tried not to stare, then gave up. A world in which Sarrask of Sask had grown thin was one in which all the laws of nature had been suspended.

No, not quite thin—there was still a lot of Sarrask. Still, he now looked like a real warrior Prince instead of an overweight and overage character actor playing one.

"I understand you've been doing good work yourself," said Kalvan. Then he added more formally, "You have Our gratitude, and you will have a lot more as soon as We're in a position to give it."

Sarrask grinned. "Thank you, Your Majesty. One thing you can do is come to a banquet I'm holding tonight. It's for the wives and children of my castellans, who sent them with me for their safety. They'd be greatly honored if you could attend."

And so will you, thought Kalvan. The idea of a banquet at this time seem like fiddling while Rome burned, but after a moment's thought Kalvan decided he'd go. He couldn't expect all his loyal followers to have the moral fiber of old Chartiphon or noble Phrames. Besides, the castellans' families were hostages for their loyalty to Sarrask, and therefore to him. Knowing Sarrask, it couldn't be any other way. They probably knew it too, and they were far from home after being dragged up hill and down dale at the tail of a beaten army. They deserved at least a visit from their Great King.

"I'll be happy to attend."

"Wonderful, Your Majesty. There are some very charming young ladies among them, too. I'm sure they'll be even more grateful than I could ever be."

Considering how Sarrask would expect them to show that gratitude, this seemed rather likely. Sarrask's tastes were not at all like Balthames's.

"How's Rylla?" Kalvan asked, to shut off that line of thinking.

"As well as any woman who's the shape of a melon can be," said Sarrask. "She wants to go out and strangle Styphoni with her bare hands." Despite his customary harsh words, there was a note of almost fatherly pride in Sarrask's voice. Kalvan wondered how Great Queen Rylla viewed her former hereditary enemy's new solicitude.

With great sufferance, undoubtedly. Kalvan forced back a laugh.

He also couldn't help thinking that Rylla might have to

do exactly that if they lost another battle, and it must have showed on his face. "You look as if you *need* a banquet," said Sarrask.

He lowered his rough voice to avoid being overheard by Ptosphes some twenty yards ahead. "Try to get Ptosphes to come too. He needs it even worse. The first thing he heard when we rode back into Hostigos was some woman crying, 'Ptosphes, Ptosphes, give me back my man,' and he looked as if he were dying of a gut wound for the next three days. I hope he hasn't taken a fever on this campaign."

No, he's just a better man than you'll ever be, was what Kalvan wanted to say, but knew it wouldn't make any sense and maybe wouldn't even be just. Sarrask would never be very likable, but by here-and-now standards he wasn't a particularly bad man—not a bad one at all, if you considered his loyalty to Hostigos had already cost him a good deal and might yet cost him his throne.

Mental memo number three thousand six hundred and two (give or take fifty): Put Sarrask of Sask on the next Honor's List. Think about something like the Order of the Garter or the Order of the Golden Fleece to reward people who already have lands, titles, and wealth—something useless but flattering to their sense of whatever they call honor.

TWENTY

I.

"Urig. One copper, two phenig."

The workman wiped his hand on a tunic that was even dirtier and held it out for the money Sirna was holding. "One copper, two phenig," he repeated, then bit into the copper to make sure it wasn't counterfeit.

Sirna smiled at his surprised look when he discovered that he hadn't been cheated. The Foundry couldn't pay more than the prevailing wages; that would make trouble with the guilds, to say nothing of making an inflation problem that was already bad even worse. They could at least use their outtime resources to make sure their workers were paid in good coin that gave them a fighting chance of not starving.

In her role as pay clerk, Sirna paid off the other eight workers from the Foundry's warehouse and was going over the scribe's soapstone tally when she heard Eldra calling her.

"I'll be back in a little while," she said to the scribe. "Don't put it on the parchment until then."

"Yes, ma'am."

Sirna hoped the scribe wouldn't disobey her by way of trying to see how much he could get away with under the nose of this new clerk. She didn't feel like punishing him or any other Hostigi when they might all be dead in a week, or arguing with the senior members of the University Team over her "weakness.'' Professor Lathor Karv would be leading the pack; to hear him talk, you'd think he'd invented the concept of wages.

As she approached Eldra, Sirna noted that several other members of the Study-Team were standing with her, and that a band of horsemen was cantering toward the Foundry from the direction of Hostigos Town. Sirna hastily moved behind her teammates to keep them between her and the horses. She'd have to get used to those great beasts before too much longer, but right now the memory of the fall she'd taken when her barely controlled mount shied at a fast-moving field gun was much too vivid.

Eldra gave her remarkably little sympathy over her distaste for horses, but then Eldra loved the perverse beasts and had an outtime ranch where she raised them. There was even a tale about how on one Fourth Level Franco-Byzantine time-line, Eldra had disguised herself as a man to win a famous cross-country horserace—the tale ending, naturally, with how the man who came in second found himself getting an unexpected but agreeable consolation prize.

The leading rider in the group was the Great King himself. Verkan Vall—Colonel Verkan—was just behind him, and on Kalvan's right—! Sirna's scream was strangled into a squeak, but it was still loud enough to make Eldra turn.

"What the—?"

Sirna pointed with a hand she was proud to see wasn't shaking. "That—it's Prince Sarrask of Sask! The Sarrask of Sask who—"

Eldra signaled her frantically to silence, then stared hard at the big man in well-hacked armor that must have once been gilded. "It can't be—well, I'll be Dralm-damned! It's our Sarrask all right, the one who belongs here, but he's trimmed down to the twin of the one you thought he was. Oh well, stranger things have happened in Paratime. And they'll happen to you, so get used to them and don't be so jumpy."

"Yes, ma'am."

Eldra looked at Sarrask again. "Definitely trimmed down. Another twenty pounds off and he'd be almost handsome. Not like Kalvan, of course, but not bad . . ."

The two rulers, unaware that they were being discussed like a couple of prize bulls, sat on their horses while Kalvan's dozen bodyguards took positions all around him. Half stayed mounted, but all looked very alert; some quietly drew their pistols without aiming them at anybody.

The two rulers, Verkan, and a young man who seemed to be Verkan's bodyguard remained mounted and conducted a long discussion that seemed to involve a lot of hand-waving. The few words Sirna overheard were all military technicalities, so she concentrated on studying Great King Kalvan without appearing too disrespectful. "A cat can look at a king," was a saying that she'd encountered; she wasn't so sure about the rights of free-traders' daughters.

Kalvan looked tired but still in fine shape physically; he obviously wasn't hiding any wounds or sickness from the campaign in Harphax. The face was certainly handsome, although it looked better when he smiled, which wasn't very often, but then why should he be smiling at all, with everything he had to worry about? It was hard to tell much about his body, as he was wearing a back-and-breast, an open-faced helmet, and bulky riding boots with pistols in them. A light cavalry trooper's outfit, from what Sirna recalled, and probably the best combination of comfort and protection he could manage.

At last the Great King signaled, and guards came to hold horses as the four men dismounted. Kalvan turned to the Foundry people.

"I'm sorry to have kept you from your work so long," he began. As if a Great King needed to apologize for anything—but then Sirna recalled that Kalvan had lived most of his life on a time-line with all sorts of myths about equality. Maybe he thought he was being gracious—although Sirna had to admit that if he thought so, he was right.

"The Foundry is going to be part of a second line of defense we're building to meet the Styphoni. We're also fortifying Hostigos Town itself, of course, and this side of Hostigos Gap. Tarr-Hostigos will keep anyone from getting through the Gap from the other side.

"We'll be wanting the Foundry workers to dig trenches and gun positions, proof against cavalry. We'll also be needing your new warehouse to store supplies. No fireseed, naturally, so you'll be able to go right on working.

"In fact, I expect you'll be able to go right on working through the whole battle. We don't intend to let Styphon's Unwholesome Host reach the second line or anywhere near it. However, even Great Kings' intentions don't bind the gods. We'll have to prepare for the worst and work for the best.

"Colonel Verkan of the Mounted Rifles has very kindly offered one of his best officers, Captain Ranthar, to command the defenses of the Foundry. He will choose positions for the trenches, train workers in arms, and take command if it does come to a fight.

"I'm trusting the loyalty you've all shown so far to continue until Styphon's wolves are driven from the land.

"Down Styphon!"

The foundry workers all repeated the cry, then someone—it sounded like Eldra—shouted, "Long Live King Kalvan!"

Kalvan acknowledged the cheers with a half salute, half wave, then Colonel Verkan helped him to remount. A moment later the royal party was riding back the way they'd come, except for Captain Ranthar and his groom, who stood holding the reins of the two horses with one hand and a roll of parchment under the other arm.

"The first thing to do is find a room where we won't be overheard—" began Ranthar, when Talgan Dreth, the Outtime Studies Director, interrupted him.

"The first thing for you to do is to explain by what authority—oh," he broke off suddenly at the hand signals "Captain Ranthar" was making.

Eldra laughed out loud at the older man's embarrassment, and even Sirna couldn't help smiling. The Director took himself *so* seriously, even though it wasn't particularly funny that the Kalvan Study-Teams were now under the watchful eye of one of Chief Verkan's most trusted—say *observers*, to be polite.

Sirna wondered how long Ranthar Jard had been Captain Ranthar in Kalvan's Time-Line. Some time, obviously, or he wouldn't be an officer in the Mounted Rifles. That was most likely a clue about what he'd been brought here to do—or prevent, but she couldn't be sure which!

Sirna began to think that perhaps she should have insisted a little harder with Hadron Tharn that she wasn't the stuff of which good spies are made.

II.

Two days after the meeting at the Foundry, word reached Hostigos Town that the Holy Host was on the march again. Kalvan's General Staff held its Council of War at Prince Sarrask's temporary residence, an inn called the Silver Stag. The improvised council chamber at least had enough chairs, as well as a table that if not exactly groaning was at least muttering darkly to itself under the weight of food and drink piled upon it. Sarrask, it appeared, was determined to be a gracious host to the end, if this was the end—and Verkan Vall was unpleasantly aware that it might be.

Not just for the Hostigi and for Kalvan, either. This was the kind of situation that had killed many a Paratimer—a fast-moving battle that could go either way on very short notice. The only sure way to be safe was to leave so soon you'd obviously be deserting your friends. If they won, you'd lose all chance of working with them again, apart from the risk of being executed for treason or desertion. If they lost, you still might not be able to deal with the victors—and you'd have to live with yourself whether you could or not.

All this was true even if you hadn't developed any deep loyalties to your outtime comrades. That happened more often than the Paratime Police liked to admit, and in fact most often happened to the best outtime operatives—one reason why Verkan Vall was Tortha Karf's third choice to succeed him. It was small consolation to Verkan that at least he'd never assumed he was immune to Outtime Identification Syndrome (as the Bureau of Psychological Hygiene's jargon called it) so he hadn't been surprised when he realized that his body might very well be one of the ones picked up after a Kalvan's Last Stand.

Prince Sarrask was the only member of the Council present when Verkan arrived. He was seated at the far end of the table, munching his way through a plate of sausages that looked large enough to put back most of his lost weight. He waved Verkan to a chair, finished a sausage, then grinned.

"I saw one of your new girls at the Foundry giving me the eye the other day," said Sarrask. "You know, the tall red-headed one with the big nose and the big—" His hands outlined in the air two of Sirna's most prominent features.

Verkan tried hard not to laugh. "I have to warn you, Your Grace, that Sirna is the daughter of a sworn blood-brother of my father. So she must be considered under my protection."

Sarrask chuckled. "Under your—your protection? Whatever would your wife Dalla say about your protecting Sirna?"

"She'd probably say that Prince Sarrask of Sask talks too much," said Kalvan, sticking his head into the room.

Sarrask grunted like a boar stuck in a bog, then shrugged. "She'd probably be right, too, Dralm-blast it! I apologize, Colonel Verkan."

"Accepted," said Verkan with a bow. Sarrask would be no problem, but it struck him that as the University Teams' strength increased, the Prince might not be only man with an eye for their unattached females. Suggest to Kalvan that the Foundry be formally declared part of the Royal Household? That would solve the legal requirements, at least, and Rylla could probably help. In the long run, it would also set useful precedents for when—call it "international trade"—really began again in Kalvan's Time-Line after half a millennium of being strangled by Styphon's House.

That was as far as Verkan's thoughts took him before the rest of the Council started arriving. By the time everyone had arrived, it was the largest and most rank-heavy Council of War that Verkan had ever attended in Kalvan's Time-Line, and was in the running for the prize in all the time-lines where he'd attended Councils of War.

There was Kalvan himself, four Princes (Ptosphes, Sarrask, Armanes, and Balthames), six Generals (Chartiphon, Harmakros, Phrames, Klestreus, Skranga, and Alkides the artilleryman), the Ulthori Count Euphrades, and at least a dozen noble and mercenary captains whom Verkan knew only by sight and name; First Level total recall didn't help with information you didn't have!

It occurred to Verkan that if the Silver Stag collapsed, the rest of the Holy Host's campaign would probably be recorded as "mopping-up operations."

It also struck him that the Council was much too large to do more than give everyone a chance to be heard, whether they had anything to say or not beyond praise for Kalvan's victory and sympathy for Ptosphes's bad luck. Kalvan had almost certainly arranged for a smaller meeting to do the real business, either before or after this huge, unwieldy Council of War.

The Council did run on until all the food was gone and everybody had said his piece or sometimes several of them. It also managed to hammer out a surprisingly complete strategy, and Verkan realized that perhaps he'd underestimated the hold Kalvan had over these people, particularly after his victory at the Heights of Chothros. That, it appeared, had been such a victory as no Great Kingdom had won over another in two centuries—since about the time Styphon's House really started clamping down on wars that threatened to create large and dangerous independent political units.

It also helped that the military situation was so simple that a nine-year-old child could probably have planned the campaign. Hostigos Town was something the Holy Host had to take and the Hostigi had to defend. There was no place farther north or farther south that let the Hostigi be as sure of meeting the full strength of the Holy Host with their own united army.

The Holy Host could not even have stayed where it had been camped much longer without sending larger and larger foraging parties farther afield. Long before Hostigos was eaten bare, the Hostigi could have marched on the weakened main body and forced it to fight against odds, then cut off the foraging parties at their leisure.

After a while it became clear to Verkan that there weren't going to be any disagreements where his voice had to be heard, or even suggestions he needed to make about the best use of the Mounted Rifles. He relaxed into the role of observer.

Ptosphes: a man who looked as if he were being eaten alive by the shame of his defeat. Sarrask: loud and lewd, but who seemed to be finding something in himself that hadn't been there before he had a leader worth following. The men Verkan had begun to call (after one of Dalla's favorite Fourth Level Europo-American novels) "The Three Musketeers"—Harmakros, Phrames, and Hestophes. Chartiphon: big and bluff, and not quite up to the demands of the new kind of war that would be fought in Kalvan's Time-Line from now on, but useful within his limits and probably wise enough to know what they were.

Balthames of Sashta, looking daggers at his father-in-law Sarrask every time he thought he wasn't observed—a prime candidate for a dose of hypno-truth drug. Alkides, who looked almost as grim as Ptosphes, after blowing up the Harphaxi artillery train—which to an artilleryman must have been like losing an adopted child. Verkan decided to keep a particularly close eye on Alkides, since he could be the key to victory in a battle where Kalvan's artillery superiority might mean everything.

Count Euphrades of Ulthor, thin and remote, with obvious plans of his own he was telling no one—another prime candidate for hypno-truth drugs. And three or four others who might prove as interesting as Euphrades once Verkan knew something about them.

A good company, not quite a "band of brothers" yet (and they were much rarer in fact than in fiction or hagiographical history, Verkan knew), but formidable enemies and fine friends.

Too fine to abandon, if it came to that. Verkan knew he wasn't going to deliberately put himself in a position where he had to go down with Kalvan. On the other hand, if he found himself in that position with no way out that let him keep a clear conscience—well, this time he was glad that Dalla wasn't with him. She wasn't Rylla, who would try not to outlive Kalvan by more than five minutes if she could help it, but she would have some hard decisions to make that he was just as glad she didn't have to face now.

TWENTY-ONE

I.

Grand-Captain Phidestros looked at the eastern sky turning pale. In another few minutes it would be light enough for his men to see him. He stood up and walked back and forth beside Snowdrift, stopping now and then to rub his knee. It had healed enough so that he could fight on foot today even in three-quarter armor if he had to.

Snowdrift whickered and nuzzled at Phidestros's belt pouch. "Very well, you godforsaken brat unworthy of either dam or sire." He reached into his pouch and pulled out a half slice of ration bread. Snowdrift whickered again and munched vigorously, while Phidestros scratched the big gelding up and down his neck the way he liked it. He hoped Snowdrift was fit to carry him through what would surely be a long and wearing battle, but hoping was all he could do.

He'd done all any man could do to make sure that his men and their mounts were properly fed after the ride from the Harph to join the Holy Host, but that "all" had not been much. He supposed he should have expected that Grand Master Soton would be pushing forward hard on the heels of the Hostigi, with as little thought for supplies as he could afford, and that any company of horse that had held together in a ten-days' ride across unknown country was worth having well up toward the front. Certainly both proved that Soton knew his business, and being toward the front had given the Iron Company several chances to fight under the Grand Master's own eye. Please Galzar that would make up for the wear on the horses and the weapons!

It was most likely the major reason why he was now a Grand-Captain, commanding a double-sized band—the three hundred survivors of those who'd crossed the Harph and four other companies. One had joined his banner on the march north, the other three two days ago when Soton raised him to his present rank.

"Grand-Captain Phidestros." It had an agreeable ring to it, but the meeting with the Grand Master had hardly been all sweetness and light. Darkness had long fallen, the candles on the table between them burned almost to stubs, the harsh planes and angles of Soton's face still harsher in the orange-red light, his voice rasping like a file with weariness and anger as he questioned Phidestros.

"Do you think yourself fit to lead a band?"

"Yes. That is, if they are horse and not too untrained or badly mounted." Something else that was the truth and would also sound well, the best combination. "I would grieve to abandon the Iron Company on the eve of victory, though. We have endured much together and know each other's ways. The Silver Wolf Company is also proving itself to be good comrades in battle and in camp."

"You would not be giving up either company. You would be leading three more free companies. They meet your conditions, I believe."

"I am honored by your confidence, Grand Master, and by theirs—if they have asked me to lead them. However, this is the first I have heard of the three companies."

"Are you sure? They are three of the companies in the service of Balthar of Beshta."

Phidestros would be too tired to think of any subtle response, but anything would be better than gape-jawed silence. "Am I to believe that the Massacre of Tarr-Catassa actually happened?"

"You thought it was camp rumor?"

"I had no reason to think otherwise. Stranger tales have crawled out of barrels of bad ale and the terrors of men far from home."

"Well, you may rest easy. It is no rumor that Prince Balthar's castellan of Tarr-Catassa killed a hundred and twenty free companions who would not swear to join the Holy Host in the service of Balthar. Their women were given to the Beshtans, then killed also."

"That castellan was a fool as well as a murderer."

By the laws governing the employment of mercenary free companies, when an employer changed sides during a war or a battle, their oath to him was still binding until he released them or their term of service expired. A wise Prince usually released doubtful mercenaries as quickly as possible, since a thousand reliable men were worth two thousand who might surrender on the slightest pretext.

If the mercenaries of Tarr-Catassa had sworn to serve Balthar of Beshta "against all enemies, in field or fortress, wheresoever he may find them," then they would have been violating their oaths to Balthar. As it was, they were a company sworn in only as the garrison of Tarr-Catassa. They could not have been a very good company, but nonetheless they had been slaughtered for refusing to do something their Prince's castellan had no right to ask of them.

"It is hardly surprising that Balthar's name now reeks to the thrones of the very gods among the free companions. The six companies who placed themselves in his pay after he joined the Holy Host do not wish to be released from their oaths, however, or to leave our ranks."

Phidestros couldn't help wondering how much choice they'd had.

"They no longer wish to serve under Balthar's Captain-General or their own elected Grand-Captain. They say both are too friendly with Prince Balthar. At the end of this campaign, it is almost certain that Balthar will be placed under the Ban of Galzar."

The Ban of Galzar meant that no free companion of the Brotherhood could take an oath to Prince Balthar, under threat of expulsion. The only men Balthar would then be able to command would be his own sworn vassals, outcasts, and criminals. The only thing worse than the Ban of Galzar was the Interdict, where no man, vassal or not, could fight for a Prince and still receive the rites of Galzar. Had Balthar ordered the slaughter himself he might have well faced the Interdict, but no sane man—even a Prince or a Great King—would so risk offending Galzar or his priests.

"The three companies I offer you have voted to follow you if you are willing. They have heard the tales of the ride from the Harph and of how under you the Iron Company won free of two lost battles—Fyk and Chothros Heights.''

Was there a note of irony in those last words of Soton? Phidestros didn't particularly care, since he'd also been freely given a knowledge he would otherwise have had to ask or even beg for. The three companies were not composed of men who wanted a safe road out of the whole war, or at least to the other side, and would shoot their captain the moment they found him barring it. They were instead merely free companions exercising their ancient privilege of choosing who would lead them into battle, a privilege only fools like Balthar's castellan denied them.

It was now light enough for Phidestros to pick out the few dark hairs in Snowdrift's mane and tail. Plenty of light to see by—and to see in the distance the banners and lance tips of the approaching vanguard of the Zarthani Knights. Phidestros swung himself onto Snowdrift's back and waved to Banner-Captain Geblon. The banner of the Iron Band rose against the dawn sky: a black iron chain breaking a gold thunderbolt on a green field.

Some of the old Iron Company troopers started to cheer. The orange sashes of Hos-Ktemnos made vivid splashes of color against their blackened armor. Phidestros waved them to silence, then pointed at the banner.

"My brothers—that is the banner of the Iron Band. Those of you who have followed it before know what it means.'' *Two well-conducted and profitable retreats, mostly, but let's not be too particular about the truth at a time like this.*

"Those of you who are following the banner for the first time in this battle—rejoice in your opportunity. You have proven comrades on all sides and a chance to add to the honor of the banner you follow. Fight as I know you can, and before another moon we will be drinking a toast from the skulls of our enemies. You are the Iron Band!''

He let them cheer freely this time. When the sound began to ebb, he cried, "To victory! To gold! To Galzar!'' As an afterthought, in case Soton or an Inner Circle spy was listening, he added, "To Styphon!''

His old troopers responded with a cheer of their own. "Phidestros! Phidestros!''

That rang even more agreeably on Phidestros's ears, but he

also knew it was the last thing Soton should hear now. He quickly silenced the men. "The Iron Band will soon become the Iron Hand around the throat of Hostigos. Furthermore, no one who has faced us in battle will find that name a matter for joking."

It had not escaped his attention that some among the free companions, jealous of his success and rapid advancement, had taken to calling the Iron Band the Yellow Hand, "first to retreat and last to advance."

"Galzar smite me if I do not speak the truth!"

Galzar, Phidestros reflected, seemed to turn a deaf ear to anything a captain said to his men before a battle. He had heard of captains being smitten down on the morning of battle by apoplexies or attacks of bile, but never by Galzar's mace.

Meanwhile, the old Iron Company was cheering again, and to Phidestros's delight the other companies joined in. They sounded like men who were ready to follow a new captain at least until he proved himself unfit to lead.

He could still wish most of them were better-mounted, though. Even Snowdrift was showing a hint of rib under his creamy flanks. As a troop of Zarthani Knights' mounted archers cantered past, a thought struck Phidestros. Could he earn enough of Soton's goodwill to be allowed to buy some of the archers' light mounts, who could feed by grazing where a charger would starve?

Such horses could hardly carry a man in armor, of course, or even press home a charge with lances. Was that so great a loss? Phidestros had begun to wonder. With the new way of war Kalvan seemed to know and Soton seemed ready to learn, speed seemed likely to prove as important as armor.

It was something to think about if he survived today with both his head on his shoulders and honor in Grand Master Soton's too-shrewd eyes.

II.

     Verkan Vall felt somewhat like an intruder as he climbed the last flight of stairs to the royal chambers at the top of the keep of Tarr-Hostigos. He also felt even more like a deserter from his post, which would normally have been at the head of the Mounted Rifles with the Army of Hostigos near the village of Phyrax to the southwest of Hostigos Town.

However, the Battle of Phyrax wasn't going to be a "normal" battle, assuming there was such a thing. By the Great King's orders, the Mounted Rifles weren't going to spend themselves scouting aginst the superior and well-trained light cavalry of the Zarthani Knights. They were going to remain in the rear and wait for the Holy Host to attack, then work around its flanks and snipe at its captains. This "assignment" had nearly provoked mutiny among some of the hotheads in the Mounted Rifles, but it made good sense considering what Hostigos was facing.

Kalvan couldn't hope to fight a maneuver battle against the Holy Host. Soton was too good, and the Sacred Squares of Hos-Ktemnos and the Zarthani Knights were the best infantry and cavalry here-and-now. They were twelve thousand men—not counting the four thousand Zarthani Order Foot—who would take a lot of killing. The rest of the Holy Host included three thousand of Styphon's Red Hand as well as two thousand of the King's Pistoleers and eight hundred Royal Guards of Hos-Ktemnos, all well above average. Even the motley array of several thousand "Holy Warriors of Styphon" might lack training, but they wouldn't lack enthusiasm.

Kalvan would still have a damned good chance if he sat still and let the Holy Host come at him. He better than matched them man for man in numbers, and the best Hostigi infantry were as good as the Sacred Squares—although he would sorely miss the two thousand veteran Old Hostigi Foot who'd perished at Tenabra. His cavalry horses were in better shape. He also would have a big edge in artillery fighting this close to home, where many of the old Hostigi bombards too heavy for campaigning could be hauled out to the battlefield and dug in.

It wouldn't hurt, either, that Kalvan would have Hostigos Unconsecrated for all his artillery and firearms, while the

Holy Host would still be firing Styphon's Best. They were making fireseed according to the new formula now in Balph, but some ecclesiastical Archbureaucrat had decided that none of the new formula could be issued until all of the old had been used up or accounted for.

That piece of bureaucracy-in-action was so far the only piece of intelligence sent by Verkan's on-the-ground agent with the Holy Host, a Paratime Policeman passing as an underpriest of Styphon, who'd finally come north with the reinforcements and supplies as part of what could laughingly be called the medical corps. Verkan had hoped for more intelligence before the battle, but even getting this little bit proved his man was alive, on the job, and might provide more later.

It also wasn't going to hurt that many of Kalvan's men were fighting on ground they knew well, with their backs to the wall and no illusions about what would happen to their homes and families if they lost. The Holy Host had only committed the normal run of here-and-now atrocities on its way north. If Kalvan lost the Battle of Phyrax, this would probably change and very much for the worse.

Ptosphes's men had a score to settle with the Holy Host. Kalvan's veterans of the Army of the Harph had a tradition of victory a whole moon old to maintain; they too would take a lot of killing.

In fact, "a lot of killing" seemed the best description of the coming battle that Verkan could think of.

Meanwhile, Kalvan's ordering him back to Tarr-Hostigos gave him a chance to pay a visit to the University people at the Foundry. They were dug in about as well as could be expected with the labor and leadership available; Ranthar Jard couldn't be in two places at once. Talgan Dreth was grumbling a lot, but at least the Outtime Studies Director was cooperating to the extent of keeping some of his people from openly obstructing the work of fortification and cooperation with Brother Mytron's University refugees. Verkan had Scholar Varnath Lala mentally tagged as the leader of that faction, who appeared to have the delusion that if they maintained some sort of "neutrality," they could continue their work under the new management that would take over Hostigos if Kalvan lost.

Verkan seriously doubted that Archpriest Roxthar, who had accompanied the Holy Host but so far had been kept on a tight rein by Soton, would agree.

At the top of the stairs Verkan stopped and cleared his throat. There was no one on duty outside the royal apartments; the last sentry post was at the foot of this flight of stairs. He could hear the low murmur of voices through the thick door, but knew that etiquette allowed him to knock only in an emergency, like the Holy Host storming the gates of the castle.

The door swung open so quietly that Kalvan was coming out before Verkan could step back to a proper place. For a moment he had a clear view into the chamber beyond, a view of something he was quite sure he hadn't been meant to see—Ptosphes kneeling on the floor in front of Rylla, with his head in her swollen lap as she stroked his tangled gray hair. Then Kalvan was past and swinging the door shut behind him, heading down the stairs without a word to Verkan.

Verkan saw in Kalvan's set face and slightly sagging shoulders a man who was suddenly feeling the full weight of being monarch and commander and husband who might lose his wife within a few days all at once. Verkan planned to ask Kalvan how much palace duty he'd planned for him; royal aide was an honorable post but obviously an impossible one for him, and he'd rehearsed a set of arguments against the honor that sounded good, even to him.

Rather, they *had* sounded good. Now, if Kalvan needed a friend—make that *when* Kalvan needed a friend—at his back for a few days, Verkan wouldn't make any arguments against taking the job for at least that long. It didn't seem very likely that anyone would have the time to be jealous of an outlander's friendship with the Great King.

Verkan hurried down the dark stone stairs. He reached the bottom close enough to Kalvan to hear him talking with young Aspasthar, the new page who'd come into royal service from Count Harmakros.

"—says the horses are ready, Your Majesty. And a messenger came who requests word with the Great King."

"A messenger from whom, Aspasthar? You should always tell me who sent a messenger if he tells you himself. Also tell me if he doesn't."

"Yes, my—Your Majesty. It's a messenger from Duke Chartiphon in Phyrax."

Verkan saw Kalvan's grim smile. "I can guess what it says.

Soton's scouts must be in sight. Thank you, Aspasthar. Tell the man he can wait for me at the stables."

"Yes, Your Majesty." Aspasthar seemed to be waiting for a word of dismissal, until Kalvan gently took him by the shoulder and turned him around. "When the Great King says what he will do, you are dismissed."

Asphasthar was too flustered to reply, and scurried off so fast he nearly stumbled. Kalvan laughed softly. "Harmakros was a little too kind with the boy's training, but he's bright. He'll learn."

"Now, Colonel. I only called you back to Tarr-Hostigos because I wanted somebody to ride up with me who'll make better conversation than Major Nicomoth. He's not stupid, but today he'll have half his mind on whether he'll get to ride in another cavalry charge. However, if you think the Mounted Rifles will need you at once . . ."

"If I'd thought that, Your Majesty, I would have said so. I'll gladly ride with you. I won't insult your army by expecting it to fall apart before we can get there or indeed at—"

The change on Kalvan's face warned Verkan to silence as Ptosphes stepped out of the doorway, buckling on his sword. He wore all his armor except his helmet and his gauntlets; the latter hung from his belt, and on his hands were new riding gloves with his device of crossed halberds on the back.

"Your Majesty, Colonel Verkan. Shall we go and kill some of Styphon's whelps?"

From the look in Ptosphes's eyes, Verkan only hoped it was Styphon's dogs that the First Prince intended to kill. Ptosphes commanded the left wing of horse, a choice forced upon Kalvan. There was no telling what Ptosphes might have done in his present condition if he hadn't been given a rank and post in the coming battle appropriate to this rank and title. Verkan was sure that Kalvan would rather have had someone else holding the crucial left wing—Harmakros, commanding the reserves, or Count Phrames, second in command of the right wing under Kalvan.

Ptosphes's mental state was going to be almost as much a factor in this battle as the morale of Kalvan's troops.

III.

Sirna saw another horse-drawn cart pull up and cursed to herself at the need to organize another working party to unload it. Then she saw Brother Mytron himself sitting beside the driver. She leaped down the embankment in front of the trench, hiked her skirts above her boots, and ran over to the cart.

"Brother Mytron! Are matters well?"

"I think we lack the time for discussing the basic nature of the universe," Mytron said with a grin. "On a more material plane, I was the last man out of the University. It seemed to me that something important must have been overlooked, and sure enough it had." He pointed to the canvas-wrapped bundles in the back of the cart, and Sirna saw the glint of metal mesh in the corner of one. Her heart skipped a few beats until she realized that this mesh was much cruder than the mesh of a Paratime transposition conveyor dome.

"What is it?"

"Two of the wire screens for the papermaking. I don't know how anyone came to overlook them after all the work it took to make them. But there they were in one corner, all ready to be melted down by the Holy Host as demonical. We loaded them in the cart and were just turning around when we saw Nostori cavalry coming back in a rush. I decided they must know something we didn't and had the driver whip up the horses."

"Dralm and Tranth bless you for that." Sirna cupped her hands around her mouth and shouted. "Urig! Bring three men out here. Another cart to unload."

While Urig was rounding up his work gang, Sirna told Mytron that the other refugees from the University were safely bedded down in an empty storeroom. Then she asked about the battle.

"It hadn't started when I passed through our army. They were all drawn up, with King Kalvan and Count Phrames on the right, Prince Ptosphes on the left, and more guns than I've ever seen in the center. I heard that Kalvan has plans for those guns, and that Duke Chartiphon with help from General Alkides will command the center. I'm afraid I have no idea what the Great King's plans are; the gods didn't make me a man of war. I'm honest enough to be grateful that I'll be spending the next few days watching over Queen Rylla."

"Is her time near?"

"The chief midwife says so, and who am I to argue with a woman sixty years at that art? All seems to be well, but—"

"Hey!" someone shouted from beyond the cart. "Either move that Dralm-blasted cart on or bring it over here and join the circle."

A mounted man was riding across the field toward the wagon, waving a cattle whip. "The Great King gave orders to —oh, your pardon, Brother Mytron!" he finished in an entirely different voice.

Sirna swallowed a laugh. Brother Myron grinned. "In fact, I'm on my way to Tarr-Hostigos to see the Queen almost at once."

"May the true gods give Her Majesty a safe birthing and an heir for the Great Kingdom," said the trooper. Then he turned his horse and rode back toward the huge circle of wagons, carts, and baggage that penned in all the refugees' cattle. They were no longer bellowing as loudly as they had at dawn, but as it grew hotter an unmistakable smell was creeping across to the Foundry. Next year some Hostigi farmer was going to have at least one field *very* well fertilized.

"Add your prayers to his," said Mytron softly. "Much of the luck of Hostigos rides with our Rylla, the gods keep her."

Sirna nodded, then turned to meet Urig and his men. "Take these bundles from the cart into the driest corner of the new storehouse and wrap them well."

Urig looked dubiously at the wire mesh. "Is it—that a weapon?"

"It is something that the Great King thinks may become a weapon in time, but only against his enemies and the enemies of the true gods," said Sirna. Urig nodded, with an if-you-say-so-Mistress expression on his face, then started shouting to his gang.

That was only partly true, Sirna realized, or at least only partly true in the short run. If Kalvan succeeded in inventing paper and following it up with printing, the processes wouldn't remain secrets for long. Styphon's House could print its propaganda just as enthusiastically as its enemies. In the long run, though, Kalvan was working toward mass literacy and mass education, which were the most potent enemies of superstitition and ignorance—and they were *his* worst enemies.

The cart was empty in a few minutes, and as it rattled away with Mytron waving farewell, Sirna made a Grefftscharri gesture of aversion. She didn't know whom she was trying to save from bad luck, but there seemed to be a lot of it going around, rather like fleas. . . .

"You made that gesture as if you believed in it," said a voice behind her.

Sirna whirled, ready to shove Lathor Karv into the nearest trench if he were mocking her tolerance toward the Zarthani. Instead she saw Eldra, and she couldn't find anything to say to the expression on the Professor's face.

In any case, before she could have said two words, they both heard a distant dull thudding off in the heat haze toward the southwest.

"Cannon," said Eldra. "That means the main armies are engaged, not just the scouts."

TWENTY-TWO

I.

From the top of a small rise at the rear of the right wing, Kalvan could see that the entire center of both the Holy Host and the Army of Hostigos were lost in a steadily swelling cloud of white smoke. From the cloud rose a continuous din of gunfire, mostly artillery, as the two armies probed each other. Kalvan was surprised by the number of guns the Styphoni had managed to haul up, almost equal to the Hostigi in numbers although decidedly inferior in rate of fire. Soton clearly learned fast.

Periodically the noise of the big guns rose as one side or the other fired a ragged salvo. It reminded Kalvan of scrap iron being dumped on a concrete floor.

Captain-General Chartiphon commanded the center, almost twenty thousand infantry with the recent Ulthori and Zygrosi reinforcements. Brigadier-General Alkides was in command of the Hostigi artillery, and Kalvan mentally wrote him down for the Battle of Phyrax Honors List, if there was one. Alkides had done everything but haul bombards on his shoulders to assemble the Hostigi artillery and the Great Battery in particular. He had thirty guns in the Great Battery, his own three eighteen-pounders, four sixteen-pounders, assorted field pieces with defective carriages, and a miscellany of heavy pieces collected from every fortress within dragging distance of Hostigos Town.

Behind the Great Battery the Hos-Hostigos regular infantry were drawn up, with the Royal Army anchoring the right and the surviving veterans of Old Hostigos holding the left. The center was composed of the veterans of the Heights of Chothros, while four thousand mercenary Ktethroni pikemen from Hos-Zygros held the rear.

The Ktethroni were a tangible sign of the support of King Sopharar; Kalvan only hoped they weren't too late. They generally reminded him of the Swiss pike squares and seemed to know their business, but pike squares were vulnerable to well-handled artillery, and in any case he wasn't about to commit untested soldiers too soon in the most important battle of his life.

If he lost this one, his allies would melt away, and there wouldn't be enough Hostigi manpower left to raise two companies. That is, if the Styphoni didn't raze every building in Hostigos to the ground and sow the earth with salt, as the Romans had done with Carthage.

So far it was a case of "Things could be better, but then again they could be worse." Prince Ptosphes, in command of the survivors of the Army of the Besh on the left wing, had on his own initiative led his cavalry out against the right wing of the Holy Host under Grand Master Soton. Kalvan was sure that Ptosphes had been drawn out by insults from the Zarthani Knights, and it was a disquieting demonstration of Ptosphes's shaken state of mind that he'd attacked without orders from Kalvan.

The Knights quickly broke Ptosphes's precipitous charge, and he was only saved from disaster by the veteran infantry of Old Hostigos, who'd quickly reformed their pike line along the left flank. They pinned the Zarthani Knights long enough for Harmakros to bring up the cavalry of the Army of Observation from the reserves. Suddenly facing the fire of fifteen hundred dragoon musketeers, Soton retired quickly but in good order. The major casualty of this action was the morale of the Army of the Besh and Prince Ptosphes, both suffering from a massive inferiority complex. Kalvan was going to either have to bolster their confidence or relieve Ptosphes of his command, something he didn't want to do unless he had absolutely no other choice.

This artillery duel couldn't go on much longer; one of them was going to have to make a major move. It looked as if it was going to be up to him; either that or wait for the Holy Host to run out of rations. He didn't know how long that would take, and in any case they might then forage until Hostigos looked

like Georgia after Sherman's march to the sea. Lord High
Marshal Mnesiphoklos wasn't about to march his Sacred
Squares up to the Grand Battery, nor was Soton about to
charge with his Knights through the Grove of the Badger King,
where Hestophes and Harmakros's pet Sastragathi were
holding back the Knights' auxiliary horse archers.

Hestophes had been wounded, but not before he'd smashed
one attack by mercenaries and a second by the horse archers.
His people were now digging in around the Grove of the
Badger King. Its name might be seen as a good omen, and its
trees would certainly keep heavy cavalry out of their hair.
Hestophes's last message before he was surrounded was that
he could hold out as long as he had fireseed and arrows, and
that fortunately Soton's auxiliaries were being generous with
the latter even if they were proving stingy with Styphon's Best.

Kalvan's remaining problem was tactical. Unfortunately,
history was short of examples of pike against bill. The bill had
been an English national weapon, and they hadn't fought
many major Continental battles during the sixteenth century.
The only major pike vs. bill engagement he could recall was
the Battle of Flodden Field, where the French-armed Scots
under James IV were shorn of their nobility by the English
bills.

Pikes were most effective against other pole-armed infantry
when moving forward in formation. Once they were halted,
they could be chopped up far too easily by the shorter and
more maneuverable bills. So at Flodden the Scots took the initiative. King James and most of his nobility led fifteen thousand men downhill in a charge against the Earl of Surrey's
seven thousand Yorkshire billmen. The shock of impact drove
the English downhill several hundred yards, but they held their
formation and took a terrible toll of the front ranks of pikes.
At close quarters, the Scots pikes and swords were overcome
by the heavier English bills, and when the battle was over,
King James and ten thousand of his subjects lay dead on the
field.

The Holy Host was also deployed with a bill-and-musket
center and cavalry flanks. The Styphoni foot, under Mnesiphoklos, were arranged in two rows. The first was made up of
the Royal Square and two lesser Great Squares, about ten
thousand men. The second row held four thousand Zarthani
Order Foot, three thousand of Styphon's Own Guard, and
three thousand assorted mercenary foot. No surprises there—

but if Ptosphes could restrain himself and Soton didn't have anything up his sleeve, Kalvan just might have a surprise or two of his own.

A shout from the sentries made Kalvan turn. An armored barrel on horseback, decorated with red plumes, was approaching. A closer look revealed Major-General Klestreus, an unwarlike figure even if his three-quarter armor was blackened.

"What the Styphon—?"

Klestreus looked mildly insulted. "My place is beside my Great King, or I am no soldier." He wasn't, of course, but why be rude?

"A messenger has just arrived from Nostor. With luck and Dralm's Blessing, he may yet outlive his horse."

Kalvan nodded. "Yes, yes." *Get on with it, man! There's a battle going on, or hadn't you noticed?*

"He says there's a great host of Styphoni on its way through Nostor. He saw the banners of Hos-Agrys and Styphon's Red Circle."

That was the reversed circular swastika that was (all too appropriately, Kalvan felt) Styphon's device and the banner of the Red Hand.

"How large is the host and did they bring their own supplies?" There would be neither food nor forage in ravaged Nostor this year.

"He said it would take two days for the wagons alone to pass. It was as if they had opened the storehouses of Balph itself."

Probably exactly what they did. That also explained the ships going up the Hudson; they'd been building up magazines of stores so that King Demistophon could fish in troubled waters at Styphon's expense. As long as somebody else was paying, his Princes would have fewer objections to his taking sides.

"How many soldiers are there in this host?"

"He had to be careful and there was not much time—"

"But?"

"He thought their force might be as great as fifteen thousand. Most were mercenaries."

"How much time do we have?"

"He doesn't know. He ran his first horse to death and had to walk two days before he found another."

"Did he give you any kind of guess?"

"Yes, Your Majesty. They could hardly come upon us in less than five days."

That was good news; they could fight today's battle without the Styphoni receiving any reinforcements. If the Hostigi won, they could turn against the Agrysi invasion with ease; if they lost, it wouldn't matter how many vultures came to pick over the corpse of Hostigos. The one question remaining in Kalvan's mind was why the Styphoni were fighting at all today, if they had a chance of being reinforced. Were they that short of supplies, did they distrust King Demistophon (who might very well have been pushed into this move to avoid drawing the wrath of the Inner Circle for allowing the Great Council of Dralm to meet in Agrys City), or had Soton and Mnesiphoklos been just slightly carried away by the chance of smashing the Daemon's host by their own unaided efforts?

No point in speculating far ahead of the facts, and in any case Klestreus wasn't leaving.

"There is more."

I don't know if I can stand any more. "Go on, General."

"Prince Armanes has been wounded in the stomach."

Kalvan winced. That probably meant a lingering, painful death for a good and loyal man. It also gave him an excuse to tether Ptosphes with Count Phrames, a much wiser counselor than poor Armanes.

"I need to ask a favor of you."

Klestreus swelled until it looked as if he might burst his armor like a lady's corset. "Anything you command, Your Majesty."

"I want you to go to Count Phrames and tell him that it is Our will that he replace Prince Armanes on the left wing."

"It is done."

"Then I want you to personally escort the Prince to the hospital and see that he receives proper care."

"With great pleasure, Your Majesty. I shall see that he knows it is your will."

That was three things accomplished: a noncombatant sent out of the way; Armanes given a fighting chance to survive, although he would doubtless not appreciate being carried away from the battle; and a general he trusted sent to keep watch on one whose judgment was no longer reliable.

As he was turning his horse, Klestreus spun around in the saddle and said, "Oh, I beg Your Majesty's pardon for forgetting. Six hundred Nyklosi peasant levies have come in. I led them to the center before I heard the news of Prince Armanes's wound. And there is word from Tarr-Hostigos. Her Majesty Great Queen Rylla has gone into labor.''

"WHAT?"

Kalvan spent a moment suppressing several unproductive urges, such as having a heart attack or strangling Klestreus with his bare hands. Finally he said, very slowly, "I wish you had told me this first."

"Forgive me, Your Majesty. It seemed—"

"Never mind what it *seemed*." Although perhaps Klestreus had a point; the outcome of today's battle did make more difference to Hostigos than the outcome of Rylla's labor. Maybe even to him, but if some god came and told him that the price of certain victory today would by Rylla's life. . . .

There were advantages to not believing in gods who struck that kind of bargain, Kalvan decided.

After a few minutes of mulling over all the terrible things that might happen to Rylla and the baby, he realized that Klestreus had left to carry out his orders. A breeze was blowing now and he was able to see the entire Styphoni center, the huge Royal Square flanked by the smaller Great Squares. A great many things could go wrong with his plans today, but somehow they seemed far less personal than what was going on in the royal chambers at this moment.

Kalvan was wrenched out of his thoughts by the harsh sounds of a badly winded horse making its way to the top of the rise.

"Did you give Alkides my orders?"

"Yes, Your Majesty," said Major Nicomoth. "Though not before he wept and ranted as though it were his own children being impaled!"

Kalvan wasn't surprised. It hadn't been easy for him to order a dozen of his mobile four- and eight-pounders spiked and rendered useless, but that was far better than having them turned and used on the Hostigi center. Besides, the Styphoni were a big fish; they needed a bait to match.

"You gave Chartiphon his orders?"

"Yes. Captain-General Chartiphon will order the center to advance as soon as you give the signal. Count Harmakros is also bringing the remainder of the reserves into position."

May Dralm be with you, Harmakros, thought Kalvan. And Ptosphes too; there would be no one to pull the Prince's bacon out of the fire if he charged the Knights again and had to fall back. Still, if Prince Leonnestros in command of the Styphoni left wing continued to be as rash as he'd proven himself in the past. . . . Kalvan was sure he knew what Soton's orders were: force the Hostigi to commit *their* army until it is worn out, then grind them into the earth without mercy.

Kalvan watched as Harmakros threaded his Army of Observation through the area between the center and the right wing. Then the wind changed direction, and all Kalvan could see was a white cloud streaked with gray and black ribs. When the smoke cleared again, he could see that Harmakros's heavy cavalry were already forming the shield for the mobile artillery.

It seemed to take an hour for the dozen artillery pieces to move into position on the knoll, but Kalvan knew it had to be only ten or fifteen minutes. Already more than half the three thousand dragoons had passed through the Hostigi lines. It was at times like this that he missed a good watch more than anything except a hot shower.

Kalvan was betting his last dollar (or in this case, Hostigos crown) that Prince Leonnestros, eager to succeed Mnesiphoklos as Lord High Marshal of Hos-Ktemnos, could not sit still under the fire of a dozen Hostigi artillery pieces. If this ruse didn't come off, Kalvan didn't want to think about what would happen to the Hostigi gunners who in blind faith were standing behind guns that couldn't fire—and they wouldn't be the only casualties.

The Army of Observation and the mobile artillery were approaching their position now. Off to the left was mostly smoke, but Kalvan thought he saw the left wing shifting again. He couldn't see clearly, and in any case there was no time to find out or do more than hope the left would hold for a few more minutes.

Kalvan raised his arm, and the primitive Roman candle he'd had Master Thalmoth make exploded over the Hostigi center. Twelve thousand musketeers and pikemen moved forward, each pikeman holding a shield as well as a pike. Some of the shields bore the devices of recently deceased nobles of Hos-Harphax. Behind them came fifteen hundred halberdiers, several thousand peasant militia, and the four thousand Ktethroni pikemen.

Kalvan raised his other arm. The second Roman candle burst, and sunlight blazed off helmets, armor, and gun barrels as the cavalry of the right wing began to mount up.

TWENTY-THREE

I.

Xykos was so tall and strong that in his home village his nickname was "the Bull." The double weight of armor and shield was still beginning to tell on him as he tramped across the rocky ground, and he wondered how the others who didn't have his strength were faring. To be sure, his shield was twice the average height, with two musketeers moving half-crouched behind it.

Halfway to the Styphoni lines now, and not a shot fired from the blue and orange squares ahead. His brothers would not falter, even when the bullets came. Were they not the survivors of twenty times their number of foot who had died at Tenabra? Xykos himself had been only one of the Hostigi militia before Tenabra; now he was one of four hundred men of the Old Hostigos regiment, the Veterans of the Long March, commissioned by Prince Ptosphes himself. He had also been blooded long before Tenabra; first at the Battle of Listra-Mouth, then later at Fyk, where he liberated his armor from the dead body of a baron of Sask.

Tenabra had been his first battle where the Hostigi lost, thanks to that Dralm-cursed traitor Balthar! The billmen of Ktemnos had mowed down the Hostigi Foot at Tenabra like a farmer's scythe in a field of rye. Somehow he knew that wouldn't have happened had Great King Kalvan been in command rather than Prince Ptosphes. Ptosphes was a fair ruler and a good leader of men, but he was no god-sent Kalvan, favored by Father Dralm and given the gods' blessing to stop the heathen Styphoni.

Xykos would have been fertilizing the fields of Tenabra now if he hadn't been lucky enough to spear a Zarthani Knight with his pike and take his mount. The charger had proved a valued friend, although he'd had to remember to stay clear of its teeth and hooves. Like a true friend it had given its life so that he might fight and see his newborn son again.

Vurth, his wife's father, had argued after his return from Tenabra that he should stay and tend his farm. Let the gods settle the matters between the Great Kings! But Xykos knew where his loyalty and his duty lay. Besides, he was now one of the double-pay Veterans of the Long March, and the extra silver would do no harm when it came to buying new stock for the farm.

Then Xykos saw a wondrous sight. From either side of each enemy Square a line of men moved out like a hinged arm. Before he'd taken a dozen more steps, there was a thunderclap of muskets and the buzz of metal hornets. He heard cries of pain all around him and staggered as his shield slowed a bullet so that it bounced off his breastplate, then he fell back into step with the men on either side.

Another volley. Xykos felt a bullet crease his high-combed helmet. How much longer before Petty-Captain Lysthog gave the order to halt and return fire? Each musketeer was carrying two or three loaded smoothbores taken from a Hostigos Armory filled to the rafters with the loot of Kalvan's victory in Harphax. A ditty sung in Hostigos during the last moon told how Kalvan took cheese and bread to Hos-Harphax and returned with steel and lead.

Two more Styphoni volleys, each more ragged than the last, then the petty-captains gave the order to halt. Xykos set his shield and waited while the musketeers planted their rests. In the third Hostigi rank, he was close enough to the enemy front to make out individual figures. They were all dressed in blue shirts and breeches, with brown boiled-leather jacks for the musketeers and polished steel breastplates for the billmen, and high-crested helmets. The Royal Square was different; they wore silvered armor and orange stripes down their sleeves and the sides of their breeches.

"Fire!"

The first Hostigi volley tore into the Ktemnoi lines as if it had been artillery firing case shot. A great cheer rose from the Hostigi rank. The second volley was almost as devastating; the third less so. Now the musketeers were supposed to sling their weapons and fall back. Instead many of them picked up pikes or drew their swords and held their places.

"Pikes advance. CHARGE!"

As he began to run toward the Ktemnoi Squares, Xykos was amazed at how quickly their reinforcements moved forward to re-form the front ranks. The musketeers fired a last ragged volley at almost point-blank range, then fell back, leaving the billmen to take the Hostigi charge.

There was a cry from what seemed like ten thousand throats.

"KILL THE DEMON'S SPAWN!"

The billmen began their charge.

The Hostigi reply came:

"DOWN STYPHON!"

The two forces collided with such a shock that the first two Hostigi ranks disappeared before Xykos's eyes. He was eight ranks keep into what had once been the Ktemnoi line before he came to a stop with his thirty-six inch pike head buried half-way to the end of its iron head into a billman's hip. He dropped the pike and drew the two-handed sword Boarsbane from its scabbard across his back. He had the six-foot blade out in time to parry a blow from a billhead. His next stroke sent the blade through the billman's shoulder, splitting him down to the belly.

Xykos was trying to free his sword when another billman charged. The billhook was less than a foot from his face when a pikehead pierced the billman's neck and the billhook clanged harmlessly against the side of his helmet. Xykos wrenched his blade free, threw it up in the air, and brought it down so hard that he split the billman's head in two, helmet and all.

He looked around to see who his friend was, but Ktemnoi and Hostigi were so tangled it was impossible to tell and so jammed together there was no hope of retreating to a better place. Maybe this place was good enough, anyway; he could kill Styphoni as well here as anywhere else!

II.

Count Phrames rode over to the left wing at the head of the King's Heavy Horse, two hundred and sixty volunteers "too thick-headed or well-born to fight in a reasonable fashion," as Kalvan put it. All of the knights wore full-plate armor, visored helmets, heavy lances, and at least one pistol in a saddle-holster—their one concession to Kalvan-style warfare. While Phrames realized their limited value, he still couldn't help respecting them for their loyalty to an older and more honorable way of war. Warfare under King Kalvan was more efficient and deadly than ever before, yet there was still something grand and noble that it would be a pity to lose in the pageantry of several hundred knights and men-at-arms in silvered or gilded armor on brightly-caparisoned horses.

It was Kalvan's hope that the Heavy Horse would give the left wing an anvil to blunt the wedge of the Zarthani Knights, who had previously cut through Ptosphes's Army of the Besh like a poignard through cheese. By Dralm's Grace, Kalvan was familiar with this novel formation and claimed there was not enough time to school the Hostigi in a counterwedge or enough room to outflank the Knights' wedge.

So there would be only the anvil of the King's Heavy Horse and the stout hearts of the Hostigi to keep the Zarthani Knights from dispersing the left wing and outflanking the center as they had at Tenabra. While he rarely wished ill of any man, for Prince Balthar of Beshta Phrames hoped there was an eternity of some special torture waiting in the Caverns of Regwarn.

Prince Ptosphes, ten years older by the day of Tenabra alone, rode out to meet Phrames with a small bodyguard.

"Reinforcements from King Kalvan, Your Grace."

"I hope we can put them to good use. I pray that King Kalvan did not give us that which he could not afford to lose."

"No, sire. If Harmakros's artillery draws off Prince Leonnestros as Kalvan believes, these men will not be needed. If not, it matters little where they fight so long as they die well."

"Well spoken, Phrames!" said Ptosphes with more fervor than the Count remembered seeing since the Prince returned from Tenabra.

Phrames outlined Kalvan's plan, and Prince Ptosphes drew up the Heavy Horse into a single line, " 'en haie" as Kalvan called it. He then formed a second line with his own and Prince Sarrask's heavily armored Princely bodyguard, and a third and even larger line with the household and noble cavalry of Nostor, Sashta, and Kyblos. The remainder of the Princely armies and mercenary horse were to follow in close order under Phrames.

At the flash of the fireseed signal, the King's Heavy Horse advanced at the center. When they had covered an eighth of the field, the heavy cavalry of Hostigos and Sask moved forward.

As the red and blue plumes of Prince Ptosphes's bodyguard began to recede, Phrames saw the Zarthani Knights begin their charge. From where he sat on the ridge, the tip of the wedge looked like a black lance tip. It almost was, for it was composed of eight hundred Brother Knights in their blackened full-plate armor with heavy lance, followed in succession by sixteen hundred Confrère Knights, as many sergeants, and eight hundred oath-brothers with javelin and sword. Against light cavalry the oath-brothers would have been leading, to act as skirmishers; today they followed in the rear to dispatch the wounded and guard prisoners.

The Hostigi third line began its charge, and at the same time Phrames saw the Knights' wedge pierce the King's Heavy Horse. The gap grew wider as the Heavy Horse pressed home their charge, but when Ptosphes and the second line hit the Knights, Phrames could see that the entire formation was being blunted and slowed down.

He signaled to his trumpeter, who blew the "Advance," and cantered out ahead of his men to indicate the proper direction. By the time he'd done that, however, the powder smoke was swirling so thickly he wasn't entirely sure himself which way to go.

He kept moving, however, and broke out of the smoke less than fifty yards behind the third line at the exact moment it struck the nose of the Zarthani wedge. This time the Knights didn't break through at once; men and horses clumped together where the two lines met. Then the front of the wedge pushed through the third line, but it was no longer a point but a truncated pyramid, obviously shaken and, Phrames devoutly hoped, at last vulnerable. He gave the signal and this time all the trumpets blew together.

"CHARGE!"

At the first shock Phrames's banner-bearer was hurled out of his saddle, impaled on a lance point but still holding the banner with the Count's device of a golden eagle. Phrames had a moment to think that this was the third banner-bearer of his to be killed or wounded this year, then had a clear shot at the Knight. He shot the man out of his seat before the other could even draw his sword, then threw the pistol away and pulled another from its saddle-holster, firing almost at once. Another Knight dropped from his white-barded horse and disappeared underneath the hooves. This pistol Phrames thrust into his red sash, then drew his sword.

Some of the Knights began to fire their own pistols, then the lines crashed together with a resounding metallic thud, so that nobody dared shoot for fear of hitting a friend. . . .

Harmakros watched with delight as Prince Leonnestros advanced from the Styphoni left wing toward the Army of Observation's advanced battery. Now, by Dralm, they had a real fighting chance, and that was all they'd ever asked for. Praise Dralm and Galzar, he promised no more prayers today! Leonnestros was leading eight hundred knights of the Royal Guard and two thousand of the King's Pistoleers forward with far more contempt for his Hostigi opponents than was prudent. He was about to learn a lesson in respect.

Harmakros's trumpets sounded the recall to the Hostigi cavalry, and he was pleased to see most of them withdrawing toward their infantry support, two crescent-shaped ranks of musketeers with two ranks of pikemen behind them. A few hotheads stayed to fight and died quickly. Before Kalvan it would have been all or most of them; once more it was brought home to Harmakros just how much they owed this man from beyond the Cold Lands.

By the time the retreating cavalry were safely behind the infantry, Leonnestros's vanguard was in range. Harmakros gave the order for the musketeers to fire. Fifteen hundred muskets went off almost as one, blowing the Ktemnoi Royal Guard out of existence as an organized military unit. Even without the King's Mounted Rifles, the Hostigi dragoons were the best mounted troops of the Great King's army and Harmakros was positive that every third shot had hit.

The Royal Guard might have been mortally wounded, but there was nothing wrong with the King's Pistoleers. They shook out their lines and charged the impudent Hostigi.

The dragoon musketeers got off a ragged second volley, then withdrew behind the pikemen to where their horses were being held. They didn't have to defeat Leonnestros, just tempt him to swallow a tasty piece of bait. The charge of the King's Pistoleers told Harmakros that the plan was working.

The pikemen held off the first charge, taking about as many casualties as they inflicted. Most of the musketeers were already mounted and withdrawing in good order. He gave the order for the pikemen to begin their own retreat.

This was the most dangerous part of the operation; the pikemen not only had to retreat, but they had to keep their formation, not let the enemy know what was happening, *and* avoid taking so many casualties that they ceased to be an effective unit. If they succeeded, Harmakros intended to recommend them for one of Kalvan's "Unit Citations."

As the Pistoleers gathered for their second charge, Harmakros gave the signal for the advance of the Hostigi cavalry. *Now, my iron-heads, you may die with honor.*

The sudden countercharge by the Hostigi cavalry took Leonnestros and the King's Pistoleers by surprise. Leonnestros, conspicuous in his black and gold armor with orange and blue plumes, tried to rally his men, but they were quickly thrown into disorder by a force less than a quarter their size. They lost several hundred men before they rallied enough to begin pushing the Hostigi back.

By then Harmakros saw that most of the dragoon pikemen were mounted and moving out. He gave the final signal. Barely half the original force of Hostigi horse broke off the action and galloped for the Hostigi lines. The artillerymen, with no support or protection at all, were the last to leave. Harmakros hoped Alkides would forgive him.

Waving and gesturing wildly to keep his Pistoleers from scattering in pursuit of the retreating Hostigi cavalry, Leonnestros directed his men toward the Hostigi redoubt. Harmakros was relieved to see that the Pistoleers saw little glory in chasing artillerymen and let most of them get clear.

Some of the Pistoleers dismounted and began to swing the already loaded field pieces around to face the Hostigi. Others crowded excitedly around the piled barrels of fireseed the cowardly Hostigi had left behind them. Leonnestros must have been preening himself on a victory that would earn him the praise and gold of Styphon's House, and better yet, the post he coveted.

Enjoy it while you can, you strutting capon! If by some undeserved miracle Leonnestros survived the battle, the only reward he was going to get for disobeying Soton's orders would be the sharp end of the Grand Master's tongue, if not the blunt end of the Grand Master's mace.

III.

Grand-Captain Phidestros began to question whether it had been a good idea after all to join the Holy Host when he saw Prince Leonnestros dash madly off toward the Hostigi battery. Grand Master Soton knew his craft, no doubt about it, but his lesser captains from Mnesiphoklos on down left much to be desired.

To do them justice, Phidestros had no idea of what he would have done himself in Leonnestros's boots, not with the Hostigi building an artillery redoubt from which they could hammer the left wing of the Holy Host at will! Great King Kalvan had turned what had once been a straightforward, honest profession into something that made the head hurt as much from thinking as the arse did from riding!

It was bad enough that the Hostigi seemed to have an improbably large number of heavy guns in their center. Worse still, the Zarthani Knights' battery was too close to the left wing for even a drinking man's comfort. One of the former Beshtan companies under his command had already lost its banner-bearer and a petty-captain to "friendly" guns.

What was he supposed to do now that Prince Leonnestros had all but deserted his post? As Grand-Captain of the largest band, Soton had put him in nominal command of the mercenary horse under Leonnestros. As he watched Kalvan's musketeers butcher the Royal Guard, he decided that it would be best to stay where he was. Men newly raised to grand-captain and given *any* charge over five thousand horse did not make great changes in Grand Master Soton's battle plans without a damned good reason!

Yet everyone else—Leonnestros and the King's Pistoleers, the Sacred Squares, and even the Zarthani Knights on the right wing—were engaged with the enemy. Here he sat with Kalvan and more horse than he liked to think about less than two furlongs away. What was Kalvan waiting for? Leonnestros to piss his men away against the new battery? Something else that only Kalvan could imagine?

Phidestros watched as the Hostigi musketeers began their retreat to the battery while Leonnestros tried to regroup his Pistoleers and the surviving Royal Guards. Leonnestros was going to have to take the battery before it opened fire or there wouldn't be enough left of him and his command for Soton to punish. Kalvan-style guns were like nothing any Ktemnoi had ever faced.

Phidestros was surprised at how quickly the Hostigi pikemen retreated before Leonnestros's Pistoleers. Surprised—and uneasy. Something was wrong there. He'd never seen Hostigi foot retreat like that, either at Fyk or at the Heights of Chothros.

It was a trap! He had to get a warning off to Leonnestros before it was too late.

"Uroth!"

"Yes, Grand-Captain?"

"There's no time to write a dispatch. Warn Prince Leonnestros to examine Kalvan's demicannon. I suspect treachery; the Hostigi yielded that battery far too easily. Now ride like the wind!"

As he watched the last of Kalvan's dragoons ride away and Leonnestros's men begin to swarm over the deserted battery, Phidestros felt a hollow sensation in his stomach. Not only had he sent a good man to a needless death, but he was about to watch the Holy Host come apart at the seams.

TWENTY-FOUR

I.

Xykos turned around warily, Boarsbane raised toward the sky. Other than the twisted husks of what had once been living men, some piled three and four deep, there was no one in any direction for a good twenty paces. Xykos set his sword down and tried to clear his head of the battle-madness that possessed him when he fought. His lungs labored like bellows, and for the first time he noticed that his breastplate was dented in half a dozen places. With this realization came the ache of bruised ribs and weary arms pushed far beyond ordinary duty.

Xykos knew this unexpected and unasked-for sanctuary would not last long. He turned around, trying to learn how the battle was going and where. Above the pikes and flailing bills, he saw the trees of the Grove of the Badger King. From where he stood, it appeared that the battle had passed over him and the Veterans of the Long March.

Within a few minutes he had located a dozen Hostigi stragglers and battle-stunned. Three or four of them had risen from the piles of dead and wounded like Hadron awakening in the Lost Mountain. One of the stragglers was Tibyon, the banner-bearer of the Veterans, still carrying the ripped and slashed flag bearing an iron boot crushing a red winged serpent. With the help of some of the Veterans, Xykos soon assembled a force of nearly thirty men, some with slight wounds but most in good spirits. Those who weren't he set to aiding the more gravely wounded.

Now the main battle was far enough away so that Xykos could see what had happened. The troops of the right and left flanks of the Hostigi center had held, while the middle had given way. The two Great Squares were no longer in any sort of recognizable formation and had apparently been well hammered by the Hostigi flanks. The Royal Square had shifted to the weakest point in the Hostigi center and was slowly chewing its way toward the Great Battery.

The Great Battery itself was almost silent, with only an occasional flash showing that it was still Hostigi-held. Xykos supposed that the two armies had become so entangled that the Hostigi gunners were afraid to fire on the Holy Host for fear of killing their own men.

It would be sheer folly to attack the Ktemnoi rear with only thirty men, especially since that meant going against Styphon's Red Hand. Instead Xykos decided to move quickly along the flank of both centers until they were in a position to help relieve the Great Battery. He hastily explained this plan to his little company and no one argued. Indeed they moved out almost eagerly, when they saw a troop of horse under Styphon's banner looking curiously in their direction.

The horse rode off without attacking, but they'd only covered a quarter of the distance to the Great Battery when a company of the Red Hand broke out of the main battle and formed a line facing Xykos's men. Their first rank let fly a ragged volley. Three of Xykos's men dropped. He measured the distance to the Styphoni with his eyes, threw up Boarsbane, and shouted, "Charge!"

Xykos was first into the Styphoni line, and their short-hafted glaives were no match for a double-handed sword wielded by a giant. Within a minute his men had joined him with their halberds and pikes and captured bills. The Red Hand still outnumbered Xykos's men four to one, and would have given better than they got if they hadn't been in three ranks instead of one.

Xykos was wrestling Boarsbane out of an enemy's corpse with one hand and strangling another man with his left, when there was an explosion so loud that he almost went to his knees. Sword and enemies forgotten for a moment, Xykos brought both hands up to his ears. One was bleeding and both were numb, almost deaf. He turned to see the barrel of a field piece flying end over end high above his head. He stared as it landed in the middle of the rear rank of the Red Hand, turning it into a mob of writhing red figures. He knew they had to be screaming and shouting, but he heard nothing.

He looked down to see both friends and enemies littering the ground like branches fallen from a tree. Some had been killed by flying pieces of iron, others knocked down and stunned by the unholy blast. Tibyon was still gripping the Veterans' banner, and Xykos helped the banner-bearer to his feet, then started rallying the survivors of his company.

He and Tibyon gathered a dozen. Meanwhile, hundreds of Styphoni all around them were still stunned or wounded, unable to rise. Many of those who had risen were lurching about as if they were drunk on winter wine.

"Attack!" Xykos shouted. Or at least that was what he thought he shouted. No one including himself seemed to hear.

Then he realized that for what had to be done, no words were really needed.

"Down Styphon!" he shouted, grabbing the hair of the nearest Red Hand. As the man dangled, feet kicking a span clear of the ground, Xykos drew his dagger with his free hand and let all his men see what he wanted done.

Kalvan watched with grim satisfaction as the tiny Ktemnoi figure at the redoubt fired the first of the captured Hostigi guns. A giant flash was followed by a deep rumble as the first gun blew up. Right behind it came another blast and then a flash and roar that made Kalvan think of a nuclear explosion, as five tons of strategically-placed Hostigi fireseed went off at once.

The mercenaries seemed to escape the worst of the damage; their commander must have guessed the nature of Kalvan's trap in time to pull his men clear. He couldn't have been able to warn Leonnestros, though, or else the Prince hadn't been willing to believe him. Leonnestros's command was gathered around the redoubt when it erupted, and two thousand Ktemnoi horse vanished as a fighting force along with the Hostigi guns.

The ringing in Kalvan's ears was so loud that he was glad he'd set up a system of hand signals for the charge. He took a final sober look at the Hostigi center, still being squeezed by the Royal Square, then raised his hand. Major Nicomoth had tried to persuade him to stay on the ridge with his Horse Guards and command the battle from there, but once again there were too many good reasons for him leading the charge himself.

Most of the battle was already in other hands, for better or worse. Ptosphes, Phrames, Chartiphon, Alkides, and Harmakros all had their own parts of it to win. Besides, who else did he have to lead the right wing, after sending Phrames to join Ptosphes? Colonel Democriphon of the First Royal Lancers was a good commander, even if he did bear an uncanny resemblance to George Armstrong Custer, with his long blond hair and flowing mustache. Kalvan had his eye on the man, but he'd need more seasoning, and there was nobody else remotely good enough except—

Kalvan realized that he'd been woolgathering with all eyes on him. No time for that now. He raised his hand again, and this time the ringing in his ears didn't drown out the shouts all around him.

"Down Styphon!"

Harmakros's head reeled. Two thousand men and horses and a dozen field pieces, all ruined in the wink of an eye. Dralm forgive him, but maybe there *was* something in this fireseed-demon tale of Styphon's House. Not that Great King Kalvan was any demon; he was human enough, as anyone knew who'd watched him suffer through one of Rylla's late-term furies. But this fireseed—that was another matter entirely. Enough of that could destroy the whole world; if he'd doubted it before, he'd just seen the proof with his own eyes.

Kalvan's charge was now halfway across the meadow, and he could make out the Styphoni mercenaries preparing their countercharge. With Kalvan commanding and the right wing outnumbering the mercenaries by at least three thousand men, there was little doubt about the outcome of that engagement.

If Kalvan wasn't going to need help, what should he do with his reserve? He had both Count Phrames in person and a messenger from Chartiphon appealing desperately for it. What he decided was likely to determine the outcome of the battle as much as anything that happened on this field today, including the fireseed surprise he'd just given Leonnestros.

"Harmakros, we need your help," said Phrames, as close to pleading as he would ever come. "When Soton struck us with his pistoleers, I thought we were finished. If it hadn't been for Prince Sarrask rallying the Saski horse, we would have broken. After Tenabra and today there won't be enough Old Hostigi cavalry to make up a full regiment. Yet Ptosphes is prepared to die with his last man rather than retreat. I'm afraid he may have his wish."

"Phrames, I can give you my two regiments of horse, but not a man more. My dragoons are needed here to reinforce the center. If the Great Battery falls, Soton will turn it on our own army. We have to hold the Battery until King Kalvan can cut his way through the Styphoni mercenaries and hit their center from the rear. I'm sorry, but that's all I can do. May Dralm and Galzar guard you and Prince Ptosphes this day."

Prince Sarrask laughed until his sides ached when his mount reared and fell upon the haunches of the Zarthani Knight's black horse as though attempting to mount it for an entirely different kind of sport than war. The Knight toppled from his saddle and fell to certain death on the ground below. That was one less of Styphon's spawn to worry about, but there seemed no end of them today!

The Knights were tough crayfish to pry open, especially the ones in full armor. His old two-handed sword and mace were all that had kept him from Galzar's side several times this day. He'd fired both his pistols until he had no more bullets or fireseed, then used them as clubs until they broke.

This was the fiercest fight he'd ever been in, as fierce a fight as a man could dream of! He'd have to thank Kalvan over some wine this evening for giving him such a gift. By Galzar's Mace—now there was a *man!*

Suddenly a roaring explosion swallowed the screaming of horses and men, the steady hammering of muskets and artillery, even the clang of steel on steel. Through his saddle Sarrask felt a rumble as though Endrath, God of the Earth, had shaken the ground itself. Every horse in sight including his own tried to rear and bolt. Without room to run, they only dashed futilely against one another, sometimes dismounting their riders. Sarrask knew that men and horses must be screaming even louder than before, but he could hear nothing except a shrill ringing in his ears.

The Knights' ranks suddenly opened and Sarrask was sure he saw Grand Master Soton, with his open helm and gleaming war hammer, staring around him in utter disbelief. Sarrask slapped his mount with his sword to get its attention, then charged toward the opening. He was pleased to note that a dozen of his bodyguards were following close behind. Then the opening closed and Soton vanished so fast that Sarrask wondered if he'd imagined both.

Sarrask shook his head to clear his thoughts. Soton might get away, but there were plenty of Knights within easy reach, ready to be killed. He whirled his mace over his head.

"Down Styphon!"

TWENTY-FIVE

I.

For as long as he lived, Grand-Captain Phidestros knew he would never forget the explosion of the Hostigi redoubt. More than a third of the left wing was gone in one earth-shattering moment—men, armor, horses, weapons, everything. If intuition hadn't told him to withdraw his own command, the casualties could have been doubled. As it was, he'd lost several hundred men and horses, killed or panicked by the blast and the flying debris from it, and it was going to be Hadron's own job getting them ready to receive Kalvan's charge. Nor was what he devoutly hoped was everybody's temporary deafness making things any easier.

When the Hostigi horse had covered about two-thirds of the distance to the Holy Host, Phidestros knew he'd done everything he could and signaled for the countercharge. His flank was organized by companies, ten wide and two or three deep, with the lancers in front. He had no illusions about turning the Hostigi wing, but he thought he could hold them long enough for Soton to come to his aid. Even a thousand fresh reinforcements could make the difference between victory and defeat.

He could see with his own eyes how the Sacred Squares were chewing up the Hostigi center. Galzar grant him the chance to do the same to the Hostigi right!

The crash of arms and armor as the two cavalry charges met

reminded Phidestros uncomfortably of the Slaughter at Ryklos Farm and the unseemly end of the Royal Lancers of Hos-Harphax. Might Ormax condemn Leonnestros to eternal torment in the Caverns of Regwarn for deserting his post!

For a moment it appeared as though Kalvan's charge might be broken; there were few heavily-armored lancers in the Hostigi front ranks. Then from the second and third ranks came point-blank pistol fire, tearing through the front ranks of the mercenaries.

Phidestros pressed his knees into Snowdrift's flanks, raised his sword, and led the Iron Band into the Hostigi lines. The Iron Band's first volley emptied fifty Hostigi saddles, including many of King Kalvan's bodyguards. For a moment no longer than the blink of an eye, the two commanders were within sword distance, then the currents of the battle took them apart before either had an opportunity to do more than stare.

Phidestros looked down at his still loaded pistol and cursed. What had stopped him from firing, or even thinking about it? Maybe it had been the dawning of recognition on Kalvan's face and his own confirming nod. There was something between the two of them—no doubt about that—but it was nothing to be settled in the heat and confusion of a battle. Kalvan had also held his pistol but not fired. For the first time, Phidestros wondered if he had picked the wrong side in this war to the death—and to the death it was, because Styphon's House would not rest until Great King Kalvan and Hostigos were no more.

There were worse ways to die than at the side of good and brave men. But there would be—could be—no parley with Kalvan until Prince Sarrask was dead, and from all reports the Prince led a charmed life, much like Kalvan himself. Maybe there was something to this notion of a War of the Gods?

Phidestros had no time to do more than ask the question, because a Hostigi captain with long fair hair and no helmet was trying to skewer him with the longest and most pointed blade Phidestros had ever seen. His breastplate turned away several thrusts, then he found himself out of reach of the blond captain. He looked around him and saw nothing but the red sashes and the red and blue plumes of Hos-Hostigos. He shot a Hostigi trooper aiming a musketoon at him and saw a red blossom appear where the man's face had been. Looking

behind him for a moment, he was relieved to see the black
plumes and orange sashes of a score of Iron Band troopers
fighting their way to his side.

Suddenly Snowdrift screamed loud enough that even
Phidestros's numbed ears could hear, then reared. He came
down on all four legs, tried to rear again, then his hind legs
crumpled and he sagged backward. Phidestros leaped from
the saddle, landing hard enough to make his knee compain
sharply. He snatched his saddle pistols free as Snowdrift rolled
over on his left side.

Blood was flowing from Snowdrift's mouth and from under
his belly; he was dying but not fast enough for Phidestros to
just leave him. He pressed his pocket pistol to the gelding's
head, closed his eyes, and pulled the trigger.

That gesture almost cost him his life. Phidestros opened
his eyes to see Snowdrift relaxing in death, but neither un-
wounded horses nor friendly riders close enough to help him
remount. Geblon was the closest, and he was forty paces
away, trying desperately to control a wounded horse without
dropping the Iron Band's banner.

While Phidestros was trying to attract Geblon's attention, a
bullet sang past his helmet. He dropped to hands and knees
behind Snowdrift and shot a Hostigi heavy cavalry man off his
horse. He looked up again to see an Iron Band lancer riding
up, leading a blood-smeared but seemingly fit mount. Too
small to carry him far, but better than remaining here.

As Phidestros rode back to his own lines, he saw several
groups of mercenaries raising helmets on sword points or
holding out reversed pistols. His only consolation was that
none of them wore the black plumes of the Iron Band.

II.

Brother Mytron clenched his hands tighter each
time he heard a scream from the royal bedchamber, now the

birthing room. He knew Rylla well enough to know that only terrible pain could wrench cries like that from her lips. It was just as well that King Kalvan had other matters of equal importance to keep him occupied. It was obvious that all was not going well in the birthing room.

If only he could see for himself! But Amasphalya, the chief midwife, had refused to allow him entrance, nor would she answer his questions the few times she came out into the antechamber for fresh air. The next time he saw the old witch he would have his answers if he had to shake them out of her!

A moment later the door flew open and Amasphalya lumbered out, followed by one of her assistants. She would have made three of even Mytron's fairly considerable figure, and thrust him aside as if he'd been a child, then stopped and looked him up and down like a butcher deciding whether or not to condemn a side of beef as fit only for dogs.

"What is it?" Mytron feared now for Rylla's life but was glad to note his voice was steady.

"I need more help. Come. You'll have to do."

Mytron put a hand on the midwife's shouler to stop her, but she brushed it off like a bothersome fly. He hurried after the women into the bedchamber, where Rylla lay sprawled in the royal bed. She was alive, but Mytron could not look at her pale, pain-lined face long enough to tell more than that.

Amasphalya and the other midwife each grasped one of Rylla's arms, while the one who'd remained in the chamber stood back.

"Take her feet, priest," snapped Amasphalya.

"But why?"

"No time for questions, priest! *Do* it!"

Mytron found himself obeying, even though he still questioned. Rylla screamed again as he gripped her feet.

"What do I do now?"

"Shake!" cried Amasphalya.

Without thinking, Mytron began to jerk on Rylla's feet in time with the two midwives holding her arms. Rylla's screams rose higher; Mytron fought an urge to faint.

I must stop them. They're killing her! What will I say to Kalvan—?

"Turn her! Turn her!" Amasphalya was shouting, apparently not to him. Then:

"Don't stop now, priest! We've almost done it!"

Done what? Mytron asked himself, but like a puppet he kept his arms moving, shaking Rylla who was now lying on her side, right or left he didn't know.

"There, the gods be thanked!" said Amasphyla. She sounded almost as if she were praying.

"Is the baby coming?" Mytron had to lick his lips three times before he could get the words out.

"Not yet, but now it's to where it can," said the midwife. The next moment her face set as if she regretted having said even so much to a man about her profession, and she growled, "Be off with you, priest. We've enough to do without picking you up off the floor too!"

Mytron was starting to reply, then took a step and realized that his knees had turned to syrup. He had to hold on to the bedpost for a moment to before he could weave his way to the door.

Looking back, he saw that Rylla's face was no longer twisted in agony and she was breathing more strongly; when the contractions came she groaned rather than screamed. Whatever had been done, it seemed to be the right thing. For the moment at least, he need not fear the burden of having to tell Kalvan that his wife and child were dead.

For the rest of his life, he would wonder why he'd been fool enough to want to know what went on in birthing chambers!

III.

"Where are the reinforcements?" asked Brigadier-General Alkides, his face and breeches black with soot. "What did Captain-General Chartiphon say?"

"The Great King told him to hold back a reserve in case the Knights defeated or outflanked Ptosphes. Which is what he intends to do, Great Battery or no Great Battery," replied Verkan.

Alkides was obviously nearly beside himself at the thought

that the Styphoni might soon be using his precious artillery. To make matters worse, the Hostigi and the Holy Host were so thoroughly entangled that the gunners of the Great Battery had been holding their fire for most of the battle.

Verkan could well understand why Chartiphon was holding back the last of the reserve, the Ktethroni pikemen. It was clearly the safest course of action. Verkan also knew that the safest course of action in a battle was not always the best.

Harmakros's dragoons had helped bring the Royal Square to a halt, but now it was advancing again. It struck Verkan that the Ktemnoi infantry were living up to their reputation. For that matter, so were the Hostigos regulars, and in any case the time for dispassionate evaluations of comparative military prowess was about over. The Mounted Rifles were the last line of defense for the Great Battery; they were either going to stop the Holy Host or die trying.

Verkan saw Harmakros lead another company of dragoon musketeers to a small barricade that had now become the next-to-last line of defense.

"Colonel," said Captain Itharos. "We should be going down to join those dragoons."

"We haven't had any orders."

"We haven't had any orders not to, either," said Itharos.

Verkan frowned. The captain had been at Tenabra and obviously wanted to avenge forty or so lost comrades badly enough to argue with his Colonel. By regular here-and-now standards he wasn't committing a serious offense, particularly against an outlander, but for the Mounted Rifles, here-and-now standards—

Another gun saved Verkan the trouble of replying. He looked down the slope. The Royal Square was still advancing slowly in the face of the fire from the barricade. Both the front ranks of billmen and the rear ranks of musketeers looked much neater from a distance than they doubtless did close up. The ground between the Ktemnoi and Harmakros's position was littered with discarded weapons, dead horses, dead and not-so-dead men of both sides. . . .

Verkan stared in surprise as four battered and battle-stained Hostigi soldiers ran up the slope toward him. The man in the lead was a giant in armor that looked as if it had been chewed on by wolves, holding in one hand a two-handed sword taller than Verkan. Behind him came two men with bloodstained halberds and a badly wounded banner-bearer, only just on his feet but grimly holding a large blue flag with a black boot stamping on a red winged serpent.

"Acting Petty-Captain Xykos reporting, sir," said the giant.

"Who ordered you here, Petty-Captain?"

"No one, sir. We're all that's left of the Old Hostigos regiment, the Veterans of the Long March. We fought our way out of the battle and I thought this is where we might be needed."

Verkan shook his head in amazement. Most NCO's here-and-now would have taken hours to answer that question, with blow-by-blow accounts of every skirmish. Here was obviously a man with some leadership potential; he'd have to talk to Kalvan about Xykos—that is, assuming all of them survived this battle.

"Captain Xykos. Why don't you and your men stay with me? I think we'll have all the fighting we want in less than a quarter-candle." *Or sooner.* Most of the retreating Hostigi had dispersed to either side of the Great Battery. Verkan hoped Chartiphon could rally and re-form them, but that couldn't happen soon enough to make up for the lack of the Ktethroni pikemen. Verkan needed all the help he could get, and Xykos looked worth a whole platoon by himself.

"Yes, sir!" said Xykos with a savage grin.

As if that was a cue, Captain Itharos came running up, followed by a messenger.

"What is it?"

"The Holy Warriors are coming against the Great Battery," said the messenger.

Itharos's jaw dropped. "Galzar have mercy!"

Verkan didn't bother replying. This meant that either Ptosphes and the Hostigi left wing were in retreat, or that Soton was so confident of victory that he'd committed what had to be nearly his last reserves to help the Royal Square take the Great Battery. Neither was particularly good news, although he preferred the former to the latter. He knew that even with Harmakros's help they couldn't stop the Holy Warriors, but they could delay them enough to buy Kalvan some more time.

"It looks as if it's mostly up to us for a while," said Verkan quietly.

Verkan moved through the ranks of the Mounted Rifles,

patting shoulders and giving encouraging little speeches while he mentally noted the number of walking wounded and near battle-fatigue cases. The Great Battery was firing more steadily, now that most of the Hostigi center was behind or around the rise. The crowd of soot-blackened figures around the guns gave the impression of a horde of demons toiling at some sinister task.

Verkan was glad he wasn't carrying any First Level gear in this battle; the odds were too good that the dead-man timer would detonate the security charge on his body among live comrades. He was willing to kill deliberately to protect the Paratime Secret; he'd be Dralm-damned if he would do it by simple chance if he could avoid it.

Verkan took his own position along with his bodyguard behind a boulder, shouted "Down Styphon!" and looked down the hill. The Holy Warriors of Styphon were mounted volunteers from all over the Great Kingdoms, most of them real believers in the Gunpowder God. Not too well mounted, he noted, or else they'd been at the back of the line when supplies were distributed. Not too well armed either, mostly swords and pistols, and few of them armored, but three thousand or more of them against five to six hundred dragoons and a hundred and thirty rifled muskets still wasn't Verkan's idea of safe odds.

Then several thousand of the Holy Warriors were coming up the slope at a trot, and Verkan stopped worrying about anything but finding a target. Harmakros's musketeers fired a volley, and the front rank swayed and shivered. Verkan sighted on a thin man on a roan horse, wearing a back-and-breast with Styphon's circular swastika painted on the chest, shifted his elbow slightly, and squeezed the trigger. The man fell forward on his horse's neck, his horse reared and lost its footing, and two more lost theirs trying to avoid the fallen ones.

A Rifleman next to Verkan picked off one of the fallen riders as he struggled to his feet. Verkan yanked out his ramrod, the next bullet, its leather patch, fumbled for his powder horn, and cursed the spectacle he must be making of himself—the outlander Colonel who wasn't as well trained as his men!

Suddenly his rifle was loaded and swinging down to firing position; he had a beautiful target in a rider turning broadside to avoid a patch of rough ground. This time he hit the horse, and someone firing wildly hit the top of his rock close enough to spray rock dust into his eyes. He found the old familiar motions coming back so perfectly that he didn't even wait to blink his eyes clear before he started reloading.

On his next reload he heard volley firing close at hand and looked around to find that his bodyguards had scrounged enough abandoned rifles and muskets to give each of them several weapons apiece. He gave them a thumbs-up signal—an almost universal signal on every time-line—and felt pleased when they responded with wolfish grins. It was almost a shame he couldn't take them along the next time he had to appear before the Executive Council!

When he looked down again, the Holy Warriors were at the barricade, in the process of being repulsed by Harmakros's musketeers and pikemen. Wielded by veterans who knew their strengths and weaknesses, the eighteen-foot pikes were deadly against the poorly equipped Holy Warriors. Verkan saw one man take a pikehead through the mouth that came out the back of his head. Others were speared out of their saddles and sent tumbling down to join the rocks under the horses' hooves.

At last the Holy Warriors retreated back down the slope out of range, dismounted, and advanced again at a dead run. Harmakros's musketeers shot them down by the dozen, but that wasn't enough; hundreds of them reached the barricade and it was suddenly every man for himself. The pikemen dropped their pikes in favor of swords and pistols, while the musketeers swung their empty weapons like clubs. Almost half his dragoons were dead or wounded before Harmakros began a slow retreat to the top of the ridge.

Verkan fired five shots and hit four men before the first wave of dismounted Holy Warriors reached his boulder. He fired a sixth shot, then clubbed his own rifle, letting his unarmed-combat training take over his muscles and reflexes. He might look a little odd if anyone was watching carefully, but he'd not lay any bets on that and he did intend to stay alive.

The rifle wasn't balanced quite like the quarterstaff Verkan knew well, but the butt end's extra weight made up for it. With ridiculous ease he brained the first man who ran at him, kicked a second in the groin, smashed a short sword or long knife out of the hand of a third, and knocked down a fourth with a butt-blow to his armored chest and finished him with another to the forehead under the rim of his helmet.

He turned to see Xykos decapitate a heavily bearded Holy Warrior with his two-handed sword. The Veterans' banner-bearer had lost one arm to an evil-looking polearm and was in the process of losing the other when Verkan shot his attacker dead with his belt pistol.

Someone was shouting in his ear and tugging at his arm. It was Itharos again, pulling him back from the edge of the slope. Xykos and one of the halberdiers were coming with him, but the third Veteran was dead and the banner-bearer was dying, one arm gone, the other crippled, but his teeth locked on the banner pole.

They cleared the Great Battery's field of fire just in time, as case shot from something heavier than a four-pounder sprayed the slope. A dozen dismounted Holy Warriors and twenty mounted ones behind them went down, and twice as many turned and ran; apparently even religious zeal had its limits.

Verkan and his bodyguards ran back another fifty yards, then stopped to make sure the rest of the Mounted Rifles were clear. They were. The number of Holy Warriors both mounted and on foot climbing the slope discouraged him from lingering to count the Rifles' casualties, particularly since the Holy Warriors were now being pushed ahead of the first ranks of the Royal Square. A company of billmen rose out of a draw, and a round shot smashed the first six of them into a bloody, screaming tangle.

Verkan started to reload his rifle on the move, and discovered the lock was hopelessly jammed with blood and hair. He made a mental note to suggest caltrops to Kalvan if he could find a noncontaminating way of doing so. Strewn over the slopes of the ridge, those multipointed hoof destroyers would have made Kalvan's Great Battery a lot more cavalry-proof.

The ground between Verkan and the Great Battery offered little cover or concealment, and he had the nasty feeling that the career of the Mounted Rifles was about to end here. A four-pounder had already been overrun, and an old-style eight-pounder was being defended by its crew against mounted Holy Warriors. What was left of Harmakros's three regiments of dragoons was manhandling two eight-pounders and the sixteen-pounder called *Galzar's Teeth* into a position where they could hit the Styphoni at point-blank range.

Alkides himself was standing on the breech of *Galzar's Teeth* in a fraction of his shirt and a smaller fraction of his trousers, defaming the ancestry and habits of his gunners for not moving faster. Behind the big gun rode Harmakros, and behind him was a line of men carrying objects the size and shape of round shot but not quite. . . .

Verkan suddenly realized he was about to see the first test of explosive shells in Kalvan's Time-Line. While he appreciated the honor, he hoped the fusing was reasonably accurate, or the shells might burst right over the Mounted Rifles.

"Down!" he shouted, gesturing frantically. The Riflemen obeyed, searching for any fold in the ground large enough to give at least the illusion of safety. The two eight-pounders bellowed together, hammering the advancing Holy Warriors. They stopped, and some of them dropped to the ground as well. The Riflemen opened fire, to encourage this notion.

With his rifle useless, Verkan was free to watch the entire process of loading the first shell, including the lighting of the fuse, the various rites of propitiation, and Alkides firing *Galzar's Teeth*. Verkan kept his head up, following the shell all the way to where it struck the ground, bounced twice, rolled under the legs of a Holy Warrior's horse—and exploded!

It took only four shells to convince the Holy Warriors that they were facing something unusual. From "unusual" to "demonic" was a short mental step for most of them. Contemplating the undignified speed of the Holy Warriors' retreat, Verkan had to admit that superstition could have its uses.

Verkan would have felt better if *Galzar's Teeth* hadn't fired a fifth shell, which burst over the Mounted Riflemen. When the smoke cleared away, he saw that Captain Itharos would never argue with him again, and the captain wasn't the only casualty.

Then the massed billmen of the Royal Square topped the rise, still in their columns of march and with a self-confident swagger that said bluntly, "Clear the way, you amateurs. The professional soldiers have arrived."

"Move out!" Verkan shouted. There weren't enough of

Galzar's Teeth to take a big enough bite out of these men. He turned to Xykos and added, "When we reach Alkides, you make sure he goes with us. I don't give a damn what he says, general or no general!"

The grin on Xykos's face told Verkan that Alkides would have an easier time avoiding the marksmen of the Royal Square than he would have escaping his burly bodyguard.

IV.

Sirna stepped out the door of the warehouse, mopped the sweat off her forehead, and looked up at the roof where Captain Ranthar was still wearing a groove in the wood as he paced back and forth, looking off to the southwest. Sirna had been up there herself earlier in the day, but the steady drumming of gunfire and the vast cloud of white smoke off toward Phyrax didn't tell her anything.

She doubted they told Ranthar very much either, and suspected that he was up on the roof because it was a way of not having to talk with the rest of the University Team. She was sure he'd sensed the hostility of some of them, and she also suspected that he felt guilty at not being in the battle with his comrades—and whom did he see as his comrades, his Chief Verkan Vall or the Mounted Rifles?

Even their military advisor Professor Aranth had admitted that it was hard to tell much from a lot of smoke and intermittent rumbling noises, without being able to see any troop movements. "At least there haven't been any wounded or fugitives coming back," he'd added. "That means *something*. Either Kalvan's army has gone into the bag without any survivors"—at which point Eldra turned pale—"or else the Hostigi are still holding on and in good order. I'd say it's more likely the second. From what we know about Kalvan and his army, it would take more than the Holy Host to wipe them up that fast."

That was typical of Aranth Saln despite his formidable appearance—polite to everybody, intelligent whenever he spoke, but committing himself only on his own speciality of Preindustrial Military Science. It was hard to trust him completely but harder still to really dislike him, even if he was a retired Army Colonel. He certainly didn't fit Sirna's image of a professional—

Ranthar shouted and ran toward the stairs from the roof. Sirna looked around and saw three bedraggled horsemen cantering toward the Foundry gate. Two rode haltingly, as though they'd never been on horseback before. All wore the colors blue and gold—which she remembered were the colors of Ulthor—and the red sashes of Hos-Hostigos. She reached the gate at the same time as the lead horseman, a tall man with a young-looking bearded face.

"Run for your life, mistress! The Styphoni have broken through the center and turned the Great Battery on our own army. King Kalvan is missing and all is lost!"

"Is the whole army running?" asked a voice behind Sirna, full of contempt and authority.

The young horseman looked as if he'd been slapped, then lunged for his sword.

Captain Ranthar had his pistol drawn and stepped forward. "I asked you a question."

The young man dropped his hand from his sword hilt and said, "I don't know, sir. I . . . guess we didn't stay around to see. We saw some of our comrades get hit by case shot and decided we didn't want anything to do with that."

One of the other horsemen cried, "I got a wife and son back in Ulthor! What do I care about Styphon's House or Hostigos?"

"That will be enough," said Ranthar.

By now the rest of the University Study-Teams and half the Foundry workers had gathered around the gate. "Let the man speak!" cried Varnath Lala. "If the Army of Hostigos is losing, then we'd better get marching."

There was a chorus of agreement.

The horseman looked encouraged and was about to speak, when everyone heard the sound of Ranthar's pistol being cocked. "You and I"—he paused and used his barrel to point to the horseman's two companions—"and these two—gentlemen—are going to go back and take another look to see what's really happening. And pick up any other stragglers we happen to find.''

"You're here to take care of us, Ranthar, and don't you forget it!" screeched Varnath Lala.

"He can take care of himself," said Lathor Karv, "but I'm for getting out of here." He set off for the stables in a wide-loping gait, followed by two-thirds of the two Study-Teams— including Varnath Lala, who only paused long enough to give Ranthar a withering glare.

Ranthar turned to Talgan Dreth, who looked as if he would have much preferred to be with the party heading for the stables. "Director Talgan, you can go ahead and prepare for Emergency Evacuation Procedure, Code Yellow. I suggest you leave a few volunteers to watch over the Foundry until I return or until it becomes apparent that King Kalvan's army really has been routed."

Rather to her surprise, Sirna found herself volunteering to stay. So did Eldra, Aranth Saln, and most of the others who weren't on their way to the stables. Ranthar put Aranth in charge of Foundry security and rode off with the three reluctant horsemen.

TWENTY-SIX

I.

The last of the mercenary cavalry held out for nearly an hour, far longer than Kalvan had expected. Most of that resistance could be credited to the big mercenary captain whom Kalvan recognized as the same one who'd escaped the envelopment at Ryklos Farm. How he had ridden from the Heights of Chothros to Phyrax had to be a story that might one day be sung by troubadours, if the man survived today's battle.

Kalvan wished the mercenary captain hadn't bothered. His stubbornness only postponed the inevitable, costing Kalvan an extra five hundred casualties and several thousand mercenary prisoners who might have been ransomed, put to work, or recruited for the Great King's army. The Hostigi still wound up with more than two thousand prisoners, not including the captain, all of whom had to be guarded and removed from the battlefield as quickly as possible. Kalvan assigned a regiment to escort them back to Hostigos Town, where they could best be split up and kept out of mischief.

All this, only to learn that Captain-General Chartiphon and the center had been pushed back and the Great Battery taken by the Holy Host! Not to mention no word about Rylla or the baby, either. If only he knew whether she was alive and doing well, or. . . . If something happened to the baby—well, they could always try again. Or adopt an heir if they had to.

No time to worry about that now. He had to relieve the pressure on Chartiphon before the center was routed. That, and pray that Ptosphes could hold back the Knights for a little longer.

Kalvan looked back at his command. It was a smaller and much less orderly group than he'd led across Phyrax pasture an hour ago. Yet their spirits were high and most of the gaps in the ranks had been closed. Since he couldn't reach the Sacred Squares, he was going to do the next best thing: hit the mercenary foot on the flank, roll right over them, and hit the Zarthani foot.

"Major Nicomoth, signal for the advance!"

Kalvan checked the loads in his pistols, raised his sword, and joined his voice to six thousand others in a single shout:

"Down Styphon!"

The mercenary infantry displayed little of the fight that the cavalry had done. Some of the pikemen stood to face the Hostigi charge, but most threw down their arms and cried "Oath to Galzar!" or simply took to their heels. About eight hundred were shot, run through, or simply ridden down; fifteen hundred surrendered.

The Zarthani Order Foot were made of stouter stuff, and they used the time it took Kalvan's cavalry to ride through the mercenary lines to wheel and face the Hostigi charge. Fortunately the Order's infantry had three pikes to every firearm, and Kalvan had another surprise for them.

Kalvan gave the order for the caracole, a difficult maneuver the cavalry had practiced but never used in such strength or on the battlefield. He knew it would need luck and the help of Galzar or Somebody to bring it off even with troopers he trusted completely; it required both discipline and iron nerves for successive ranks of cavalry to ride within twenty yards of the enemy line, fire both pistols, then wheel away to let the next rank follow.

Galzar or Somebody helped; the caracole went off as close to a textbook exercise as could ever happen in combat. The Zarthani Knights' arquebusiers emptied a good many Hostigi saddles at first, but the effect of such continuous heavy fire beat them down, then began to shred the ranks of the pike-men. Their ranks showed gaps, wavered, and began to leak deserters. Finally the pikemen could stand it no more and charged wildly, in no particular order and hardly under the control of their officers.

This was what Kalvan had been waiting for; pikemen on the move who weren't keeping their ranks tight were comparatively easy meat for cavalry. He ordered the countercharge.

The Hostigi cavalry smashed through the disordered Zarthani Foot and rode them into the ground. Few asked for quarter, fewer still were granted it. Most died where they stood. Kalvan watched from the rear, knowing that whoever won today, Grand Master Soton would never forget the price his Order had paid.

II.

"Fire!"

The gun must be close for his battle-numbed ears to hear that command, Harmakros realized. A moment later the crash of the gun proved him right. The ball gouged a huge clod out of the slope, spraying the Sacred Square of Imbraz with grass, dirt, and pebbles. It bounced high, crashed through a cluster of billheads with a weird clanking, then dropped to the ground out of Harmakros's sight. He couldn't see or hear if it did any damage.

That was probably the demicannon that had run out of case shot. It wasn't the only one, not after the Great Battery had been lost and then retaken. Fireseed and shot were running low for the whole Great Battery. The Ktemnoi infantry must be running short too; their musketeers were only firing a squad or so at a time, and aimed fire instead of volleying by ranks. Not that aiming at two hundred yards with a smoothbore did much good, but it couldn't hurt, and Harmakros had been knocked on his back once since they'd recaptured the Grand Battery.

He wasn't exactly sure in the confusion who was responsible

for the temporary retreat of the Holy Host. One messenger said that Kalvan had attacked their rear, but if that were true, why had the retreat stopped so quickly? It was Chartiphon's Ktethroni pikemen who had brought the Holy Host to a standstill in the first place and given the battered Hostigi infantry time to regroup and mount their own counterattack. It was during the counterattack that the Styphoni had begun to fall back, but he was sure that something other than the battered Hostigi infantry was responsible for that retreat.

Now the Holy Host was back on the march. So far they hadn't reached the top of the slope again. They formed a gigantic arc with the Royal Square now on Harmakros's right, stretching through the Second Great Square to the First on the left. Right in front of Harmakros the ground was mostly defended by the fire of the Great Battery itself, but he could see the surviving Mounted Riflemen and his own dragoons tying in with the First Foot beyond.

Another gun fired, a sixteen-pounder, and this ball cut a bloody furrow in the Sacred Square of Cynthlos. Another far-off gunshot came like an echo to the first. The Great Battery's few remaining guns on the left were firing occasionally, to do what they could to discourage the Zarthani Knights. From what little intelligence Harmakros had been able to gather in this potmess of a battle, the Knights had run Ptosphes and most of the left wing into the forest. Phrames, Sarrask, and maybe fifteen hundred troopers were all that was keeping the Grand Master from committing his Knights in support of the Sacred Squares. When that happened, neither Great King Kalvan nor Dralm himself would be able to save the Army of Hos-Hostigos.

Harmakros heard the sixteen-pounder fire again, then a great shout.

"Long live King Kalvan!"

He turned, raised his hands to shield his eyes, and saw in the distance the red plumes of Hostigos pushing into the black plumes of the Zarthani Knights.

Praise Father Dralm and Galzar Wolfshead, was Harmakros's one thought.

He watched for a moment longer, then knelt and said a short prayer of thanks to gods who had clearly not forgotten Hostigos.

•   •   •

Soton muttered curses under his breath as he saw the shrunken circle of Hostigi defenders once again re-forming to meet the Knights' charge. He would have cursed at the top of his lungs, but after nearly two watches of continuous fighting, he had little voice left and needed to save that for giving orders.

How in the name of all gods and everything else a man might swear by, could hardly more than a thousand men go on holding against three times their number? Yet they were doing so; this was the Knights' fourth charge, when Soton had begun the attack certain that one or two would be enough.

And there was that madman Prince Sarrask and the noblemen of his household, countercharging with sword, mace, war hammer, and pistol butt! Soton remembered his first sight of the Saski at Tenabra, when their armor looked like trophies or even table service. Now, if it looked like table service, it was the sort of ware provided for the lesser servants in a cheap inn. Sarrask and his men had been to the wars, and what were the gods thinking of, to let a man who could have been a pillar of the God of Gods become instead a pillar of the Usurper's cause?

There were no answers to that question, Soton suspected, and certainly none to be found on this battlefield. He took a two-handed grip on his war hammer and guided his lathered mount to the left, where there seemed more likely to be room to swing his favorite weapon.

The two masses of horsemen collided, the clang of steel on steel rose, and for perhaps an eighth of a candle Soton's world narrowed down to the man he was facing and perhaps the Knight on either side of him. When the two sides lurched apart again, Soton was pleased to see that the Hostigi were leaving the better part of two hundred men on the ground as they withdrew.

He was not so pleased to see that nearly the same number of Knights had gone down. At least the Knights were still mostly mounted, while the Hostigi now had no more than one horse for every three men. Now, if that messenger he'd sent to the rear for a few mule-loads of fireseed would just do his work. . . .

Fireseed or no, another charge or two should be enough, unless they really were facing a demon in the shape of Sarrask of Sask. Then the Knights could ride the Hostigi into the dirt and ride to support the Sacred Squares. Please Galzar that would finally break the Hostigi center and *end* this Ormaz-spawned battle!

"Grand Master! Grand Master! We are doomed!"

Soton raised his war hammer and turned. He saw Knight Commander Aristocles, his face white with more than the day's accumulation of dust.

"What is it? Speak, man, speak!"

Aristocles paused to catch his breath, then said, "It's the Daemon Kalvan! He's ridden down the Red Hand and is attacking us from behind!"

Soton slammed his left gauntlet into the pommel of his saddle, causing his mount to whinny in surprise. "What about the Order's Foot?"

"Dead. Crushed. Not enough left to make a small band."

Soton sagged in his saddle. To himself he murmured, "All is lost." Then he straightened. "Commander, summon the trumpets and give the order to form up. It's time to leave."

Relief was written all over the Knight Commander's face as he turned to ride away and attend to the Grand Master's orders.

Soton felt no such relief. He could either stay here and fight to the last man, a disaster from which the Knights might never recover, or retreat and live to fight again. As much as it gnawed at his pride, he really saw no choice. Only the Knights stood between the nomads and tribes of the Lower Sastragath and the fertile lands of the Five Kingdoms, and now the barbarians of the Valley of the Great River were on the move as well. With the losses at the Heights of Chothros and the slaughter of the Order's Foot, every man-at-arms he could bring back from this disaster would be needed, regardless of what it cost him.

And cost him it would. Even if he went unpunished by Mnesiphoklos and Prince Leonnestros, there were still many in the Inner Circle who would savor his failure and see it as a slap in the face to the First Speaker and his supporters.

III.

From her post on the Foundry roof, Sirna was the
first to see the six horsemen riding toward the Foundry gate.
She sighed with relief when she saw they were wearing the
colors of Hos-Hostigos. She reached the gate just moments
ahead of the leading horseman, a broad-beamed captain in
yellow and gold Saski colors as well as the red sash.

"What's the word from the battle?" she asked.

"They're sending back the captured mercenaries and the
Foundry's to take five hundred."

"But what about the battle?"

The Saski shrugged. "Well enough. We chewed up the
Knights and sent them packing back to Tarr-Ceros. Our
Prince did the biggest share of that, let me tell you. If only
you'd seen him after Prince Ptosphes fled the field, rallying
the Saski and Nostori cavalry. Well, it's true Count Phrames
helped, but our Prince—"

He went off into rambling praise of a paragon of the
military virtues who was obviously supposed to be Prince Sarrask of Sask. This gave Sirna many useful insights into how
romances of chivalry get started, but very little knowledge
about whether the Foundry people should be prepared to
celebrate or to run for their lives. With Captain Ranthar still
gone. . . .

Finally a voice from behind Sirna interrupted the captain's
steady flow of praise for Sarrask. "Is His Majesty sending the
mercenaries back to split them up and protect them from any
rescue attempts?"

The Saski captain looked down at Aranth Saln, obviously
relieved at being able to deal with a man who appeared to be a
fellow soldier, even if he was only an outlander. "That's most
likely the way of it. But the Great King doesn't sit down with
me over the wine to tell me why, he just gives orders. Our own
Prince has much the same—"

"We have no room to house all these soldiers! Kalvan will
have to come up with some other place to quarter them," said
Talgan Dreth.

The captain, obviously shocked by such open disrespect for
his superiors, started to draw his sword. Then he stopped, as

though realizing he was dealing with outlanders who really couldn't be expected to know any better. "You are speaking of our Great King. Great King Kalvan to you." He touched his sword hilt for emphasis.

Talgan Dreth turned pale as he realized what had gone through the captain's mind and how close he'd come to a quick end to his long life. "My apologies, Captain."

Sirna and Eldra smiled at each other behind Talgan's back. She doubted they were the only ones enjoying the Director's predicament.

"It's not what you want or what I want that matters," continued the captain as though the interruption had never happened. "It's what Great King Kalvan wants that matters, and what he wants is to split the mercenaries up and give some of them to you. They've sworn Oath to Galzar, so they won't be troublesome."

He fixed Talgan Dreth with a singularly cold eye. "If you don't treat them right, they may think they're released from their Oath. If five hundred mercenaries run wild in Hostigos Town because you mucked your job, you'd all better run like the flux before the Great King wins the battle and comes looking for you!"

"We shall do the Great King's will," said Aranth Saln. "Remember that if we treat the men well while we have care of them, we will find favor in the eyes of Galzar and his priests. We shall have reason to expect honorable treatment."

"Please yourself, as long as you please King Kalvan," said the Saski. "Now I'll assume you'll be ready for them and don't need any more dry-nursing. Farewell," he said with a wink at Sirna, then was off in a spray of clouds.

"He said '*before* Kalvan wins,'" began Sirna. "Does that mean—?"

"Very little," said Aranth. "He didn't mention their having broken the Sacred Squares of Hos-Ktemnos, who won the decision at Tenabra. Meanwhile, we'd better get ready for our guests. Most of them can camp in the courtyard, but the wounded will need shelter."

"You take care of this, Aranth," said Talgan Dreth. "I've got more important things to do than worry about somebody else's prisoners."

"We'll need more guards, too," said Eldra. "We don't want anyone wandering inside and seeing the equipment."

Aranth looked around to see that all the Foundry workers were out of hearing. "It might be better if they saw everything except the papermaking equipment," he said. "The more they see, the more they'll realize that it's just an improved version of a regular cannon foundry. Not a demon in sight."

Eldra looked ready to argue about betraying Kalvan's secrets when Doctor Sankar Trav broke in. "If we're going to be treating wounded, I suggest we start cleaning out one of the storerooms about ten minutes ago! Sirna, you'll be my assistant, although they'll probably have at least one priest of Galzar with them and some mercenaries trained in first aid. Break out that medical kit of yours, then go to the kitchen and have every pot we have filled and put on to boil."

Sirna looked a question. The doctor shook his head. "Not full antisepsis, no. But you can boil the Styphon out of the instruments and dressings. Also, they understand removing foreign matter from a wound. But we're servants of 'the servant of demons,' and Mytron really hasn't persuaded even the Hostigi that antisepsis is a Dralm-sent blessing." He shrugged. "A pity Kalvan wasn't able to introduce distilling. Then we'd be able to sterilize, anesthetize, and toast Kalvan all at once!"

TWENTY-SEVEN

I.

Kalvan watched from the top of the Great Battery as the recently resupplied Hostigi artillery raked furrows through the Sacred Squares of Hos-Ktemnos. After the Zarthani Knights retired, Kalvan and the right wing had reunited with what remained of the right wing. Kalvan had put Count Phrames in command of the cavalry with orders to hit the Squares from the rear. The time had come for him to return to the role of supreme commander, rather than the more exciting one of cavalry general.

As an eight-pound ball rolled through the Ktemnoi ranks, knocking aside men like bowling pins, Kalvan wondered just how much more punishment the Sacred Squares could take. Their claws were not yet blunted, he noted, as a cluster of horsemen drew a series of volleys from below. A couple went down; the rest dismounted and came toward Kalvan.

Prince Ptosphes in his battered armor was in the lead. Blood had trickled from a scalp wound down into his beard and caked there. He was carrying an antique battle-ax instead of a sword, and as he drew closer Kalvan was startled to see streaks of white running through his hair.

"Welcome, Prince Ptosphes. Are you all right?"

Ptosphes looked around wide-eyed, as though waking from a dream. "I am still alive."

"Yes, and we are on the verge of a great victory."

"It is your victory, Your Majesty." Ptosphes held out his hand. "Not mine. I am sorry that I have failed you once again, letting the Knights drive my command from the field."

"You owe me no apologies, Father. I didn't expect you to hold the Knights for the entire battle. No man could have done any better with the forces you had."

In a low, toneless voice, Ptosphes said, "Phrames did."

Kalvan pretended he hadn't heard and turned the conversation to a topic where they both felt the same. "Have you heard anything of Rylla?"

"No. Has—she died?"

"No! She's gone into labor. At least she had, according to the last message I received several hours ago."

"May Yirtta Allmother keep watch over her and the baby."

"Amen," said Kalvan. "Other messengers could have been killed or lost their way, but I'm beginning to wonder . . ." He kept the rest of his thoughts to himself. If Brother Mytron was hiding bad news to keep his Great King and Prince in shape to win their battle, he might soon find himself guest of honor at a hide-pinning party. But why assume the worst?

Why indeed? Nonetheless, Kalvan knew that if he could have sold his soul for Rylla's safety, he would have signed on the spot. If the deal had also included ten rifled sixteen-pounders and a thousand shells with reliable fuses, he wouldn't have bothered reading the fine print.

"I had hoped to die before I gave way to the Knights again, but Galzar did not hear my prayer," said Ptosphes.

"Do not despair, Father. You were not the only one today who gave way before the Holy Host. Captain-General Chartiphon was forced to give up the Grand Battery."

Which he probably could have held if he hadn't waited too long to commit the reserve of Ktethroni pikes. Memo: Find an honorable way of kicking Chartiphon upstairs to where he won't be commanding in the field.

The Duke seemed to be developing General Longstreet's problem: obeying orders in his own sweet time. Robert E. Lee had tolerated Longstreet and probably lost a war because of it; Kalvan I of Hos-Hostigos—

From below Ktemnoi trumpets sounded. They had a deep bellowing tone, like the ancient *bucinae* of the Roman

Legions. Ptosphes hefted his ax.

"That's their signal for the charge. They must know it's madness now."

Maybe, but what a magnificent lunacy, thought Kalvan.

"It sounds as if they're using the last of their fireseed—"

Ptosphes's voice was lost in musket volleys from below and answering fire from both muskets and artillery from above. Kalvan dismounted and ordered his horse led clear. No doubt some day this would be written down as a heroic gesture; right now it was more the old infantryman's instinct to stay as low to the ground as possible when there's shooting going on.

The Sacred Square of Imbraz was the one coming at Kalvan. The musket bullets whistled about him, *spanged* off the rocks, *thuked* into the ground, and occasionally made the unmistakable noise of sinking into flesh. Ptosphes let out a yell as a bullet struck the head of his ax, jarring his whole arm. A Hostigi heavy gun fired, and Kalvan saw the white smoke-puff of a shellburst in the Royal Square. *Galzar's Teeth* would be a lot sharper for about ten or twelve more rounds—

Case shot smashed into the front ranks of the Imbrazi from several guns at once. Bodies and parts of bodies, weapons, and pieces of armor flew in all directions. The front ranks were suddenly a mob, but they were an armed and dangerous mob—and they were still coming on.

Kalvan shot one musketeer, felt a hammerblow across his ribs as another hit him with a glancing bullet, shot that man, then dropped his empty pistols and drew his sword. A billman swung but misjudged his distance and sank the billhead into the ground. Kalvan slashed at him, but the man jerked up his weapon, and the shaft knocked Kalvan's sword up and to the side, while another billman ran in, too close to swing at but not too close to thrust hard enough to dent Kalvan's breast-plate—

Ptosphes charged from Kalvan's right, swinging his ax and shouting what Kalvan hoped were war cries. The first billman had his bill chopped in two with one blow, his arm chopped off with the next, his helmet and head split with the third. That gave Kalvan a chance to run in under the second man's guard as he raised his bill and thrust him through the face. He fell, and both Great King and Prince gave ground with more concern for haste than for dignity.

To the left the Imbrazi seemed to be carrying everything before them, although it was now bills and clubbed muskets, with nobody stopping to reload. Kalvan backed away to the right without looking behind him until he tripped over a dead body and fell hard enough to knock the wind out of himself.

He sat up to see Ptosphes crouched beside him, shielding him and looking anxious. On the other side was Harmakros, lying behind a dead horse and carefully picking off Imbrazi with two pistols and a musketoon. A cluster of his troopers lay just behind him, reloading the weapons as fast as he emptied them and passing them back to him.

Improbably, Harmakros was smoking one of the royal stogies from the box Kalvan had given him for his good work at the Heights of Chothros.

Then Kalvan's ears rang to the sound of massed musketry and the war cries of the Ktethroni pikemen as their counter-charge went in. The dragoon pikemen were fitting themselves into the Ktethroni lines wherever they could, while the musketeers darted along the flanks, firing volleys by platoons and companies.

Kalvan decided he'd better mount up and show himself to his men, even if that meant withdrawing a short distance. Otherwise someone would be sure to start a rumor that the Great King was dead or captured or missing or carried off by ravens or something; he could imagine a number of consequences of that, all of them unpleasant—and not just for the Hostigi.

It took less than fifteen minutes for the Ktethroni to break the Ktemnoi charge and another fifteen to drive them back downhill. By the time they'd done that, Phrames was hitting the Squares from the rear. Kalvan waited until he saw that Phrames had thickened up his cavalry cordon enough to block any attempts at a breakout, then ordered the trumpeters to ride down under a white flag and sound for a parley. Ptosphes stared.

"They can't get away, and I suspect their captains know it," Kalvan said. "I'll offer reasonable terms—honorable ransoms for the nobles and captain, good treatment for the men, an escort out of Hostigi territory after they're disarmed. It will be as big a victory as killing them, and cheaper."

"Shouldn't we wait until the prisoner guards return?"

That would give the Army of Hostigos fresh fireseed, which it desperately needed, and six or seven hundred fresh cavalry, which it needed almost as badly. The victory was going to be sweet, but tallying the losses—well, many more victories this costly and there wouldn't be an Army of Hos-Hostigos.

"If we wait," said Kalvan, "the rain will hit and that may give them ideas about trying to break out with cold steel." The sky over the Bald Eagles had turned black in the last half hour, and it was no longer just his weary imagination that saw flashes of lightning.

Ptosphes sighed. "Very well. If you've gone mad, I'll pretend to go mad along with you so that people won't talk."

"Or they may think the Great King's madness is catching."

Kalvan couldn't admit now or perhaps ever his real reason for the parley. He didn't want to kill any more of these men. They were too good—too much like the army he wanted to lead someday, that he would *have* to lead someday if he was to survive here-and-now.

Down the hill, bills and muskets were being lowered, and someone waved a white flag on a pole that held a Square's banner. Kalvan and Ptosphes took off their Hostigi sashes and put on white ones, then gathered Major Nicomoth and the escort troop of Horse Guards and rode down the hill.

A large man in plain three-quarter armor that showed fine workmanship under the powder smoke rode out to greet them.

"Prince Anaxagron . . . ?"

"No." The man's face seemed to work briefly at the mention of that name, then he said, "Baron Phygron, Grand-Captain over the Sacred Square of Sephax and Marshal of the Second Great Square of Hos-Ktemnos. Do you speak for the ruler of Hos-Hostigos?"

Kalvan grinned and lifted off his helmet, ignoring Ptosphes's stifled gasp. "I *am* the Great King of Hostigos. In my own name and that of the Princes, nobles, and people allied with me in defense of the True Gods, I offer you terms."

Phygron swallowed and pushed up his visor. "May I hear those terms, Kalvan?"

"The correct term of address is 'Your Majesty,'" said Ptosphes.

Kalvan nodded. "If I am not 'Your Majesty,' then obviously I can't be the Great King of Hos-Hostigos. If you are going to argue over names, we shall have no time to discuss more important matters, such as the surrender of your Squares. I assure you that there is no other alternative for them but destruction."

Phygron looked like a man who wished the earth would open up and swallow him. "I do not admit that. But, King—Your Majesty—"

A musket blasted from the Ktemnoi ranks, followed by two others. Major Nicomoth twisted toward Kalvan, one eye staring, the other replaced by a red-rimmed hole. Then he toppled from his saddle.

Kalvan heard shouts of "Treachery!" from the Hostigi lines, then another shout:

"They've killed the King!"

There was the fat in the fire, or it would be if he didn't get back uphill and show those damned fools that he was still alive! In the twilight before the oncoming storm it was an easy mistake for tired men, since he and Nicomoth were not only about the same size and wearing similar armor but were now riding similar horses.

Kalvan turned his mount and dug in his spurs. As he did, Baron Phygron clutched at his chest as three bullets punched through his armor—rifle bullets, they had to be, at this range! He was going to have to speak to Verkan about discipline in the Rifles. . . .

If he got back alive, that is. The Ktemnoi were cursing, shaking their fists, and drawing swords. Kalvan and Ptosphes waited until their Horse Guards were all on the move, then put their heads down and their heels in and galloped up the hill. At any moment Kalvan expected to feel a bullet smash into his back or at least into his horse, but they reached their own lines in one piece, with only three empty saddles among the Guardsmen.

As they reined in, a heavy gun fired, followed closely by a distant rumble of thunder. Then the musketry started up again, an irregular spattering from the Ktemnoi as the desperate let fly, followed by the solid volleys of the Hostigi.

Kalvan closed his eyes and wished he could close his ears. "Dralm-dammit!"

Ptosphes was gripping his arm. "Kalvan, it was more my fault than yours. I should have remembered that Styphon's

House doesn't recognize your title, and that even a Ktemnoi Marshal in the Holy Host—"

"Should have had better sense than Phygron," Kalvan finished. He wondered if this were true, but he'd be damned if he were going to let Ptosphes start blaming himself for this too!

Side by side, they rode back toward the Great Battery.

II.

The moon came out just after Verkan Vall sighted the Mounted Rifles' campfires. Trust his men to be as good at scrounging little comforts such as dry wood as at fighting or at caring for their dead and wounded. He rode slowly toward the fires, hoping the moonlight would keep his horse from stepping on dead bodies even if it didn't do anything about his exhaustion. He felt that about a week's uninterrupted sleep, preferably with Dalla—except that then it wouldn't be uninterrupted. . . .

A sentry challenged him.

"Halt! Who's there?"

"Colonel Verkan of the Mounted Rifles."

"Pass, Colonel."

Verkan rode into the firelight; the faces it showed were almost as dead as those he'd seen on the corpses, except for the red-rimmed eyes and the slowly working jaws as they munched salt pork and hard cheese. Someone took his horse's bridle and two other someones helped him dismount, which saved him the embarrassment of falling flat on his face.

Neither firelight nor moonlight lit up the open ground between the foot of the slope and the woods. Verkan was just as happy about that. Before nightfall he'd seen enough of that field to last him a thousand-year lifetime. For hundreds of yards a man could walk from body to body without touching the muddy ground. Six thousand of the Sacred Squares lay there; about a third as many had escaped, including both of the Ktemnoi Royal Princes—if they'd been with the Squares in the first place. About fifteen hundred had been taken prisoner after the Hostigi had worked off their rage at the treachery and both sides were too exhausted to lift their weapons.

That was just the beginning of the casualty list for the Holy Host: three thousand of Styphon's Own Guard dead to a man, over three thousand Zarthani Order Foot, a thousand to fifteen hundred Knights, most of Leonnestros's Pistoleers and Royal Guard (along with Leonnestros himself), thousands of mercenary dead, and two thousand Holy Warriors who would never again fight for Styphon or anybody else.

Nor were all the bodies down there Styphoni, of course.

A hundred Mounted Riflemen, close to two-thirds of Harmakros's Army of Observation, half of Phrames's troopers. Count Euphrades of Ulthor, who'd charged a little too far, all his plots and schemes now forever beyond the reach even of hypno-truth drugs, unless one encountered him in his next incarnation. Thousands of Chartiphon's men, and far too many of the Hostigi regular infantry. Verkan recalled seeing toward the last the standards of five regiments flying over a body of men hardly large enough to make three. Much of the fighting nobility of Ulthor, Sashta, and Sask were no more, and as for the Nostori, Verkan doubted there was enough left of cavalry, infantry, and militia put together to make a single respectable regiment.

Eleven or twelve thousand Hostigi casualties was the estimate Verkan had heard, and it matched his own. Too many more such victories and Kalvan would be ruined, no matter how many more opponents he smashed as thoroughly as he'd smashed the Holy Host. Their casualties might run to twenty thousand dead or missing and eight thousand prisoners, with two-thirds of the survivors under Soton's command.

They would get away; the Hostigi were not only exhausted, but very nearly out of fireseed. In fact, Hos-Hostigos was practically where Old Hostigos had been pre-Kalvan—not enough fireseed to load all the artillery at once. Cleitharses the Scholar would have his sons back, but not his Lord High Marshal or much else of what he'd sent north. He and his ministers would certainly have no more illusions that making war on behalf of Styphon's House was a cheap way to win friends in the Inner Circle.

Over the crackling of the fire and the distant moans of the dying, Verkan heard a horse approaching. Kalvan or a messenger, probably. He forced himself to his feet, saw the rider take shape at the edges of the firelight, and noticed that both mount and rider seemed oddly shrunken. The rider reined in, and Verkan recognized young Aspasthar.

"Good evening, Colonel Verkan," said the boy. "I bear a message for the Great King. Do you know where he is?"

"Out there, somewhere," said Verkan, pointing along the ridge. He'd last seen Kalvan riding that way and hadn't seen him riding back, although it would have been easy to miss a whole regiment in the darkness before the moon came out. "If you'll tell me what the message is, I'll carry it. You don't want to be riding around in the dark on that pony by yourself."

Too late, Verkan realized that he'd just mortally insulted the boy. Aspasthar bristled like a cat with his fur stroked the wrong way. "It is a message for the Great King's ears alone, Colonel Verkan. I cannot entrust it—"

Verkan felt his stomach drop to the level of his bootsoles. There was only one message he could think of that would be for Kalvan's ears only, and he'd be damned if his friend was going to learn about his wife's death from—

Aspasthar underestimated the speed of Verkan's movements and the length of his arms. Suddenly he found himself hauled from the saddle and dangling with his collar firmly gripped in two strong hands and his feet well clear of the ground. He kicked futilely at Verkan's shins, then used a number of words that suggested he'd been associating with too many cavalry troopers.

Verkan waited until the boy ran out of breath, conscious of the snickers of the Riflemen and not quite sure he wasn't making an awful fool of himself. "Let's compromise. You tell me the message privately and I'll ride with you to find the Great King."

The peace offering fell flat. The boy took a deep breath, then shouted, "Colonel Verkan has no honor, but his brave Riflemen do, so I will tell them all. Queen Rylla is safe and well and delivered of a daughter!"

Verkan's hands opened by sheer reflex, and Aspasthar dropped to the ground. He bounced up in a moment, grinning impudently and brushing off his trousers. Verkan stood stiffly, now sure that he'd made a fool of himself, then was cheering along with everyone else. Someone started beating a drum, two or three men leaped to their feet and started a Sastragathi war dance, someone else began to sing "Marching Through Harphax" in a voice that had to be drunk with fatigue because there wasn't anything stronger than water within miles—

"Long live Queen Rylla and the Princess of Hostigos!" shouted Verkan. He heard the cheering taken up as the word spread, and suddenly he felt as if he could ride twenty miles and fight another battle at the end of the ride. He knew the feeling was purely an adrenaline fantasy, but he did think his new strength might last long enough to find Kalvan.

"Aspasthar, if you don't mind the company of a man without honor—"

The boy bowed with a positively courtly grace. "I have cast doubts on my own honor by doubting yours, Colonel." Then he was wide-eyed and eager again. "Don't worry about Redpoll, Colonel. He's very sure-footed."

III.

The musketry in Phyrax was dying down as Harmakros's men drove out the last of the Zarthani Knights' auxiliary horse archers, the rear guard of the Holy Host. So far Kalvan could see only two or three small fires in the village; the heavy rain had soaked the thatch and shingles enough so that they would not burn easily. Not that either side was actually trying to set it on fire; though the Zarthani horse archers were devilishly hard to kill, they were only fighting to give the survivors of the Holy Host a head start, while Harmakros was mostly trying to keep them from advancing beyond Phyrax back on to the battlefield.

Torches glowed on the battlefield itself; the Hostigi search parties were collecting enemy wounded. They also had orders to keep away the local peasants until the fallen weapons and armor could be gathered in, but so far the peasants didn't seem to be a problem. Maybe the sheer size of the battle had scared them away—the usual here-and-now battle involved fewer men than either of today's two armies.

Against the torchlight Kalvan could see a rider making his way up the ridge. As he reached the crest, Kalvan recognized Phrames, undoing his red scarf. That scarf had been one of Rylla's name-day gifts to Phrames; on any other man it might have been a calculated insult to Kalvan, but on Phrames it was a symbol of his loyalty to his Great Queen.

"Well done, Phrames. I think in another moon you can have Rylla embroider the arms of Beshta on that scarf." Kalvan's mind shied away from the thought that even now there might not be any Rylla.

The silence was so long that Kalvan wondered if perhaps he'd overestimated the wits Phrames had left after today's fighting. The moon was disappearing again and another thunderstorm seemed to be building in the southwest, so he couldn't make out Phrames's expression.

Then he heard the Count clear his throat. "Your Majesty— Kalvan. I—I am your servant in—all things." Then a soft laugh. "But don't you think this is selling the colt before the mare has even been brought to stud?"

"No. We're going to have to take Balthar's head—if it's still on his shoulders. We haven't found his body, and most of the Beshtans ran like the blazes as soon as it was safe to do so. I suspect he'll be giving the executioner some business, and all his kin and ministers—"

"Don't forget his tax gatherers."

"Especially his tax gatherers. That means nobody of the House of Beshta left except his brother Balthames. He's going to be content with Sashta or he'll join his brother. That leaves the Princedom vacant, and if there's anybody else who deserves it more, I'd like to hear who you think he is—"

"There are many, Your Majesty. Harmakros, Alkides, even Prince Sarrask—"

"Yes, Harmakros and Alkides were invaluable. So was Sarrask. But it was you who held the left wing together after Ptosphes's retreat."

Kalvan held up his hand to block further argument. "I know the First Prince did everything that was humanly possible. You performed a miracle. If the Knights had hit our center in the flank—well, right now there wouldn't be any Great King of Hos-Hostigos to reward his brave and loyal subjects. Besides, if we want to win this war, we're going to need all the miracle workers we can get.

"Furthermore, announcing the new Prince of Beshta before we've settled accounts with the old one has a couple of other advantages. First, it will keep people from worrying that I'm the kind of Great King who likes to collect vacant Princedoms. I understand they are not popular." *An understatement if there ever was one.* "I'll expect a share of vacant estates and the treasury, but that's traditional."

"Second, you're popular in Beshta, Phrames. The people and even some of the nobles may rise against Balthar as soon as they know who they're rising *for*. That may save us the trouble of his execution. It will certainly save us a good deal of fighting and some lives. If I asked them to rise without naming a new Prince, I might look as if I liked starting rebellions. That would make me even more unpopular. But naming a successor to a Prince attainted for treason—again, that's traditional."

"There's wisdom in all that you say, Your Majesty, but—what's that?"

It sounded as if the battle were starting all over again for a moment, then Kalvan recognized cheering. A moment later he saw two familiar riders approaching at a trot, both carrying torches. One was Verkan, the other Aspasthar, and both of them had grins that practically met at the backs of their heads.

"Queen Rylla and the baby are safe!" shouted Aspasthar.

Kalvan was struck speechless.

Aspasthar gentled his horse, then dismounted and knelt to Kalvan.

"Yes, Your Majesty. Both the Great Queen and the Princess of Hostigos are well."

"How—how did they choose you as messenger?"

Aspasthar blushed. "Your Majesty, they didn't exactly—
you see, I was listening outside the birthing chamber. When I
heard everybody being so happy, I knew what had happened.
In the excitement it might take a while before they told someone else to ride to you, and I thought you would want to know
right away, so I got on Redpoll and rode off. But I became lost
and had to ask Colonel Verkan for help—"

"And insult my honor into the bargain," said Verkan,
laughing. He told the rest of the story, while Aspasthar
blushed even brighter.

Kalvan wanted to run around waving his arms and shouting
at the top of his lungs, but he did have his royal dignity to
preserve. The boy also had a reward coming.

"Aspasthar. You have earned yourself a good-news
bearer's reward. Twenty ounces of silver. It shall be paid to
you tomorrow, and then you will take it to your—to Count
Harmakros and give nineteen ounces of it to him for safekeep-
ing. You are also to say that it is the Great King's command
that you be thoroughly thrashed for riding out as you did with
no authority or permission, putting yourself in danger, and insulting Colonel Verkan!"

Aspasthar only had to gulp twice before he stammered,
"Y-Yes, Your M-M-Majesty!"

Kalvan turned away and took a few stumbling steps. *If there
is anybody to thank—thank you for Rylla and our daughter.
Now, what to name her—?*

Kalvan took the offered jug and swigged from it without
thinking. He felt as if he'd swallowed a mouthful from one of
the crucibles at the Foundry. Nothing was this strong except
high-proof whiskey! Had they gone and invented distilling
behind his back while he was off fighting the war?

He sniffed at the neck of the jug. Not bourbon or any other
kind of whiskey, just good winter wine. It was only fatigue
and strain and not having eaten or drunk anything for twelve
hours that made the winter wine taste so potent.

"Aspasthar has good sense in one thing," said Verkan. "He
tied two jugs to Redpoll's saddle, and took some cheese and
sausage as well. Probably stole them from the kitchen, of
course. Drink up, Your Majesty."

Kalvan took another sip, then felt rain on his face and
shook his head. If he drank any more, he'd either have to be

carried back to Tarr-Hostigos or else stand here in the rain like a barnyard turkey, his mouth upturned until the rain filled it and he drowned.

IV.

The door to the royal bedchamber that had become a birthing room was closed when Kalvan reached the top of the stairs. One of the midwives and a maidservant were slumped on the bench outside the door; another maidservant was sprawled on a pallet under the bench, snoring like a small thunderstorm. Softly, so as not to wake the sleepers, Kalvan knocked. The door opened a crack, and the bulldog face of old Amasphalya, the chief midwife, peered out.

"You can't come in, Your Majesty. Both Rylla and the baby are alseep, and they need the sleep more than they need you."

Kalvan felt his mouth open and shut several times without any sound coming out. He was glad the antechamber was dark and the three women asleep, because he knew he must be making a thoroughly nonroyal spectacle of himself.

He thought briefly of battering rams. He thought somewhat less briefly of summoning Brother Mytron and having him negotiate a passage for the Great King. Then he remembered that Brother Mytron was also enjoying a well-deserved sleep after a day not as dangerous but certainly as long as his King's.

He was thinking that he really didn't know what to do next when he heard Rylla's voice from inside the chamber. "Great Dralm, Amasphalya, let him in! That's an order."

"Your Majesty—"

"*Let him in*. Or I'm going to get out of bed and open the door myself."

Kalvan would have very much liked a camera to record the expression on Amasphalya's face. If nothing else, he could have used the picture to blackmail her into better manners the next time she decided that she outranked a Great King.

Then he let out a great whoop of laughter. Until now he'd only been *told* that Rylla was alive and healthy; in his exhaustion he'd had moments of believing that everyone was lying to him. Now he'd heard her voice, and more than her voice, her old familiar impatience with fools.

Amasphalya sighed and stepped out of Kalvan's path without opening the door any wider. Kalvan kicked it open all the way and ran to the bed. He kissed Rylla several times and ran his hands through her hair before he realized how fortunate he'd been to hear her voice before seeing her. With dark circles under her eyes, pain-carved lines in her pale face, and hair matted to the consistency of barbed wire, she looked like a stranger.

No, not a stranger. Just a woman who'd been through a long hard labor, and he'd seen them before, but he hadn't been married to any of them and the baby wasn't his—

"Kalvan. Look."

He looked where a too thin, too pale hand was pointing. At first he saw nothing but a pile of furs and linen, then—

"By Galzar's Mace! I didn't know babies came that big!"

Rylla laughed and Amasphalya was bold enough to say, "Oh, she was a fine big lass, that's for certain. All of three ingots. It's no great wonder that she was hard in coming, but all's well now. She's already eaten once and—"

Kalvan wasn't listening. In fact, as he stared down at his ten pounds of daughter, he wouldn't have heard Dralm himself coming to announce that Balph had burned to the ground and Styphon's House was surrendering unconditionally to the will of Great King Kalvan. All his attention was on the baby, red-faced and wrinkled as she was, with a snub nose that looked more like Rylla's than his—

Under her father's scrutiny, the Princess of Hostigos opened large blue eyes that were her mother's and nobody else's. Then she opened her mouth and let out an earsplitting howl.

"She wants another meal, the greedy thing," clucked Amasphalya. "I'd best summon the wet nurse."

She bustled off to do that, while Kalvan held out his thumb to the baby. Her fingers curled firmly around it, but she went right on squalling. Kalvan grinned.

"I suppose it's going to be a while before she can be impressed by Great Kings or anybody else who can't provide food."

Rylla smiled and silently gripped his free hand. Then the door opened again as Amasphalya led a hefty peasant woman into the chamber. Kalvan was looking her over to make sure she'd bathed properly when he saw two men silhouetted in the doorway. Something about them looked familiar—

"Count Phrames. Colonel Verkan. Welcome. Come in."

The two soldiers followed the wet nurse. Amasphalya took a deep breath, then appeared to think better of whatever she'd been about to say. Instead she looked toward the ceiling with an expression that was clearly a silent prayer to Yirtta Allmother to guard Rylla and the baby, since her own best efforts to keep the birthing chamber free of fathers and other useless men had failed.

Kalvan straightened up, although for a moment he wondered if he would need to ask for help. Something seemed to have happened to his spine.

"How is the army?"

"Harmakros, Ptosphes, and Sarrask have things well in hand," said Verkan.

"I don't know what that Sarrask is made of," added Phrames. "He fought all day, worked all night, and now he and his guardsmen are having a drinking party with some captured beer!"

"Maybe he wants to forget the battle," said Verkan softly. "The gods know I wish I could."

Phrames looked oddly at the Rifleman for a moment, then nodded slowly. "It could be." Obviously the idea of Sarrask of Sask having some virtues was still novel, but no longer completely unthinkable.

The baby's howls had died to an occasional squeak or gurgle as she snuggled against the wet nurse's breast and went to work on her meal. Kalvan found himself swaying on his feet, even after Phrames put a hand on his shoulder to steady him.

"Come on, Your Majesty. We've arranged a bed for you in

the shrine-house. All the wounded are under tents in the courtyard, and Verkan has twenty of his Riflemen guarding the shrine-house. You'll be able to sleep in peace."

Sleep seemed like an excellent idea, but he had to talk to Rylla about the baby's name. He shook off Phrames's hand, turned, swayed so violently that he nearly fell, and saw that Rylla was asleep again.

A *very* excellent idea, for everybody. "Princess of Hostigos" would be good enough for the baby for the next few hours.

He cautiously placed one foot in front of another, then felt Phrames gripping him by one arm and Verkan by the other as they led him toward the door.

TWENTY-EIGHT

I.

"At the trot—forward!" Baron Harmoth shouted. With a great thudding of hooves on stony ground and the rattling of harness brass and armor, the Old Hostigos Lifeguards put themselves into motion. Baron Harmoth looked behind him to make sure that nobody was moving faster than a trot, then pulled down his visor.

Prince Ptosphes left his own visor up. He had this whole battle to observe and command, not just a single cavalry regiment with a single fairly simple mission. He was riding with his Lifeguards, newly reinforced after losing half their strength at Phyrax and Tenabra, because that seemed the best way to move far enough forward to see what was going on without making himself easy prey to the Agrysi.

Of course, the Agrysi might have run out of either fireseed or the will to fight in the last two days, after the capture of their main wagon train. The loss of their train made three successive defeats for them in the ten-day since Ptosphes led the newly organized Army of Nostor into the Princedom to clear it of King Demistophon's gesture of friendship toward Styphon's House.

They might have, but Ptosphes wasn't going to wager his life on it. The Army of Nostor's sixteen thousand men had begun with no great advantage in numbers, and those three

victories had all been hard fought and fairly won; regiments
that had been weak when he led them into Nostor were now
mere skeletons. Yet Dralm be praised, winning those victories
had made Ptosphes really want to go on living for the first
time since the dreadful day of Tenabra.

Furthermore, it was too beautiful a day to die with his work
unfinished. There was so much more to be done, such as
casting down Styphon's House of Iniquities, watching his
granddaughter grow up. . . .

White puffs of smoke from the thicket of trees to the left
were followed by the bee-hum of bullets passing close by.
Three riders and two horses went down; Ptosphes heard Harmoth shouting, "Keep moving! Don't bunch up!" and saw
the Lifeguards obeying. The mounted nobles and gentry of
Old Hostigos still knew only one operation of war—how to
charge—but they knew several different ways of making that
charge more dangerous to the enemy and less dangerous to
themselves. Teaching them more would have required the
command of a god, not merely of a Great King.

Prince Ptosphes turned in his saddle and shouted to a
messenger to bring up a squadron of the mercenary dragoons
riding behind the Lifeguards and have them clean out the
woods. If the Agrysi detachment there was more than a single
squadron could handle, the rest of the mercenaries and the
Royal Lancers would be within what Kalvan called "supporting distance." Ptosphes hoped they wouldn't be needed in
the woods; he wanted to push home this charge right into the
Agrysi rear and that would surely need more than a single regiment.

By the time the messenger was gone, the Lifeguards were
over the crest of the little rise and Ptosphes could see the entire
Hostigi battle line—his own left-flank cavalry, seven to eight
thousand infantry in the center, and the mercenary, Saski, and
Ulthori horse on the right. The guns were barely visible in the
rear of the infantry, staying limbered up and well protected
until they had good targets. Ptosphes would have given a
couple of fingers for three sixteen-pounders to add to his
mobile four-pounders, but Kalvan needed all the ones that had
survived Phyrax to dispose of the Beshtans.

A little further, and Ptosphes could see the Agrysi—a thick
but rather ragged line of mercenary infantry drawn up behind
a farm and a stone wall, with old-fashioned guns, small bom-

bards, and demicannon in the gaps, and the cavalry behind either flank. Black-streaked white smoke rising from the farm told him of a concealed battery opening fire; a moment later whirrings and thumpings told him that its target was his cavalry. Then a solid mass of horsemen was shaking itself loose from the Agrysi right and coming toward the Hostigi.

The Agrysi weren't quite stupid enough to ride down their own gunners, but they did manage to mask the farm battery's fire completely. The hedges and outbuildings around the farm also broke up their formation, so that it was half a dozen separate squadrons rather than a solid mass that reached Ptosphes. By that time the Hostigos Lifeguards were a solid but flexible wall of steel and horseflesh, and another messenger was riding back to bring up the Royal Lancers.

The two cavalry forces collided with a sound like a cartload of anvils falling onto a stone floor. Ptosphes saw men hurled from their saddles by the sheer impact of the collision, to die under the hooves of their comrades' horses. He shot one of those horses, used up his other pistol on the horse's rider, saw a knot of men growing behind the fallen horse, and lifted his battle-ax.

"For Hostigos! Down Styphon!"

"Prince Ptosphes!" the shout came from behind him, as his Lifeguards dug in their own spurs and drew steel. Now it was just a matter of straightforward fighting, and Ptosphes had no doubts who would win such a contest. Few of his Hostigi veterans did not owe Styphon's House a debt for dead kin or burned homes or both, and no one was disposed to be merciful to the Agrysi and their hired soldiers merely because King Demistophon had been stupid rather than evil.

How long the hewing and hacking lasted, Ptosphes never knew precisely. He did know that a moment came when he saw there were no enemies within reach who weren't shouting "Oath to Galzar!" and holding up helmets on sword points or snatching off their green sashes. Beyond the surrendering cavalry Ptosphes could see the Agrysi infantry doing the same. Colonel Democriphon, recognizable by his unhelmeted head and flowing blond hair, was riding through the farm battery as if on parade. On either side and to his rear the Royal Lancers rode as if invisible ropes tied them to their Colonel.

Ptosphes hoped they wouldn't ride into more than they could handle, but that would be quite a lot. Democriphon loved to make a show of his swordsmanship and riding, but Kalvan said he was probably the best Colonel in the Great King's regulars.

Ptosphes dismounted to spare his horse and made sure that none of the blood that spattered his armor was his. Except for a nick beside his left knee, he turned out to be intact. He was drinking water laced with vinegar and refusing a bandage when he saw Democriphon riding back around the farm. With him rode a handful of Agrysi horsemen in rich three-quarter armor and etched and gold-filled morions, under the red-falcon banner of Prince Aesklos of Zycynos.

By the time the riders reached him, Ptosphes was in the saddle again.

"Hail, Prince Ptosphes," said the leading horseman. "I am Count Artemanes, Captain-General to Prince Aesklos of the Princedom of Zycynos. In his name I yield all the men sworn to Great King Demistophon of Hos-Agrys on this field."

"Where is Prince Aesklos?"

The Count swallowed, letting Colonel Democriphon speak first. "He's about to have his leg taken off, back there around the hill," he said, pointing with his sword. "There's another whole wagon train back there, four guns, and a lot of wounded. Five hundred at least."

"We'll have our priests take care of them as soon as they're through with our own wounded," said Ptosphes. "They may be able to save the Prince's leg."

"With some demon-taught trick—?" began the Count, then quickly broke off as he saw faces harden around him. "Very well. I don't suppose a priest of Dralm can really be brought to harm a wounded man."

"Of course not," said Ptosphes irritably. The last thing he wanted to waste time discussing now was the nonsense Styphon's House had been spouting about Kalvan's demonic wisdom. "Now—is there anything you need other than aid for your wounded?"

The Count looked around, as if he wished he could speak to Ptosphes privately, then shrugged. "Somebody to keep the Styphoni off our backs. Three bands of Styphon's Own Guard from the Great Temple at Hos-Agrys came with us. They're not more than half a candle's ride north along the High Road. If they think we've surrendered without cause, they may try to retake the camp and kill any of our men as well as yours they find."

Ptosphes nodded. Styphon's Red Hand hadn't done this sort of thing to friendly soldiers thus far during the Great Kings' War, but their reputation more than justified fearing it. "Is that why you fought us?"

"That, and not knowing how many you were. We thought we'd done enough damage the last two times that you'd be licking your wounds. Has the de—Has Kalvan taught you how to make armies invisible?"

"Great King Kalvan, to you. No, he hasn't. Just how to move them so fast and so far that they're hard to see unless one is looking in the right place. You could learn those arts too, if you gave the Great King cause to see you as a friend rather than an enemy."

The Count's frozen face told Ptosphes he was in no mood to listen to that kind of suggestion. In any case, there was no time to make it.

"Colonel Democriphon," said Ptosphes. "Take your Lancers, two bands of mercenary cavalry, and two guns up the High Road. Find the Red Hand and block the road against them, but don't engage them unless they advance. If they do, I'll bring up the whole army and we'll see about collecting their heads as a name-day gift for Princess Demia."

"My Prince!"

Democriphon wheeled his horse and trotted off. The Count sighed and seemed to sit more easily in his saddle. "Thank you, Your Highness. I wish—well, it seemed better to have my men die at your hands than at the hands of Styphon."

"Better still if they had not died at all," said Prince Ptosphes. "Now, if you would care to sit down with me over some wine, I think we can put an end to this war in Nostor . . ."

II.

—on terms which you will see in the enclosed copy of the Truce Agreement. It is hard to believe that anyone not a minion of Styphon's House will consider

*them other than honorable, or even generous for a host so
thoroughly defeated as that of King Demistophon.*

Kalvan quickly looked over the other sheets of parchment
with Ptosphes's letter. The Agrysi were to retain all their small
arms and such fireseed and food as they could carry on their
persons or mounts; those taken prisoner in the earlier battles
were to be released on oath to pay token ransoms before next
spring; petty-captains and above were to retain their armor.

> *These terms cover the lawful subjects of King Demi-
> stophon and his Princes. The mercenaries have given
> Oath to Galzar in the customary manner. It appears that
> not less than three thousand of them and perhaps more
> could be persuaded to take Hostigi colors. With the cap-
> tured supplies and this addition to our strength, we are
> more than fit to stand against any treachery by Styphon's
> House, without eating Prince Pheblon's lands any barer
> than they are already.*
>
> *From the speed with which the Red Hand retreated, I
> much doubt that they had orders to slay the Agrysi for
> yielding untimely. Such an act added to Prince Balthar's
> folly at Tarr-Catassa would drive many mercenaries into
> our service—or at least out of Styphon's—and end the
> war at a blow. Grand Master Soton would have the wit to
> see this, if none of the Inner Circle did.*

Kalvan's mouth made an O and a soundless whistle. A
casual, even complimentary mention of the man who'd
defeated him twice showed just how much Ptosphes had
recovered his morale. He wondered if he should include in his
reply the rumors that the Grand Master was in serious trouble
with the Inner Circle for pulling his Knights off the field of
Phyrax instead of keeping them there to die to the last man.

Best not. Letters could be captured, and so far the rumor
was just that, apart from also being something the Styphoni
might not know had reached Hos-Hostigos. Right now the
Styphoni seemed to be running around like the proverbial
chicken with its head cut off, and any precaution that con-
tributed to their confusion and ignorance was justified.

And speaking of precautions—Kalvan rose to his feet and
shouted at the gunners who were digging a pit out of the side

of the trench toward Tarr-Beshta. "That's deep enough, you Ormaz-spawned idiots! Any deeper, and the gun will be firing straight up. The shells will land on the heads of the men in the forward trenches! If they landed on *your* heads it might not be so bad, because I don't think you keep anything important there, but I wouldn't swear to that with your comrades!"

"Your Majesty?" said several bewildered voices at once.

Kalvan sighed, cursed Styphon's House for discouraging the art of siegecraft, and stood up. He spent a moment studying the scarred gray walls of Tarr-Beshta for any signs of unusual activity that might mean a sortie, then scrambled down into the trench without regard for his dignity or the ability of his guards to keep up with him.

Five minutes with the gunners who were digging the pit was enough to give him some hope that they almost understood most of what he'd been trying to tell them. To be sure, the old twelve-pounder they were using as an improvised mortar would have a longer barrel and therefore more range than the mortars he hadn't been able to cast reliably yet, but why take chances? Only one or two shells on the heads of the infantrymen doing the dirtiest work of the siege, and the whole concept of indirect fire would be distrusted and despised so that not even a Great King could get it easily accepted.

On the other hand, if those shells landed in Tarr-Beshta—it would take more than one or two, but not many more before it would be safe to storm the castle, end the siege, and let a Great King who was also acting as his own Chief of Engineers get more than three hours' sleep a night!

Kalvan finished Ptosphes's letter over lunch in his field headquarters, a tent pitched a good thousand yards outside gunshot from the castle. He remembered the fate of Richard the Lion-Hearted, who'd ridden into crossbow range of a French castle he was besieging. On the way, Kalvan had to explain several times to digging parties the reason for zigzags in siege trenches and above all the reason for *never* digging them straight toward the enemy's walls and the enemy's cannon.

The letter concluded almost jauntily:

> *Prince Aesklos's leg is being treated with your new healing wisdom about cleanliness by Brother Cytiphrax, an underpriest of Galzar. There is some danger in this, because if the Prince dies or loses his leg, we shall be*

*blamed for setting demons upon him. However, Brother
Cytiphrax says that the bone of the leg is not so badly
broken that if the flesh wound does not fester, the Prince
need fear neither for life nor limb. We are more likely to
heal than to harm him, and as he is much respected both
as Prince and war leader in Hos-Agrys, we will have in
our debt a man whose voice will carry much weight in the
councils of Demistophon the Short-Sighted.*

*When the danger from Styphon's Own Guard is past, I
intend to use such of the Army of Nostor as can be supported with our available supplies to rebuild and garrison
some of Prince Pheblon's abandoned strongholds, and
after that to root out the bandits who have become a veri-
table plague in the countryside. Thanks to their wagon
trains, the Agrysi made few demands on the Nostori, although most prudent men and women fled from their advance. What is more likely to prevent a proper harvest in
Nostor this year, besides the number of farmers who died
in the wars or protecting their holds, is the bandits, and it
seems to me that the best work for me is seeing that they
are destroyed.*

*With good fortune and the aid of the True Gods, I may
return to Hostigos within a moon. Amasphalya should be
warned that at that time I shall pick up my granddaughter
and hold her, and Hadron take anyone who stands in my
path. Perhaps Amasphalya dares to stand against a mere
Prince, but if she stands against a grandfather she shall
suffer for it.*

*With best wishes for Your Majesty's continued health
and success and for that of our well-beloved Queen Rylla
and Princess Demia, I remain,*

> *Your obedient humble servant*
>
> *Ptosphes*
> *First Prince of Hos-Hostigos*

This time Kalvan whistled out loud. It was hard to believe
that this letter was written by the same man he'd seen off to
Nostor a moon ago, who'd looked as if he were going to his
execution. Kalvan had been torn between sending someone to
keep an eye on his father-in-law and keep him from getting
killed unnecessarily and fearing that doing this would be an in-

sult that would make Ptosphes certain he was incompetent and dishonored even in the eyes of his son-in-law. After listening to Rylla, he'd decided to let Ptosphes go without a watchdog and keep his fingers crossed—a gesture that the True Gods or Somebody seemed to have rewarded.

It was a real pity that so many men wound up being killed in the process of restoring Ptosphes's morale. Not that the war with Hos-Agrys was Ptosphes's fault, however—or Kalvan's, or anybody's except Styphon's House and to some extent King Demistophon, who had fallen upon Hostigos like a wolf upon a wounded bear and learned to his cost that the bear was still full of fight.

Kalvan saw no reason to quarrel with Harmakros's epitaph on Demistophon's campaign in Nostor:

"The stupid son of a she-ass should have known better."

Not to mention that some of his nobles apparently *had* known better, or at least were having second thoughts, and if antisepsis saved Prince Aesklos's life and his leg as well. . . . Kalvan decided not to uncross his fingers until he heard how Aesklos was doing.

He was reading Ptosphes's second enclosure, a list of booty collected and honors he wanted awarded, when he became aware of someone standing in front of him. He looked up and stifled a groan when he saw Major-General Klestreus. The Chief of Intelligence could hardly have come down from Hostigos Town without neglecting his duty, so he'd better have a damned good excuse for the trip.

"Yes, Klestreus?"

"Your Majesty, the convoy with the shells for the—the *mortar*—has arrived. Great Queen Rylla rides with it, and Princess Demia, so it seemed to me that a man of more rank than the captain of the convoy should accompany—"

Kalvan made a strangled noise that he'd intended to be the word "What!" and jumped out of his seat as if his pants had caught fire.

"Rylla? And the baby? *Here*?"

"I told Your Majesty—"

"Yes, you did. Now tell me—are they well?"

"I am no judge of such matters, having always believed that saddles were made for horses, not men, and that if the True Gods—"

"Get on with it, man!"

"Yes, yes. The Queen rode all the way, and Her Royal Highness cries most lustily and keeps the wet nurses awake much of the night."

Kalvan thought of telling Klestreus that he was not a lot of other things besides a judge of the health of babies, then decided to save his breath for the inevitable fight with Rylla. This time he was going to have to lay down the law, and if she threw tantrums or anything else, he'd just duck and go on until he'd spoken his piece.

He practically leaped down the stairs from his War Room and reached the door of the house just in time to see Rylla dismounting from the big roan gelding who had the easiest gait of any horse in the royal stables. She looked pale, but she was still so damned *beautiful* that before he could think of royal dignity he was running toward her.

She ran to meet him, and a moment later he was glad he was wearing a back-and-breast, because otherwise he would have felt his ribs cracking. He was hugging her back with one arm and stroking her hair with the other and saying things he hoped nobody else was hearing until he ran out of breath.

At last he held her out at arm's length and saw beyond her grinning face most of his guards trying very hard *not* to grin. Farther out, he saw a trio of horse litters and a long string of pack animals surrounded by at least two hundred mounted men all armed to the teeth. A fat, gray-haired woman was dismounting from one of the litters, carrying a wailing bundle as delicately as if it had been a basket of spiderwebs.

Rylla hadn't just ridden off on a whim; she'd come with a proper escort and a regular traveling nursery and generally done things the way he would have told her to do them—assuming that he hadn't been able to keep her from coming at all, which knowing Rylla was a pretty safe assumption.

Besides, a second look told him that Rylla wasn't pale because she was still sick. She'd just been inside so long that she'd lost her usual tan. In fact, she looked even better close up than she had from a distance.

Not to mention that after he'd made this kind of a spectacle of himself, she'd never believe a single harsh word he said. She'd break into giggles, and in the face of that, Kalvan doubted he could keep either the last shreds of his royal dignity or even much of a straight face.

III.

From behind Kalvan and Rylla the converted twelve-pounder went off with a sound like a bull running into a wooden fence. They watched the shell trail sparks as it soared overhead, rising toward the peak of its trajectory and then dropping toward the walls of Tarr-Beshta.

With the previous two shells, the spark trail had died on the way down as the fuse went out, and the shells fell as harmlessly as stones. At least that was better than the shell bursting over the Hostigi trenches, which had only happened once—a damned good record for the gunners, considering that the fusing of shells was still very much a matter of by guess and by gods.

The trail of sparks lasted all the way down to the shell's bursting just above the breach in the curtain wall. The Beshtans working in the breach didn't panic; they'd learned by now that shells were not a demonic visitation but only a new use of fireseed. They still hadn't learned one of the basic rules of night combat: when suddenly illuminated, *don't move.* Hardly surprising, either, since this was the first night bombardment with shells in here-and-now history.

In the glare of the bursting shell, Kalvan could see men with picks and sledges running for cover. He also saw the Hostigi in the forward trenches raising their muskets. Two volleys crashed out, the second fired into darkness, drawing a couple of screams from the Beshtans. Two or three slow shooters let fly after the volleys; they drew the voice of a petty-captain describing explicitly where he would put their muskets the next time they fired without a target.

From the battered walls of Tarr-Beshta came only silence.

"They must be short of fireseed," said Rylla.

"That, or saving it for when we storm the walls."

"They still can't do much harm—seven hundred against six thousand."

"They can do enough," said Kalvan. "Not to repel the attack, probably, but certainly enough to send our men out of control."

"Does that matter? The Beshtans have no right to quarter."

Kalvan shook his head. "If it will save our own men—"

"It won't, Kalvan. All it will do is make other rebels think that the Great King is too weak to punish them as they deserve. Then they will think that rebellion is perhaps not so foolish, and we will have more Balthars and more Tenabras. That is *not* saving our men."

The hint was about as subtle as the chamberpot lid she'd once thrown at him. Kalvan looked to his right and left along the earthworks. Count Phrames stood to the left, Captain Xykos, promoted and made a Royal Bodyguard for his work at Phyrax on Colonel Verkan's recommendation, stood to the right. They were keeping the guards out of earshot, Phrames would sooner be burned alive then embarrass Rylla, and Xykos had an intelligent peasant's common sense about ignoring the indiscretions of his betters. As long as he and Rylla didn't start shouting at each other, they could have it out here and now.

"All right. I'll consider not giving them another chance to surrender."

"It would be better not to do it at all."

"I'll think about it. Men who ignore three chances to surrender aren't likely to have the wits to recognize a fourth."

"That is certainly true."

"But I *won't* take Tarr-Beshta the way Styphon's Red Hand took that temple of Dralm in Sask. I'll cut off my hand and cut out my tongue before I write or speak the orders to do that."

Rylla shook her head in exasperation. "What's more important to you, the Great King's tender conscience or the Great King's justice? And the Great King's head, and the Great Queen's, and our daughter's? All of them will rest uneasy on their shoulders if you are weak toward traitors. This is a time for death warrants, not pardons!"

"Rylla—" Kalvan began, then stopped, shaking his head as he realized the futility of the argument. She was right, of course. He'd even said something like that himself, last fall when he considered how many kings had lost their thrones through signing too many pardons and too few death warrants.

That was before the Great Kings' War, though, with its hundred thousand or more soldiers dead or maimed between spring and autumn, not to mention the-gods-only-knew how many civilians! That was also before he faced the need to sign the death warrants himself.

"All right. I won't summon them to surrender again. Custom would require I give them a day to answer, and that means putting off the assault when we have a breach already. I still won't stand for a massacre of every living thing in the castle, either. Let's figure out a way to prevent that, because I'm going to do so and Styphon fly away with anybody who argues the point!"

He heard Rylla's hiss of indrawn breath and braced himself for anything from a curse to a slap. Instead he heard silence, then a small sigh.

"I'm sorry, Kalvan. I shouldn't have called you weak. You were just trying to do something new, or something old in a new way, as you always have. But if you'd seen my father's face when he came home from Tenabra . . ."

Kalvan resisted rubbing in the fact that he'd seen Ptosphes even before that, and there wasn't much she could tell him about the price the First Prince had paid for Balthar's treachery. A moment later she spoke as briskly as ever.

"There is a way. You can proclaim that the women and children are the Great King's personal charge, for his judgment. Anyone who rapes a woman or murders a child will be usurping the Great King's justice, and his own life will be forfeit. You can also have Uncle Wolf Tharses administer an oath to the storming parties."

Kalvan nodded. He would have liked to have Chancellor Xentos do the oath-binding as well, but Xentos was in Agrys City, involved in the interminable wrangling of the Council of Dralm. Xentos had provided useful information about Great King Demistophon's attack on Hos-Hostigos, but there hadn't been any formal denunciation of it by the Council itself. A fact that did not bode well for his future relationship with the Council or even Xentos.

Chartiphon was with Prince Ptosphes, Verkan was on his way back to Greffa, and in general too many of his best people seemed to be anywhere and everywhere except where he needed them! Oh well, at least he still had Rylla, and she would have been worth any two of the others even if he hadn't been married to her in the bargain.

"I'll do that, Rylla. But then what should I do with the women and children?"

Rylla laughed. "The Sastragathi will probably be thinking you're planning to set up a harem. What I would suggest is that you turn them over to the new Prince of Beshta for his justice. That way you will assure the other Princes that you will not be taking away their right of High Justice.''

Kalvan had no intention of doing anything of the kind, but it was likely that some of them wouldn't believe that without tangible proof. After all, hadn't the Great King already taken away serfs, slaves, and private warfare? What might his fingers itch for next?

A moment's suspicion struck him. Of all the people who might have rights over the prisoners, Phrames was the one most likely to listen to Rylla. What would she advise?

In the next moment Kalvan realized he was doing both Rylla and Phrames an injustice. Rylla might think that the only good traitor was one whose head was on a spike outside the Great King's gate, but she was hardly likely to order a cold-blooded massacre of women and children. If she did, Phrames would listen politely because of his regard for her, then refuse, because—well, because he was Phrames.

"Very well. Phrames is going to be leading one of the storming parties, though. It would be best if you took charge of the women and children until Phrames is free.''

"This, of course, will also keep me off the scaling ladders on the day of the storming?''

Kalvan heard the strained laughter in Rylla's voice and was glad it was too dark for her to see his face. "I couldn't help thinking of that, I admit.''

"Don't worry, Kalvan. I can ride and sit in council, but I can't wear armor yet, let alone climb a scaling ladder in it.''

Kalvan kissed her and toyed with the idea of proclaiming a National Day of Thanksgiving in Hos-Hostigos for the first time in her life that Queen Rylla was careful of her own safety. Instead he changed the subject.

"What do you think of your father's using the Agrysi mercenaries who've taken our colors to reduce Nostor to order?''

"Something has to be done about all the bandits and brigands, but I've heard Harmakros complaining that he'd like about a thousand of the horse down here to reinforce the Army of Observation. I was surprised to hear he was short of cavalry. I thought the Beshtans ran rather than fought.''

"After Galzar's Ban stripped them of their last mercenaries, they were too weak to face us in the field. They did run. But when they ran, we had to chase them, and chasing men running for their lives wears out horses. Harmakros told me yesterday that half the Mounted Rifles were on mules, and he was going to have to dismount one regiment of dragoons completely.''

"Then by all means let's give him a thousand Agrysi. They'll have to bring their own supplies, because Sask has been eaten bare and we have our own army to feed in Beshta. . . .''

TWENTY-NINE

I.

"THE TIME HAS COME TO PUNISH THE FALSE GOD DRALM AND KILL HIS TOOL, WHO GOES BY THE NAME OF KALVAN. ALL OF DRALM'S TEMPLES MUST BE PULLED DOWN, BURNED, AND SOWN WITH SALT. HIS PRIESTS MUST BE BLINDED, CASTRATED, AND STRANGLED. KALVAN, HIS WIFE AND SEED, MUST BE SLAKED WITH LIME AND THEN BURNED UNTIL ONLY ASHES REMAIN. THESE ARE TO BE CAST INTO THE OCEAN SEA. ALL THOSE IN HOS-HOSTIGOS WHO DO NOT FORSAKE THEIR FALSE GOD MUST BE HANGED AND THEIR BODIES THROWN TO THE WOLVES AND CARRION BIRDS. THOSE WHO ADMIT TO THEIR ERRORS AND FALSE WAYS MUST BE RESETTLED IN THE SASTRAGATH TO LIVE AS BARBARIANS.

"THIS WILL BE DONE. I HAVE SPOKEN."

The great bronze idol of Styphon, rising eighty hands above its worshippers, fell silent. From ten thousand voices in the Great Temple of Styphon's House on Earth came the reply:

"Kill Kalvan! Kill Kalvan! Kill Kalvan!"

Anaxthenes had once worked the mechanism that moved the mouth and the bellows that amplified the image's voice. He still felt a chill as the giant bronze jaws snapped shut. More

than fifteen years had passed since the last Proclamation from
Styphon's Great Image, and that had been nothing more than
a short blessing to the underpriests and deacons for their good
works in collecting Styphon's offerings. Never in his lifetime
had the Great Image spoken to a lay crowd, which it did only
in times of grave crisis.

Anaxthenes stepped down from the dais and held out his
arm to support Sesklos. Followed by six Temple Guardsmen,
the two men left the Temple through the rear door.

As soon as they were alone in the carriage, Sesklos turned to
Anaxthenes. "What *are* we going to do about Grand Master
Soton? Archpriest Dracar and his followers want him stripped
of his offices and expelled from the Order."

"Then they're even bigger fools than I'd thought," snapped
Anaxthenes. "Excuse me, Father, but they're not dealing with
some backwoods Blethan underpriest in Soton. The Grand
Master rules as much territory as most Great Kings, and with
more unquestioned authority. If he gives up his offices, it will
only be willingly. And I don't believe that it's in the Temple's
best interests that he do so."

"You believe he is innocent?"

"Innocence has nothing to do with it. Certainly the charge
of cowardice is absurd. The only thing Soton is guilty of is
being a realist; he knows when it's time to pack up and go
home. From what my informants tell me, the battle was all but
won until Leonnestros fell into Kalvan's trap. After that,
everything came unraveled, until Soton had to retreat to save
the entire army from being destroyed. He saved himself too,
but he's the only commander we have capable of defeating
Kalvan. We owe Soton a great deal for proving to the world at
Tenabra that Kalvan's men *can* be defeated."

"There is much in what you say. But I doubt that your
words will sway Dracar and his faction. Even your true believers blame Soton for retiring from the field of battle. It
would not be so had you accepted my blessings."

Anaxthenes turned and looked at the old man, his slender
fingers trembling with palsy, who had offered him the highest
and most powerful office in Styphon's House and the Five
Kingdoms. He felt a trace of affection stir and promptly ignored it. Sesklos's wits were declining, or he would have fallen
into an apoplexy before admitting such sentiment.

"I declined because there are too many unpleasant things to

do and no one else to do them, because I have earned too many enemies, and because there is too little time to do all that must be done if the House of Styphon is to triumph over Kalvan and its many enemies. As Styphon's Voice there is too much ritual, too many meetings, too many audiences. . . . Why go on? You know the burden much better than I."

Sesklos nodded wearily. "Yes, my son, there is a great weight upon the shoulders of Styphon's Voice. There are times when it seems that only death itself will ease my burdens."

"When will Soton be brought before the Inner Circle?"

"Two ten-days. That is as long as I can put off Dracar and his followers. What will you do?"

"I don't know," said Anaxthenes, although even if he had known, he would have said the same. Maybe a miracle would happen—

Of course, said a voice in his head. *And maybe Styphon's Great Image will speak on its own and walk off its pedestal.*

II.

The sky to the northwest was turning gray as Count Phrames rode up to the house where Kalvan had his head-quarters. By the time he'd dismounted and climbed to the royal observation post on the roof, he could see occasional flickers of lightning in the gun-metal sky. Phrames hoped the storm would hold off until after they'd taken Tarr-Beshta; he had no wish to lead his men forward through flooded trenches with useless guns and no artillery to keep the traitors' heads down.

The head of the stairs was held by Aspasthar the royal page and Captain Xykos, Rylla's new Bodyguard. Xykos wore only a back-and-breast and an open-faced burgonet with a high-comb; his famous two-handed sword and ax were nowhere in sight. The armor was richly decorated, and Phrames won-dered which Ktemnoi nobleman who no longer had any use for armor had donated it to sustain Xykos's new dignity.

Xykos certainly made a fine sight in silvered breastplate with tassets, dark blue velvet breeches, slashed and paneled, and red and white striped hose. He also seemed to have a natural instinct for dealing with his superiors. He would need every bit of that and more the first time Kalvan ordered him to keep Rylla from doing something she really wanted to do.

Guarding Rylla was not so much a matter of fighting off enemies; any who sought her life would first have to hack their way through the entire Army of Hos-Hostigos and Phrames himself if she had the sense to stay safely under their protection! If she went back to her old habits, on the other hand—well, if all else failed, Xykos was big enough to pick up Rylla under one arm and carry her out of danger.

If he did that, of course, he'd be wise to spend the rest of his life among the Ruthani of the Great Mountains; anywhere closer Rylla might track him down. Phrames knew that he would love no other woman than Rylla till he'd drawn his last breath, but on occasion he'd found himself blessing the wisdom of the gods in sending Kalvan to protect both Hostigos and Rylla.

"Welcome, Phrames," said the Great King. "Are the storming parties ready?"

"As ready as I think we can make them," replied Phrames. That was much readier than they would have been before Kalvan; the Great King had taught captains to see that their men each had a spare flint, dry socks, a bandage, and many other things that might not be needed if they were ready at hand but infallibly would be needed if left behind.

Phrames thought of quoting Prince Sarrask's doubts about the brushwood and timber that were supposed to fill up the moat for his men's scaling ladders. Then he realized that he would be doing that for the dishonorable purpose of trying to make Kalvan doubt Sarrask's faith in the Great King's weapons. Kalvan didn't expect blind obedience, Phrames had his own doubts, and—Galzar moved in mysterious ways, but moved he had!—if the Saski storming party died in the moat, their Prince was very likely to die there with them.

After years of knowing Sarrask as a deadly enemy, it was not easy to turn around and accept him as an ally. He would have to try harder in the future to make Sarrask feel welcome. But the gods have mercy on him if he turned out to be the kind of "ally" that Balthar had been at Tenabra!

Rylla stepped up to Phrames. For a moment he felt his heart stop, then took a deep breath and disciplined his thoughts and body.

"Phrames, I wanted to give you that scarf embroidered with the arms of Beshta to wear today, but that seemed like tempting the gods. Xykos has something, though, that I'd like you to wear in place of any favor from me."

"Yes, my—I mean, Your Majesty." Phrames fought to keep the color from his cheeks.

The big man pulled a long strip of bloodstained, ragged cloth out of his sash. "My lord—this is what's left of the banner of the Veterans of the Long March. It's not much, but then we aren't much either. Not enough to make a half company, with most of those too hurt to be fighting here today.

"If you could see your way to wearing this onto the walls— well, a lot of us who aren't here because of that pig-spawn Balthar will sleep easier." Xykos held out the cloth, and Phrames tried to ignore that both his hands and the big man's weren't entirely steady.

"I would be honored, Captain," he said. Rylla stepped closer, kissed him lightly on the cheek, and helped tie the banner around his helmet. This time there were no betraying blushes or stammers. Rylla had just finished the last knot when Kalvan raised his hand to the signalers at the far end of the platform. A fireseed rocket spewed green smoke, then soared into the darkening sky, trailing more smoke behind it.

Phrames saw ripples of movement in the gun positions between the headquarters and the trenches—then involuntarily flinched as every gun in the Hostigi siege batteries fired as one. By the time Phrames was mounted and riding back toward his men, the fireseed smoke had completely hidden the Hostigi cannon.

When Count Phrames and his banner-bearer took their place at the head of the breach-storming party, the combination of smoke and darkening sky had cast a sinister twilight gloom over Tarr-Beshta. On Kalvan's orders the men of the storming parties had chalked or painted white squares on their helmets so they could tell friends from enemies when the fighting moved indoors; Phrames suspected those white marks would now be useful the moment battle was joined.

Meanwhile, the guns were falling silent one by one and a faint breeze was beginning to thin the smoke. It would have done more if the Beshtan hadn't been busy proving they weren't out of fireseed, guns, or even determination. Marksmanship was fortunately another matter; most of the fire from the breach and the walls on either side of it was going a bit high to hit Phrames's leading regiment, the dismounted Royal Musketeers, although his golden-eagle banner had a couple of new bullet holes. The regiments to the rear were out of range of everything except a two-pounder in the breach itself, which was firing too slowly to be a problem once the men started moving forward.

A final shell burst against the face of the keep itself, spraying chunks of masonry into the courtyard, then the guns were silent. Kalvan had spoken of the guns of his homeland, which could actually keep firing over the heads of the infantry as they advanced on the enemy, and General Alkides had sworn that his gunners could do the same if they were allowed to. Phrames had politely refused; Prince Sarrask had refused somewhat less politely.

"I know all you gunners think you can drop a ball into Styphon's chamberpot if you have the chance!" the Prince had growled. "Maybe you can. And maybe you'll just drop the ball on my head, and while maybe it isn't the greatest head Dralm ever made, it's the only one I've got!"

A minute later the Beshtan fire seemed to slacken, as arquebusiers, musketeers, and gunners reloaded or shifted position to meet the attack they had to know was coming. Phrames decided it was safe to climb out of the trench for a better view. He'd reached open ground and was rising to hands and knees when a bullet *wheeted* past his ear. A second *spanged* off a stone by his left hand—and then, with a crash of thunder louder than the Great Battery at Phyrax, the skies opened and poured rain.

Phrames had never been in such a storm; it was more like being under a waterfall than being out in the rain. He felt as if he were lifting a tangible weight as he struggled to his feet, his boot soles sinking into suddenly muddy ground. As the thunder rumbled away into silence, he heard someone squalling in panic:

"The gods are angry! This is a warning from Lytris not to fight today!"

One such idiot could be more than enough to start a panic. Phrames drew his sword with one hand and gripped his banner-bearer's helmet to urge him upward with the other.

"Traitor! Fool! This storm is the gods themselves fighting for us! Dralm and Galzar and Lytris have sent this storm to soak the Beshtan fireseed. We outnumber them ten to one; with no fireseed they're doomed. We can take the castle with our bare hands!"

Phrames gave one final heave to his banner-bearer and saw the man struggle up beside him. Then he raised his sword high and ran forward toward the breach without looking back to see if anyone was following him.

At first he didn't look back because he didn't want to give the impression of doubting his men's courage. Before long he didn't look back because he had to look where he was going to keep from falling over his own feet. He'd been noted both as a runner and a climber as a youth, but he'd never tried to both run and climb at once, over muddy ground strewn with rain-slick stones and shot, in a pouring rain, and wearing three-quarter armor. He began to wonder if broken ankles would account for as many of his men as Beshtan fire would have otherwise.

By the time Phrames was actually at the breach, enough of his men had caught up so that while he was certainly the first there, it wasn't by much. He counted forty or more Hostigi scrambling over the rubble that had filled the moat, sometimes falling but helping each other up and always going on.

A few Beshtans had kept their fireseed dry; Phrames's banner-bearer went down with a bullet in his left leg halfway up the breach. Phrames caught the banner before it fell and made a mental note to set up a special fund in the Princely treasury to support the kin of his banner-bearers; the job seemed unreasonably dangerous.

Being one-handed through holding the banner nearly cost Phrames his life. Many of the Beshtans who'd lost their dry fireseed hadn't lost their courage; they swarmed down from the top of the breach, swinging muskets, arquebuses, half-pikes, swords, and maces like madmen. Phrames had to use the banner pole like a spear to impale one swordsman, then dropped it and laid about him with sword and pistol butt. He made another mental note to carry a mace the next time he had to storm a breach. His sword was a fine weapon for use from horseback, but on foot he needed something that would stop an opponent as well as just kill him.

The second regiment of Hostigi came pouring up through the breach, and for a moment Phrames was wedged so tightly between his own men and his enemies that he couldn't have wielded a feather, let alone a mace. Then sheer weight of numbers pushed the Beshtans back. The gunners around the two-pounder gave up trying to find dry fireseed, drew swords or picked up their tools, and waded into the fight.

Phrames chopped through a rammer with one swordcut and through the gunner's raised arm with the next, then thrust the man in the face. *Thank Galzar most of these people don't have swords with points!* In this kind of close-quarters brawl, the Hostigi ability to thrust was a large advantage.

With lines being drawn now so that friend could be told from foe, the Beshtans on the wall were joining in. Some were leaping down to thicken the defenders' line, others adding bullets, arrows, and even thrown stones from above. The number of fallen Hostigi began to increase at a rate that did not meet with Phrames's approval, and not all of them were men who'd slipped on wet stones or tripped over a comrade's feet.

Someone was shouting in his ear about bringing up the pikemen of Queen Rylla's Foot, the third regiment in the storming column. Without bothering to turn and face the man, Phrames bellowed, "Great Galzar, no! The pikes are the last thing we need until we're down in the courtyard. They won't have room to use their pikes or even defend themselves up here." A pikeman needed firm ground for both feet and both hands for his pike; if he lacked either, he was just an easy victim instead of one of the deadliest kind of soldiers ever to march.

The Beshtans were falling faster than the Hostigi; in places their dead and dying now lay three deep. Reinforcements were still coming up; it looked as if the defenders were staking everything on holding the breach and the walls and not worrying about a second line of defense in the keep.

A man Phrames recognized emerged from the Beshtan line—a baron who'd commanded a Beshtan cavalry squadron on the Great Raid into Hos-Harphax in the spring. He'd done a good job, too; why had he chosen to follow his damnable Prince into treason? No one would ever know, most likely; all the man could be given now was an honorable death. Phrames shouted a war cry and raised his sword.

For about a minute it wasn't entirely clear who was going to give whom what sort of death. The baron's sword was heavier and his reach longer than Phrames's; three times he beat down the Count's guard and would have finished him if his armor hadn't been sound. Finally Phrames hooked a foot behind the baron's leg and sent him crashing down, then thrust him in the throat through his mail aventail. When he stepped back from the dying man, there seemed to be as many Beshtans as ever, and he began to wonder if maybe he hadn't been a little hasty in dismissing the pikes. They wouldn't help to get through the breach, but as for holding it against the Beshtans. . . .

As Phrames completed the thought, a new uproar of screams, war cries, curses, and the crashing and clashing of weapons and armor burst out behind the Beshtans. Somebody was taking them in the rear. By the time Phrames had caught his breath, that somebody had opened enough of a gap in the Beshtan line to let him see men in Saski green and gold swarming across the courtyard. At their head was a bulky figure in freshly regilded armor, wielding a bloody mace and defaming the sexual habits of the Beshtans, their parents, and their illegitimate offspring by an astonishing variety of mothers, not all of them human or even earthly.

For a moment Phrames wanted to curse. To owe his success at the breach to Sarrask of Sask—! Then he sighed. His honor was one thing; the lives of his men another. He could not throw the second away because of some whimsical notion of the first. Besides, it began to seem that Dralm and Galzar had so made Sarrask that there *was* some good in him—or at least a fighting man's courage that the right leader could bring out, and then Dralm and Galzar sent Kalvan. . . .

No good ever came of questioning the judgment of Father Dralm or Galzar Wolfshead, even when one did not understand it.

So Phrames walked down the rubble into the courtyard to greet Prince Sarrask with outstretched hand. The big man grinned, clapped Phrames on both shoulders, then unhooked a silver-stoppered flask from his belt.

"You look like a man who could use this."

"After we've cleared the courtyard, I won't say no."

"Then drink up, Count. We've got everything except the keep already."

Phrames looked toward the keep and realized that the downpour had passed almost as quickly as it had come. He could see the whole castle and the trench-carved ground beyond it. The courtyard swarmed with Sarrask's men, and the walls were crowded with the Sastragathi irregulars who'd followed the Saski up the ladders. True to their habits, the Sastragathi were busily stripping what Phrames hoped were the corpses of the defenders and tossing them into the moat or into the courtyard. On top of one of the gate towers a little knot of defenders was still holding out, but below a gang of Saski with sledges was already trying to free the portcullis and lower the drawbridge, to let Alkides bring in his artillery and finish off the keep.

"Hope those poor bastards in the keep have the sense to yield before Alkides brings in a bombard," said Sarrask, waving the flask at Phrames again. This time the Count took it. "Otherwise you'll be a Prince with no place to sleep. I could knock that (guilty of fornication with a barnyard fowl) pile down with my mace! Drink up, Count."

Phrames drank. It was extraordinarily good wine. "Thank you, Prince. Your own stock?"

Sarrask shook his head. "Made in Ktemnos. Those Ktemnoi believe in bringing all the comforts of home with them when they go to war. Some nobleman had a cartload of it in a wagon train that passed too close to one of my castles. The castellan was out raiding that day and bagged the lot. He couldn't drink it all before we saw the Styphoni out of Sask. Sent over a barrel last night. Come around tonight; there's plenty left."

Phrames drank again, considering that Sarrask of Sask accusing another nobleman of being too comfortable in the field was the pot calling the kettle black but hardly inclined to say so out loud.

Then a Saski captain was coming over to tell his Prince that the portcullis was hopelessly jammed; did he and Phrames think the gate should be blown up or did Alkides want to get his guns through the breach?

"Galzar strike me dead if I know," said Sarrask. "I'm no damned gunner! Phrames, do you mind a few more holes in the wall of your new seat? I'll hand over a few ransoms to you and see that Balthames does the same, since the gods didn't finish the little bugger at Tenabra or Phyrax! If you need to rebuild . . ."

Phrames wasn't listening. He was instead looking at the top of the keep, where a white flag was now hanging down over the battlements. A moment later a second joined it, then a third.

"Never mind, Prince Sarrask. I don't think we're going to need any artillery in here at all. Just someone to parley with the men in the keep. Would you care to join me?"

"My pleasure, Count Phrames."

THIRTY

I.

The screams and groans of the dying were fading behind Kalvan as he descended the winding stone stairs in the northwest tower of Tarr-Beshta. They weren't fading fast enough, but he couldn't move any faster. The stairs were crumbling and treacherous—more of Balthar's cheese-paring! Besides, Captain Xykos was just ahead and determined to slow his Great King to what he considered a proper pace. Since Xykos filled the stairs from top to bottom and nearly from side to side, his determination counted for a great deal.

After what seemed like enough time to reach the bottom of a mine shaft, they reached the tower cellar. Here, so it was said, lay the door to Balthar's treasure rooms, whose riches had grown with soldiers' imaginations until they rivaled Styphon's House Temple Treasury in Balph. Kalvan hoped the soldiers were right; from first to last Balthar had cost Hos-Hostigos too Dralm-damned much to be paid for with nothing but his head and those of his kin who hadn't been able to cross into Hos-Harphax before the Army of Observation swept into Beshta!

The cellar was already crowded, with Phrames and half a dozen of the King's Lifeguards. They held either drawn swords or torches, except for one who was bending over a dying woman, trying to work a dagger out from between her ribs. Two men and another woman lay sprawled in a corner, already dead.

"Your Majesty," said Count Phrames. "One of the men seems to have been the keeper of the—of whatever lies beyond that door." He pointed to an oak door bound in tarnished brass to the left of the stairs. "He had a key to it. We unlocked the door but thought you should have the honor of being first in."

It was on the tip of Kalvan's tongue to remind them that men who'd seen Leonnestros's cavalry massacred by the explosion of the artillery redoubt at Phyrax should be aware of booby traps. The words died there; they were doing him an honor and besides, he'd be drowned in mare's milk if he'd abandon "Follow me" leadership, even here in the bowels of Tarr-Beshta. Kalvan drew his sword, thrust hard against the door, and when it squealed open on rusty hinges stepped through the gap.

It took a moment for Kalvan's eyes to adjust to the thick darkness inside. It took several more moments to believe that what they were showing him was actually there.

Several tunnels ran off in different directions from a stone-walled circular room. On either side of each tunnel sacks, boxes, and kegs were piled as high as a man, except where cloth or wood had rotted and let the piles collapse. There the tunnels were completely impassable, knee- or even waist-deep in fragments of rotting cloth or wood and gold and silver!

Kalvan heard blasphemous mutterings behind him as the Guardsmen pushed in through the door and stared around them. He also saw more gold and silver gleaming in the chinks and rents in the many boxes and bags. The torches now lit one tunnel; he saw that not all the piled gold and silver was coin. Most of the silver was, but a lot of the gold was rings, cups, bowls, plates, even ingots, not to mention swords and daggers and armor plated with precious metals, bags of pearls, ornamental boxes inlaid with gold and coral, what looked like uncut emeralds—

Kalvan's head spun, and not just because so many torches were burning in an unventilated room. The treasure of Beshta was no soldier's tall tale. It was real, and enough to buy a Kingdom—or save the one he had already. Three generations of miserliness. . . .

Kalvan took another step, to see if what looked like

emeralds really were, then saw for the first time the man sitting in the tunnel just beyond the emeralds.

Prince Balthar sat cross-legged, back braced against a keg, running silver coins through his fingers like a child playing in the sands. "Yes, yes, my pretties," he said in a cackling voice that made Kalvan's flesh crawl, "Dada will see that the evil Daemon won't hurt you."

Balthar wore nothing but one of his threadbare black gowns, and even from a distance Kalvan could tell that both the gown and its wearer stank as if they'd been fished out of a midden pit. Kalvan stepped forward to look into Balthar's face, then turned away, very much wishing that he hadn't or at least that his stomach would stop twisting ominously.

He felt a hand on his shoulder and heard Rylla's voice. "I came as quickly as I could. I see you found the traitor. It seems he will escape the Great King's justice after all."

Frustration filled Kalvan. What good would it do to put a madman on trial for treason? Balthar wouldn't understand what was happening to him, and would be more likely to end up an object of pity than anything else. As for caring for him until his body was as dead as his mind—what would that accomplish, except insulting the memory of all the men Balthar's treachery had murdered, men whose widows and children would not be living nearly as well?

Balthar deserved to die, if only in the same way that a mad dog run over by a car but not yet dead deserved to be put out of its pain. Kalvan drew his pistol and was cocking it when Rylla gripped his arm.

"No, Kalvan."

"We can't have the farce of trying—"

"You don't understand. A Prince has to die by steel."

Kalvan nodded, half his mind wondering why he hadn't asked first and the other half replying that he'd never expected to need to know. He started to draw his sword, then doubted it would be heavy enough for the job. His stomach twisted again at the thought of hacking Balthar's head off or running him through. What they needed was a heavier blade—

"DOWN, YOUR MAJESTY!" shouted Phrames.

Kalvan twisted around, knocked Rylla off her feet, then looked up to see an orange-robed figure emerging from one of the darkened tunnels. His face was distorted by a triumphant grin, and the muzzle of the horse pistol aimed at Kalvan's head looked as wide and deep as a well.

"For the God of Gods! Die, Daemon!"

On the periphery of his vision Kalvan saw Xykos, Phrames, and two guards running toward the highpriest. They were going to be too late, Kalvan realized. His mind seemed to be working faster and more clearly than ever before; he noted dispassionately that he'd dropped his own pistol out of reach when he'd fallen on top of Rylla. At least she would survive and maybe all of his work wouldn't be undone. So much to do and now no time—

A sharp explosion, a bright flash, and a high-pitched scream. Then the room was filled with fireseed smoke.

"Are you all right?" screamed Rylla.

"Fine, darling." He patted himself to make sure.

The highpriest must have been sent by Styphon's House to keep watch on Balthar and make sure he didn't change sides again. Now he was waving all that was left of a hand peeled to the wrist by the explosion of his pistol. One of his cheeks was open to the bone from a flying fragment, leaving red streaks all over his orange robe. A shot from Phrames's pistol ended the screams.

A thunderstruck Xykos turned back to Kalvan and roared, "A miracle! Bless the Great God Dralm! Great King Kalvan is unhurt!"

Phrames vanished into the tunnel, returning a moment later with a powder horn. He poured some on his hand, then tasted it.

"Hostigos Unconsecrated. The poor fool probably thought it was only Styphon's Best and overloaded his pistol. Thanks be to Dralm and Galzar!"

"It's still a miracle," said Xykos more quietly.

Rylla rose shakily to her feet and nodded. "Xykos is right. The True Gods have once more shown that their blessing is on Great King Kalvan and his war to rid the Six Kingdoms of false Styphon and his priests."

Kalvan started to reply, but Rylla's hand cut off his voice. "Let them think what they will," she whispered. "It's best for our cause and for our daughter. Look, see Xykos's smile."

Another instant legend, thought Kalvan. *Now all I need is my own press secretary!*

"Who dares to blaspheme my Treasure House?" cried Balthar. "I command you to leave at once, on pain of my displeasure." Then he whispered, "I told you I would protect you, my pretty ones."

"Xykos," said Kalvan.

"Your Majesty?"

"Will you execute the Great King's justice on Prince Balthar of Beshta for his treasonable conduct on the field of Tenabra and his armed resistance to the lawful summons of his Great King?"

Balthar suddenly screamed in terror. Kalvan wondered if he was really as insane as he'd been acting, or was it possible that even a madman could understand and protest his own death sentence?

Xykos would have drawn himself up if there'd been room overhead. Instead he nodded. "Gladly, Your Majesty."

Wrinkling up her nose, Rylla lifted the Princely circlet from Balthar's head. Then she and everyone else hastily stepped back as Xykos drew Boarsbane from its sheath on his back. There wasn't room for Xykos to swing properly, but Boarsbane was sharp and heavy, Xykos was as strong as a bull, and Balthar's neck was thin.

The Prince's head had only just stopped rolling when Rylla was handing the circlet to Kalvan. Kalvan wiped it off on his sleeve, then held out the gold ring with both hands. Nervously Phrames knelt.

"Count Phrames, from the hands of your Great King receive this, the token of Princeship over Beshta, truly earned by good and faithful service." The circlet settled into Phrames's hair.

"Arise, Prince Phrames of Beshta!"

Then everyone was shouting, "Long live Prince Phrames!" Rylla was kissing both men impartially, and Xykos was waving Boarsbane around so that Kalvan was afraid he'd accidentally behead someone else.

Most of his mind was on one thing. The dirty work was done, Balthar was dead, and if the Great King really wanted to, he could now slip off somewhere and be sick to his stomach!

II.

Anaxthenes's mood was somber as he watched the orange-robed Archpriests filing into the circular chamber at the heart of Styphon's Great Temple. He had used all his influence, but this time with little success. The Inner Circle was as determined as a lodge of Mexicotal priests to have a sacrificial victim for the Temple's losses. It appeared that Grand Master Soton was to be that victim. Nothing short of divine intervention seemed likely to make the slightest difference.

Today even Anaxthenes's usual supporters were wavering. This meeting could well see the end of his short dominance of the Inner Circle, as well as Soton's career. Sesklos looked weary and refused to meet his eyes. Archpriest Dracar's face was set in a triumphant gloat that did nothing to raise Anaxthenes's spirits. Dracar's ascendancy here today could well signal the sunset of Styphon's rule over the Five Kingdoms.

When all the Archpriests were seated, Grand Master Soton was brought into the chamber by two of the Temple Guardsmen. Soton's grim face was set, but his eyes darted about, searching out enemies and allies, and he strode ahead of the two Guardsmen as though he were leading them against the Sastragathi. He still wore his badge of office, a large hammered-gold sunwheel suspended on a heavy gold chain, and a plain white tunic with the orange trim that showed his rank as an Archpriest of Styphon's House.

Soton was taken to a marble dais at the center of the chamber. Anaxthenes noted that both his sword and dagger scabbards were empty. Some of the Archpriests were fingering their own poinards as if they expected at any moment to rise up and hack the Grand Master to pieces.

Sesklos's voice boomed through the chamber, thanks to the use of the echo chamber behind his seat, as he brought the meeting to order. "Soton, Grand Master of the Holy Order of the Zarthani Knights. You are brought before us on charges of insubordination, cowardice in battle, and desertion in the face of the enemy. What is your defense?"

Soton's weathered face paled—with rage, Anaxthenes was sure. "My orders were to support Lord High Marshal Mnesiphoklos and help him defeat the Usurper Kalvan. I did as I was ordered until I saw that the fool Leonnestros had disobeyed orders. Fortunately for him he died of his folly, or I would have hacked him limb from limb with my own sword.''

Anaxthenes groaned. Such words from Soton would only make Dracar's job easier. Nor were his endless details of Kalvan's movements through the mercenaries into the rear of the center any more helpful to his cause. Anaxthenes had the impression that right now Soton would like to hack his way through the Inner Circle as though it were Kalvan's Life-guards. If others noticed it, Soton's fate would be sealed.

''. . . when I saw that there was no more center to support and that it would be a waste of manpower to continue, I ordered the Knights to retire. That they did so in order and in no little haste was the sole reason for more than a third of the Holy Host escaping death or capture by Kalvan's forces. Were the same circumstances to arise again, I would not change my orders, regardless of my own safety.

''Usurper or Daemon, Kalvan is the greatest war captain I have ever seen. We are going to need every man in our service to have any chance of defeating him and his perfidious ideas.''

''Is that all you have to say?'' asked Styphon's Voice.

''It is.''

''Is there anyone who would like to speak?''

''Yes,'' said an older Archpriest. ''I would like to address the Grand Master. Is it not true that when you—recalled—your Knights, the Squares were still fighting Kalvan under Marshal Mnesiphoklos, your commander?''

As Soton answered, Anaxthenes remembered that the elderly Archpriest had once served as Mnesiphoklos's personal healer and household priest, and as a result considered himself something of an expert in matters of war.

''Yes, they were still fighting. They were also trapped between Kalvan's battery on one side and his cavalry on the other.''

''Is it not true that they also wrested control of that battery you mentioned from Kalvan's gunners and turned it upon his army?''

''I do not know. I was engaged elsewhere.''

''Then you really didn't know whether Mnesiphoklos was winning or losing when your Knights deserted their post.''

''Of course I knew!'' Soton seemed to be begging the gods

for patience. "Battery or no battery, Kalvan had the center enveloped. Sooner or later it was going to be defeated. There were not enough men under my command to affect that outcome. I ordered them to retire while I could still have my orders obeyed."

"There are a number of the late Lord High Marshal Mnesiphoklos's captains who would willingly debate you on that point. The Lord High Marshal himself would probably do so had he survived the battle!"

"Mnesiphoklos was a doddering old fool and Leonnestros was a dithering idiot. Had either survived the battle, I'd personally crack his joints on the rack!" Roxthar's voice cut through the objections like a knife blade.

"You are out of order!" cried Sesklos.

"No!" shouted the Guardian of the Faith. "The entire Council is out of order! I was there at Phyrax. *Where were the rest of you?* I watched the entire battle from the baggage train, while you were no doubt counting your offerings and lamenting at how small they were.

"I tell you, were it not for Grand Master Soton our defeat would have been complete, final disaster, and Kalvan would now be knocking at the gates of Balph instead of Tarr-Beshta!"

As Roxthar continued, Anaxthenes was reminded of the pilot of a galleass he'd been aboard when she ran hard aground on a sandbar in what the pilot had thought was a clear channel. The same combination of fear, incredulity, and surprise he'd seen on the pilot's face was now showing on the faces of most of the Archpriests.

If his own face had been allowed to reflect his feelings, it would have worn a triumphant grin. Clearly Roxthar was turning the tide, and Soton would not be thrown to the wolves, leaving them free to rend Styphon's House any time Kalvan chose to whip the pack. Anaxthenes's supporters were rallying, as were the true believers. Those who feared Roxthar too much to go against him over what they could easily persuade themselves was a minor matter would join next. No one would be left opposing Soton except Dracar and his most determined supporters, who would gladly see Styphon's House fall into the ruins as long as Anaxthenes was buried in these ruins.

As Roxthar paused for breath, he looked toward Anaxthenes and a brief smile flickered on his thin lips. Anaxthenes's urge to grin suddenly vanished. Roxthar would demand his price for today's work—and what that price might be, for him and for the whole Temple, Anaxthenes did not really care to contemplate.

THIRTY-ONE

I.

Verkan Vall yawned and looked up at the chronometer over the control panel of the paratemporal conveyor. It showed that five minutes passed since the last time he looked at it, what seemed like several hours ago. He yawned again.

What was making this trip home from Kalvan's Time-Line seem to last forever? He doubted if the fatigue was helping; he felt as if he hadn't slept in a week—and come to think of it, he very nearly hadn't, making sure everything in Greffa would last through the winter without any further supervision by him.

This was his last trip to Kalvan's Time-Line until next spring, and he was quite sure that had more to do with his boredom and frustration. It bothered him to be leaving a friend before he'd done everything that could be done for him, even though common sense told Verkan that he himself couldn't do much more for Kalvan and indeed not much more needed to be done.

Ptosphes was cleaning out Nostor very nicely; by the time winter came Prince Pheblon should be ruling over an untroubled Princedom—one still almost a desert, but a peaceful desert. The succession to Nyklos was giving no trouble; Armanes's eldest son was not only the lawful successor, but fit for the job.

In Hos-Agrys, Prince Aesklos was going to have to spend the winter by the fireside recovering, but he would be spending it with both legs—a near miracle for this time-line. His voice would be heard against the notion that there was anything demonic about Kalvan's knowledge, and since King Demistophon still seemed to be of at least two minds about which side he was on. . . .

In Beshta, Prince Phrames was taking charge with a vengeance, and Harmakros and Hestophes were commanding the Army of Observation on the border with Hos-Harphax. Not that they had much to do; Galzar himself couldn't have made an army out of men who wouldn't stand and fight, guns that wouldn't shoot even if there was fireseed to load them, and beasts who wouldn't carry or draw a load, which was all the Harphaxi had left.

The only man who might have tried, Grand Master Soton, was on his way back to Tarr-Ceros and his Knights for the coming campaign against the nomadic tribes. Verkan had hoped Soton would be returning in disgrace with Styphon's House, although it would have been moumentally unjust to disgrace a fine soldier for common sense and loyalty to his comrades. Instead, so rumors ran, Soton was considered the appointed champion of Styphon's House against the servant of demons.

That was probably true, and there was nothing to be done about it either way. What bothered Verkan more was another rumor that Soton had been saved from disgrace at the price of an alliance with Archpriest Roxthar. If the best soldier and the most fanatical Archpriest of the Inner Circle were now working together, the war would do worse than go on; it would very likely take an extremely ugly turn the next time Styphon's House marched.

Better send Ranthar Jard a few more men for his Paracop squad assigned to the University Study-Teams before that happened. Then he'd have enough people to take care of that majority of the University Teams who couldn't take care of themselves, and meanwhile he'd be able to keep people like Varnath Lala and Gorath Tran from committing any egregious follies—or at least he'd be able to try harder. If nothing really nasty happened, he'd at least have more people to carry messages, which would reduce the need to use possibly contaminating First Level techniques and leave the Paratime

Police smelling a lot sweeter legally.

Whatever happened, Ranthar Jard was going to be much more on his own next year, because his Chief was going to have to spend most of his time on First Level until the Dralm-damned business of pulling out of Fourth Level Europo-American was settled, one way or another. The Study Group had been appointed, and it was now sitting and talking. It showed signs of being willing to go on sitting and talking until entropy reversed itself, and meanwhile all Verkan Vall's enemies would be sharpening their knives and loading their guns to take advantage of this situation. He was just going to have to keep a close watch on the Study Group in order to get anything useful out of it, or look like a fool for appointing it in the first place.

What else could he do on Home Time-Line? Pick some more reliable subordinates who could be trusted to hold the fort when he had to go outtime, for one thing. Otherwise, it would be mostly a question of looking as though he were on the job, an image he could present much more effectively from behind his desk—a desk that didn't need a power excavator to be dug out from under accumulated paperwork.

The thought of that paperwork made Verkan look at the chronometer again, then at the display showing the parayears remaining to First Level. He'd thought of going straight to his office and making a start on at least sorting the backlog into broad categories. He'd be too tired to do even that unless he took a nap in the conveyor, and there wasn't enough time to make that nap a good one.

He'd do better to go home, get a good night's sleep in a proper bed, and make his start at getting back to work in the morning. Sleep was something too precious to sacrifice to presenting an image, and if he ever forgot that the Paracops would not only need a new Chief fairly soon, they'd deserve one.

11.

Outside the keep of Tarr-Hostigos, the autumn wind rose until Kalvan could hear it moaning past the battlements. From somewhere a draft found its way around the wooden shutters over the windows. One of the candles on Kalvan's table flickered and went out. He contemplated relighting it with a coal from the brazier, then decided he could finish the letter with the light from the remaining candle.

Two wax candles would have been extravagant for anyone but the Great King of a victorious but battered Kingdom. Kalvan hadn't entirely mastered the art of writing with a quill pen, he didn't want to risk spoiling parchment, and above all he couldn't entrust this letter to Colonel Verkan in Grefftscharr to a secretary.

Kalvan moved the wine cup and jug so that they stood between the nearest window and the candle, then went on writing:

> The most recent shipment of grain has arrived safely in Ulthor and is now on the road to us. One of the shipmasters who rode ahead with the messenger said that the sailing season on the Saltless Seas may end before another convoy of grain can make the voyage from Greffa, let alone go and return.
> I have promised him, and through him his fellow masters, that any of them who are obliged to winter over in Ulthor shall have the wages and rations of their crews paid out of the Treasury of the Great Kingdom. I have also indicated that I will buy outright any sound ships whose masters may wish to sell them. The masters and crews may take Hostigi colors, or return home at the expense of the Crown.

That would be a start on the Royal Navy of Hos-Hostigos. Only a start, and indeed he couldn't hope for anything more as long as the Great Kingdom didn't have a port on the Ocean Sea, but it was better than nothing. Much better than nothing, considering that the grain route to the Middle Kingdoms looked as if it were becoming the lifeline of Hos-Hostigos, and

that the Prince of Thagror (here-and-now Detroit) was showing signs of taking his nominal allegiance to Hos-Agrys more
seriously than before.

> We will not be too badly off even if there is no more
> Grefftscharri grain this year. In those parts of the Great
> Kingdom not involved in the fighting, the harvests were
> good. The worst of the fighting was over well before
> harvesttime, and we were able to release many more of
> the troops than we'd expected. In addition, many of the
> mercenaries who remained in our service were willing to
> work in the fields for extra pay. We have been able to ship
> some of the surplus food to Old Hostigos, Sashta,
> Beshta, and Sask.
>
> Prince Phrames is also hopeful that he can purchase
> grain in Harphax through the same grain merchants who
> supplied the late lamentable Prince Balthar last winter.
> Phrames has been granted one-fifth of Balthar's hoard to
> begin his reign, and he should be able to accomplish much
> with that.

Since Balthar's hoard had been counted at three hundred
thousand ounces of gold and more than a million ounces of
silver, Kalvan was quite sure that Phrames would be able to
buy quite a lot of grain with his share. What gold and silver
couldn't do would be done by less polite means; it was no
secret that most of the grain merchants had private stockpiles
ready for the expected famines. Kalvan remembered listening
from behind a tapestry to Phrames's explicit lecture to the
grain merchants about the penalties for hoarders and specu-
lators. Afterward, he stopped worrying about Phrames being
too noble to make a good here-and-now ruler. Where his new
subjects were concerned, Phrames had the determination of
an old cat with one kitten and the ruthlessness of an Archpriest of the Inner Circle.

> It also seems unlikely that anyone in Harphax will be
> able to prevent Phrames from purchasing grain where he
> will. King Kaiphranos is generally rumored to have col-
> lapsed both mentally and physically after the death of
> Prince Philesteus, Prince Selestros is no more fit to rule
> than ever, and Grand Duke Lysandros appears to rule in

*all but name. He is far abler than Kaiphranos, but it
seems unlikely that he will be able to do much soon to put
in order a Great Kingdom with no army, no treasury, no
revenue, many enemies, and few allies. From the rumors
we hear in Hostigos, the Electors Princes of Hos-
Harphax would as soon put one of Styphon's fireseed
demons on the throne as Lysandros. The succession crisis
in Thapigos, brought about by the death of Prince
Acestocleus, is the most serious of the problems Lysandros faces, as it threatens to embroil the Harphaxi with
Hos-Agrys, but it is far from the only one.*

*Lysandros has the open support of Styphon's House,
to be sure, but this does not seem likely to be an unmixed
blessing. A good many Harphaxi are convinced they lost
because the Inner Circle would not send the Holy Host
north to march with the Army of Hos-Harphax. On the
other hand, Grand Master Soton is said to be bitter about
the loss of his Lances through what he feels was inex-
cusable incompetence on the part of the Harphaxi. Since
his word now carries much weight in the councils of the
Inner Circle, his ill will toward the Harphaxi is not
something Lysandros can ignore.*

It was more than ever a pity that there was no way for Hostigos to take advantage of the mess in Harphax this winter, but
the year's battles had just cost too much. Half or more of the
men who'd marched out under Hostigi colors in early summer
were dead or wounded, and the cost in gold, silver, weapons,
fireseed, cavalry horses and draft animals, even in things like
bandages and canteens. . . . Kalvan now understood exactly
how King Pyrrhus had felt.

The second sheet of parchment was almost filled; Kalvan
drew a third toward him, smoothed it out, and checked it for
tears or thin spots. At least the work at the paper mill was
beginning to show some results; Ermut had kept at his ex-
periments right on through the summer, only leaving the mill
when the Holy Host was less than an hour's ride away. He had
had all his results written down, too, although he himself was
illiterate; work was already starting up again where it left off.
By next spring maybe, just maybe, they'd have usable paper.

Then they'd need iron or steel pen nibs, because if paperwork multiplied the way it usually did, there wouldn't be

enough geese in the six Great Kingdoms and Grefftscharr put together to supply quills! Not to mention more schools to produce literate clerks to do all the paperwork, and those schools would need teachers, who could probably be trained at the University. That would mean more work for Mytron that wasn't connected with his duties to Dralm, and what Xentos would have to say about *that*—

"Kalvan, are you writing a letter to Verkan or a chronicle?" Rylla's voice from the curtained bed had the note of a woman with a grievance.

Kalvan looked back over the pages to see if he'd left out anything. Nothing that couldn't wait, or that wasn't too sensitive to be written down in a letter even to somebody as trustworthy as Verkan. A letter could go astray on the way to Greffa, and it would do no good if the world learned, for example, that Chartiphon's elevation to the rank of Great Captain-General of Hos-Hostigos was intended to keep him off future battlefields.

No, there was one thing he'd forgot to mention, and not a little thing, either. He dipped his pen and wrote:

> *Prince Phrames has finished dividing the estates of the Beshtans who died without heirs or who were executed and attainted for their treason to the Great Kingdom. He has granted one-third of them to the Great Crown*—a useful step toward giving Kalvan his own lands—*"one-third to loyal Beshtans, and one-third to distinguished soldiers of the realm. These include Duke Chartiphon, Duke Harmakros, Baron Alkides, Baron Hestophes, and yourself."*

Being able to promote Harmakros and give Alkides and Hestophes titles had been the second happiest moment of the year. The only happier one had been when he first saw Princess Demia.

> *I have been assured that the patent of gift for your new Beshtan estates has been drawn up and should be on the way to me even now. If the weather holds so that the roads do not dissolve in the next two days, I may be able to send it along with this letter. If not*

"Kalvan! My feet are getting cold!"

*rest assured that you now have lands of your own in Hos-
Hostigos, which you have served so well and so valiantly,
along with the rank of Baron. Her Majesty joins me in
wishing you and your lady wife health and prosperity this
winter and a swift return to us in the spring. Farewell.*

Kalvan

The Great King sprinkled sand on the last few lines, then
shook it off, slid all three pages into a pile, weighted it down
with the wine cup and jug, and blew out the candle.

MORE SCIENCE FICTION

ADVENTURE!

☐ 20726-X	**ENSIGN FLANDRY**, Poul Anderson	$2.50
☐ 21889-X	**EXPANDED UNIVERSE**, Robert A. Heinlein	$3.95
☐ 01685-5	**ALIEN ART & ARCTURUS LANDING**, Gordon R. Dickson	$2.75
☐ 73296-8	**ROCANNON'S WORLD**, Ursula K. Le Guin	$2.25
☐ 65316-2	**THE PATCHWORK GIRL**, Larry Niven	$2.50
☐ 78435-6	**THE STARS ARE OURS!**, Andre Norton	$2.50
☐ 87305-7	**THE WARLOCK IN SPITE OF HIMSELF**, Christopher Stasheff	$3.50
☐ 80698-8	**THIS IMMORTAL**, Roger Zelazny	$2.75
☐ 37066-7	**IF THE STARS ARE GODS**, Gregory Benford & Gordon Eklund	$2.25
☐ 89853-X	**THE WITCHES OF KARRES**, James Schmitz	$2.75

Prices may be slightly higher in Canada.

Available at your local bookstore or return this form to:

ACE SCIENCE FICTION
Book Mailing Service
P.O. Box 690, Rockville Centre, NY 11571

Please send me the titles checked above. I enclose _____ . Include 75¢ for postage and handling if one book is ordered; 25¢ per book for two or more not to exceed $1.75. California, Illinois, New York and Tennessee residents please add sales tax.

NAME _____

ADDRESS _____

CITY _____ STATE/ZIP _____

(allow six weeks for delivery.)

SF 10